"Brilli... storyte...ling on the next to this timely original series!..."   —Julie E. Czerneda, author of *A Turn of Light*

"Mara's personal growth is a delight to follow. Sharp characterization, a fast-moving plot, and a steady unveiling of a bigger picture make this a welcome addition to the genre."   —*Publishers Weekly*

"Encapsulating the best features of a good teen title, *Masks* is sure to resonate with readers. . . . An intriguing setting and a suspenseful story line."   —*Library Journal*

"Fans of *Masks* will not be disappointed with Blake's amazing sequel, *Shadows*. The magic continues in this enthralling adventure, grabbing the reader's interest and holding it until the final page. Each chapter brings a new twist in the already sensational story."
                    —*RT Book Reviews* (top pick)

"Not since the likes of *Lirael* or *Sabriel* have I enjoyed a YA with a female protagonist to the extent I did *Masks*. . . . A novel that will emotionally touch you and leave you reeling through it."   —Fantasy Faction

"Tension building that will curl your toes and amazing worldbuilding!"   —My Shelf Confessions

"Blake brings his fantastic world to life through offbeat links between magic, nature, and human behavior in a caste-ridden society."   —*Locus*

"It's a clever and unique fantasy world . . . . I loved *Masks*, and thoroughly enjoyed this second installment in the series. Full of suspense, mystery, magic, and a bit of romance—the intensity builds to a climactic ending."
                    —SciFiChick

Novels of
The Masks of Aygrima
from E. C. Blake

MASKS
SHADOWS
FACES*

SHADOWS

E. C. BLAKE

DAW BOOKS, INC.

DONALD A. WOLLHEIM, FOUNDER

375 Hudson Street, New York, NY 10014

ELIZABETH R. WOLLHEIM
SHEILA E. GILBERT
PUBLISHERS

www.dawbooks.com

First Paperback Printing, May 2015
1 2 3 4 5 6 7 8 9

This book is dedicated to the only member of my family I've never yet dedicated a book to: Shadowpaw the Siberian cat, who, after all, shares part of his name with the title.

♦ ♦ ♦

Acknowledgments

My heartfelt thanks to my publishers, Sheila Gilbert and Betsy Wollheim of DAW Books, for allowing me to share Mara's adventures with my readers, and especially to Sheila, my editor, who has an extraordinary knack for spotting, not only what works, but, more importantly, what doesn't work, in her authors' tales—and an even more extraordinary knack for helping them discover how to fix those problems.

A special thanks to my agent, Ethan Ellenberg, who looked at several different ideas I was toying with and urged me to focus on what has become *The Masks of Aygrima*. If not for his initial enthusiasm, this series would never have been born.

And finally, all my love and gratitude to my wife, Margaret Anne, and daughter, Alice. I love being a writer. I love being a husband and father far, far more.

ONE

The Stranger from the Sea

THE MASK GLEAMED WHITE against the dark
surface of Mara's workbench, like a pearl in an eb-
ony box. It looked perfect, priceless, a masterwork of the
Maskmaker's craft . . .

. . . and it was completely, totally, fatally *wrong*.

"It looks good," Prella said from behind her. The other
girl, the same age as Mara—fifteen—but smaller, had taken
to spending all her free time hanging around Mara, ever
since Mara had saved her life by healing her with magic after
she'd suffered a terrible injury. Mara understood that, and
ordinarily was rather touched by it, but she would have been
just as happy not to have a witness to her repeated failures.

Like this one. "It isn't," she growled. "Watch." She
reached out and poked the Mask's gleaming cheek. As

though her touch had infected the shining face with some terrible disease, the Mask cracked at that point . . . and kept on cracking, a spiderweb of black lines spreading out across all of the shining surface, until the entire Mask abruptly fell apart into dust and flinders.

Prella gasped. "Oh!"

Mara gazed glumly at the ruined Mask. She didn't even swear . . . this time. She'd used up her entire vocabulary of obscenities (of which a childhood spent playing in the streets of Tamita had given her a surprising number) the first . . . what? twelve times? . . . something similar had happened. Although at least this one had *looked* like a Mask. The first half-dozen had looked more like something intended to frighten small children.

She lifted her gaze from the crumbled clay and stared out through the narrow slit of the window cut through the rock wall above the bench. Her work chamber was on the topmost level of the Secret City, a long climb from the Broad Way that ran from the main entrance down to the underground lake that was the City's source of water. From up here, she looked straight across the big horseshoe of the cove into whose walls the City was carved, all the way to the cliff on the far side. Snow glistened on the trees that capped it, white as the failed Mask had been before it crumbled.

Six weeks had passed since she had returned to the Secret City from the disastrous attempt to rescue her friend Katia from the terrible mining camp to which the unMasked were exiled. Six weeks since she had discovered her ability to harness enormous amounts of magic, and to pull that magic, not from the stores of it painstakingly collected from the black lodestone to which it was drawn when living things died, but directly from other human beings. Six weeks since she had ripped magic from scores of people—men, women, boys, girls, Masked and unMasked alike—and contained the force of an explosion that should have leveled the mining camp and killed everyone aboveground within it.

Six weeks since she had discovered that she had the rare form of the Gift that had produced the greatest monsters in the history of Aygrima . . . the same Gift, but to a far greater degree, as the Autarch himself, the tyrant to whose overthrow the unMasked Army dwelling in this Secret City was devoted.

She rubbed her tired eyes. "And a fat lot of good all that power is doing me right now," she muttered.

"You'll figure it out," Prella said, and Mara started. She'd momentarily forgotten the other girl was there.

"I hope you're right," she said. She tried to give Prella a smile. It wasn't very successful.

She looked down at the crumbled Mask once more. Growing up, she had watched her father, Charlton Holdfast, Master Maskmaker of Aygrima, make many, many Masks. She knew how to shape the clay, how to fire it, how to do everything except for one little thing . . . how to infuse the Mask with magic.

Catilla, the elderly woman who had founded and still commanded the unMasked Army, had seen no difficulty with that little fact when she had kidnapped—*rescued*, Mara reminded herself—Mara and four others who had just turned fifteen from the wagons taking them to the mining camp in the wake of their failed Maskings. Catilla didn't *want* real Masks, Masks that would reveal any traitorous leanings on the part of their wearers to the Autarch's ever-present Watchers, Masks that would shatter completely if the magic within them judged that the wearer posed a threat to the Autarch's rule.

She wanted even less the new Masks, those made within the last year or two, which not only revealed incipient sedition but allowed the Autarch to draw magic out of the Masks' wearers for his own use, a process which also weakened the wearer's will to the point where he or she literally could not conceive of any rebellion against the Autarch. As a side effect, the new Masks altered the personalities of those wearing them, making them almost unrecognizable to their friends and loved ones. But what was that to the Autarch, desperate for more and more magic to stave off the ravages of old age and keep himself firmly in control?

All *Catilla* wanted were believable semblances of real Masks, Masks that her followers could wear as disguises, enabling them to safely enter the towns and villages of Aygrima, and even Tamita itself, to . . .

To what? Mara asked herself, not for the first time, and, also not for the first time, had no answer. Catilla had not confided in her what she intended her followers to do once they could enter those towns and villages.

But then, it doesn't really matter, does it? Mara thought, still looking down at the failed Mask. *I can't make the counterfeits she wants.*

The Mask in front of her *should* have been nothing but inert clay. She had put no magic into it—she *had* none, without reaching into the bodies of those around her. And since she had almost killed those whom she had treated as her personal storehouses of magic before, including her friend Keltan, she wasn't about to do it again.

No matter how tempting it was . . . which it was, despite the agony she had felt when she'd stripped magic from living people, despite the warnings of Ethelda, the Palace Healer who now dwelt in the Secret City and had been tutoring Mara in the knowledge of magic (though not in its use, since the Secret City had no store of it with which to practice), despite the soul-sapping, nightmarish images of those she had killed with magic that had driven her to the edge of ending her own life before she had Healed Prella.

That act of Healing had somehow eased the nightmares, as if it had salved some internal injury she had done herself through her use of others' magic. Ethelda had warned her, though, that those horrors were not gone from her mind: her power meant that every person she killed with magic, or even those who simply died in her presence, imprinted themselves on her, their final agonies mingling with her own imagination to produce hallucinatory horrors that could threaten her sanity if fully unleashed.

She knew all that. She *knew* it. And yet ...

... and yet, despite it all, she longed to touch that raw power again, to see what else she could do with it.

She could *feel* the magic inside Prella's skinny little body. It would be so easy to reach out and tug it to herself, use it to try to make the *next* Mask succeed where all the previous attempts had failed. Prella might not even notice what she had done, if she was—

No! She clenched her fists. *No.* Keltan had been unconscious for hours after she had sucked him dry of magic that night in the camp. It had taken him days ... *weeks* ... to recover fully.

I will not do it, she told herself. *I will* not.

It wasn't the first time she had made herself that promise, and so far, she had kept it.

So far.

She shoved the thought aside, hard, like an annoying branch on a forest path. In any event, she had put no magic into this Mask, or any of her previous attempts: and that, apparently, was the problem.

She had very carefully left out the "recipe," as her father had called it, the black lodestone dust, infused with magic, which the law required each Maskmaker to include in every Mask he or she made. That "recipe" imparted to the Masks their traitor-detecting, and more recently Autarch-feeding, capabilities. Without it, she had thought the Mask clay was perfectly ordinary.

But clearly it wasn't. The clay the Maskmakers shaped into Masks *also* came from the Palace . . . and though she could shape it and fire it in the Secret City's own kilns, used by their own potters to make ordinary pots and plates, and though it always looked, when she drew it out, as though it had fired successfully, one touch, and . . .

. . . *that*. She stared down at the remnants of her latest failure for another long moment. Of course she'd known that making real Masks required magic from the Maskmaker. What she hadn't realized was that that magic was required simply to keep the Mask from falling apart. And she had no idea how to use her magic to accomplish that, nor any magic she dared draw on to attempt it.

She sighed and swept the ruined Mask into a dustbin, where the dust and shards of her previous three attempts still rested. "Are you going to try again?" Prella asked.

"I don't think I can," Mara said dully. "I'm almost out of clay." She crossed the small chamber to a chest in the corner, Prella trailing her. She lifted the chest's lid, revealing a smallish lump wrapped in wet sackcloth, all that remained of the clay she had been provided by the unMasked Army, which had raided (and then burned to cover their tracks) the Maskmaker's shop in the nearest village, Stony Beach. "I can't make more than three Masks out of that."

"But surely you'll figure out—"

"I already *have* figured it out," Mara snapped, suddenly annoyed beyond reason. "Don't you get it? *I can't do what Catilla wants me to do.* And you and your stupid questions and your stupid chatter and your whole stupid always being there, joggling my elbow, aren't helping. Go away!"

Prella's eyes widened, her lip trembled, and Mara had an instant to feel terrible before the smaller girl turned and ran from the workroom, slamming the door behind her.

Great, Mara thought. *Just great.* She felt like she'd kicked a puppy. *I'm a failure as a Maskmaker* and *a friend.*

She sighed. *I'd better go apologize. And then I'm going to have to face Catilla. I'm going to have to tell her I can't do what she wants me to do. What she rescued me to do. What people have* died for *me to do.*

She felt sick.

She slammed the chest shut, then raised her eyes to the wooden shelf above it. Three clay faces stared back at her, blank eyeholes and mouth openings filled only by the shadows behind them. As sculptures, they were rather good, she thought. But as Masks, they failed utterly. Made of ordinary clay, they were monstrously heavy, whereas a true Mask felt light as a feather on the face. And a true Mask also simply clung, clearly another function of the magic within that accursed special clay, or the magic provided by the Maskmaker. The fake Masks could not be held onto a face without an elaborate system of leather straps. It seemed to Mara that she had somehow managed to carve disappointment and reproach into the expressions of each one.

Prella, she thought again. *Catilla.*

But at that moment, she didn't think she could face either. Or anyone else: not Alita, or Simona or Kirika, the other girls rescued from the wagons along with her; not Keltan, whom she had met in Tamita, who had fled the city rather than be Masked, and who had almost died when she pulled magic from him; and definitely not Hyram, great-grandson of Catilla, whose father, Edrik, was second-in-command. Alita would be contemptuous, Simona uninterested, Kirika sullen, Keltan and Hyram would fall all over themselves trying to outdo each other in compassion, and none of it would change anything.

She had failed. All she really wanted was to be alone, and she knew just where to go to achieve that.

Her fur-lined leather coat hung on a peg by the door; she grabbed it and left her workroom. Beyond the door a corridor ran left and right, parallel to the cliff face. Other doors led to other workshops—those of the blacksmith and the regular potters, a few others—all located on the topmost level of the Secret City for the simple reason that they all needed fires and the smoke from those fires could be most easily vented through cracks in the ground at the top of the cliff. Mara had worried that that smoke, and all the other smoke from the heating and cooking fires down below, might lead Watchers to the City, but Hyram had explained that the many hot springs in the area (like the one that heated the women's bathing area in the underground lake) vented steam through similar cracks scattered over a wide area. From a distance, there was nothing to distinguish the smoke of the Secret City from the natural vapors of the landscape. "Provided they don't get close enough to smell the smoke," he'd added. "And nobody will get that close without one of the patrols seeing them."

Mara knew that down the corridor to her left, stairs led up to the "back door," a concealed entrance through which foot patrols came and went, but she turned right and instead took the stairs down. The next two levels of the Secret City were mostly living quarters, including, on the lower of the two, the room where she slept with Kirika, Prella, Alita, and Simona. From there, the stairs led straight down to the Broad Way.

Everyone was busy with their various chores and tasks, or on patrol, and so she met no one during her descent. A young man coming up the Broad Way with a bag of grain slung over his shoulder nodded to her as he passed; a moment later an identical copy of him passed her in the other direction and did the same. "Hi," she said to each of them in turn. She'd known them for weeks, and they'd been part of the disastrous rescue attempt at the mining camp, and she *still* couldn't tell Skrit apart from Skrat.

Skrit/Skrat turned into the Great Chamber, taking his grain to the kitchens, but she pulled on her coat, tugged on the hat and gloves she took from its pockets, and hurried out into the bright, cold afternoon.

The days had grown shorter and shorter over the past few weeks, until now, though it was only about four hours past noon, the sun was already dipping toward the horizon, casting long blue shadows on the snowdrifts, crisscrossed by trampled paths, that filled the cove. In ten days it would be Midwinter. Just a year ago she had celebrated it with her parents, their home alight with candles and hung with evergreen boughs. She could still remember how their fragrance had mingled with the delicious smells of cooking ham and baking cakes, how everything had felt beautiful and warm and safe. This year . . .

This year, there seemed little to celebrate, even if the unMasked Army marked the day. So far she'd seen no sign of it.

The ocean thundered, tall breakers racing in to batter themselves into white spray against the stony shore, the sea still unsettled from a violent storm that had blown through the night before. Mara, seeing the height of the waves, hesitated; in storms the water sometimes reached the path along the beach she meant to travel. But she decided to walk down to the water's edge at least, and once there, looking north, she saw that the path was open. *Must be low tide*, she thought, for though the water roared against the shore, only the occasional blast of spray made it as far as the cliff face.

The path looked grim, gray, cold, and lonely.

Perfect, Mara thought, and set out along it.

Her feet crunched over the salt-rotted ice covering the sand-and-pebbles beach. Just before the curve of cliff face hid it from her, she glanced back at the Secret City. Two dark figures trudged across the open space, presumably heading to the Broad Way from the stables carved into the base of the cove's northern cliff. She recognized them instantly as Keltan and Hyram, but they had their backs to her and didn't see her . . . which suited her fine.

Ten more steps and they, and the cove, were lost to sight. Alone with her thoughts, she wended her way north along the narrow strip of land between the pounding waves to her left and the gray stone cliff to her right, past the entrance to the mine from which the Secret City drew the gold it occasionally used to purchase goods in the villages via children too young to be Masked.

I can't make the Masks Catilla wants, she thought again as she walked. Spray touched her face. She licked salt from her lips, but lowered her head and trudged on, her breath forming white clouds, the crunch of her footsteps echoing from the cliff to her right. *I don't know how. I need to talk to someone who knows more. I need to talk to . . .*

Her thoughts and her feet stumbled. She caught herself with a hand on an ice-coated outcropping of gray stone.

I need to talk to my father.

Her father had deliberately sent her into exile. At great risk to himself—uncertain if his own Mask, modified though it was, might reveal his betrayal to the Watchers—he had crafted her Mask to fail at her Masking on her fifteenth birthday . . . and then had sent word to the unMasked Army that someone with the ability to make Masks would be in the next wagonload of un-Masked children sent north from Tamita to the mining camp.

Father must have known I couldn't really make counterfeit Masks, Mara thought. *Which means he lied to the unMasked Army, tricking Catilla into saving me.*

But now that lie was unraveling. With the stolen Maskmaker's clay all but gone, she could hide the truth no longer. She would have to tell Catilla that she could not provide her with the counterfeit Masks she needed.

Unless Mara could talk to her father.

She wanted that; wanted it so much that she wondered for a moment if she had subconsciously *made* her Masks fail. *Of course not,* she told herself: but having wondered it herself, even for a moment, she knew there was little doubt Catilla would ask her about it point-blank.

No, she thought. *I did everything I could. I did. I just don't have the knowledge . . . or the magic. Catilla will have to see that. She'll* have *to. And then she'll have to figure out some way for me to go back to Tamita . . . some way for me to see my father again. She'll* have *to.*

Won't she?

Mara stopped her northward wandering and wiped water from her cheeks. She told herself it was spray from the sea . . . but it was warm.

She looked around. She'd gone past the narrow defile in the cliff that, providing the only access up from the beach for horses, led to the Secret City's grain fields and pastures. She'd never walked any farther. The cliff curved out to sea in front of her, and the beach narrowed, so that at the tip of the headland the waves appeared to be crashing across it. *Time to head back,* she thought. *Time to face Catilla.*

She tugged her rabbit-skin hat tighter onto her head, shrugged her coat more firmly into place, started to turn ...

... and then froze as a stranger came around the shoulder of the cliff.

TWO

Chell

MARA'S FIRST INSTINCT was to flee. But then an extra-large wave rolled in from the sea, doused the stranger in spray as it smashed into the rocks, and washed around his feet as it receded. He stumbled and fell, splashing into the water . . . and didn't get up. She hesitated, torn between fear and compassion.

Compassion won.

She hurried forward, not quite daring to run on the ice-slicked beach. As she got closer, she saw the stranger try to get to his hands and knees, but he collapsed forward, head turned, his cheek pressed against the stones.

His *unMasked* cheek, she realized with a thrill.

Another wave splashed over him, and receded.

Just because he wasn't wearing a Mask didn't necessarily mean he was *really* unMasked, of course. Like the Watcher who had found her in the magic-collection hut the morning after she had slain her kidnapper and would-be rapist, Grute, with magic—blowing off his head in a gruesome fashion that continued to haunt her dreams—this young man might merely have removed his Mask while he wandered the Wild, intending to don it again whenever he got back to civilization.

But she didn't really think so. The young man wasn't carrying anything with him, and anyone Masked would keep his Mask close at hand at all times: the Masks would crack and crumble if they were abandoned and that would be a death sentence should the wearer encounter a Watcher.

The stranger wore dark blue trousers, a heavy leather coat, and black boots, all soaked through. His pale hair—Mara had never before seen anyone young with such pale hair, so blond as to be almost be white—was plastered to his head in lank, dripping strands. At his side he wore a sword with a strange, basket-shaped hilt.

She took all that in as she ran up to him. As she reached his side, she was able to see around the shoulder of the cliff for the first time. Debris lay scattered along the shore, bits and pieces of planking and rigging, clearly the remains of a wrecked boat. Debris . . .

. . . and corpses. Her breath caught. She counted five, all dressed in nondescript clothing like the young man at her feet. She didn't have to go close to them to know they were dead: her Gift told her. When living people were near, she could always—always—feel the magic within them, the magic she sometimes had to fight not to draw on. She could feel no magic from those sprawled, wave-tossed bodies.

But she could feel it in the young man. She could do

nothing for the others, but him, she might still be able to save.

She knelt, the icy pebbles digging painfully into her knees. The stranger's face was white as the ice all around, his lips the color of a bruise. His eyes fluttered open, startlingly blue in his white face, framed by that astonishing pale-gold hair. "Help . . ." he whispered.

"I will," Mara assured him. *But how?* her mind whispered, as panic fluttered in her chest. If she ran for help, he might freeze to death before she returned. She had nothing with which to make a fire.

Magic, she thought. *If only I had magic . . .*

But she had none, except for what she sensed in the shivering frame of the frozen youth, and if she drew on that, she'd likely kill him.

Not to mention what it might do to her.

"I'll help you," she said again, "but you have to help me do it. You have to walk."

"Don't know . . . if I can," he said. His words were oddly shaped, vowels elongated, consonants clipped.

"You have to," Mara repeated firmly. "You can lean on me."

A brief smile flickered across his white face. "I'll t-t-t-try," he said through chattering teeth.

She helped him to a sitting position, then slipped his arm over her shoulder. "We'll stand together," she said. "On three. One . . . two . . . three!"

She struggled to rise and he struggled to rise with her. Mara's foot slipped on an icy rock and they both collapsed back into a heap, Mara on top of the youth, who grunted at the impact. "Sorry!" she said, and they tried again. This time they managed it. Another tall wave doused them both with spray and sluiced freezing water around their ankles, almost tugging them down again, but Mara held on, though she was now so thoroughly soaked that her teeth, too, were chattering. "Hold on t-t-to me," she gasped out.

"Right . . ." he mumbled.

Together, they began struggling back toward the Se-cret City. The young man . . . *he can't be more than twenty*, Mara thought, glancing sideways at his smooth-shaven, unlined face, *maybe younger* . . . was a head taller than her, but thin enough that she was able to support him without trouble.

Even as she thought it, his feet slipped on the ice and he fell, dragging her down with him so that she sprawled across him once again, this time over his back. Her knees had both cracked hard against the ground as she fell, and she sat up and rubbed them. "Ow," she said.

The youth rolled over. "S-s-s-sorry," he said.

"It's all right," Mara said. "We're alm-m-m-ost th-there."

"Where?" the youth said as she helped him stand again.

"The Se-secret Ci-city," Mara said, then clamped shut her chattering teeth, wondering if she'd said more than she should.

Well, he's going to see it for himself soon enough, isn't he?

"What's your n-name?" she said as they struggled along, the going a little easier now they were past the defile leading up to the pastures. "I'm Ma-ma-mara Holdfast."

"Chell," he said. "Royal Korellian Navy." The chatter of his teeth had stopped, but his speech was slurred. "At your service. May I have this dance?" He blinked sleepily at her. "Actually, rather tired. Think I need a nap. Dance later."

The name was outlandish, the rest gibberish; clearly the cold was making him delirious. *Catilla will have to figure this one out*, Mara thought.

The youth leaned harder and harder against her, his weight dragging at her, and then, with the cove still a hundred yards away, slipped away from her entirely. She clutched at him and managed to slow his fall, but when he hit the ground he lay motionless, eyes closed, cheek pressed against the icy stone.

Mara straightened and ran for the Secret City, slipping and sliding and shouting for help.

As bad luck would have it, there was no one in the drifted space between the cliffs, but when she dashed into the Broad Way she saw Hyram and Keltan coming toward her, hair wet, faces shining, carrying towels; they'd obviously just come from bathing in the underground lake. "Hi, Mara!" Keltan said cheerfully, and then his eyes widened as he took in her soaked clothing and red face. "What's wrong?"

"Stranger," Mara gasped out with what little breath she had. At least the exertion had stopped her teeth from chattering. "On the beach ... freezing ... hurry!"

The two boys exchanged startled glances, then dropped their towels on the floor and ran after her into the cold. The Broad Way was cold enough that they wore proper boots and light jackets, despite having just come from the baths, and they followed her across the snow-covered space between the cove, then outdistanced her and ran ahead, leaving her to pant along in their wake, when they spotted the strange golden-haired youth's dark form on the beach.

Within minutes they had carried him inside and up the stairs to the chambers of healing, where Mara had spent far too much time herself. Asteria, granddaughter of Grelda, the Secret City's nonmagical Healer, looked up from chopping herbs as Hyram and Keltan carried the unconscious stranger into the whitewashed chamber. Lanterns and firelight provided the only illumination, since the shutters over the narrow window slits had been closed to keep out the chill. "Go get your grandmother, and Ethelda," Hyram shouted at her. "And my father and great-grandmother!"

Asteria said nothing—a rare occurrence—and dashed out. Hyram and Keltan carried the stranger through a red curtain into a chamber beyond with four beds, all empty, and placed the youth on the same bed in which Prella had been laid when she had been brought in with the terrible wound, inflicted by Kirika, that Mara had healed with magic.

I healed Prella, I could heal the stranger, Mara thought. *I know I could.* There was magic in Keltan, magic in Hyram. She could draw on it, use it to warm the cold body of the unconscious youth. *I wouldn't need much. They'd hardly ...*

She clenched her fists against that insidious desire. *No!*

Hyram was kneeling by the boy, pulling off his boots; Keltan was tugging at his coat. "Mara, blankets," Hyram snapped without looking at her, and Mara, startled, shook herself and went out into the main room. There were stacks of thick blankets in a tall wooden cabinet; she grabbed two and went back into the other room.

Hyram and Keltan had finished stripping the stranger, and were just covering his pale, naked body with the blanket already on the bed. Mara held out the extra blankets to them, painfully aware her ears were flaming with embarrassment. "Here," she said.

"Thanks," Hyram said. He spread the additional blankets on the youth, while Keltan went to the fire and put on a new log.

The red curtain swirled aside and Grelda came in, followed by Ethelda. The former had been one of the handful of people who had originally fled to the Secret City, then a smaller warren of caves left by some long-gone tribe of ancients, sixty years ago when the rebellion against the Autarchy had failed. The latter had been Chief Healer of Aygrima—and a secret ally of Mara's father—until she had been kidnapped by the unMasked Army to heal Mara . . . and, hopefully, tutor her in the use of her powerful Gift.

The two Healers had come to an uneasy truce. Grelda did not have the Gift, and so her Healing was based on her knowledge of the body and its ills, and the uses of herbs and potions. Ethelda had the Gift, but in the Secret City she had no magic to work with. She was not without knowledge of the other kind of Healing, however. "I've learned a lot from her, but she's learned a lot from me, too," Ethelda had told Mara. "And we're both better Healers for it." She'd grimaced. "If you can call it Healing when no magic is involved. The body does whatever healing takes place. All you can do without magic is try to keep the body alive long enough for it to heal itself."

"Let me see him," Grelda said now as she entered. Mara stepped back into the corner as Grelda pulled back the blankets and examined the youth. She could feel herself blushing again, but she didn't look away.

The youth was thin, but not emaciated: his muscles stood out like thick cords beneath his skin. *Wiry*, she guessed was the word that would apply to him best. He showed no signs of having been wounded. The only mark on his skin was a curious tattoo on his left breast, just above his heart: a circle, a crescent, and a star all in a line, in red, green, and blue, respectively. His limbs trembled visibly as shivers racked his body.

Grelda pulled the blanket back over him, felt the pulse in his neck. "Nothing wrong with him that warming up won't fix," she said. "He's shivering; that's a good sign."

"It is?" Mara said, startled into speaking.

Grelda ignored her, but Ethelda gave her a quick smile. "Shivering is the body's way of trying to stay warm," she said. "When the shivering stops, death is very near."

Grelda had turned to Asteria. "Bladders of hot water," she said. "Three of them. One to his groin, one under each armpit."

Asteria nodded and hurried out, almost colliding with the tall man just hurrying in: Edrik, Hyram's father, second-in-command of the unMasked Army behind his grandmother Catilla. He stopped in the doorway. "It's true?" he said. "A stranger from the sea?"

"Yes," Mara said. "I found him. Just past the horse path. There's a wrecked boat. And . . . bodies."

"Other survivors?"

Mara shook her head. "No."

Edrik stared at her, eyes narrowed. "You're sure?"

"I'm sure." She didn't want to say it was because of her Gift, but he took her meaning.

He grunted. "I'll send a retrieval party. Give them a proper burial. And see if that wreckage can tell us anything more about where they came from . . . and who *this* is." He stared down at the shivering youth.

"Look at this, Father," Hyram said. He had been examining the stranger's trousers; now he held them out. "Look at the button."

Edrik took the pants and examined the fly, frowning. "It's embossed with letters . . . R . . . K . . . N?"

"Royal Korellian Navy," Mara said.

Everyone turned to look at her.

"He introduced himself," she explained. "Just before he passed out. He said his name is Chell, and then he said 'Royal Korellian Navy.'" They all stared, and for some reason she added, "And then he asked me to dance."

"He's a lunatic," Keltan said, then stopped, flustered. "Um, not for asking you to dance. Fine thing to do. I'd do it myself. But not when I was half-frozen on a strange shore."

"Mental confusion is one of the effects of loss of body heat," Ethelda said.

"Royal Korellian Navy," Edrik said slowly. "That's . . . unexpected."

"You've heard of it?" Hyram asked.

Edrik put the coat down on the back of the chair. "I must go talk to the Commander," he said. "And organize that retrieval party."

"Isn't Catilla coming herself?" Grelda said sharply.

"She's not feeling well today," Edrik said. "One reason I was close at hand when your granddaughter came looking for me. My grandmother had asked me to fetch you."

"Is it . . . ?" Grelda said, her eyes on his face.

He nodded once, without expression.

"I'll go at once," Grelda said. She glanced at the sleeping stranger. "Once we get the hot water bladders on him, he'll recover quickly. But he'll probably sleep for hours."

"Hyram, Keltan, stay here," Edrik ordered. "One of you come get me the minute he's awake. The other keep an eye on him. I'll be in the Commander's quarters." He followed Grelda out.

Asteria came back in with three bloated pig bladders in a basin. "Armpits and groin, Grandma said," she said cheerfully. She gave Mara a sideways look and a wink. "Want to help?"

"No, thank you," Mara said hurriedly, blushing again.

Asteria laughed. Ethelda pulled back the blankets, Asteria placed the bladders between the youth's legs and under his arms, and the blankets went back into place.

"There," Asteria said. "Nothing to do but wait. And I'd better get back to chopping those herbs." She swept out through the red curtain.

Ethelda glanced at Mara. "Will you still be coming to talk to me tonight?"

Mara nodded. She had been meeting with Ethelda every two days since she'd returned from the mining camp. Catilla had commanded Ethelda to teach her how to use her magic more safely, but since they had no magic to practice with, the sessions had become more a mixture of history lessons and counseling. "Yes," she said. "I have . . . something important to talk to you about."

Ethelda's left eyebrow lifted, but she simply nodded once, and then went out.

That left Hyram, Keltan, and Mara alone in the room with the unconscious Chell. "My father knows something about this 'Royal Korellian Navy,'" Hyram said. "I could see it in his eyes."

"Still don't believe in other lands beyond the seas?" Keltan teased. Hyram had been known to call tales of other lands nothing but children's stories.

"We don't know he's from beyond the sea," Hyram said stoutly. "He might just be from farther up the coast. Maybe there are people north of the mountains."

"Nothing up there but frozen wasteland," Keltan said.

"And maybe the Lady of Pain and Fire," Mara said.

Keltan snorted. "That's about as likely as a mysterious hidden kingdom we've never noticed before. She's a myth!"

No, she's not, Mara thought. *She's what I could become.* But she didn't want to tell them *that*. Instead she moved closer to the sleeping stranger and looked down at his white-gold hair. "I've never seen hair that color before. Have you?"

"Only on an ear of corn," Hyram said. He sounded

grumpy. "You're not going to make a habit of this, are you?"

Mara glanced at him, puzzled. "Of what?"

"Fishing handsome young men out of the sea. You've got me. You don't need to go looking."

"What do you mean, she has *you*?" Keltan said. "Don't you mean she has *us*?"

Mara rolled her eyes. The two boys were the best of friends . . . except when it came to her. They'd already had at least one fistfight over her. If she even *looked* at one of them too long, the other got jealous. And if she went so far as to hold one's hand, or give the other a hug . . .

One of these days I'll kiss one of them just to see what the other one does, she thought. Her mouth quirked at the thought. *But which one?*

That was the problem, wasn't it? She liked both of them. But she wasn't sure she was ready to *kiss* them. Or . . . other things.

Well, not yet.

"Stop it," she said out loud. "I don't *have* either of you."

Hyram leered. "Don't you mean you haven't 'had' either of us?"

"She better not have," Keltan growled.

Mara sighed. *Boys*, she thought. She looked down at the golden-haired youth. *He looks nice*, she thought. *Awfully pale. But kind of handsome. And that hair . . .*

She reached down and brushed a wet strand out of the stranger's face, then suddenly realized silence had fallen in the room. She glanced up to see Hyram and Keltan looking at her with identical expressions of narrow-eyed suspicion. "What?" she said.

And then the stranger moaned, coughed . . . and opened his eyes.

Mara, caught with her hand on his forehead, froze for a moment, then snatched her fingers back as though his cold wet flesh had burned her. The youth blinked up at her sleepily. "Pim?" he said. "Is that you?"

Who is Pim? Mara thought. It wasn't a girl's name . . . at least, not in Aygrima. "No," she said. "I'm Mara. I found you on the beach. Do you remember?"

"Mara?" The boy frowned. "Mara . . . the beach?" His eyes almost fluttered closed again, then snapped open. "Beach. The boat. Boat capsized. All of us, in the water. Trech . . . Bariss . . . helped me . . . but so cold . . ."

"He talks funny," Hyram said. "'Boot cahpsized . . . soo kahld,'" he mimicked.

"I'm surprised we can understand him at all," Keltan said. "If he's really from beyond the sea . . ."

"Hush, both of you!" Mara said. She knelt beside the bed to bring her mouth closer to the youth's ear. "Do you know where you are?" she said.

His eyes fluttered again. "Aygrima," he said. "Kingdom of magic . . ."

And then his eyes closed and he fell back into unconsciousness.

"'Kingdom of magic'?" Hyram said. "Who calls Aygrima *that?*"

"He does, apparently," Keltan said. He gave Hyram a look. "And aren't you supposed to be running off about now to tell your father he's waking up?"

"He's not awake, he's asleep," Hyram said, but he was already getting to his feet. "All right, all right, I'm going." He gave the prostrate youth a sour look, gave Keltan an even sourer one, and went out.

"I thought he'd never leave," Keltan said.

Mara got up from her knees and sat beside him on the bed next to the stranger's. She shivered.

"You're wet through yourself," Keltan said. "You should take off your clothes."

Mara gave him a look, and he threw up his hands with a laugh. "I didn't mean *that*!" Then, as though compelled by honesty, he added, "Well, not *entirely*. But seriously, you need to put on something dry."

"I will," Mara said. "But I want to be here when he wakes up for real."

"At least wrap this around you," Keltan said, grabbing one of the blankets she'd brought in earlier, one they hadn't put on Chell. He put it around her shoulders and tugged it tight around her. "Better?"

"Better," she said, and gave him a smile. "Thank you."

"I live to serve." They sat in silence for a moment, staring at the youth. "What did you say his name was?" Keltan asked after a minute or so.

"Chell," Mara said.

Keltan snorted. "Chell? What kind of a silly name is that?"

Mara gave him a withering look. "Says the boy who's named after the Autarch's horse?"

"Well, yeah, but that's, you know . . ." his voice trailed away.

"Different?" Mara finished sweetly.

"Exactly!"

"Well, so is he," she said. "Different, I mean."

Keltan said nothing, although somehow he managed to be grumpy about it.

For ten minutes they silently watched the stranger sleep. Then the red curtain swept aside, and Edrik came in, followed by Hyram. Hyram's eyes narrowed at the sight of Keltan and Mara sitting on the bed, but then swung to his father as Edrik said, "Has he said anything else?"

"No," Mara said. "He fell asleep again."

Edrik frowned. "If he woke up once, he's ready to wake up again. And I want some answers." He leaned down, gripped the youth's shoulders through the blankets covering it, and shook him. "Wake up, Chell of the Royal Korellian Navy," he said. "Wake up, and give an account of yourself."

The youth groaned. His eyes flicked open and this time focused. He blinked. "Who are you?" he asked. "Where am I?"

Edrik grunted. "The classic questions," he said. "But I think I get to ask mine first. Who are *you*? And where did you come from?"

The boy hesitated. Edrik's hands tightened on his shoulders. "The *truth*."

"I . . . I already told *her*." His eyes flicked to Mara. "My name is Chell."

"And you're in the Royal Korellian Navy. Yes, I heard." Edrik released him and straightened. "But you'll forgive me if I find that hard to believe . . . since the Sea Kingdom of Korellia sank beneath the waves four centuries ago."

Mara, Keltan, and Hyram exchanged startled looks.

"I assure you, it did not," said Chell. His voice sounded stronger now. "Not literally, at least. Though I suppose, figuratively, that's not a bad description of what happened . . . to Korellia, and all the other kingdoms."

"Explain," Edrik snapped.

Chell shook his head. "Look, I'll gladly answer all your questions and explain who I am and why I'm here . . . but do we have to do it this way? It's a bit awkward discussing ancient history when one is naked in a bed—" His eyes flicked to Mara, who looked away. "—with bladders of hot water under your arms and on your . . ." he let his voice trail away.

Edrik gave a quick nod. "Very well. If Grelda gives you leave, you may get up and get dressed." He looked at Keltan. "Fetch the Healer."

Keltan scrambled to his feet and hurried out. To Hyram, Edrik said, "He looks to be about your size. His clothes won't be dry for hours. Fetch him some of yours." Hyram scowled, but followed Keltan.

Edrik glanced at Mara. "You should go get some dry clothes of your own."

"I'm fine," Mara said.

"I insist," said Edrik, and his tone made it clear that she had no choice but to obey. She let the blanket slide from her shoulders onto the bed, got up, and went to the red curtain.

Glancing back just before she went out, she saw the strange young man's eyes following her.

THREE

"I Have to See My Father"

"IT'S NOT FAIR," Mara said, sitting in the Grand Chamber that night, pushing redroots around on her plate. "I found him. They should have let me be there while they questioned him."

"You make him sound like a stray puppy," said Alita. "He's not yours."

She and Simona were the only ones at the table with Mara. Hyram had been sent out on evening patrol and Keltan had probably scraped the very redroots Mara was pointedly not eating—much as she liked them—since it was his week for kitchen duty. Prella . . .

Prella was the other reason Mara was pushing her red-roots around instead of shoveling them into her mouth. Prella had come in with Alita, taken one look at Mara already sitting at their usual table, and gone off to sit with Kirika who, as usual, was sitting by herself at a table near the door instead of joining the others. That was good in a way, Mara thought; the dour, prickly Kirika had warmed up to, and *opened* up to, Prella far more than any of the rest of them, *mostly out of guilt at having almost killed her with a spade*, Mara thought, then felt her own pang of guilt for being so uncharitable. But she knew the main reason Prella had gone to sit with Kirika *tonight* was that she had hurt the other girl's feelings badly in the Mask workshop.

I have to apologize, Mara thought. She gave Prella and Kirika a sideways glance. They were leaning toward each other, heads almost touching. *I should go over there and do it now*. And she honestly was about to, except just at that moment Simona, in response to Alita, said, "I wish he was *mine*. He's cute."

"How would you—" Mara began, and then broke off, because she had followed Simona's gaze and seen what she'd seen: Chell, entering the Grand Chamber with Edrik and Edrik's beautiful black-haired wife (and Hyram's mother), Tralia. Though dressed in what were definitely not Hyram's best clothes (in fact, judging from the patches, not even his second- or third-best), the strange, slim young man stood out in the Chamber with his pale face and white-gold hair.

"Well, he's not a prisoner," Alita said.

"Looks more like an honored guest," Simona said. Her voice had a dreamy quality.

Mara gave her a disgusted look, then turned back to follow the stranger's procession through the Grand Chamber, heads—including Prella's and Kirika's—turning as he passed, to the tables at the far end where the highest-ranking members of the unMasked Army typically gathered, presumably to discuss important matters over dinner.

Matters too important, apparently, to involve Mara.

Well, she thought, *I've got my own important matter to discuss.* And before she was even fully aware she was doing it, she found herself on her feet and following Edrik, Tralia, and Chell the length of the Grand Chamber. "What are you doing?" she heard Alita whisper behind her, but didn't look back.

As the trio seated themselves, Chell was the first to see her, and her heart, oddly, skipped a beat as his face split into a huge grin. She felt herself echoing that smile with one of her own. "Mara! My rescuer!" Chell said. "Come and join us!"

Edrik turned his head sharply toward him. "No," he said. "I'm sorry, Mara, but the Commander has ordered that we not discuss—"

"I'm not here to ask anything about Chell," Mara said. She turned resolutely away from him. "I need to see Catilla."

Edrik frowned. "The Commander is not well," he said. "Is it urgent?"

"It's about . . . what I've been ordered to do," Mara said, some belated sense of caution reminding her that she knew nothing about Chell and so perhaps should not be too open in his presence. "I need to discuss with her how I am to proceed."

Edrik chewed on his lower lip, a nervous reaction Mara could never remember seeing from him before. "All right," he said at last. "I'll arrange it as soon as possible. I'll send word. Now if you'll excuse us—"

"Please," Chell said. "May she not join us? I promise I will be discreet in what I say. But I would like to thank her properly for saving my life."

"The Commander—" Edrik began again, but Mara got support from an unexpected quarter.

"Edrik," Tralia said. "Let her stay. I hardly think letting her eat with Chell will pose a threat to security. We're both right here."

Edrik glanced at his wife. "Well . . . all right," he said, reluctantly.

"Thank you!" Mara said to Tralia, who smiled at her.

Chell moved over to make room for her beside him on the bench on his side of the table.

"How are you feeling?" she asked him as she sat down.

"Perfectly all right now," he said. His accent was still strange, but easier to understand now that it was not slurred by the chill that had almost claimed his life. "Thanks to you. If you had not happened to walk that way along the beach, I would have fallen where I fell and either frozen to death or been carried out to sea by some rogue wave like the one that capsized my boat." His face turned grim. "And drowned all the rest of my party. As I would have drowned, had not two of them boosted me onto the boat's hull. I tried to pull up others, but the cold took its toll so quickly . . ." He fell silent.

Mara swallowed a sudden lump in her throat, thinking of those gently bobbing corpses on the beach. They had had names, families, lives. They had been Chell's friends. She managed a tentative smile. "Good thing I was feeling restless, then."

Chell swallowed hard himself, then managed a small smile in return, a smile that revealed dimples in each cheek that made him look even younger. "A very good thing indeed." He glanced up. "Ah! They're bringing food. I'm starving."

Mara looked up, too.

Keltan, hurrying toward them with a tray containing clay plates and bowls, almost stumbled when he caught sight of her, coming within a hair's-breadth of dumping his whole steaming load on Tralia's head, but he caught himself and instead placed the tray on the table, shooting Mara one astonished—and more than slightly outraged—look before turning away. While Edrik, Tralia, and Chell helped themselves, Keltan returned with a bottle of wine and three clay mugs, which he slammed down onto the table with rather more force than was necessary.

Chell watched him go, then glanced at Mara with an amused expression. "A friend of yours?"

"Sort of," Mara mumbled.

"Just sort of?" Chell leaned closer. "He looks jealous to me," he whispered teasingly. "Boyfriend?"

"No!" Mara said, more loudly than she intended, and felt her face flame with embarrassment. At that moment she could cheerfully have stabbed Keltan to death with her butter knife.

Chell sat back. "You're not eating?"

"I already ate," Mara said.

"Wine?"

Mara shuddered. "No, thanks."

"We discourage the younger ones from drinking wine," Tralia said conversationally. "Although I daresay they manage it anyway." She gave Mara a wink, and Mara, whose first experience with wine just a few weeks before had been humbling, looked down.

Why did I come over here? she thought miserably. *They treat me like a child. Even after what I did in the mining camp.*

What I could do right now . . .

She suddenly felt the power all around her, the magic in all the bodies crammed into the Grand Chamber at the height of the dinner hour, feeling it strongest from Edrik, Tralia, and Chell. She could draw that power to herself, show them she was no child, show them she was to be taken seriously . . .

She swallowed hard.

"I . . . I think I'd better . . ." She got to her feet. "I promised Ethelda . . . meet with her . . ."

Chell stood, too, and bowed to her courteously. "Then a good evening to you, fair lady," he said. "And my thanks again for the rescue." He glanced at Edrik, who had remained seated, stoically shoveling food into his mouth, and Tralia, who gave her husband a slightly exasperated look before smiling at Mara.

"Run along, then, dear," she said.

"Sure," Mara said. "'Bye." She walked away as quickly as she could, ears burning, certain that if she looked back she'd see Chell, Edrik, and Tralia laughing at her as she went.

She didn't look back.

Simona and Alita's eyes tracked her as she approached—and then passed—their table. Prella looked up as she neared, and then immediately looked away again. Kirika barely glanced at her, her face stony.

Keltan angled across the floor with a laden tray as though intending to intercept her, but she quickened her steps to avoid him, emerging into the quiet dimness of the Broad Way a moment later. There she paused, wrapping her arms around herself and pressing her back against the stone wall. *What's wrong with me?* Drawing magic from other people . . . it was *wrong*, it was *evil*, and it *hurt*—hurt worse than any other pain she had ever experienced. It should be the last thing she ever wanted to do again. And yet, day after day, she felt the urge to steal others' magic. Day after day, she pushed that urge away, but it always came back . . .

. . . and it was getting stronger. Just now, in the Grand Chamber, stung because she felt she'd been treated like a child, she'd come perilously close to giving in.

And if she gave in once . . . would she ever be able to stop?

Ethelda, she thought. *I must see Ethelda.*

She hurried across the Broad Way. The stairs she climbed led up to the girls' room on the second level, but carried on past that to the third level, where Ethelda had been given quarters down at the far end. The Healer opened the door at once when Mara rapped, and ushered her into the small room beyond, furnished with bed, chair, table, and chest. A cozy fire burned in the small hearth, and a white-painted shutter on the single slit-like window kept out the wintry sea air.

"I thought you'd forgotten," Ethelda said. A small woman with blue eyes and a round, pleasant face, she smiled as she spoke, leeching any possible sting from the words.

"Something reminded me," Mara replied. She stepped into the room, and Ethelda closed the door behind her, her expression concerned.

"What's happened?" Ethelda said, taking a seat in the chair by the table.

Mara sat on the edge of the bed and poured out what she had just felt. "It was the strongest it's ever been," she said miserably. "I felt hurt, and embarrassed, and angry, and I wanted to ... I wanted to show them, to prove to them I'm not a child, to show them I'm powerful ..."

"But you didn't," Ethelda said quietly. "You resisted."

"Barely."

"It doesn't matter if you 'barely' dodged a sword stroke or dodged it by a mile, you still dodged it," Ethelda pointed out.

"But what if I don't dodge it next time?"

A candle burned in the middle of the table; Ethelda reached out and passed her hand back and forth through the flame, too quickly to get burned. "Mara," she said at last, "the fact is ... I don't know how to help you."

Mara's stomach twisted. "What?"

Ethelda pulled her hand back from the flame and stared at her open palm for a moment. "You have reached the limit of my knowledge." She closed the hand into a fist, then opened it again and drew it back to her. She looked up into Mara's eyes, her expression grave. "You are Gifted, in a fashion that is rare ... not *unique*, perhaps, but almost. I know what you can do ... but I don't know how you do it. I do not know how you draw magic from others. I do not know what it means that you can see and use all 'colors' of magic at will, or what is truly possible with that kind of power. I do not know a great many things."

"But you're the Master Healer of Aygrima!" Mara cried. "If *you* don't know—"

"I *was* the Master Healer," Ethelda said, a hint of sharpness in her tone for the first time. "And I know a great deal about the use of magic for healing. But I have never had to heal, or help, one with your abilities ... or problems. If I were in the Palace, I would delve into the ancient books in the Library ... but I do not have access to the Library. All I have is the knowledge I have managed to sequester in my own brain over the years. And that is depressingly little."

Mara felt cold, though the fire blazed as hot as ever in the hearth not six feet away. "But ... what do I do? How can I learn to control these ... urges? What if I can't? I'll start hurting people. I might kill someone again. I might—"

"Might, and might, and might," Ethelda said. "Might is not the same as 'will.'" She raised her hands in a placating gesture. "I know. That is still no guarantee that 'might' won't *become* 'will.'" Then she spread her hands. "Mara, all I can say is ... resist."

Mara looked down at her own hands, twisting together in her lap. "This ... Library," she said. "In the Palace. Do you really think it might contain information that might help me control this?"

"I think there's an excellent chance," Ethelda said. She sighed. "Catilla would have been better served kidnapping Shelra, the Mistress of Magic, than the mere Master Healer. Shelra is extremely learned in all lore pertaining to the Gift. No doubt if she were here, she would know exactly how to help you . . . and train you. Or, if she did not, she would know exactly where to look in the Library for the knowledge she required."

Mara clenched her hands into fists and looked up. "Does my father have access to this Library?"

Ethelda's eyes narrowed. "Yes," she said slowly. "Mara, what are you . . . ?"

"I have to talk to Catilla," Mara said. "Now, more than ever. I have to talk to the Commander."

Ethelda looked away, into the fire. "That might be difficult," she said after a moment. "Catilla . . . is very ill."

Mara blinked. "I knew she wasn't feeling well," she said. "Are you saying it's something serious?"

Ethelda didn't look at her. "It is not common knowledge," she said in a low voice, "not yet, and you are not to tell any of your friends . . . but she is suffering from far more than just an autumn ague." Now, at last, she met Mara's eyes again. "She is dying."

"Oh, no," Mara whispered. She had no great love for Catilla, but she respected the old woman, who had led the first members of the unMasked Army to the Secret City in the wake of the failed rebellion six decades previously. And besides, she was Hyram's greatgrandmother. "But . . . you are . . . were . . . the Master Healer. Can't you—?"

"If I had magic, I might be able to do something, but without it . . ." She shook her head. "Grelda is of more use than I am. At least she has potions that can ease

Catilla's pain. But a cure is beyond her abilities. Catilla suffers from a tumor, blocking her esophagus."

"Her what?" Mara had never heard the term before.

Ethelda gestured at her throat. "The tube that runs from the mouth to the stomach. Already she finds it hard to swallow more than thin gruel, and even that pains her. She is losing weight, and she had little enough to lose to begin with."

"But you could cure her, if you had magic?" Mara said.

"I don't know," Ethelda said. "Tumors are difficult. Often they spread throughout the body, so that even if you eliminate one, there are others growing you cannot see. But she would at least have a chance." She sighed. "But I have no magic."

Mara felt the flow of magic within Ethelda herself, magic she could seize if she wanted, and said slowly, "I have."

Ethelda looked up sharply. "*No*. Mara, we've discussed this. If you give in to the urge to use the magic you can draw from others, even once . . . it will be that much harder to resist the urge the next time, and the next time, and the time after that. You will become as addicted to it as the Autarch . . . or the Lady of Pain and Fire. Do you want to become like *either* of them?"

"No," Mara said. "But if I could help Catilla . . ."

"You might just as easily kill her," Ethelda said flatly. "You were lucky with Prella: lucky, *and* using magic filtered through black lodestone. You could see the damage the spade had caused and you had a clear image of what an uninjured, healthy Prella looked like. The magic did your will, and returned her to that image. But the tumor that is killing Catilla is inside her. Do you know what an undamaged esophagus looks like? Can you tell diseased tissue from healthy? If you strike at the tumor with magic, you might just as easily blow her chest apart."

Mara winced, remembering when she had done just that to a Watcher in the camp, a Watcher threatening Keltan. That Watcher, a bloody hole torn straight through his body where his heart should have been, featured prominently in the nightmares that still sometimes fought their way through her drug-aided sleep. She remembered the glisten of organs in the firelight, the red gleam of the severed ends of ribs and spine, superimposed that horrific image on Catilla's frail frame, and thought she might be sick.

"I see in your face that you understand the danger," Ethelda said softly.

"But . . . couldn't we get magic for *you*?" Mara said desperately. "The hut—"

"The hut where you killed Grute is now guarded constantly," Ethelda said. "As are the other magic-wells in the vicinity. As is the cavern where you found magic for the Autarch's geologists. Already the Watchers are building permanent shelters there. By spring they will have unMasked mining it." She shook her head. "No. We have no way to get magic. Not in the quantities we need."

"But there must be *something* we can do!" Mara cried.

"I do not believe there is," Ethelda said. She sighed. "I'm afraid, child, that one of the hardest truths you learn as a Healer is that there are times when there is nothing you can do."

Mara sat in silence for a moment, staring down at her folded hands. "But . . . I still have to see her," she said in a low voice.

"Why?" Ethelda asked, her own voice gentle.

Mara looked up. "I have to go back to Tamita," she said. "I have to talk to my father."

Ethelda blinked, then snorted. "I hardly think you need to see Catilla to know what she's going to say to *that*."

Mara shook her head stubbornly. "It's the only way. If Catilla wants me to make counterfeit Masks, she's got to let me see my father. There's some . . . trick, some bit of magic, that must be performed to make the Masks work, even the counterfeit ones. Only my father can tell me what it is."

Ethelda opened her mouth to protest further, but Mara rushed on. "Then there's the matter of my own magic. You said yourself there might be knowledge in the Palace Library, and that my father has access to it. He might be able to—"

"At what risk to himself?" Ethelda reminded her sharply. "Yes, he has modified his Mask so it is not as sensitive as most to disloyal thoughts, but if he starts actively aiding the unMasked Army . . ."

"He would be aiding *me*," Mara said. "His daughter."

"Catilla will never agree!" Ethelda repeated. "She—"

"And," Mara said, "to make the counterfeit Masks will require a store of magic. My father can provide that, too. And if he provides enough . . . you might be able to use it to heal Catilla."

She stopped. Ethelda stared at her; she pressed her lips together and stared back.

"It would be . . . incredibly dangerous," the Healer said after a moment. "You are unMasked—"

"But I can still pass for a fourteen-year-old," Mara said. "So can Keltan. It's been less than half a year since either of us turned fifteen. And *he* knows how to get into and out of the city without being seen—he escaped it once already. We can slip inside. I know Catilla has a way to get a message to my father. She can send ahead, arrange the meeting. The Watchers will never know. And when we get back ... I'll be able to make the Masks, you'll be able to heal Catilla, and I'll know how to fight this ... addiction." *Or maybe even how to use my Gift safely*, she added to herself but did not say out loud.

Ethelda looked away, staring at the fire. "I don't know what Catilla will say," she murmured. "But ... all right. I'll take you to her."

Fifteen minutes later, Mara faced the Commander of the unMasked Army in her tapestry-hung chamber deep in the rock. This night Catilla did not sit at the golden-hued table where she had greeted Mara the first time they had met there. Instead, she lay in the four-posted bed, her gray hair unbound and spread on the pillow, her hands, blue-veined and pale, plucking restlessly at the pale blue counterpane. Grelda rose from the chair beside the bed. "I gave orders—" she said dangerously.

"The watchers on the door know I am a Healer, too," Ethelda said.

Grelda's frown only deepened. "You have said you can do nothing. Why do you trouble Catilla's—"

"Enough!" The new voice, thin and tired but with the hard edge of command in it, stopped Grelda's protest. Catilla's eyes, which had been closed, were now open, and whatever drugs for pain she had been given, however much she hurt inside, those eyes remained bright, clear, and cold. "Grelda, I have told you before. *I* will decide who may and may not see me."

"I'm your healer," Grelda said. "It is my decision to make, not yours."

"No," Catilla said softly. "It is not. I am still Commander, while I live and while I am in my right mind. Do you deny either of those conditions exist?"

Grelda let out her breath in an explosive sigh and threw up her hands. "Fine! Talk to them. But don't complain to me if you take a turn for the worse afterward."

She sat back down on the chair, folded her arms, and glared at Mara and Ethelda.

Catilla ignored her. Her eyes were now on Mara. "Maskmaker," she said. "How goes the effort?"

Mara remembered asking Catilla much the same question about how successful the efforts of the un-Masked Army to overthrow the Autarch had been, and on a whim, startled by her own boldness, she gave the same reply Catilla had given her. "Like shit," she said.

Ethelda shot her a startled look and Grelda frowned. But Catilla barked a hoarse laugh. "A . . . direct response," she said. "Very good. Since I have no strength or time for beating around the bush." Her eyebrows drew together. "Explain."

Mara told Catilla what she had told Ethelda . . . and what she proposed they do about it. Catilla listened without comment. Ethelda and Grelda stood — and sat — silently by. When she had finished, Mara watched Catilla's face while she waited for a response.

The old woman took a long, shallow breath, grimacing as she did so. "Sneaking into Tamita . . . is not something we have ever done," she said. "Into the villages, we have risked it, using children or, where Watchers are few and unwary, those whose Masks have not yet crumbled. But Tamita . . ."

"Sneaking into Tamita is why you want the counterfeit Masks in the first place," Mara said. "If you ever hope to send in a force large enough to do whatever it is you plan to do there, then you must let me sneak into the city now."

Catilla pressed her lips together against a silent cough that shook her slight body. When it passed, she lay with her eyes closed, breathing in quick, shallow gasps. Grelda got up and turned to her. "Catilla, you should — "

"I should finish this conversation, is what I should

do," Catilla snapped without opening her eyes. Grelda, lips drawn in a thin white line, plopped herself back onto her stool.

Catilla's eyes opened again, locked onto Mara. "Very well," she said. "I will send a message, through our secret channels, to your father, telling him when to expect you, and what you expect from him. You may dictate it to Edrik, once I have told him of my decision. And then ... you and Keltan will go to Tamita." A faint smile twisted her lips. "With Chell."

Mara's jaw dropped. "With ... Chell?"

"Edrik will explain." She closed her eyes again. "Now get out. Ethelda, please send someone to fetch my grandson." Another cough racked her. Grelda got to her feet again and leaned over the bed, muttering something Mara couldn't hear. Ethelda took Mara's arm and ushered her out, but just before they reached the door, Mara glanced back ... and caught a glimpse of the cloth Grelda had used to wipe the Commander's mouth in the wake of the cough.

Even from across the room, Mara could see the bright red blood that stained it.

FOUR

Forgotten History

HYRAM SQUEEZED SNOW between his clasped hands, forming it into a ball. "I should be going with you," he said plaintively. "Why aren't I going with you?" He threw the snowball as hard as he could: it splattered against a pine tree, leaving a white lump stuck to the dark bark.

"Good shot," Keltan said. "Did you picture your father's face when you threw it?"

Mara, sitting on a rock in the forest above the Secret City, said nothing. She was looking down into the cove, down to the beach, where Chell was examining one of the unMasked Army's small fishing boats. It had been a week since she'd found him on the beach, half of him frozen, the other half drowned. Soon she'd be traveling with him and Keltan to Tamita to see her father. It didn't seem quite real.

"Anyway, you know why," Keltan continued. "This is a stealth mission. The fewer the better. Mara has to go, obviously. I have to go because I know how to get into Tamita unseen. As well, if we *are* seen, we can both pass for fourteen. You can't." *Keltan's a better actor than I would have given him credit for*, Mara thought. *He almost doesn't even sound smug.* But she thought it rather absently. Chell was climbing over the boat, which had been pulled high enough onto the shore that even storm-driven waves couldn't touch it, and she was admiring the confident way he tugged on ropes, felt spars, ran his hands over the painted flanks . . .

"Neither can *he*," Hyram said. He was already forming another snowball, and he looked down into the cove with eyes narrowed, as if wishing he could throw it far enough to hit the stranger.

"Yes, well, he doesn't have to, does he? He's not coming into the city with us. He's just scouting."

"For the Royal Korellian Navy," Hyram said. "If it even exists." He turned and threw his new snowball even harder than before. It hit the tree trunk just below the first one.

"Your great-grandmother and your father are both convinced," Keltan said. "Why aren't you?"

"I don't know," Hyram growled. "I just don't like Chell."

"I do," Mara said, and then reddened, suddenly aware that both boys had turned to look at her. "I mean," she hurried on, "he seems trustworthy enough."

"Really," said Keltan.

"You don't say," said Hyram.

"Oh, stop it," Mara snapped. "I'm not your personal property, you know, either of yours. I can have other friends."

"Nobody's denying it," Hyram said, though it sounded as if he would have liked to. "But you hardly know Chell. Just because you saved his life doesn't mean you can trust him."

"I just don't feel like he's lying to us," Mara said. "That's all."

"Is that part of your Gift?" Hyram said. "You can *feel* when someone is lying?"

Mara flushed again. "You know it isn't."

"Then you'll forgive me if I don't take your *feeling* as very strong evidence for Chell's trustworthiness," Hyram said. "Because *my* feeling is just the opposite."

"*Your* feeling is just jealousy," Mara said. "You've been expecting me to throw myself at you since the moment I arrived at the Secret City."

Keltan snickered; Mara turned her glare on him. "You're just as bad," she said. "You're both so convinced I'm going to pick one of you as a boyfriend. You even got in a fight over me. But did either of you ever think to ask me if I was interested in either one of you?" And with that she jumped up and stomped away through the snow, half-surprised it didn't sizzle away from the heat of her anger.

The trouble is, she thought grumpily a few minutes later as she lifted the branch-covered trapdoor that opened into the corridor leading to her workshop, *that I don't know I can trust Chell. I just* want *to.*

And there it was. It made no sense, none at all. He was just a young man. A very handsome young man, but just a young man.

Yes, that's right, she thought. *A young* man. *Not a boy like Hyram or Keltan . . .*

She shook her head sharply. *And there you go again. What's gotten into you?*

She went into her workshop and closed the door firmly behind her. Her kiln was cold, her tools untouched for days; she saw no point in wasting clay on yet another Mask that would surely fail the same as all the others. *Father can help*, she thought, for the hundredth time. *But will he?*

She had dictated her message to Edrik, sitting at his table in the Grand Chamber the night after her meeting with Catilla, choosing her words carefully in case they went awry. "Father," it began. "I cannot do what I have been asked to do without your help. May we meet? Send word by this messenger." Then, on impulse, she had added, "I am well. I love you both."

Edrik had written down what she'd said without comment. The message had gone out the next day. How it was being conveyed, and at what risk to the messengers, no one told her. There had not yet been time for a reply; they could not start for the city until there was.

Mara went to the window slit and looked down into the cove. Chell now stood a few feet away from the boat, talking to Edrik. As she watched, he threw back his head and laughed. *He's not evil*, she thought. *He can't be. He must be telling the truth. It all makes sense . . .*

Hyram and Keltan, of course, had only heard his tale as it had been passed on by Edrik. *She* had heard it from Chell himself, on the night after her meeting with Catilla.

First, though, she had heard from Edrik. Once she had dictated the message, she had stood up, intending to rejoin her friends at their usual table far down the Chamber, but Edrik had indicated she should stay, and she'd sat down again, though not very comfortably, wondering what he had to say to her.

"The Commander has asked me to explain to you why we are allowing Chell to accompany you to Tamita," he said, in a tone she thought implied he would much have preferred to keep her in the dark.

"It surprised me," she admitted. "I didn't think you'd

trust him." *Catilla certainly didn't trust* me *when* I *first arrived,* she thought with more than a trace of bitterness.

"His story rings true to us."

And mine didn't? she thought. "*What* story?" she said out loud.

Edrik flicked his hand as though shooing a fly. "That's not important. I'll let him tell it, if he chooses to. All you need to know is that he will be coming with you, but he will *not* be entering Tamita." He leaned forward. "And you also need to know this. You are *not* to tell him you have the Gift. He knows that magic exists in Aygrima, but he does not know that *we* have anyone with the Gift, about you and Ethelda. He does not know you are attempting to make Masks for us. All he knows is that you must speak to your father in aid of our cause. He does not know who your father is."

Why the secrecy? Mara wondered, but, "All right," she said out loud. "But you know how hard it is to keep a secret in the Secret City. Are you sure no one else has told him?"

Edrik flicked his hand a second time. "We are not fools. He is guarded at all times, and no one is permitted to speak to him without permission."

"He could lead the Watchers here, if he is captured."

"He will not know where 'here' is. He will be blindfolded for the entire first day of your journey. And he will not be alone. I had thought to send Tishka with you, but now I've decided to come myself."

"He knows we're on the coast," Mara said. "All the Watchers have to do is sail far enough north—"

Edrik glowered at her. "Enough! The Commander and I judge the risk acceptable, and that is all you need to know." He leaned forward. "He has asked to speak to you, and I have agreed that he may do so. But I repeat: *do not tell him that you have magic. That* secret we are not prepared to share."

And then, an hour after that, Tishka, a tall, thin woman who wore her long red hair in a braided ponytail, one of those who had accompanied Mara on the disastrous attempt to rescue her friend Katia from the mining camp, and who had been coldly formal to her ever since, found Mara in her workshop. Without speaking, Tishka led her to one of the windowless storerooms along the Broad Way, which was emptied of bags of grain and turned into a cell for Chell.

Two other storerooms nearby, she knew, were also being used as cells: they held Turpit and Pixot, the Autarch's geologists, captured when the unMasked Army had rescued Mara for the second time from the clutches of the Watchers, at the mouth of the magic-filled cavern that would soon be Aygrima's second magic mine. Mara had tried to speak to Pixot once or twice—he had seemed almost friendly when they'd first met—but he had refused to see her. Both of them wore their Masks every day, though there were no Watchers to see. Mara suspected they were convinced they'd be rescued and they were afraid of doing anything that might get them labeled traitors once the Watchers finally arrived.

As they might, if this mission goes horribly wrong, she thought, and then pushed the uncomfortable thought firmly away.

The only furnishings in Chell's chamber were a wooden chair and a narrow bed. Chell pointed Mara to the chair; he sat on the bed. Tishka stationed herself at the door, silent, but watching and listening. *Making sure I don't say anything I shouldn't*, Mara thought. *I wonder what her orders are if I do? Kill Chell?*

She couldn't dismiss the possibility out of hand. *Be careful*, she warned herself. *Be very careful.*

"Thank you for coming to see me," Chell began. "I've

been wanting to thank you again for saving my life. If you had not come along when you did . . ."

"Anyone would have done the same," Mara said, though in fact she was uncomfortably aware she had almost turned and run back for help . . . in which case, given the way the waves had been washing across the beach where Chell had fallen, they probably wouldn't now be having this conversation.

"Perhaps. But you *did*." Chell gave her a crooked grin, and once again she was struck by how handsome he was, and how much more *mature* he was than Keltan or Hyram. His lean face, stubbled this late in the day, had lost the boyish softness their countenances still bore. "And in return, I want to tell you in person how I came to your shore."

"I've been wondering about that," Mara said. "It seems an awfully big coincidence that your boat should capsize so close to the Secret City."

"Not really," Chell said. "We knew the Secret City was here. Well"—he held up his hands hastily—"not the Secret City as such, but some sort of settlement. We saw what we thought was smoke, from far out at sea." He shook his head. "Now, of course, I know that most of what we saw was really steam from the hot springs. Nonetheless, it drew our attention."

Mara remembered wondering just a day or two before if it were really safe for the Secret City to allow so much smoke to escape from the cliff above her workshop. "You were looking for a settlement?"

"Yes," Chell said. "I . . . *we* . . . came to Aygrima in the hope of contacting its people . . . if any still survived."

"You sailed across the ocean in that tiny boat?"

Chell laughed. "No, of course not. We marked the location of the smoke and sailed north until we found a better harbor for our ship. Then the scouting party set out in the boat along the shore." His smile faded. "But the storm caught us in shallow water. The waves . . ." He shook his head. "Again, I thank you for saving me. I wish you could have saved the others."

"If you have a larger ship, why not sail *it* along the shore?" Mara said. She heard the almost accusing tone in her voice, and recognized it as the same one she'd used with Edrik earlier. She didn't seem to be able to take anything at face value anymore.

Well, there were reasons for that.

"We did not want our approach to seem threatening," Chell said. "A small party, in a small boat, could be travelers from farther up the coast rather than from across the sea. And we had no idea what we might find here. Caution seemed in order."

"And when will your ship come looking for you?" Mara said. "You've been gone for several days already."

"Not for some time," Chell said. "We were equipped for several weeks. We intended to scout as far as we could before returning with our report."

"So you're a scout," said Mara, "for the 'Royal Korellian Navy.' What *is* that?"

"Ah." Chell looked embarrassed. "I shouldn't have mentioned it. But apparently almost freezing to death didn't do much for what little brainpower I possess. So I guess that secret is out." He leaned forward. "Catilla and Edrik had heard of Korellia. You haven't?"

Mara shook her head. "Another land, beyond the sea? There are tales about such places, but most people"—*like Hyram*, she thought—"don't even believe they're real."

"They're real," Chell said. "Four or five hundred years ago, there was a great deal of trade between Aygrima and Korellia. And many other island nations. But then came the Great Plague."

"Plague?" Mara stared at him. She'd never heard any of this in her history classes. She glanced at Tishka, but her face remained impassive.

Chell nodded. "It swept the world like a hurricane. Whole kingdoms were wiped out. Others, like Korellia, survived, but with only a tenth of their previous population. All trade ceased, for once the plague had burned through a country, no one dared travel anywhere it might still rage. In Korellia, and I suspect in many other lands, even the building of ships suitable for long-distance voyages was prohibited: only small fishing vessels were allowed.

"But as time went by, Korellia revived and, eventually, prospered. A few years ago, the King changed the law, not only permitting the building of ships, but commanding the construction of a whole new fleet, to explore the sundered world. But for fear the plague still lurks, we are cautious in our approach to new lands—which is another reason for only a small party coming ashore, rather than the entire ship's company."

"We have no plague here," Mara said. "I do not believe we ever did." She glanced at Tishka once more, but again got no response.

"Oh, you did," Chell said. "I am sure of it. But you had something else, and I think that is why here, unlike in every other land we have rediscovered, the plague is little remembered."

"What?" Mara asked.

"Magic," Chell said softly. "Alone in all the world, Aygrima has magic."

He doesn't know I have the Gift, Mara reminded herself. She glanced again at Tishka. The red-haired woman's gaze had sharpened; her eyes, bright in the lamplight, focused on Mara like a hawk's. *Nor am I allowed to tell him.*

"You don't have magic in Korellia?" she said instead.

He shook his head. "No. But we know of it from our own histories, which clearly are more complete than yours. Once upon a time the ships of Aygrima traveled the world, their holds filled with urns of magic, their Healers and Engineers in great demand. They were welcomed everywhere ... but also resented; and when the plague broke out, there were some who claimed it wasn't natural, that it had been created and unleashed via dark magic, concocted by the evil mages of Aygrima. Aygrima's ships were seized and sunk. Not surprisingly, soon enough they stopped coming. Many of our people now believe, as yours do of Korellia, that Aygrima never really existed, and that the magicians of Aygrima are mere fairy tales. Indeed, they've become just that, featuring in fantastical stories told all over the islands. There's a particularly popular musical play you'd probably enjoy." He grinned. "Maybe I'll have the chance to take you to see it someday."

Mara digested all that for a moment. "You're lucky you found us first," she said at last. "If you had appeared in any other village, not wearing Masks, the Watchers would not have welcomed you."

"So I have been told," Chell said. He shook his head. "The Masks sound evil."

"They are," Mara said flatly. "But not as evil as the Autarch who commands them to be made and worn."

"And that," Chell said, "is why I am going to accompany you to Tamita. To see this evil for myself."

"Why?" Mara said. "You know it will be dangerous." *For all of us*, she added silently to herself. *Keltan and I can at least pass for unMasked children, but you ...*

"I have told Catilla," Chell said carefully, "that Korellia might be willing to aid the unMasked Army in its effort to ... improve the political situation in Aygrima."

Mara's eyes widened. "You'd fight for us? Against the Autarch?"

Chell held up his hands. "I cannot make such a commitment," he said. "I do not have that authority. But I *do* have authority to open diplomatic channels with the peoples I encounter, and the autonomy to decide with whom our initial discussions should be conducted."

Mara stared at him, startled. *He looks about twenty*, she thought. *And he has that much authority?*

They must do things differently in Korellia.

"Assuming what I see in Tamita confirms what I have been told here," Chell went on, "then I think I am right to say it is far more likely Korellia will side with the un-Masked Army than with the Autarch." He made a face. "We overthrew a tyrant of our own once. We have little stomach for the tyranny of others."

"That would be . . . wonderful," Mara breathed. *An ally against the Autarch! An ally with seagoing ships, weapons . . .*

. . . facing magic? She felt her first qualm. What could the Autarch do with all the magic at his disposal if faced with an enemy from the sea?

She had her own memory of an explosion contained, a glass-walled crater, and a towering pillar of flame and smoke to hint at the power that could potentially be unleashed in defense of the Autarch. Could the Korellians really face *that*?

"But I cannot make any recommendations until I have scouted further," Chell continued. "And reported back to my ship." He cocked his head. "So what do you say, Mara? Will you permit me to accompany you?"

She snorted. "You don't need *my* permission. Unlike you, I don't get to make my own decisions."

He shrugged. "It's true Catilla and Edrik have both agreed to let me go . . . albeit with certain conditions on the early part of our journey. But even though they've granted *their* permission, now I'm asking *you*. This journey is for your purposes more than mine ... a journey to see your father, I am told. You must decide if my presence will endanger that task. I would not do that for the world, and if you do not want me to accompany you, then I will find some other way to complete my mission. I owe you that consideration, and more, for saving my life." He smiled that crooked smile. "After all, I definitely wouldn't be completing my mission if I were a blue frozen corpse bobbing in the sea!"

"What have they told you about my father ... about why I must see him, despite the risk?" Mara asked slowly.

"Only that it has something to do with the effort to overthrow the Autarch." Chell studied her face. "I am curious, of course."

Mara very carefully did not look at Tishka. "I'm afraid I can't tell you anything more."

"Pity." He kept his eyes locked on hers. "Well, Mara? May I come with you?"

Even though she really had no choice, even though the choice had been made by Catilla and Edrik without the slightest thought of asking her, it warmed her heart that this strange young man thought highly enough of her opinion to ask. "Of course," she said.

He smiled a smile so broad that it seemed to brighten the dim room. "Excellent! I look forward to getting to know you better during the journey."

For some reason, Mara felt herself blushing. She jumped up so suddenly the chair teetered and Tishka had to step forward to keep it from clattering to the floor. "Fine. Wonderful. Um ... good night." *Why is my face so red? Can he see how red my face is?*

How embarrassing. Her face flamed even hotter.

"Good night," Chell said courteously, getting to his

feet. Tishka opened the door for her and she fled into the cool dimness of the Broad Way.

Tishka closed and locked the door behind her, then trailed Mara down the wide hallway. "He is very handsome, isn't he?" she said nonchalantly from behind Mara.

"Is he?" Mara kept her gaze resolutely focused ahead. "I didn't notice."

Tishka chuckled, but Mara wouldn't give her the satisfaction of looking back.

FIVE

The Journey South

FOR THREE WEEKS, Mara waited for a response from her father. Without her work on the Masks to occupy her, she was assigned more mundane tasks: cleaning tables, sweeping chambers, changing beds. She hardly saw Chell, who seemed to spend all his time either sequestered with Catilla or Edrik or locked in his cell.

Midwinter Day came and went, and it turned out the unMasked Army *did* mark it: they didn't do much decorating, but there was a feast and some of the more musical residents of the Secret City gathered at the head of the Grand Chamber to sing and play drums and flutes and various stringed instruments. What they lacked in skill they more than made up for in enthusiasm.

The best thing about Midwinter Day, though, was that Mara finally had the opportunity to apologize to Prella. She found herself next to the other girl during the concert. Prella wouldn't look at her, constantly turning the other way to talk to Kirika instead, and Mara's first thought was to move; but then she steeled herself and spoke. "Prella," she said.

The smaller girl turned to look at her, expression cool.

"I'm sorry," Mara said. "I'm sorry I snapped at you. You didn't deserve it. I was just frustrated by my own failures with the Masks. I didn't mean what I said." She took a deep breath; this was harder than she'd thought. "Will you forgive me?"

For a moment Prella's face remained unreadable; then a small smile flickered. "Of course I will," she said. She looked a little shamefaced all of a sudden. "I shouldn't have taken it so hard. It was just . . . unexpected."

Mara looked past Prella at Kirika, staring coldly at Mara through narrowed eyes. There was still no love lost there. *She probably thinks I'm trying to steal her only friend away from her*, Mara thought. *Well, maybe I can put her mind at ease*. She stood up, though she'd just sat down. "Well, I'll . . . see you around, Prella," Mara said. "You too, Kirika."

"See you," Prella said, sounding a little puzzled by her abrupt departure.

Kirika said nothing, but Mara thought she could still feel the other girl's stare as she wove her way across the Grand Chamber.

More days slipped by. And then finally, almost a month after Chell's arrival, on a night when a howling wind lashed snow around the cliffs and rattled the shutters on every window, Catilla finally summoned her.

The Commander looked even frailer than last time:

new lines on a face already as wrinkled as an old apple, skin chalky except for the dark shadows under her eyes. She motioned Mara to her bedside. "A message has come from Tamita," she said, voice hoarse. "Grelda, please."

The Healer gave Mara a dark look, but took up a small square of paper from the table by Catilla's bed. "Midnight, thirteenth of Winterwhite. Beneath the skylight," she read, then looked up. "That's it."

"You understand, child?" Catilla said.

I'm not a child, Mara thought automatically, but distantly, because all her thoughts were focused on that message.

Beneath the skylight. Her old room.

Home.

"Yes," she said. "I understand."

• • •

Two days later, on the morning of the seventh of Winterwhite, Mara sat astride the sleek chestnut mare that had become her favorite horse in the Secret City stables—not that that was saying much. Mara's riding skills had improved somewhat with a few more weeks of practice, but she still envied Edrik's comfortable way with the animals—a skill apparently shared by Chell who, despite the black hood encasing his head, sat at ease astride his bay mare. Keltan hadn't had much more riding practice than she had, but even he, atop a rangy gray gelding, looked far more comfortable than she felt.

Mara's mare gave her a look over her shoulder as if to say, "You again? Are you going to stay on this time?"

"I'll do my best," Mara told the animal. Keltan gave her a sidelong look.

"Talking to horses is just a little . . . odd," he said.

"Not as odd as naming yourself after one," Mara replied sweetly. Keltan laughed.

They took the "back door" path up to the top of the cliff, first riding along the same beach Mara had walked just before discovering Chell, then up the narrow defile in the cliff face while the ocean thundered behind them, the waves today unsettled by the echoes of some storm far out at sea. At the top, they rode for several minutes past corrals, pastures, and grain fields before plunging into forest.

Even though she *wasn't* blindfolded, Mara suspected she would have had no more luck than Chell finding her way back to the Secret City if Edrik were not with them. It seemed that every time she left or returned to the place it was by a different route.

Of course, on at least two occasions she'd been unconscious during the final parts of the journey, so she supposed she had some excuse for not having it fixed firmly in her mind. But even when she was awake and alert, every bit of the forest looked the same as every other, as far as she could tell: the same dark trees, the same snow-laden branches, the same sound-deadening blanket of white covering the ground, so that they rode in an eerie hush broken only by the jingle of harness and the occasional blowing of the horses.

The snow seemed to smother conversation as much as any other sound, so they mostly rode without speaking. Mara would have liked to talk to Keltan about what they would do when they got to Tamita, but she didn't dare while Chell rode alongside them. At some point they'd have to find a chance to talk in private, she thought, but the opportunity didn't come that day—or night. They camped, made a fire, and huddled around it. Chell's hood came off, and he blinked around him, face flushed. "Well, that's better," he said cheerfully. "Good thing it's so cold or I might have smothered in there."

Mara's own face felt dry and chapped from a day in the open. "Can I wear it tomorrow?" she asked.

Chell laughed. "Be my guest." He glanced at Edrik. "I presume I *will* be free of it tomorrow?"

Edrik nodded. "I doubt you could find your way back to the Secret City now."

"I know I couldn't," Mara said, and Chell laughed again.

Keltan, for some reason, glowered.

The next morning, the eighth of Winterwhite (the date was the first thing Mara thought of every morning now, as the days counted down toward the thirteenth, when she would see her father again), they rode on through a forest that dripped: a melting wind had blown in overnight. When they camped that night, in the lee of a small bluff of weathered gray stone, Edrik made another fire, then announced, "Enjoy the warmth tonight. No more fires. There are few enough people up here, but the lands become more inhabited with every mile we make toward Tamita."

Tamita. Mara felt a kind of shiver at the name. The city she'd grown up in. The city she'd thought she'd never leave. The city where her mother and father still lived.

The city of the Autarch. And the city in which she was forbidden to show her unMasked face, on pain of death.

She glanced at Chell, who was talking in a low voice to Edrik. She looked back at Keltan, and jerked her head toward the shadows beyond the circle of firelight. He frowned at her. She jerked her head again, harder, and finally he understood, and followed her into the brush surrounding their camp.

"What is it?" he said. "It's cold out here."

"I need to know your plan for when we get to Tamita," she said. "How do we get through the wall?"

He looked annoyed. "I could have told you that by the fire."

"No, you couldn't," she said. "Not while Chell is there."

"I thought you trusted him."

"I do," she said. "At least, I guess I do. But Edrik doesn't. Not completely. I don't think he'd want us talking about our plans in front of him."

Keltan shrugged. "It's not much of a plan. There is a place where you can get under the wall; you and I crawl through, then go to your old house. We meet your father. We leave again. That's the plan."

"Well, Chell doesn't know it. And now we do."

Keltan laughed. "I'm pretty sure he's guessed we've got some way to get through the wall. It's pretty obvious, isn't it?"

For a moment Mara considered slugging him. "I just . . . look, we need to decide other things, right? So we get through the wall. Where will we come out, exactly?"

"In the river," Keltan said.

Mara blinked. "What?"

"That's how you get under the wall. The river flows through an arched passage, blocked at both ends by metal grates. Someone, at some point, cut holes through those grates, just big enough to slip through, and built a narrow wooden walkway between the grates, above the river. There isn't room to stand up; that's why we'll crawl. Once we're through the inner gate, there's a small gap between the wall and South Bridge . . . and a path we can scramble up. It's screened from the bridge by some willows. And then . . . we're in the city."

"South Bridge," Mara said. "I don't know that part of the city."

"I do," Keltan said. "I can get you safely back to that basement where you found me. And from there I presume you can find your house, since you did it once before."

Mara nodded. "The Night Watchers will be our biggest threat . . . but I'm used to avoiding them." She didn't tell him about the time she and Sala were caught skinny-dipping by the Night Watchers and dragged home in disgrace. She'd face far worse than embarrassment and her parents' displeasure if she were caught this time.

And if the Watchers learned she'd met with her father . . .

Her breath caught in her throat. *He* was risking more than she was. If the Autarch discovered his Master Mask-maker was actively working against him . . . had subverted his own Mask so he could do so, and was helping rebels create counterfeit Masks that would allow them to infiltrate the City . . . he would surely make an example of him, an example so terrible that no Maskmaker would ever be tempted to alter his Mask again. "Let's get back to the fire," she said, suddenly craving warmth and light.

As Edrik had promised, the next day's travel (*the ninth of Winterwhite*, Mara thought as she awoke) took them out of the Wild and into more settled lands. They entered the broad, shallow valley through which flowed the Heartsblood River, the very river they would follow under the city wall. Farms spread out across the valley floor on both sides of the river, and occasional villages huddled next to it. But even here the land was far from completely cleared; heavy woods cloaked the valley slopes, as Edrik pointed out as they sat astride their horses below the ridgeline they had just crossed, so they wouldn't be silhouetted against the sky. "We'll stick to the trees as much as we can," he said. "We can manage pretty well today and tomorrow. Farther down the valley there is a long stretch with no cover at all except for hedgerows. We will cross that the night after next, in the dark. Beyond that, the Heartsblood flows through woods that provide some cover, almost as far as Tamita; but there will also be far more Watchers. They patrol the lands within a day's ride of the city on a regular basis." He glanced at the others. "We have no Masks, nor any counterfeits of them," he said, his eyes flicking for a moment to Mara. "Mara and Keltan could pass as too young to be Masked, but you and I"—he nodded at Chell—"cannot. Keep your hood up. If someone does see us from a distance, we should attract little attention as long as they do not realize our faces are uncovered."

"Why do the Watchers patrol?" Chell asked. Edrik frowned at him; Chell returned a sunny smile. "The Autarch has everyone in these Masks, and so no one dares to rebel, right? So why bother patrolling? What are the Watchers looking for?"

"Bandits," Edrik said. "Those who fled their Maskings, or whose Masks shattered but who managed to escape, and scrabble for survival in the Wild."

"Why would they come so close to the city?" Chell said.

"Because they are starving," Edrik said. "And the richest farmland and wealthiest villages are closest to Tamita."

"But there are also villages farther north. Why not limit their raids to those?"

"They raid those, too," Edrik said. "But we make sure they also raid villages closer to Tamita. We want the Watchers patrolling down here rather than closer to the Secret City."

Chell raised an eyebrow. "Ah," he said. "You have some influence over these 'bandits.' Useful."

Edrik turned away without replying. "Let's move out."

They picked their way down the slope, and for the rest of that day and the next day (*the tenth of Winterwhite,*

Mara thought) rode through the woods along the east side of the valley, without seeing anyone or, they hoped, being seen. At nightfall they stopped their travel only long enough for a cold, cheerless supper and to rest the horses, then pressed on. As Edrik had warned, the trees petered out. In the moonlight, stubble-covered fields stretched away in front of them, broken only by dark lines of hedges or stone fences. Edrik glanced up at the star-strewn sky. "Bad luck it's so clear," he said. "Still, it's unlikely anyone will be abroad. It's a cold night."

Mara had to agree with that. The temperature had dropped again in the wake of the one-day thaw, and her nose felt like a lump of ice glued to her face. She kept reminding herself not to lick her burning, chapped lips— and then licked them anyway.

Edrik led them a little farther to the left, until they intersected one of the stone fences. In its insubstantial shadow—it was only about four feet high—they rode out of the forest.

They moved from fence line to hedge line, zigzagging back and forth through the fields, like ghosts in the night. But though they seemed to be the only humans abroad, their horses weren't the only animals. Trouble came as they skirted a village. Edrik led them into a stand of woods . . . but the trees ended suddenly, and without warning they emerged into a farmyard. In the moonlight Mara glimpsed a tidy stone hut, a thatched roof, a low fence, a cowshed . . . and then a huge black dog exploded from the shadows, white teeth gleaming as it charged toward the horses, deep, bone-shaking barks shattering the still of the night.

"Back!" Edrik cried, and wheeled his horse and galloped back into the trees. Chell followed, Keltan turned with a little more difficulty and did the same . . . and Mara, somehow, between the onrushing dog, the skittish horse, her own pounding heart and her own inexperience, suddenly found herself sliding sideways in the saddle ... and then fell heavily to the ground, the impact knocking the breath from her. As she lay trying desperately to draw air into her lungs, the horse reared and galloped after its stable mates ...

... and the black dog reached her and stood slavering over her, drool dripping from its fanged, snarling mouth.

SIX

Warm Bed, Cold Steel

"STAFIN! HEEL!" a voice shouted. The dog growled once more at Mara, then turned and trotted back to the owner of the voice, just emerging from the cottage. Mara turned her head and saw a big man wearing an improbable patchwork robe lumbering toward her, a stout wooden cudgel in one hand. "What have you got, boy?" he said as the huge dog, so terrifying to Mara a moment before, romped around him like a puppy.

The man came closer. Mara, still struggling to breathe, couldn't say a word. He bent over. "Why, it's a girl!" he said in astonishment. His hand went to his unMasked face. "And me without . . . girl, what on earth are you doing out in the middle of the night?"

"I . . ." Mara began. "I . . ." It was no use. She still didn't have the air.

"You'd best come inside," the man said. "Filia!" he called over his shoulder. "It's a girl! I think she's hurt!"

"A girl!" A woman's voice came back. "Well, bring her in, Jess, you big lump. Let me get a look at her."

Jess tossed aside the club, leaned over, and picked Mara up as though she weighed no more than a baby. He carried her toward the house, while Mara, helpless, looked over his broad arm at the dark forest where Edrik, Chell, and Keltan must just be realizing she was missing.

Light flared in the doorway as Filia lit a lamp. "Take her into Greff's room, Jess," the woman said. Mara could see her face now, unMasked, lined, a kind and friendly face filled with equal parts concern and bewilderment.

Jess turned to the right, ducking through the low door into a lean-to of a room, obviously a later addition to the original farmhouse, since its walls were of plastered timber rather than stone. It had two big windows, both shuttered, a chest, a small table, and a long, narrow bed. Her breathing was coming easier now, which allowed her to feel more clearly the sharp pain between her shoulder blades. Jess started to place her on the bed, then stopped. "She's bleeding, Filia!"

I am? Mara thought.

Filia bent closer, and made a tsking sound. "Looks like you fell on something sharp, love," she said to Mara. "But not to worry, it doesn't look too serious from what I can see. Hold her a moment more, Jess." She bustled out and returned with a ragged blue blanket, which she spread on the bed. "There now," she said. "I don't mind getting blood on that. Put her down."

Gently, Jess lay Mara down. She gasped as her back

touched the blanket, and sat up again in a hurry. "Ow," she said.

"I'd best take a closer look," Filia said. She waited a moment, then gave her husband an exasperated look. "That means taking off her jacket and blouse, you big lummox," she said. "Which means you have to leave."

"Oh!" Jess said. His face turned red. "Of course. Sorry, miss. I'll . . . I'll just go retrieve my stick." He went out.

Filia shook her head in a bemused sort of way. "Not the smartest wolf in the pack," she said to Mara, "but a wonderful man, all the same. Now, let's get a look at you . . ."

With Filia's help, Mara slipped out of her jacket and blouse and undertunic, then hugged her arms across her breasts while the farmwoman examined her back. "How . . . how bad is it?" Mara said, the first sentence she'd managed to speak since falling from the horse.

"Naught but a nasty scratch," Filia said. "From a sharp rock or a bit of root, most like. I'll have it cleaned up and bandaged in a jiffy. You just sit tight for a moment." She got up and went out, closing the door behind her.

Mara, still hugging herself, looked around the little room. Besides the bed and chest and the little table on which the lantern rested, she saw a shelf attached to one wall. On it were half a dozen wooden carvings of birds. They weren't extraordinarily wonderful carvings: Mara had seen far better in the Outside Market, never mind the high-end shops of the Inside Market near the Palace gate. But she thought, from looking at them, that they had probably been done by a child; and as the work of a child, they definitely held promise. She could have done better, but then, she'd had a lot of practice sculpting as apprentice to her father.

Her father. He would be looking for her the very next night. How was she going to get away?

She shivered, and wished Filia would hurry up. The room was warmer than the air outside, but not by much. It was certainly too cold to sit around half naked.

Fortunately, Filia returned within five minutes, with a basin of steaming water and a folded-up piece of white cloth from which she tore several strips. The first she used as a rag to clean the wound Mara couldn't see but could certainly feel; she gasped. Then Filia tore three more strips from the cloth and had Mara lift her arms so she could wind them around her chest and back. When she was done, Mara looked down and sighed. Bound in the bandages, she was even more flat-chested than usual.

I could pass for a boy, she thought.

"I'll need to wash the blood out of your clothes," Filia said. She frowned. "I've got mint tea brewing in the kitchen," she said, "and that's where we'll want to hear your story. But you'll need something to wear . . ." She got up and went to the chest, opening it to reveal neatly folded clothes. "You're about the same size as my son . . . was." Her voice caught before the last word. She pulled out a brown shirt and held it up. "You can wear this."

Mara pulled it on, grateful for the warmth, then followed Filia into the kitchen, where Jess already waited at a well-made table of dark wood. The fire had been stoked and blazed cheerfully in the hearth, and a kettle hanging over it issued a steady stream of vapor. A tub in the corner steamed, and Mara, glancing in, saw her jacket and shirt in the pink-tinged water. "I'll pull those out to dry," Filia said. "Jess managed to rub most of the blood out of them, I think. You just sit at the table."

Mara sat. Filia pulled the dripping jacket, blouse, and undertunic from the tub. "Don't just sit there like a frog on a log," she said to her husband. "Work the pump. I need to give these a rinse."

Jess, as obedient to his wife as the big black dog had

been to him, got up and began cranking the wooden pump handle. Water poured into a wooden trough that guided it out through the wall. Filia worked the clothes under the clean water for a few moments, then said to Jess, "That's enough. Now you pour the tea while I hang these up, and then we'll talk."

While Filia draped the clothes on a rope strung across the kitchen in front of the fire, where they hung, dripping onto the stones of the hearth, Jess took the kettle from the fire and poured clear green tea into three clay mugs already sitting on the table. Mara wrapped her hands around her mug to warm them, and took a long sip of the blessedly hot liquid, trying to look unconcerned and at home, while all the while her heart fluttered. What could she tell them? What *should* she tell them?

Filia sat down next to her husband. He looked far less frightening in the light than he had as a dark shadow in the farmyard. His bald head glowed in the firelight and his gray-bearded, bushy-browed face was as lined and kindly as his wife's. "Now, then, child," said Filia gently. "What's your name?"

"P . . . Prella," Mara said. The real Prella, far away in the Secret City, surely wouldn't mind.

"Prella," said Filia. "And how old are you?"

"Fourteen," Mara said, thankful once again to Ethelda, who had been present at her Masking on her fifteenth birthday and had healed her torn face so well after the Mask failed that no scars remained.

"Not long until your Masking?"

"Not long," Mara said. "Two months. Fourteenth of Waterspring." That was her mother's birthday.

"Where do you live?" Jess rumbled. "You're not a local girl."

"Riverwash," Mara said. It was the only village name she could be sure of; one of her classmates had had an aunt there and had told tales, after returning from a midwinter visit, of how impossibly dull a place it was. Located on the river, just as the name implied, it lay a few miles north of Tamita. She hoped it was still far enough away that neither Jess nor Filia knew its inhabitants well.

"Riverwash?" said Jess, frowning. "That's a long walk from here, girl."

"I wasn't walking, I was riding," Mara said. "When your dog came charging out, my horse threw me. Then she galloped off."

"Riding? At night? Through the woods?" Jess shook his head. "Of all the fool . . . why weren't you on the road?"

"I got lost," Mara lied. "I was riding with my brother, and we were late setting out, and he said he knew a shortcut to a village where we could find an inn, but then it got dark and somehow I lost him and then I didn't know where to go and then I came on your farm and then your dog came out barking and I fell and . . ." Cold, hurting, and worried, she didn't have to work very hard to conjure up a few tears. Sniffling, she swiped the sleeve of her borrowed shirt across her nose.

"Your brother must be worried sick!" Filia said, voice full of concern. "But I'm afraid we can't do anything about that until morning." She leaned forward and patted Mara's hand. "You sleep in Greff's room tonight. Tomorrow we'll take you into Yellowgrass. Like as not your brother will be there waiting for you."

Mara nodded, still sniffling. "Won't . . . won't Greff mind? His room, I mean?"

Filia smiled a sad smile. "Greff's not here," she said. "He turned fifteen a year ago and was chosen to join the Child Guard. A great honor. We were very pleased." She didn't sound pleased. She sounded on the verge of tears herself.

And she doesn't even know what I know, Mara thought, feeling ill. *She doesn't know that the Autarch is sucking magic—sucking* life—*right out of the Child Guard, that none of them thrive while in his service, that some of them die.*

Ethelda had told her that. She'd also told her, in one of their recent conversations, that as time went along, she feared *all* of the Child Guard would die: that the Autarch, needing to draw ever more magic to stave off his own aging, wouldn't be able to help himself. "He'll suck them dry and discard the husks," she'd told Mara. "It's already starting to happen. Any child taken into the Child Guard now I fear is as good as dead, if the Autarch remains on the throne."

"How wonderful," Mara forced herself to say to Filia.

The farmwoman said nothing to that. "Into bed," she said. "We'll talk in the morning and figure everything out."

She showed Mara to the lean-to room, said good night, and went off to bed with her husband.

Mara wanted nothing more than to lie down on that inviting bed, pull up the covers, and sleep until morning . . . but instead she sat, waiting, thinking she would sneak out as soon as they were asleep.

Her plan survived only as long as it took for her to crack open the door and peek into the hallway.

The big black dog lay across the threshold of the main door. His eyes locked on hers as she peered out. He growled.

Swallowing, Mara eased the door closed again. For a moment she considered trying to climb out the window, but the dog would surely bark if she did that, and Jess had only to let him out the door and he would have her again.

Looks like I have no choice but to spend the night, Mara thought.

She undressed and climbed beneath the covers into that warm, dry, blissfully comfortable bed. *Well, it could be worse*, was her last thought before sleep took her.

She woke refreshed, hungry . . . and even more worried. (*It's the eleventh of Winterwhite! Only two more days . . .*) Sometime before she'd awoken Filia had brought in her own clothes, neatly mended and dried; she wondered how the farm wife had had the time. She dressed, then asked diffidently where she might "refresh" herself and was pointed to an outhouse a little way down a path through the farmyard. The big black dog was nowhere to be seen, and neither was Jess. *Probably busy with farm chores*, she thought.

The outhouse wasn't as bad as she'd thought it might be, but as she came out, blinking in the morning sun, she almost jumped out of her skin as a voice from behind her said, "Are you all right?"

She shot a quick look around to make sure Jess wasn't in sight, then sidled around to the side of the outhouse out of view from the house. "I'm fine," she said to the lurking Keltan. He looked cold and dirty and miserable and she felt a little bit guilty to be clean, well-rested, and about to be well-fed . . . but only a little.

"Good," he grunted. "Grand. Now let's go."

"Not yet," Mara said. Struck by sudden inspiration, she said, "Come inside with me. Filia will feed you."

Keltan started. "What? No!"

"No, it's perfect," Mara insisted. "I told them I was out riding with my brother and I got lost. And just look at you! You obviously were searching for me all night. Now you've found me, we'll be able to ride calmly away and they'll never question the fact we were here . . . or tell the Watchers about it, which is more to the point. Otherwise they're going to take me to the village."

Keltan glanced back at the forest, where no doubt

Edrik was watching and fuming. Mara followed his gaze, plastered a big grin on her face, and gave a cheery wave in that direction. "Come on," she urged. "A hot breakfast? It could be the last one for days. And then we'll get my horse and be on our way."

"Edrik will kill us," Keltan muttered.

"Hot food," Mara countered, and clearly she had the better argument; Keltan heaved a huge sigh and walked up the path toward the house with Mara. "Oh, and by the way," Mara added brightly, "we're from Riverwash, and my name's Prella."

"River—?" Keltan began, but then they were in the hallway and Mara was introducing Keltan to a surprised Filia, although she called him "Hyram," since even Filia might be expected to know the name of the Autarch's horse.

The breakfast went well, with Filia apparently perfectly willing to believe Keltan was Mara's brother and had been searching for her all night. "You look very close in age," Filia commented.

"We're twins," Mara offered, earning another startled glance from Keltan. "Fraternal, of course."

"Of course," Filia said dryly.

"May I have another slice of ham?" Keltan said quickly.

Less than an hour after they had entered the farmhouse, they were on their way again, Filia waving goodbye to them, and Mara, the cut on her back covered with a fresh dressing, feeling full, contented, and generally pleased with herself.

Edrik did not share her high opinion of how things had gone. "What if they had gone straight to the Watchers while you slept?" he said coldly. "What then?"

"Nice to see you, too," Mara said. "Why would they have gone to the Watchers? I'm clearly just an unMasked child, harmless and lost. But if I *had* disappeared suddenly in the night, or if I had run off the moment Keltan appeared this morning, then they really *might* have gone to the Watchers, because they would have been afraid something bad was happening to me. Instead they fed us both and sent us happily on our way." She gave him a bright smile. "See? It all worked out perfectly."

Edrik grunted but said nothing more. Chell and Keltan both gave her smiles as they mounted their horses.

They moved well back in the woods and spent the day holed up in the trees, keeping watch in case someone came along. They didn't ride again until nightfall. "We're behind our time now," Edrik growled, "thanks to your adventure. We'll have to travel all night and through tomorrow with only short rests if you're to make your rendezvous."

Mara just nodded.

That night's travel passed without untoward encounters of either the human or canine kind. Daybreak of the twelfth of Winterwhite found them in rougher country, with plenty of stands of trees through which to pick their unobserved way. But by the end of the day, broken only by brief rest stops, the refreshing sleep and hot meal in Filia and Jess' house seemed like something Mara had experienced only in a dream. Reality had always been this, jolting along on the back of her mare, almost falling from her saddle from weariness.

The others had to be even wearier than she was, since none of them had had even *one* peaceful night in a soft bed. Perhaps that was why Edrik, as they neared the edge of a wood, for once did not slow and scout, but simply rode out into the open.

They emerged into no ordinary clearing, but into a swath cut through the forest to allow the passage of a road: and there, in the middle of the road, astride a white stallion, black-Masked head turning toward them as they crashed out through the undergrowth that had screened him from them, rode a Watcher.

The Watcher reined in the horse and stared at them. He took in their unMasked faces in an instant and his sword slithered from its sheath. "Hold!" he shouted.

Edrik uttered one startled, disgusted oath, then clapped heels to his horse and galloped forward, drawing his own sword. The Watcher's stallion reared. Edrik reached him. Steel crashed.

Keltan, face white, drew his sword, too, and started forward, but Chell was faster. Though he had no weapons at all, he, too, dug his heels into his horse's flanks and charged forward. As the Watcher's stallion, bigger and stronger than Edrik's mare and doubtless battle-trained to boot, shouldered the unMasked Army's second-in-command back, Chell flung himself from his saddle and crashed into the Watcher. Both of them thudded to the ground. The Watcher's stallion, suddenly riderless, galloped away. Edrik brought his own horse under control and spun to assist Chell, but there was no need. Chell got to his feet, wincing. The Watcher lay still, head twisted at an unnatural angle. As Keltan and Mara rode up, his black Mask crumbled away . . .

. . . and Mara gasped. A ghostly image of the Watcher, a gleaming, multicolored ghost, rose into the air, wavered . . . and flowed into her.

She swayed in the saddle. The world whirled around her.

And then she fell into darkness.

SEVEN

Return to Tamita

MARA OPENED HER EYES. She lay where she
had fallen, but now Keltan knelt behind her, cra-
dling her head in his lap. She blinked at his upside-down
face, his eyes wide and warm with concern. Edrik stood
behind him, staring down at her; Chell stood to her left,
looking puzzled.

"She's awake!" Keltan said, sounding relieved. "Mara,
what happened?"

Groaning, Mara sat up. "I . . ." She looked past Edrik at
Chell, who did not know of her Gift and was not to be told.
"I . . . I fainted." She hated making herself sound so weak,
but she saw no alternative. "The . . . the Watcher . . . his
neck . . . it was horrible."

"I did not mean to kill him," Chell said. "Just to knock him from his horse. But he landed badly."

"You could say that," Edrik said dryly. "But I *did* mean to kill him, so I won't fault you for it." He glanced over his shoulder. "I wish his horse had not escaped. When he is retrieved, riderless, they'll come looking for this one . . ."

Chell shrugged. "He fell off his horse. Broke his neck. It happens."

"Not with the tracks of other horses nearby," Edrik said. "The Watchers are many things, but they—well, at least, most of them—are not stupid. We must move on. And we must do our best to cover our tracks." He sighed. "And that, I think, means giving up our horses. They will follow them . . . and not us."

Mara got to her feet. She felt . . . odd. Tingling. *Magic,* she thought. *When the Watcher died . . . the magic he contained didn't just . . . evaporate. It flowed into me. I've got his magic inside of me. Magic I can use.*

"I may have a better solution," she said softly, and Edrik gave her a sharp look. She glanced meaningfully at Chell, and Edrik, rather to her surprise, took her hint. His eyes narrowed.

"You're sure?"

She nodded.

He grunted. "Very well. Mount up," he said to Chell and Keltan. He glanced at Mara. "I'll lead your horse . . . ?"

She nodded again.

Keltan shot Mara a startled look. She winked at him. His eyes widened, and he turned to his mount.

Only Chell protested. "We can't go on without Mara—"

"We're not going far," Edrik said. "Mount up. Now."

Though obviously sorely puzzled, Chell did as he was told. He, Edrik, and Keltan rode down the path, disappearing around a bend in moments.

Mara turned back to survey the scene. She considered the power lurking under her skin, the magic the Watcher had released as he died. It . . . fizzed, a sensation not even close to the agony she had felt when she'd actively pulled magic from living people to contain the explosion at the mine, but irritating, like an itch she couldn't scratch. She had to use it, had to get it out of her, and she thought she knew how to do it.

She looked at the earth beaten down by their horses as they rode out of the forest, at the trampled undergrowth beneath the tall trees. She pictured it undamaged, unmarked. *That's what I want*, she thought.

She released the magic.

Red and green, blue and gold, yellow and purple, and other colors she didn't even have a name for seemed to explode from her skin. She gasped: for an instant her skin felt on fire, as if the power had burned as it rushed out of her. But the pain only lasted an instant. Then it was gone, and the tingling irritation with it . . . and so were the marks of their horses. Grass, earth, and trees alike looked unmarked. Neither hoofmark nor manure remained. Not a blade was bent, not a twig was broken.

Mara took a deep breath. She started to follow the others, then, struck by a sudden thought, turned back to the dead Watcher and carefully slid his sword back into its sheath. *So they won't realize he was facing an enemy*, she thought. She looked down at his corpse. His dead eyes stared sightlessly from his pale face into the forest she had just restored, the shards and dust of his crumbled Mask clinging to the black stubble on his cheeks. With a shudder, she hurried away.

Her companions awaited her just out of sight. "Done," Mara said to Edrik as she climbed wearily into the saddle of her patient mare.

Edrik nodded. "Excellent," he said. "We'll risk riding

along the path a bit farther, then we'll take to the woods again."

Chell was staring at her with bright, narrowed eyes. She gave him an innocent smile. A flash of irritation crossed his face as he reined his horse around to follow Edrik.

Keltan rode up close beside her, and leaned even closer. "Are you all right?" he murmured. "You used magic, didn't you?"

She nodded. "I had to do something with it," she murmured back. "When the Watcher died . . . his magic leaped to me." *As though I were made of black lodestone,* she thought. "But it . . . itched. I had to get rid of it."

"But Ethelda said—"

"I know what Ethelda said. I didn't have a choice," she snapped.

Or was I just looking for an excuse to use magic again despite the warnings?

It had felt good . . . *right* . . . to use her Gift. But what other surprises did it have in store for her? When Illina had died in front of her during the raid on the mining camp, Mara hadn't received *her* magic. What had just happened with the Watcher had never happened before.

But then, when Illina had died, she hadn't yet drawn any magic from others. That had happened spontaneously when she had contained the explosion in the mining camp. Perhaps that had also awakened *this* new ability, but since then no one had died in her presence until now, so she had been unaware of it.

She wondered if there really were books in the Palace Library that could explain her strange power . . . and tell her how to control it. *I'll ask Father when I see him,* she thought. *He could look it up . . . send a message . . .*

But she felt uneasy even as she thought it. She was

already putting her father into terrible danger by meeting with him. How much more could he risk? How much more did she *want* him to risk?

He put you *in terrible danger by arranging to have your Mask fail and the unMasked Army rescue you!*

The harshness of her own thought surprised her, and not for the first time, she wondered what she would say to him when she saw him again. She wondered what he would say to her.

She'd find out soon enough, if all went well.

Possibly a big "if," she thought, thinking of the dead Watcher by the side of the road.

She thought of that Watcher a great deal more than she wanted to later that night, for as she slept, he came to her, head flopped over, tongue extended, blood dripping from the corner of his mouth, eyes glazed. He could not speak from his twisted throat, but he made strange grunting noises, and his hands reached for her—

She woke with her own scream echoing in her ears, and jerked upright to see Edrik, who was on watch, on his feet, hand on his sword hilt, eyes wide; looked right to see Keltan, lying on that side, gasping with the fright of one woken suddenly from sleep . . . and looked the other way to see Chell lying still, but with his eyes open, studying her.

"Sorry," she gasped out. "Sorry. Bad dream." She got up and stumbled to her pack. The fire had burned down to coals, but there was enough heat there to boil water in one of their cooking pots and pour in one of the packets of herbs Ethelda had prepared for her. Keltan, who had come to the fire with her, wrinkled his nose and drew away as steam rose from the pot, but to her it smelled like spring and flowers and baking bread and every other lovely smell all rolled together. She poured the hot liquid into a mug and drank it too fast, burning her tongue.

When it was finished, she lay back down, the memory

of the nightmare receding. "Will you be all right?" Keltan asked her softly.

She nodded, and he returned to his own bedroll. She lay down, but could not sleep.

Just as Ethelda had warned her, the Watcher's death had left an imprint on her mind. Using the magic that had flowed into her from his body to erase their tracks hadn't removed that imprint. The Watcher with the broken neck now lingered inside her mind, joining all the others, Grute, two other Watchers, Illina, the Warden ... Katia. The imprints of those earlier deaths had faded enough with time that she had stopped her once-daily brewing of the potion Ethelda had provided her. Apparently that had been a mistake.

She stared up at the star-bright sky, but the diamond glitter blurred and faded as tears welled in her eyes. *What am I?* she cried out silently to those distant lights. *What kind of freak am I?*

The stars offered no answer, and she had none within herself. She could only hope that *somewhere* there was one.

She thought her sobs silent. Certainly Chell did not stir again and Edrik did not look around. But Keltan must not have been able to fall back to sleep either. He got up and came over to her, lying down beside her, his body warm against hers. She turned to him, suddenly sobbing uncontrollably, and he put his arm under her head and cradled her on his shoulder. "Shhh," he said. "Shhh. It's all right."

"I don't have much of that potion," she said in a choked whisper. "If the dreams come back ... I'll run out ... I can't bear ..."

"No dreams will come back tonight," Keltan whispered in return. "I'll stay right here to keep them away. Now go to sleep."

She nodded, remembering when Illina had held her after she woke screaming during the journey to the mine.

Illina, who had also died, and whose image had also haunted her dreams . . .

She shuddered, and Keltan's embrace tightened. "Shhh," he whispered again. "Shhh . . ."

She closed her eyes. It felt good to be held.

She slept.

• • •

On the morning of the thirteenth of Winterwhite, they finally caught sight of Tamita.

They came over a rise and there it was in the distance, walls of yellowish stone surrounding rank on rank of houses and other buildings, climbing the terraced slopes of Fortress Hill to the gleaming white towers of the Palace, whose blue banners, snapping in the sunlight, were only occasionally visible through the wreaths of steam and smoke from the city's thousands of hearths, all alight to ward off the wintry chill. (*Though if they think* this *is cold*, Mara thought, *they should visit the mountains*.) The Heartsblood flowed toward Tamita and, eventually, into it, passing beneath the walls, as would she and Keltan when they entered the city that night. The ridge they had climbed held the last bit of forest cover: only brown stubble-covered fields and the occasional farmhouse remained between them and the city walls.

"This is as far as Chell and I go," Edrik said to Mara. "Once it is dark, you and Keltan can enter. But it's too exposed to go any closer until sunset."

"I cannot learn anything of the city from here!" Chell protested. "If I am to report—"

"This is all you get to see," Edrik said flatly. "It's too dangerous for us to go closer."

Chell's jaw set, but he nodded, once.

"We'll camp here for the rest of the day," Edrik continued. "No fire."

Mara sighed. The warm night in the farmhouse seemed an eternity ago.

The day crawled by. Clouds rose in the west and swept over the sky as the hours passed, swallowing the sun shortly after noon. The temperature rose slightly but the air became damp, making it feel colder rather than warmer.

Chell sat by himself, writing in a small notebook, presumably making notes about what he had thus far seen in Aygrima. Edrik stood watch, staring out over the plain below, where nothing moved except a few cows and, once, a lone farmer trudging along a path through the fields, his Masked face a white dot beneath a brown hood.

Keltan sat close beside Mara, gazing at Tamita. "I never thought I'd be going back in there," he said in a low voice. "I never wanted to."

Mara said nothing. She knew that Keltan's life in the city had been hard, his father abusive, their home a hovel. She, on the other hand, had longed to return since the day her Mask had failed, had dreamed of her own room, her own bed, her mother and father, of life as it had been for the first fifteen years of her existence, the life that had been torn away from her in one horrifying moment of blood and pain.

Now she *was* returning home, to her own room, to her father . . . and though she had longed for it, now it terrified her. She wasn't the little girl who had once slept in the room where she would meet her father that night, and she could never be that little girl again. She was . . . whatever she was now, with her strange, terrifying Gift. She had seen and experienced things she had never dreamed of in her worst childhood nightmares. Her faith in her father had been shattered along with the Mask he had so carefully crafted to fail. She understood that he had judged the fear and agony of that moment worth the possibility of freedom if the unMasked Army succeeded in rescuing her, but at the same time, he had sentenced her to all the terror, pain, and degradation that had followed. And he had made that choice *for* her, hadn't warned her what was to come, hadn't discussed it with her. She knew he had had to protect himself and his own Mask in order to protect her, but still, she wished he had been able to give her some kind of warning, some kind of reassurance. And she still remembered the screams of her mother, being forced from the Maskery after Mara's Mask had shattered. Her father had caused his wife to suffer, too, and hadn't confided in her, either— at least not before the fact. Whether or not her mother knew the truth now, Mara didn't know.

What she really wished, she realized, was that her father had treated her like a grown-up instead of like a child. The irony was, a hundred times since she had wished she could go back to being a child.

Is growing up this hard for everyone, she wondered, *or is it just me?*

At last, the sun, though unseen behind low, scudding clouds, set behind the hills to the west. Beneath the overcast, twilight faded quickly to darkness. Shadow swallowed the lands below the ridge, but the city glowed in the dark, streetlamps turning the smoke and steam from the innumerable hearths into long orange plumes rising toward the streaming clouds. White, star-bright lamps in the Palace, shining out above the walls through tower windows, seemed to float over everything else, like fireflies hovering above the city.

"You have five hours to make your rendezvous with your father," Edrik said to her and Keltan. "We will wait here through tomorrow and tomorrow night. If you have not returned by morning on the fifteenth of Winterwhite, or if we see any sign of alarm . . ." He said nothing else, but he didn't have to.

Mara nodded to him, and then to Keltan. Without a word, the two of them began their descent.

Though neither starlight nor moonlight penetrated the clouds, the city-glow provided ample light to keep them on track. Keltan led the way, down to the river and along its western bank, the city looming ever closer until at last, an hour after they had left the ridge, they stood at the base of the towering wall, its yellow hue faded to dark gray in the dim light. The river, a hundred feet across, swept silently through a low arch. Willows grew close to the massive stones of the wall, built without mortar (but with magic). Keltan knelt and pushed aside trailing branches to reveal the nearest corner of the arch . . . and the dark space beneath it, just above the level of the rushing waters. "In here," he whispered. Mara nodded and eased her way down the slippery bank, her feet finding rough wood at the bottom: a walkway (crawlway, really, for there was certainly no room to stand between it and the top of the arch) disappearing under the wall. She waited there for Keltan to descend, steadying him with a hand on his arm as he slid down beside her. He crouched and looked beneath the arch. "All clear," he whispered. "Let's go."

"Wait!" Mara grabbed his arm. "Listen!"

Keltan's head shot up, and then turned sharply as he heard what she had just heard: the crunching of footsteps through the stubble at the top of the bank.

Keltan's sword whispered from his sheath as he turned to face the sound. Mara stared up, too, willing whomever was up there to turn and walk away down the wall, but half-expecting the black-Masked face of a Watcher to suddenly appear among the willow branches.

An instant later, a face did appear: but it was un-Masked, and clear enough in the dim light that Keltan lowered his sword. "Chell!" he whispered furiously.

"Found you," Chell said cheerfully. He slid down the bank to join them on the narrow walkway, grinning.

"What are *you* doing here?" Keltan demanded.

Chell's grin instantly slipped away. "My duty," he said. "I was sent to scout out this land. I cannot do that from a hillside two miles from the capital city."

"Edrik would never—"

Chell shrugged. "I didn't ask him. Went to relieve myself in the woods. Didn't bother going back."

"He'll come after you."

"How can he?" Chell said. "He doesn't know for certain where I went, and he dare not come closer to the city. He said so himself." He leaned over, looking past Keltan and Mara at the archway. "Shouldn't we get under this wall? You have an appointment to keep."

Keltan didn't move. "You're unMasked. You can't pass for a child. You're risking—"

"I'm risking," Chell said, his voice suddenly cold and hard as bared steel, "my life to do my duty. As I always have, and always will. My duty requires me to enter this city, no matter the risk; and I will do so . . . whether you approve or not." His eyes, black pools in the dim light, looked down at Keltan. "Do you plan to try to stop me?"

Keltan's hand went to his sword. Without looking around he said, "Mara, this is your mission. What do you want me to do?"

Mara stared over Keltan's shoulder at Chell. The young man met her gaze, face impassive, jaw set. *He's so sure he's doing what he's supposed to do. No doubts, no second-guessing. He has his duty, and his way is clear. And I'm . . .*

I'm making it up as I go.

"Leave him alone," she said tiredly. "But, Chell, you cannot come to the meeting with my father. The danger is too great, for you, for us . . . and for him. Keltan," she added, without taking her eyes off the stranger from the sea, "if he *does* try to follow us to my father's—*then* I *do* want you to stop him."

"My pleasure," Keltan growled, and Mara heard the dislike in his voice.

If Chell did, too, it didn't seem to bother him. His grim expression dissolved into his usual lighthearted smile. "Fair enough," he said. "I don't really care whether I meet your father or not, though I'm sure he's a fine gentleman. I have other whales to chase."

"We're wasting time," Keltan said. He sheathed his sword. "I'll go first." He got down on his hands and knees and crawled along the wooden walkway.

Mara went next, with Chell behind her.

The boards of the walkway, crudely hacked out of lumber by someone with no interest in finesse, made Mara glad she was wearing gloves; otherwise she would surely have had splinters in both hands within the first few feet. The low, curving ceiling of stone, glistening wetly even in the almost nonexistent light seeping into the tunnel from both ends, amplified the noise of the river. The water poured by not only to their left but also directly beneath them, for the walkway clung precariously to the sharply sloped wall of the arch, creaking and swaying as they made their way along it. Here and there boards had fallen away, and Mara eased her way over them, breathing hard, thinking what would happen if they fell into the ice-cold water. How far would it sweep them before they could climb the bank? Would they be *able* to climb the bank? Or would the water simply pull them under, suck heat and breath from their bodies, and spit them up as blue-skinned, bloated corpses for some farmer to find miles downstream of the city?

You're way too morbid for someone so young, you know that? Mara told herself, and concentrated on crawling instead of worrying.

Though the city wall was only twenty feet thick, the walkway went on for more like fifty, taking them not only through the wall but then, almost before Mara realized there was open sky above her, under another, higher arch, which she realized must be South Bridge, by which the Great Circle Road that encompassed the city just inside the wall crossed the Heartsblood at that point. When at last they reached the end of the second arch, the wooden walkway likewise ended, two posts anchoring it to the muddy riverbank. Keltan crawled out into that mud, rolled over onto his back, and eased himself out from under the arch, looking up at the bridge. After a moment he flipped back onto his stomach, made a sharp "come on" gesture, and slithered out of sight. Mara followed, the mud squishing like Mask clay between her gloved fingers.

At the top of the bank Keltan scrambled to his feet and dashed across a narrow footpath and a stretch of brown grass to a cobblestoned street, and across that into a dark alley. Moments later all three of them were crouched together in its shadows, breathing hard.

"Welcome to Tamita," Mara whispered to Chell.

"Worst place in the world," Keltan growled.

Chell laughed lightly. "I doubt that," he said. "I am sure I have seen far worse."

Mara, thinking of the mining camp, had to agree.

Keltan glanced at her, his face a pale oval in the dim light reflected from the clouds. "We're going to have to hurry to make the meeting," he said in a low voice. "And we must be very careful of the Night Watchers. We can't be certain they still follow the patterns they did when I fled the city weeks ago. And after what happened at the mine, they may also be on high alert."

Mara nodded impatiently. "So let's go."

"Not me," Chell said.

"You can't wander these streets at night," Keltan snapped. "The Night Watchers—"

"We each have our missions," Chell said. "You be about yours . . . and I'll be about mine." And with that he leaped to his feet and dashed away. Keltan scrambled up, hand on his sword hilt, but Mara put a restraining hand on his forearm.

"Let him go," she said. "It's his funeral."

"It may be ours if we're wrong and he can lead the Watchers to the Secret City," Keltan snarled. "*Dammit*, I should have knocked him down and tied him up outside the walls."

Mara, with great restraint, forbore pointing out that Chell was taller, older, stronger, and no doubt better trained than Keltan. "We can't do anything about him," she said instead. "And we *cannot* miss this meeting with my father."

Keltan swore again, but led Mara back to the cobblestoned road, turned right—the opposite direction to that taken by Chell—and took her deeper into Tamita.

Toward home, she thought, heart beginning to beat faster than even fear and exertion could account for.

Home!

EIGHT

Homecoming

L IKE WRAITHS, they slipped through the silent
streets from shadow to shadow, occasionally climbing steep stairs as they moved higher up in the tiered city,
ever alert for the Night Watchers. No one else would—or
at least *should*—be abroad; children had a sundown curfew and even the Masked were prohibited from traveling
anywhere within the city except the broad, well-lit bou-
levards of the entertainment district east of the Palace . . . and the less well-lit, officially frowned upon but
unofficially sanctioned streets to either side of it where
the entertainment was of a sort usually provided behind
closed doors.

They were in luck. Though the Night Watchers were
surely somewhere about, for they always were, they

heard nothing except for one lonely dog howling at the clouds. They gave the sound a wide berth not just because it gave Mara the shivers, but also for fear his howls might turn to intruder-warning barks if they strayed too close. There was no law against people looking out of their windows, after all, even at night.

About half an hour after crawling under the wall, they reached streets Mara knew well. Now she took the lead, creeping along fences, crawling through bushes, dashing across streets only when it could not be avoided. At last she reached the corner of a particular brick wall where a particular tree grew. "Here," she panted to Keltan.

He looked around, obviously puzzled. "Here what?"

Mara grinned. "Watch." Quick as a cat, she scaled the tree and swung herself onto the top of the wall. Straddling it, she looked down at Keltan. "Can you do that?"

He snorted. "Watch me." Sure enough, in a moment he was beside her on the wall, although he hadn't exactly been catlike about it; he swiped a hand across a bleeding scratch on his cheek. "Now what?"

"This way." Mara stood and walked along the top of the wall, balancing easily enough in her boots, though she didn't quite dare to run along it as she had in bare feet so many times as a child, albeit on warmer nights than this. The thrill of slipping out of her warm bed and into the forbidden streets had never seemed nearly as inviting when her breath came in clouds.

The wall enclosed the back garden of two houses. The second was Mara's. She looked down into the enclosed space, barely visible in the cloud-glow. In hot summers she had practically lived there, playing and reading in the evenings, even sleeping outdoors in a hammock slung between those two trees in the corner when the heat became unbearable in her room upstairs. Now it looked alien and forbidding.

Of course, she knew well enough it hadn't changed.
She had.

The wall ran up close under the eaves of her old house. She stepped lightly off the bricks and onto the rounded green tiles, clambering up them to the skylight. *I wonder how long Father has known about this way into the house?* she thought as she reached for the glass window. *Did he know about all the times I sneaked out when I was supposed to be asleep?*

It wasn't an altogether comforting thought.

Normally, when she had come back to the house, the window in the skylight was out of its frame, lying on her bed where she had placed it before escaping into the night. She wasn't sure she'd be able to remove it from this direction, not without risking dropping it into her room to possibly shatter on the floorboards; but as she drew nearer to the skylight, she realized she needn't have worried—the window was already out of its frame.

And that could mean only . . .

Her breath suddenly caught in her throat. Her heart fluttered. "Daddy?" she whispered.

"Mara!" The voice that came back from the darkness, deep, rough, warm, flooded her with so many memories of her lost childhood that she instantly burst into tears. Suddenly not caring in the slightest about stealth, she lowered herself into the darkness, ready to drop onto her bed—but she didn't have to. Strong hands took her waist and guided her down, and then she turned and flung her arms around the man she had once thought could do no wrong, the man she had loved and admired above all others . . .

. . . and the man who had sentenced her to pain and exile, a cold core of her soul reminded her, but she brushed that aside. All that mattered now was that she had returned to her father. All that mattered now was that she was *home*.

"There, there, Mara," he murmured, big hand stroking her hair. "There, there."

She heard the bed creak behind her as Keltan dropped down into the room, and felt her father stiffen. She pulled back, raised a hand to dash the tears away from her face. "It's all right, Daddy," she said. "This is Keltan. He's my friend."

"Keltan? That's the name of the Autarch's—"

"It's not my real name," Keltan said.

Mara looked at her father. He had lit no lamp, and so was little more than a shadow, but she didn't need to see him clearly to know exactly what he looked like. "Where's Mother?" she said.

Her father hesitated. "Mara . . ."

"What's wrong?" Mara said. "She's not sick? She's not . . ." Her throat closed on the final word.

"No, no, nothing like that," her father said. He laid a reassuring hand on her shoulder. "No, it's just . . ." He took a deep breath that shook a little. "She left me, Mara. She went back to her old village, to the old house there. She was devastated when your Mask failed. She blamed me." He swallowed. "And of course she was right to blame me, since I made your Mask to fail. But I couldn't tell her that, and I couldn't tell her why, or her Mask might have failed, too . . . maybe even mine, despite the way I modified it." His voice fell to a shaken whisper. "So it's been . . . hard."

Mara couldn't speak. By now her mother must think her as good as dead, and she could do nothing to disabuse her of that notion. Even if she could somehow get to her mother's village, far to the south, to tell her anything that had happened might risk her mother's Mask.

And Daddy did it. The thought was bitter as curdled milk. *He not only forced me into exile, he plunged Mother into the hell of thinking I'm gone forever.*

She wanted to shout at him, ask him if he really thought it had been worth it, if he really understood how much pain he had caused her and her mother . . . but there was, simply, no time.

As if her father had read her mind, he took another deep breath, then rushed on. "You must not linger. It's too dangerous. I received your message and have prepared your answer." He turned away and picked up something from the worktable along the wall where Mara had spent many hours writing and drawing when she was a schoolgirl. "This should answer any questions you have about the making of Masks. It is a copy of *The Book of Masks*, the secret manual of Maskmaking. Ironically, it was made for you with the full approval of the Palace, for me to present to you when you became a full apprentice, after you were Masked. If things had gone as . . . as we once hoped, you would have begun learning the knowledge it holds at my side." He held it out, and Mara took it. It felt heavy in her hand. "Now you must learn on your own. But you should find therein the knowledge you need to enable you to . . . do whatever it is you are trying to do."

"I'm trying to make—" Mara began, but her father flung up his hand.

"No! *I must not know.* My Mask is forgiving, but I cannot be certain *how* forgiving. The less I know, the less likely I am to cross some threshold that will cause it to crack. And if it cracks . . ." His voice trailed off.

If it cracks, Mara thought, remembering her fears of earlier in the night, *he will face the Autarch's fiercest retribution for betrayal.*

She turned and handed *The Book of Masks* to Keltan, who slipped it silently into his backpack. Then she turned back to her father.

"There's one more thing," she said.

"Mara, there's no time—"

"This is important!" As quickly as she could, she told him about her Gift. "But I don't know how to control it," she finished. "And the nightmares are ... terrible. Ethelda said there might be answers in the Library. She said ... you have access ..."

Her father stood silent in the dark for a long moment. "I had hoped that Gift ... that *curse* ... had died out," he whispered at last. "Mara, I'm so sorry."

Mara stared at his shadowed face. "You've heard of this?"

He nodded. "There have been a few, in my family line, with the ability to draw magic directly from others. But not for decades. I never thought it might afflict you."

"It's not an 'affliction,'" Mara snapped, strangely angered. "It's a Gift. It's a particularly powerful Gift. I've saved lives with it." *And taken them*, that cold spot in her heart reminded her, but she pushed that thought away. "I just need to learn how to control it. If it's appeared before in our family ..." Hope kindled suddenly. "Do you know how to control it?"

That little flame died as her father shook his head. "No," he said. "I don't know if anyone does. But yes, *if* such knowledge exists, it may well be in the Library." His voice dropped. "It will be risky for me, Mara. A close watch is kept on the Library and those who use it. But I ... will do what I can. For you."

Mara flung her arms around him. "Thank you, Daddy," she whispered.

He returned the embrace. For a long moment they stood there, warm in each other's arms, and for that moment all the horrible things that had happened since Mara's Mask had failed receded into the mists, like a dimly remembered dream, and she was just a child again, safe in her father's love.

But the moment passed. Her father released her, stepped back. "Go," he whispered. "Go now. Get out of Tamita. Get far away. I will send a message when . . . when I have something to tell you." He glanced at Keltan. "Take care of her, son." His voice broke. "Take care of my little girl." And then he turned, dashing his sleeve across his face, and went out, closing the door gently behind him.

Mara's legs felt weak. She sat down on her old bed, felt a lump beneath her, reached down, and pulled out a stuffed cat, one eye missing, whiskers akimbo, striped pelt moth-eaten and bare in places. "Stoofy," she whispered, and hugged it to her chest.

Keltan sat down beside her. "Stoofy?" he said, tone gently mocking.

"I've missed Stoofy," she whispered.

"And your father?" he said, no longer mocking.

"And my father," she said. She hugged Stoofy even tighter. "I may never see him again." The lump in her throat threatened to choke her.

Keltan looked around the dim room. "If I had lived *here*," he said, "I might not have fled to the unMasked Army."

"I had no intention of fleeing," Mara said. "I was forced out." She looked at the closed door, outlined by the dim yellow light of some distant candle. "By *him*."

Keltan sighed. "Feelings are complicated things."

"You can say that again," Mara said. She wiped her nose with the back of her gloved hand, then held Stoofy out to Keltan. "Put him in your backpack. I am *not* leaving him behind again."

Keltan bowed slightly to her. "Milady." He stuffed the cat out of sight.

She stuck her tongue out at him, then looked up at the skylight. "All right," she said. "Homecoming's over. Time to get out of Tamita."

Climbing out proved easier than it had been the last time she'd done it, the night she had met Keltan in the basement coal room where he had taken refuge while on the run from the Night Watchers: the ceiling seemed closer to the bed than it used to be. On the other hand, as she had noted slipping in, but hadn't really registered in the rush to meet her father, the fit was tighter, too.

From the roof, they hurried back onto the wall, down to the tree, and down into the street, retracing their steps to South Bridge. Once more they slipped through the shadows as silent as hunting cats . . .

. . . but even cats could be taken unawares.

They were almost free, hurrying toward the bridge along the footpath that followed the river, when suddenly Mara heard, from just the other side of a fortuitous screen of bushes, the sound of running, booted feet, and then a breathless voice. "I saw something, sir! Couple of blocks back. Just a glimpse of movement. Could have been a dog."

"Could be something else," growled a second voice, almost on top of them, though they'd seen no one. "Check along the river. Start down there."

Footsteps clattered . . . away from them for the moment, but that wouldn't last. "Hurry!" Keltan said, his mouth so close to Mara's ear his lips tickled it and his breath raised goose bumps on her arms. "Once we're under the bridge we're safe."

They sprinted forward.

They almost made it. Keltan reached the place where the slippery path led down to the walkway under the bridge, slid down it like a child on a slide, and vanished from sight. Mara dashed after him . . . but a root she did not see in the near-darkness caught her toe. She fell headlong, thudding to the ground, unable to bite off an involuntary cry of pain.

"There!" shouted a voice behind her. Footsteps thundered along the path. "Hold!"

Mara saw Keltan's pale face, eyes wide and horrified, slip back into the sheltering darkness of the bridge. Then two Night Watchers reached her, and gloved hands seized her arms.

NINE

Taken!

"**C**HECK UNDER THE BRIDGE!" shouted the Watcher who had grabbed Mara.

Mara caught her breath as the other black-Masked man cautiously picked his way down the slippery bank and knelt, holding onto one of the barren willow branches with one hand, to peer under the bridge. He grunted. "Some kind of walkway," he said. "Made by kids, from the look of it." He knelt even lower, and swore. "Damn thing goes right under the wall!"

"Anyone on it?"

"No." The Watcher straightened and turned around. "Looks like she was alone."

"We'll have to tear that out," the Watcher said. "And make sure the river passage is properly barred again, both ends." He shook Mara. "That's a security risk, that is."

The Watcher by the bridge snorted. "Risk from whom? That's what the Masks are for." But he was unsheathing his knife as he said it. He reached down under the bridge and flicked the blade once, twice. The ropes holding the walkway parted and Mara heard the splash as the nearest end dropped into the river. Several planks of wood swept into view and floated downriver. "Done for now," the Watcher said. "Take iron bars to rip it out proper." He sheathed his knife and scrambled back up the ridge. "Now, who have we got?"

"Another damn kid breaking curfew," growled the Watcher holding Mara.

The other Watcher took Mara's chin in his gloved hand and forced her head up, turning it this way and that. "Pretty," he grunted. "How close are you to your Masking, girl?"

"Close," Mara said. Her heart was pounding and her head felt light. Keltan must have made it to the far end of the walkway before the Watcher cut it, or he would have been seen ... but he couldn't get back in. He couldn't help her. No one could.

Once more she was in the hands of the Watchers, and this time, unlike in the mining camp, there was not even the slightest hope of rescue from the unMasked Army. And the risk wasn't just to herself, but to her father. She couldn't let them know who she was. "It's next month."

The Watcher didn't seem to have heard her. He was peering closer at her face. "Wait a minute," he said slowly. "I've seen you before."

Mara's heart stopped, restarted with a painful lurch. "My name's ... Kirika," she said. "My father is a ... a ..."

"You're Mara Holdfast," the Watcher growled, releasing her chin. "You're the daughter of Charlton Holdfast, the Master Maskmaker. I caught you and your friend swimming in the pool behind the Waterworkers' Hall." He snorted. "I haven't just seen you, I've seen you naked. Gave you my cloak to wear."

"No," Mara said. "That wasn't me. I'm not—"

"Don't lie, girl." He looked at the Watcher holding her in an unyielding grip. "And there's more," he said. "Her Masking has come and gone ... and she failed. Big surprise to everyone. She's not a kid. She's unMasked." He frowned. "And I sense ..." He drew back from her, then reached inside his cloak. When he took out his hand, she saw that his fingers were sheathed in glowing purple light.

Magic! she thought. *If he has more, I could—*

But she never finished the thought. The Watcher flicked his fingers as though flicking away water. The purple light leaped from him to Mara ...

... and she gasped, and sagged in the clutches of the Watcher who held her, because she suddenly felt as if she had gone blind, deaf, and dumb.

Her Gift was gone. Just like that, it was gone!

The grip on her arms tightened even more. "She's Gifted?" gasped the Watcher who held her. "UnMasked, and still Gifted?"

The first Watcher nodded. "I've blocked her, for now."

For now? Mara thought, and though her thoughts felt strange and sluggish in her own mind, she felt a surge of relief. *Then it's not permanent!*

The Watcher who had just used magic on her glanced back down the riverbank at the bridge. "She came in under the wall, obviously." He turned back to her again, his Masked face a black void in the dim light. "The question is, why? How did she get back here from the mining camp? And why does she still have magic?"

"What do we do with her?" said the Watcher holding her.

"She's not a kid," the other said grimly. "Out in the streets at night, unMasked? That's a death sentence, that is."

Mara swallowed.

"But that's not our call," the Watcher went on, and Mara felt a quick surge of probably unwarranted relief. "There's something strange about this. More than strange. And that means we kick it up the chain of command." He looked over her head at her captor. "We take her to the Palace."

The two Night Watchers led her up onto the Great Circle Road, and moved along it at a brisk pace, the city wall towering over them to the left, blank-faced warehouses and shuttered shops to their right. Lamps hung periodically on tall posts, though here and there they had guttered out, so that they passed from pools of light to pools of deep shadow as they made their way around the city.

High above them, at the peak of Fortress Hill, the Palace glowed orange in the light reflecting from the still-scudding clouds. Its towering curtain wall hid the lights that Mara had seen from the ridge south of the city. She wondered if they were going to go all the way around to the Palace's main gate, if the Watchers would parade her down that well-lit boulevard. This late, it would be mostly deserted, but not entirely; there would still be citizens emerging from the pubs and other establishments—and her father moved in the highest circles of Tamita society. There were many who knew her face, many who knew she had failed her Masking, many who would take note that she was in the hands of the Watchers and being taken to the Palace . . . many who would tell her father. And then what would he do? What would he risk? And at what cost?

There was nothing she could do but keep her head down in the hope no one recognized her; but in the end, the Watchers began the climb toward the Palace long before they reached the main boulevard. At first Mara felt relieved as they led her up a narrow alley that climbed steeply, long stretches of staircase followed by terraces where rather mean and run-down houses huddled together; but as they continued to climb, she realized where this path must lead, and sick terror gripped her again, for it ended, not at the grand main gate, gilded and glowing, but at a much smaller one made of unadorned, solid iron, rusted the color of blood.

Traitors' Gate.

Forbidden as a matter of course from going anywhere near it, she had, also as a matter of course, sneaked up there: less than a year ago. She had had nightmares about it; nightmares that paled in comparison to the ones generated by the horrors she had encountered since, but they had left an indelible impression on her.

And *there* was why.

She didn't want to, would have preferred to look anywhere else, but she could not climb the stairs without keeping her head up, and looking up, she could not help but see the tall wooden structures erected on both sides of the path on the last terrace beneath the Palace walls: two score in all, a dozen on each side of the road.

She was thankful for the dim light. She only wished it could be dimmer, for even in the slight glow from the clouds and those buildings still showing lights behind them there could be no mistaking what hung from those structures: corpses, the decaying remains of those deemed traitors to the Autarchy, hanged from these gallows and left to feed the crows until, picked clean, their bones were at last taken down, and, it was rumored, ground to provide fertilizer for the Palace gardens.

There were eight in all, two more than when she had sneaked up there last. Six were already little more than skeletons hung with strips of dry flesh and skin. But two ... two were fresh. Both were naked, the final humiliation for those whom the Autarch had declared to be his enemies and therefore less than human. One was female, the other male. The woman was older, in her forties, perhaps, but the male ... the male was only a boy, no older than Hyram. His purpled, bloated face stared at her, swollen tongue protruding from the corner of his mouth.

He had no eyes. The birds always took those first.

Swallowing hard to keep from throwing up, Mara tore her gaze away and focused grimly on Traitors' Gate itself: the gate through which traitors emerged, but never re-entered. She dreaded it opening for her now, but in fact it didn't. The Watchers, swearing under their breaths at the stench from the bodies, took her instead to a small door next to the gate. The one who had recognized her rapped sharply on it with his gloved fist. A panel slid open and a black-Masked face peered out. "What is it?" the new Watcher said. Then he saw Mara. "Who's this?"

"UnMasked," the first Watcher said. "But I know her. Mara Holdfast."

"Holdfast? The Master Maskmaker's daughter?" Mara could hear disbelief in the Watcher's voice. "But she—"

"Failed her Masking," said the one on her side of the door. "Was sent to the camp. And now ... she's back. *And* she still has her Gift. Blocked for now."

The Watcher inside swore, then stepped back. The panel slid across the peephole again and a moment later a bolt crashed open, and then the heavy wooden door swung inward. Beyond was a short, dark tunnel through the walls, leading into a room aglow with fire- and lamplight, almost blinding to Mara after so much time in the darkness. She squinted and blinked watering eyes as the Watcher who had opened the door stepped aside so that she and her two captors could enter.

He closed and bolted the door behind them, then followed them into the room. Scattered chairs and tables gave it the look of an inn's common room, as did the huge hearth in which crackled the remnants of a once much-larger fire. Lamps hung on the walls and stood on a couple of the tables, and stairs led up from one corner. To Mara's right, another heavy, bolted door presumably opened onto to the path the condemned followed to Traitors' Gate.

"Sit her down," said the Watcher who had let them in. Mara's captors shoved her into one of the wooden chairs at a table near the fire. She savored the warmth despite the fear and despair gripping her.

None of the Watchers sat. They stood, looming over her like the gallows loomed over the path to Traitors' Gate. "You were at the camp?" the one who had recognized her said in a low voice.

Mara hesitated. Should she tell the truth?

And then, like a ray of light breaking through the clouds, she felt a surge of hope—probably unreasonable hope, but hope nonetheless. *Everyone in the Palace must be frantic to understand what happened at the camp. They know magic was involved, but they don't know where it came from. And no one who was there can tell them a thing: everyone aboveground collapsed when I sucked in their magic to stop the explosion of the rockbreakers. There were no witnesses.*

They need *me. They need to question me. They won't kill me.*

Not yet, anyway.

"Yes," she said. "Yes. I saw what happened." Her brain seemed to be fizzing, bubbling, working frantically to construct a tale that might get her taken somewhere else, anywhere else, away from the Watchers and Traitors' Gate and the horrible "fruit" hanging from the black gallows-trees outside. "The gates were open, I ran . . . I've been . . . living in the villages, passing as a child. But I know I can't keep that up. I'm getting too tall, too . . . too much older.

"So I thought . . . I thought . . . maybe if I came back, I could, I don't know, bargain. Tell what I know in exchange for not being killed. For not being sent back to that horrible camp."

Were they believing her? The black Masks gave no clue. "And you just happened to know a way into the City?" said the one who had let them in, whom she gathered must outrank the others.

"Under the wall," said the Watcher who had recognized her. "Along the river."

"That walkway's been there for years," Mara said. "A lot of kids know about it." She suspected that was a lie, but not one they could easily check, without interviewing every child in the City.

"If you sneaked in to turn yourself in, why did you run when you were seen?" the commander said skeptically.

"I . . . I panicked. I *thought* I wanted to turn myself in, but then, when I saw the Night Watchers . . . I've always run from Night Watchers. They've . . . chased me before."

She glanced at the one who had recognized her, the one who had said he had seen her naked the night he'd caught her and Sala swimming behind Waterworkers' Hall, and gave him a slight smile, hoping it looked like she was flirting, though she didn't really have a clue how to flirt and he was the last person she would have flirted with if she had. *But anything to make them think a little more kindly toward me . . .*

He rewarded her, if that was the word, with a grunt. "It's true," he said. "She's been in the night streets before. That's why I recognized her."

The higher-ranking Watcher regarded her for a moment. "You've clearly got a story to tell," he said at last, slowly. "Whether it's a true story or not isn't for me to judge." He turned to the others. "You two get back on patrol," he said. "I'm taking her to Lord Stanik."

Mara's breath caught. Lord Stanik was the Guardian of Security, a member of the Autarch's Circle. He was also her father's boss. If she was being delivered to *him*, then they were taking her tale seriously indeed.

Whether she should respond to that with hope or despair, she didn't know.

She tried in vain to sense the magic in the Watchers' bodies, or the magic the Watcher who had flicked purple at her obviously carried with him in his cloak. Surely they also kept a store of magic within the guardhouse. But she could feel nothing. She was still blocked.

She'd had no idea the Watchers had that power. What *other* powers did they have? Could they force her to tell the truth? Force her to reveal what she knew about the unMasked Army and the Secret City?

The Watchers who had captured her nodded and went back out the way they had come in. Their commander grabbed her arm, jerked her to her feet, and propelled her toward the other door. He unlocked it with a big brass key from a ring at his belt, pulled her through, closed and locked the door behind them, and then turned left down a passage open to the sky above but hemmed in on both sides by high walls. After fifty feet or so it ended, and Mara and her captor stepped into the open.

Mara stared around in wonder. She had never been inside the Palace walls before. But her father had been, many times, and had told her something of it. This had to be what they called the Great Courtyard, which surrounded the Palace proper. Paved with massive flat slabs of white stone, each as wide as her outstretched arms, lit by lamps on posts all around its perimeter, it was large enough to accommodate a crowd of thousands. Light glowed through the doors and windows of numerous buildings constructed along the inside of the curtain wall: stables and smithies and storerooms, Mara guessed. In the center of the courtyard, water plashed endlessly down the sides of a large tiered fountain, from basin to basin, four in all, each progressively larger, at the bottom spouting through the mouths of carved mountain cats into a walled pool. Atop the fountain glowed an enormous glass ball, yellow and gold, lit from within: the sun symbol of the Autarch. *Amazing how someone so foul can be represented by something so pure,* Mara thought bitterly.

To her left she could see a long line of lamps, leading down a broad path to the main gate, closed this time of night. But her captor led her straight across the courtyard, the sound of their footsteps echoing back from the walls all around them.

As they drew nearer to the Palace, Mara stared up at it. Though the curtain wall made the Palace look like a fortress—and since it was built atop Fortress Hill, presumably it had once served as one—from here, the Palace looked more like a mansion than a place of protection. Surely a building constructed primarily for defense would not have such enormous glass windows. Their panes, the largest and clearest she had ever seen, gleamed with lamplight from within, all around the lowest story.

On the second story and higher the windows had diamond panes, and were much smaller, but despite the lateness of the hour they still glowed with the lights she had seen from far away, where Edrik still waited in the camp to which she would never return. Mara wondered if anyone were really still awake behind those arched windows or if the light were meant as a message for the city below: *The Autarch is always watchful. The Autarch is always alert. The Autarch never sleeps.*

What if he really is *awake?* Mara thought then, as she stared up—and up!—at the Palace, four towering stories in all, topped with turreted spires on all four corners that climbed another two, and centered by one enormous tower four stories taller than that. *He has the same Gift I do, or something like it. He can sense the magic in others. Can he sense mine? Does he know I've arrived? Is he tossing and turning in his bed, aware that someone potentially as powerful as he has just entered the Palace grounds?*

She snorted at her own folly. As powerful as the Autarch? Maybe in potential, if Ethelda were to be believed, but right now she had no power at all. The strange magic of the Watcher had seen to that.

The Palace awed her with its sheer size. As they drew nearer, and she could see the intricate carvings in the shape of twining vines in the stone around those windows, the fluted columns, the silken surface of the polished white stone, her awe only increased. She had never seen anything so beautiful: and yet at the heart of all this beauty, she knew, lurked the Autarch, a venomous spider sucking the life from his people to feed his insatiable need for magic.

A need she was in danger of coming to share. Every time she drew magic from others, Ethelda had warned her, however much it burned her, she would strengthen her desire for its taste. Do it too often, and she might never find her way back, might give in to her need and rip it forcibly from anyone who crossed her, leaving them broken in her wake. "You might even come to love the nightmares," Ethelda had warned her in one of their sessions. "You might lose the shame and horror they engender now, see them only as a sign of your power, as bloody trophies of your hunt for more and more of that power."

If the Watcher hadn't blocked me, she thought, *I might have given in to temptation back at the bridge. I might have escaped . . . but at what cost?*

That thought was almost enough to make her welcome the Watcher's magic that had temporarily robbed her of her Gift. But if . . . *when* . . . she regained the ability to draw on the magic that would surround her within the Palace, would she be able to resist the temptation to use it . . . especially when it might be the only way to avoid execution, or the betrayal of the unMasked Army?

And if she gave in to that temptation, what then? How would the Autarch react?

And what would it do to *her*?

The Watcher pulled her onward even as all those thoughts spun through her head, and took her up a flight of steps onto a porch on the side of the Palace and through a bronze door into a long hallway, paved with glistening marble, paneled in rich red wood, bright-lit by golden chandeliers that hung from beams carved like tree branches, the ceiling between painted and hung with leaves of green cloth to give the illusion of a forest canopy.

She only had a moment to gape at the almost ridiculous beauty of it all before the Watcher opened another door and took her down yet another hallway. The tall windows she had seen from outside were now on their left, the view through their giant panes of glass astonishingly clear and undistorted, almost as though the glass wasn't there at all. Lamps blazed all along the hallway, showing doors on their right. Rich tapestries hung above those doors, and a series of larger-than-life sculptures, mostly of the heroically nude variety, stood between those doors. *No Masks*, Mara thought, glancing at one of those stern stone visages as they passed it; a reminder that the Autarchy had not always relied on that controlling magic to maintain order.

At the end of the hall, the Watcher took her through another bronze door, this one opening into a stairwell whose steps spiraled up into one of the towers. Up those steps they climbed, Mara in front. On the fourth landing, they left the tower, though she was so turned around by the climbing she wasn't sure in which direction, and entered another hallway, paneled in more of the red wood, the floor an intricate mosaic of small white-and-gold tiles. The hall had three thin windows, like the ones cut through the stone cliff in which the Secret City nestled; but unlike those, which let in the free, fresh air, these were barred by horizontal rods of iron and blocked with red-stained glass that allowed no view from inside or out.

Wooden benches of that same red wood ran down both sides of the hall, interrupted halfway down the side opposite the windows by an imposing black door with lamps burning on either side of it. The Watcher shoved Mara down onto the bench next to the door, then knocked. He waited a long moment, then knocked again.

The door opened a crack. "Do you know what time it is?" said a peevish voice from the darkness beyond. "This had better be important."

"It is," said the Watcher. "Wake Guardian Stanik. Tell him . . ." He glanced down at Mara. "Tell him we have captured someone who witnessed what happened in the mining camp. Tell him we have Mara Holdfast."

A moment's silence. "Wait here," the voice said, and the door closed again.

The Watcher sat down next to Mara on the bench. He said nothing.

Heart beating fast, Mara stared at the floor and waited to learn her fate.

TEN

The Examination

TEN MINUTES PASSED, then fifteen, with no change: Mara waited, the Watcher watched, the door stayed closed. The minutes crept by with such excruciating slowness that the opening of the door at last came as a relief, no matter what might follow after, simply because it broke the suspense.

A thin man wearing a belted night robe of deep purple velvet, his face hidden in a white Mask marked with golden links of chain on the forehead and cheeks, turned sideways and gestured them in. "Please step into the parlor," he said. "Guardian Stanik will join you momentarily."

The Watcher stood, unlocked Mara's manacles, and then propelled her through the door into the hallway beyond. Dark wood sheathed the walls. A round black table embossed with a gold-and-silver sun emblem stood in the precise center of the black-and-white-tiled floor. Doors opened to left and right, and the hall ended, after perhaps twenty feet, in another door. The white-Masked man opened the door to their left and ushered them into a room perhaps thirty feet wide and twenty deep. To Mara's left, it extended to a tall, diamond-paned window through which she could see the windblown, city-lit clouds. To her right, sideboards bearing decanters and flagons of silver, crystal, and gold flanked another door. Directly across from her, in a large brick hearth, a fire crackled cheerily, clearly recently laid, for the logs were just beginning to char.

Arranged around that fire were three chairs and a small couch just wide enough for two grown-ups (perhaps three of Mara's size), all made of black wood, their cushions of scarlet velvet. The Watcher pointed her silently to one of the chairs. He remained standing, going to the window and staring out. Mara sat obediently and looked around her, taking in the thick red carpet underfoot and the wooden beams overhead that were intricately carved into the shapes of twining vines. She was studying the painting over the hearth, which showed the Autarch, resplendent in his golden Mask, driving an army from a battlefield with streaming rays of magic that made him strongly resemble the sun come to Earth, when the door behind her opened.

Mara turned.

A tall, thin man stepped inside, pulling the door closed behind him. Gray hair, beginning to thin but carefully combed to hide that fact as much as possible, showed above a gleaming silver Mask. A gray beard and a hint of mustache partially covered the thin lips visible through the Mask's mouth opening. Though from their greeter's comments Mara suspected Stanik had been roused from bed, he wore a snow-white tunic and perfectly pressed trousers, the gold stripe down the outsides of the trousers and the golden sleeves of the tunic, though made of woven cloth, somehow catching the light exactly like the actual gold of the buttons down his chest.

"Captain Daneli," said Stanik, "I understand you have a matter of some urgency to discuss with me." *It had* better *be urgent*, his tone implied, and she shivered. She wouldn't want to be the one who woke Stanik from a sound sleep without a good reason. Her father, though hardly in a position to criticize, had mentioned Stanik once or twice. "An . . . intimidating man," he had said. "And a hard one. He is well suited to the task the Autarch has set him."

His task, Mara knew, was the keeping of order and the squelching of dissent. Those naked corpses outside Traitors' Gate had been sent there by Stanik. She could still join them, if she did not convince the Guardian of Security she deserved leniency.

Captain Daneli turned and saluted, placing a clenched fist on his heart. "Guardian Stanik," he said as he lowered his arm and relaxed his hand. "Earlier this evening two Night Watchers discovered this girl trying to sneak out of the city through the river passage via a crude walkway, since destroyed. One of them recognized her as Mara Holdfast, daughter of the Master Maskmaker." He indicated Mara. "She says she witnessed the events that occurred in the mining camp, which she fled during the confusion. She claims she returned to Tamita to turn herself in, in the hope that what she can tell us about what happened might earn her mercy." Captain Daneli glanced at Mara. "But the strangest thing of all, Guardian, is that her Gift survives. She has been placed under a temporary block." He turned back to Stanik. "I apologize for disturbing you so late . . . or so early . . . but I believed that you would not want me to treat her as an ordinary unMasked, and that you would want to be informed about her apprehension at once."

"You judged correctly," Stanik said softly. "Good work." He came around the end of the couch and stared at Mara with disconcerting intensity, his blue eyes cold as the mountain snows. "Thank you, Captain," he said without shifting his gaze from Mara. "You are dismissed."

"Yes, sir," said Daneli. He saluted again and went out. The white-Masked man who had greeted them, who stood in the hallway outside, closed the door softly behind him. It shut with a subdued click.

Stanik stared at Mara for another long moment, then sat down in another of the chairs, facing her. "I'm astounded to see you here, Mara," he said. "The last time I saw you, in the kitchen of your home, you were barefoot and in pigtails and begging your mother for an extra helping of mashed redroots." Through his Mask's mouth opening, she saw his lips curve into a slight smile.

Mara didn't know how to respond. She remembered that day; her father had been nervous about Stanik coming to their house, but Stanik had insisted on trying on his new silver Mask—the very Mask he wore now—in private in her father's workshop before taking it back to the Palace. No doubt the Guardian of Security had had other matters to discuss with the Master Maskmaker while he was there, for he and Mara's father had been cloistered in his workshop for a long time, and had descended to the kitchen just as, as Stanik said, Mara had been begging for a third helping of her favorite food. She had been . . . what? Nine? Ten?

And he remembered?

"I was shocked to hear you had failed your Masking," Stanik went on. "Of course we had no choice but to send you into exile: the law is the law. Regrettable, but I confess I thought no more about it at the time, except to urge those who know about such things to redouble their efforts to discover why so many of our youth are failing their Maskings—especially so many of the Gifted. The Autarch himself has expressed his concern, since several failings of the Gifted have occurred when he was in attendance at the ceremony."

Mara stared at him. Stanik's voice betrayed nothing, but Mara didn't believe for a moment that Stanik didn't know *exactly* why so many Maskings were failing: because the Masks had been changed to feed more magic to the Autarch, and to rob the newly Masked of even more of their ability to think and act for themselves.

As for why so many Gifted were failing their Maskings, with the Autarch himself in attendance . . . well, that was because the Autarch was so eager to seize the Gifted's magic for himself that occasionally he tugged too hard and suddenly, shattering the Mask in the process. Mara knew that. Ethelda knew that. Her father knew that. Stanik *must* know it.

But if he did, he gave no sign of it. He continued, "Then came word of the bandit attack on the wagons taking the latest unMasked to the labor camp, word that you were among the missing . . . and then word that you had been found and returned to the camp by one of the magic-harvesters. I wondered then if I should have you brought back to Tamita for questioning, but the Warden insisted he could question you more effectively there. And then came the strangest news of all: that you, alone of all the Gifted whose Masks have failed, retained your Gift." He glanced at the closed door. "Poor Captain Daneli no doubt intended to startle me with that revelation. I fear I disappointed him."

He looked back at her. "The Warden asked permission to make use of your miraculously surviving Gift to prove out what he hoped was a substantial find of magic-bearing black lodestone, and we granted it: he had often asked for young Gifted to be sent to him before for that task, but since it seemed a dangerous and uncertain pro-posal, and Gifted are precious, we had always rejected it." His voice betrayed nothing more of his inner thoughts than his Mask did, but Mara suspected there had been more to it than that; that the Warden, for whatever rea-son, had made enemies in the Palace who had *wanted* him to fail and so had found reasons not to grant his re-quest, which surely wasn't as outrageous as all that.

"We had no reports from the camp for some time af-ter that," Stanik went on. "When we did get another . . ." He cocked his head to one side. "When we did," he con-tinued softly, "it was almost impossible to believe. It was not the Warden who sent it, but the captain of the camp guard. He told us the events of that strange day began when you returned alone from the expedition to the pos-sible new mine site, pounding on the gate and demand-ing to be let in, claiming bandits had attacked the geologists and Watchers who had accompanied you to the potential new mine, and that only you had escaped.

"That night, fire broke out in the stables, and at the same time, bandits were seen inside the walls, breaking into the Warden's house. One was killed. The others es-caped. But down by the stables . . . down there, another Watcher died, his chest blown apart in what could only be a magical attack. And then the fire spread to the hut housing the explosives known as rockbreakers. Had they all detonated, the camp would have been leveled.

"But something very, very strange happened instead. Everyone aboveground in the camp blacked out . . . and when they woke up, feeling drained and weak, they dis-covered the rockbreaker hut had vanished, replaced in-stead by a pit lined with black glass: and far overhead and to the east, an enormous black cloud of smoke drifted slowly away.

"Of the Warden, there was no sign. You, too, had vanished, as had Katia, another young unMasked with whom you had worked in the mines. We had a dead bandit, a dead Watcher, a missing Warden, two missing girls, a hole in the ground, and a mysterious bout of unconsciousness, and no good explanation for any of it.

"Now here you are, turning up in Tamita as strangely as you turned up at the camp, once more, metaphorically at least, pounding on the gate." He leaned forward. "*What happened in the camp?*" His voice was soft. It was also terrifying, like the quiet hiss of a venomous snake.

Mara opened her mouth to speak; closed it again. She looked down at her fingers, twisting them together in her lap.

"Need I remind you, Mara Holdfast, that your life is forfeit?" Stanik said in that same soft voice. "You may still look like a child, you may be only scant weeks past the time when you *were* a child, but you are an adult in the eyes of the law, and that law demands your death. But I am the Guardian of Security, and I am the one who enforces that law. If I decree it, you will live. Do you want to live, Mara?"

Mara nodded. "Ye . . . yes," she said, through a throat that tried to close on her words. "But . . . I'm afraid."

"As you should be," said Stanik. He smiled behind the Mask, the red light from the fire turning his teeth bloody and kindling small flames in his eyes. "Unless you have me as an ally, rather than your judge."

"It's . . . it's just what I told the Watcher," Mara said. "I was there, when the . . . when whatever it was happened. There was a . . . an explosion, but it didn't destroy the camp. It just went . . . straight up, into the clouds, as though something had . . . contained it."

"And how is it you were running free in the grounds of the camp to see it?" Stanik said. "Why weren't you locked up like the rest of the prisoners?"

"When . . . when the bandits entered the house, they broke in all the doors, including mine," Mara said. "I . . . I was frightened. It was the same bunch . . . the same ones who'd attacked the wagons, who attacked the Watchers and the geologists. I recognized the leader . . . a . . . a tall man, a big man, with a scar, maybe a sword scar, across his face, like this." Mara made a slashing movement across her face and prayed her tongue was not weaving a net of lies that would ensnare her later. "I hid under the bed, they didn't find me, but they left my door open. When they went down the hall, I scrambled up and I ran. They heard me, they came after me, so I ran toward the fire, where all the Watchers were. That's how I saw what happened. Everyone down by the gate was lying on the ground by the time I got there, after the explosion. I thought they were dead."

"This . . . contained explosion," Stanik said. "This interests me. Your Gift survives. Did you see magic?"

She nodded. "A lot of it. But I don't know where it came from."

He cocked his head to one side. "Go on."

"I . . . I thought the bandits were still after me. I wanted to escape. I wanted to escape them . . ." She decided a little bit of honesty couldn't hurt. "And I really wanted to escape the camp," she said in a low voice.

Stanik shrugged his shoulders. "You need hardly apologize for that. Perfectly understandable. The late Warden was not overly solicitous of his charges." He regarded her another long moment. "And what of Katia, the girl with whom you worked in the mine, and who shared the room with you that night? You have not mentioned her. Did she hide, too? Did she escape?"

Mara's mind raced. "She . . . she didn't want to go anywhere near the Watchers. After . . . she'd been in the barracks . . ." She let that unfinished thought lie there for a moment, then said, "So she wouldn't go toward the gate. She ran off somewhere else. I don't know what happened to her. Maybe the bandits took her."

"Maybe," Stanik said, his voice noncommittal. "Let us return to you, then. You escaped, you say. Into the wild. And you came here how . . . ?"

"I just kept heading south. I sneaked onto farms, slept in barns. A couple of times I pretended to be a child who was lost, and people helped me. Somewhere along the way I realized I couldn't keep hiding forever. Sooner or later, I wouldn't be able to pass as a child. And I knew . . . what I had seen . . . I knew someone in the Palace must want to know what had happened at the camp. So that's when I decided to come all the way back to Tamita. I knew I could get into the city through that walkway kids had built along the river. I'd found it a long time ago, on one of those nights when I used to sneak out of my house after curfew. I thought I'd wait until morning. I thought I'd go home, talk to my father, and he'd take me to the Palace. But I'd barely come into the city when the Night Watchers saw me, and they chased me, and I panicked again and . . ." She let her voice trail away. "And that's how I came to you."

Stanik said nothing for a moment. "An interesting tale," he said at last. He studied her for another long moment. "There is much to consider in it. But what intrigues me most . . . and what will intrigue the Autarch most . . . is the strange matter of your Gift surviving the failure of your Mask. *That* intrigues me a great deal."

Mara felt sick to her stomach. If Stanik discovered her father had deliberately made her Mask fail . . .

Stanik stood. "My secretary will escort you to one of

my guest rooms for the remainder of the night. In the morning, we will discuss things further ... and I will decide what is to be done with you." He went to the door and stepped out into the hall. Mara heard a low murmur of voices, then Stanik walked down the hall and the secretary entered.

"This way," he said, standing aside and gesturing her out into the hall. He led her to the door at its end, through which Stanik must have just passed. There was no sight of the Guardian beyond: just another corridor, much longer and more utilitarian than the foyer, studded with half a dozen doors, two on the left and four on the right. He took her to the last door on the right, unlocked it with a key he took from his belt, and, much to her astonishment, showed her not into the grim cell she'd half-expected, but rather into the most beautiful room she had ever seen: paneled in richly grained golden wood, thickly carpeted in blue, the window curtained with gold. The bed boasted four massive posts, carved like twining grapevines, supporting a canopy of blue-and-gold brocade. Two white chairs faced a glowing hearth, another table and chair of white stood in the corner by the window, and just beyond a massive wardrobe of the same golden wood as the walls another door, standing open, revealed gleaming marble and gold ... a bathroom?

She blinked, then glanced back at the secretary. "Sleep well," he said, and closed the door.

The snick of the lock as he turned the key reminded her that, no matter how palatial her surroundings might be, she was still a prisoner: trapped in the Palace with no prospect of ever leaving it, unless it were through Traitors' Gate.

But as she soaked in the bath she filled from golden taps that provided both hot and cold water, washed her hair and body with lavender-scented soap (she was pleased to find it stung only slightly in the mostly healed cut on her back), pulled on a thick white dressing gown, ate some of the bread and cheese she found under a domed dish on the table by the window and drank chilled juice from a silver flagon, then finally took off the gown and crawled between clean sheets into the most comfortable bed she had ever known, even that grim thought could not lessen her pleasure. She fell asleep at once . . .

. . . and woke screaming from a dream of the Watcher Chell had killed along the road south. But tonight, there was no one to comfort her.

Where is Keltan? she wondered as she stared up into the darkness, breathing hard, waiting for her heart to slow. *Where is Chell? What will Edrik do?*

And what will happen to me tomorrow?

She had no answers, and despite the comfortable bed, more sleep eluded her for a very long time.

Eventually, of course, fatigue won out; but it seemed she had barely closed her eyes before she woke to daylight and a knock on her door. She climbed out of bed, pulled on the dressing gown, and padded barefoot across the thick blue rug. "Yes?" she said.

"I have your breakfast," said the voice of the secretary. "May I come in?"

Mara cinched the dressing gown tighter, then stepped back. "All right."

The door opened, and the secretary entered bearing a tray that he took to the table, placing there a steaming bowl of porridge, a small loaf of white bread, a silver bowl of butter, another of some kind of purple jam, a white plate with strips of bacon, and a moisture-beaded glass of juice. He nodded to her and went out without another word, closing and locking the door behind her.

Mara ate, and wondered what would happen next . . .

and wondered, too, what Keltan and Edrik were doing this morning, out on the ridge overlooking Tamita. *What can they do?*

And then another thought struck her, so hard the bacon she had been contentedly munching turned suddenly to sawdust in her mouth. Keltan, she knew, had gotten out through the wall. But when Chell had returned to the bridge—he would have found the walkway gone. He was trapped as surely as she, unMasked in the daylight—and unlike Keltan or her, he had no hope of being taken for a child. The Watchers would arrest him, if they hadn't already.

She knew *she* would not betray the Secret City and the unMasked Army. But she couldn't be as certain about him.

Can I even be sure about myself? she thought uneasily, once again wondering if the Gifted of the Palace had some method of using magic to extract the truth.

Her own Gift remained blunted. She had felt nothing of the magic within the secretary's body that morning. It was like a part of her had been amputated. It felt *wrong*.

Whatever that Watcher did, it won't last forever, she thought.

But the block was still there some two hours later when, as she paced the room, once more dressed in her own clothes, filthy with mud and grass stains and horse sweat and who-knew-what-else, a Watcher suddenly opened the door. "Come with me," he growled, and Mara, after a moment's start, followed, her heart racing.

The secretary moved into the room behind them as they left. Mara glanced back to see him already pulling at the sheets of the rumpled bed. She had the sinking feeling she wouldn't be spending a second night in luxury.

The Watcher took her out of Stanik's apartment and

back down the stairs to the Palace's main floor. Again she walked down the long hallway beneath the high, glass-paned windows, showing blue sky this morning, the wind having blown the clouds away overnight, but they went only a short distance before they turned onto a side passage. A moment later they passed through a double set of ironbound doors into the smaller central courtyard enclosed within the Palace's four tall wings.

The Great Courtyard outside the Palace was paved in stone; the Garden Courtyard was grass-covered, though the grass was brown and sere now, so soon after Midwinter. Winding pathways of white stone led between flowering bushes now wrapped in sackcloth as protection against winter blight. But even without their blooms, even with the many flower beds lying fallow and bare, the Garden Courtyard made Mara gasp. Her attention flitted from wonder to wonder: evergreens cleverly carved into the shapes of animals and people, fountains of marble and glass and gold and silver, statues of astonishing artistry.

Here and there people moved among the walkways. Almost all of their Masks bore at least a hint of color, marking them as Gifted. Almost all of those Masks turned toward her as she crossed the courtyard, then immediately turned away again, as if their owners knew better than to look too closely at any prisoner a Watcher brought among them.

To her left, an arched passageway led through the Palace's west wing, the sharp spikes of portcullises showing above it at both ends. Beyond that passage she saw the path down to the main gate of the Palace's curtain wall. Standing open, it offered a breathtaking view down Fortress Hill to the city's main gate and beyond it the brown fields of the wintry farmlands. *Keltan and Edrik are out there somewhere*, Mara thought.

And then she thought, *Keltan can still pass for a child. He could come into the city if he found another way in. He might be in the city now. If I could just escape . . .*

She thought about making a break for it, turning and running away from the Watcher as fast as she could, pictured herself dashing down the path to the main gate, down the boulevard, ducking into an alleyway, twisting and turning through the streets, losing herself in the city's bustle . . .

But that foolish fantasy died as she spotted the Watchers standing guard at the far end of the archway, and others by the main gate. *Even if Keltan's out there*, she thought dully, *it won't do me the slightest bit of good.*

She looked right. There, at its western end, the Garden Courtyard culminated in a broad flight of stairs, leading up to a massive portico supported by four three-story-tall pillars of white marble. Behind the pillars rose golden doors, wide as a house, tall as a tower, bearing the sun emblem of the Autarch. Behind those doors, which faced the rising sun, lived the Autarch. There the Circle met and deliberated. There dwelt the Child Guard, always in close proximity to the ruler, always at hand to provide the magic he needed to stave off the ravages of advancing age, no matter what the cost to themselves. It was beautiful and awe-inspiring—and the abode of a monster.

A monster like I have the potential to become, she thought. She stared up at the tall windows above the portico. Was the Autarch even now looking down into the courtyard, watching with narrowed eyes as she crossed his garden? She felt cold. And if he were, could he sense her magic, so rare and powerful, so akin to his own? Did he see her as a threat? The Autarch dealt severely with those he saw as threats, as Traitors' Gate attested.

My magic is blocked, she thought. *Maybe he can't sense it. Maybe he doesn't know what he's got in his hands ... not yet.*

Not yet. But for how long?

She turned her eyes forward again, following the Watcher to a plain black door recessed into the southern wing of the Palace, through it, and then down stairs whose worn stone steps had nothing of luxury about them, stairs that led her into the great warren of tunnels and chambers that honeycombed Fortress Hill beneath the Palace, and where she had been once before: on the day her Mask failed and she was sent into exile.

No one knew everything that was down there, deep beneath the city; or rather, those who knew did not talk of it. Rumors abounded. One thing everyone agreed on was that there were dungeons. Everyone had heard of someone vanishing into the Palace one day never to be seen again, not even as a corpse outside Traitors' Gate.

Like me? she thought.

However, the hallway they entered at the bottom of the stairs, though utilitarian, at least did not look like she'd always imagined the Autarch's dungeons would look. It was simple white stone, like the tunnel beneath the Maskery. Doors punctuated it at irregular intervals. After perhaps forty feet it ended in a T-intersection. They went right a short distance to another door, somewhat grander than the others they had passed. The Watcher knocked.

The door opened. A man in a yellow Mask, dressed in a long yellow robe sashed with gold, looked out. Mara gasped and glanced down. Sure enough, she saw gold-painted toenails on feet resting in golden sandals. She flicked her eyes back up. A Masker. Perhaps even *the* Masker, the one who had presided over her Mask's failure. *Unless they* all *paint their toenails*, she thought.

"Ah," said the Masker. "Mara, is it?"

"I'll wait here," said the Watcher. "Outside the door. In case of trouble."

"I hardly think—" began the Masker, but the Watcher cut him off.

"Orders," he said. He pushed Mara through the door, then reached in and tugged it closed.

Mara looked at the Masker. He looked at her. When he didn't say anything for a moment, she looked around the room instead.

There seemed to be nothing special about it except its shape. Like the Maskery, it was round. Unlike the Maskery, it did not have an artificial moat, water pouring from the mouths of snarling cats carved in stone, or an enormous representation of the Autarch's Mask, complete with glowing eyes. It *did* have a circular white dais at its center, but unlike the Maskery, this dais bore, not a table for the Masks of the candidates, but a black stone basin, covered with a wooden lid.

Mara's breath caught. *Magic! That basin must be full of magic—normal magic, magic filtered through black lodestone, not ripped directly from the living. Once this block fades, maybe, just maybe, I can . . .*

She thought of the Watcher outside. *What? Escape?* It seemed a ludicrous hope.

So what? she thought defiantly. *Before I stopped that explosion, I would have thought* that *was impossible.*

Without a word to her, the Masker went to the basin. He turned to face her, his eyes sparkling behind his yellow Mask with the reflected light of the lamps hung at regular intervals around the circular room. He locked those eyes on her face. Then he reached out and lifted the lid of the basin . . .

Mara gasped, her throat closing on the sound so that it came out as a strangled sob: for she saw nothing. *Noth-*

ing. Not a glimmer of light, not a gleam of color: only blank, black stone.

The Masker nodded once, and replaced the lid. "You saw no magic," he said. "I could see it in your eyes. The Watcher's block continues to work."

"I didn't even know you *could* block the Gift," Mara said. Her voice sounded sullen and defeated in her own ears. There was magic in that basin, magic she could use without fear of becoming a monster . . . and she could no more see or shape it than . . . than Keltan could.

"It is not something that is widely known," said the Masker. "But it is, obviously, an important ability for a Watcher to have, since they must occasionally arrest those who have some measure of the Gift." He studied her. "I think you had better sit down for this next bit." He indicated one of a row of four chairs set haphazardly against the wall, as though they had been hastily pushed out of the way. She sat where she was told. "You may feel dizzy," he said, as he turned back to the basin. He removed the lid once more, reached in with both hands, and turned and came back to her with his hands outstretched. To Mara, they looked bare, though she knew they must be coated with magic. *So this is what it means to be unGifted.* She didn't like it. And then she thought of Prella and Alita, who had also been Gifted, but whose Gifts had died when their Masks shattered, and felt ashamed of how little sympathy she had had for them. *I didn't understand*, she thought. *I didn't understand how horrible that would be . . .*

And then what the Masker had said registered. "Dizzy?" she said. "Why should I—"

He reached out and took hold of her head, placing his hands on her temples. Pain ripped through her skull, the room whirled around her, and then everything went black.

When she came to, she was sitting on the floor and leaning up against the wall, the Masker standing over her. The chair she had been sitting in lay on its side. Her left elbow hurt. The Masker's Mask had the same expression as always, of course, but his voice, when he spoke, was shaken. "Are you all right?"

"What . . ." Mara's throat was dry. She swallowed hard a couple of times, and finally managed to croak out, "What happened?"

"I've never seen that reaction before," said the Masker. "Your Gift . . . it's strong. Very strong." He hesitated for a moment. "I think . . ." He turned and went to the door. Opening it, he said to the Watcher outside, "Fetch the Mistress of Magic."

"My orders are to stand guard here—"

"Do as I say," the Masker snapped. "I'll take responsibility for the change in your orders. Fetch the Mistress of Magic. Fetch her *now*!"

A pause. "Very well," growled the Watcher, then strode away.

The Masker came back to Mara, who still felt no inclination to get up, what with the room spinning slowly around her. It took most of her willpower just to keep from throwing up. *I threw up at the Masker's feet the day of my Masking*, she thought distantly. *He'd hate me if I did it again . . .*

The Masker righted the chair she had fallen from and sat in it, leaning over her. "Listen to me," he said swiftly, voice low and sharp. "We have only minutes before the Mistress of Magic arrives, and your life may hang in the balance. You have a powerful Gift, a rare Gift, the ability to see and use all colors of magic . . . but you are un-Masked. And you escaped the mining camp. The Autarch will order you executed unless you can convince him you will use your Gift in his service. And that means you must first convince the Mistress of Magic." He touched his yellow Mask, whose calm smile belied the urgency of the words spoken through the hole of its mouth. "You must swear to serve the Autarch. Swear it with all your heart. Swear it and mean it when you swear it. If the Mistress of Magic has any doubt ... then you will leave the Palace the same way you came in: Traitors' Gate. But you will not go far." He leaned close and spoke in a voice barely above a whisper. "But remember this: the magic of the Masks has already rejected you ... and that means the Mistress of Magic cannot use magic to determine if you swear true. The magic of truth-testing and the magic of the Mask are one and the same, and you are immune to both."

Mara stared at him. "What? But ... why are you telling me this? Your Mask ..."

"*I am telling you to serve the Autarch*," said the Masker, low and fast and hard. "Why should the Mask question that? As for the other ... you can thank your father for that."

"My ... father?"

"He is the Master Maskmaker. We have worked closely together for many years. I count him as a friend. I would not see his only daughter hanging outside Traitors' Gate."

Mara struggled to sit up—and winced; more than just her elbow, the whole left side of her body felt bruised after the fall from the chair. "Please," she said urgently. "Please ... don't tell my father I'm here. Don't tell him I'm a prisoner in the Palace. I don't ... he shouldn't have to go through that. He can't do anything, and he's already lost me once."

The Masker studied her for a moment. "I will not tell him," he said at last. "But I do not know what the Mistress of Magic or the Autarch might do."

"I understand," Mara said. She swallowed, her gorge

rising. "I . . . excuse me . . ." She turned her head, and threw up all over the white stones.

When she had brought up everything that was left of that wonderful breakfast she'd been served by Stanik's secretary, she leaned her head back against the cold stone and closed her eyes. "Sorry," she mumbled. "Sorry for the mess . . ."

"You are not the first to vomit in this chamber," said the Masker. "Nor will you be the last. I'll summon a servant."

She didn't open her eyes, so she didn't see how he did it, but a few minutes later a young girl, not yet Masked, bustled in and silently cleaned up the mess with rags, mop, and pail. Mara gave her a weak smile. "Sorry," she said again.

The girl looked frightened at being spoken to. She put her head down and finished the job at breakneck speed, then scurried out without a word. The Masker shut the door behind her. Mara closed her eyes again and waited for the Mistress of Magic to arrive.

She must have slipped back into semiconsciousness, for no time at all seemed to have passed before someone else stood over her. She blinked at more painted nails, these a glimmering green and belonging to far more slender toes than the rather blocky appendages of the Masker, and then looked up past the hem of a green robe to a Mask of a kind she had never seen before, though her father might well have made it: it appeared to have been carved intact from a giant crystal, so that its glittering surface was all sharp angles that cast back the lamplight in glimmering rainbows. She squinted: she found it strangely hard to look at, hard to even see it as a face. "I must Test her myself," said a feminine voice, hard and sharp as the crystal of the Mask from which it issued.

"Mistress," said the Masker, "I object. I am fully confident in the results of my—"

"I said I will Test her myself," the woman snapped. "Get her up."

The Masker shook his head. "Best to let her stay there," he said, his own voice cold with disapproval. "She passed out when I Tested her the first time. Again, and so soon—I cannot be responsible."

"I can," said the woman. "Uncover the basin."

Mara watched, feeling oddly detached, as the Masker removed the wooden lid from the basin. The Mistress of Magic plunged her hands into the black stone bowl, then turned back toward Mara. Once again, she could see nothing. But as the crystal-Masked woman approached her with hands outstretched, she suddenly realized what was about to happen, and tried to struggle up. "No!" she gasped. "No, please—"

The Mistress of Magic came inexorably on. She touched the sides of Mara's head. And Mara, who had once blown apart the head of a boy trying to rape her, discovered, as near as made no difference, what it was like to be on the receiving end of such magic. White fire flashed and agony shredded her thoughts. She felt her back arch, felt her mouth stretch achingly wide in a scream that could not escape from lungs frozen in the act of taking breath, felt her arms and legs and fingers snap rigid as iron rods, felt the back of her head crack against the stone wall . . .

. . . and then, blessedly, felt nothing at all, as she fell into oblivion.

ELEVEN

Before the Sun Throne

MARA WOKE, and was rather surprised by that fact as she remembered what had plunged her into unconsciousness. *I'm so glad I'm Gifted*, she thought as she scraped sandpaper-lined lids open over itching eyeballs. *Every day brings another wonderful new experience.*

At first her eyes wouldn't focus, and were so gummy anyway that everything around her seemed shrouded in a gray fog. She blinked hard, blinked again, and finally managed to clear her vision enough to make out a dark-beamed plaster ceiling that she didn't recognize. She looked right, and saw two empty beds between her and a white plaster wall; looked left, and saw three more. She looked down the length of the blue blanket that covered her past the lump of her toes to a closed door of simple wooden planks.

Beneath the blanket (she lifted it to check) she wore only a thin white shift. *Great*, she thought. *Who undressed me* this *time? The Masker? The Watcher?*

She shuddered and took another look around. There were small tables between the beds, and on the bed to her left, clothes were spread ... for her, she hoped, though they weren't the ones she'd been wearing. And at the end of the hall she saw a young woman seated in a chair, reading a book bound in blue leather. "Hello?" she croaked.

The woman's head came up sharply. She wore the blue Mask of a Gifted Healer. "Well, hello!" she said cheerfully. "I *thought* you'd wake up this afternoon. Nothing really wrong with you, after all. Just simple magic shock." She put down her book and came to Mara's bedside, sitting on the next bed over. "How are you feeling?"

Mara considered that question. "Um ... all right. I guess." At least her head didn't hurt any more. "What did you call it? Magic shock?"

"Kind of an all-purpose description," the Healer said. "Too much magic running through your brain ... not good. Even when you're Gifted. Worse when you're not. And probably worst of all when you're Gifted, and under a Watcher's block." She shook her head. "Don't know what they were thinking of, putting you through that *twice*," she said. "Lucky they didn't kill you. But, here you are!"

Lucky, Mara thought. *That's me. So lucky* ... "So ... what happens next?"

"What happens next," said the Healer, "is you drink the restorative I've had ready for you for the last four hours, waiting for you to wake up. And then you sleep.

After that..." She shrugged. "After that, I tell the Masker and the Mistress of Magic that you can be released. And then you are no longer my concern."

Mara licked dry lips and nodded.

The restorative, she was pretty sure from its dark-green appearance, was the same brewed first by Grelda and later by Ethelda back at the Secret City, the first time she had ended up in a Healer's Hall suffering from ... well, Grelda hadn't called it "magic shock," she had called it "a surfeit of magic," but clearly it was the same thing. She had drunk the potion many times since.

But there was a difference this time. Before, her Gift had been operating. Now ...

Now, she was clearly still blocked, because the restorative, which always before had smelled heavenly to her, now smelled like ... well, Grelda had compared it to the sickroom chamber pot after a week's run of sourbelly, and though Mara had no personal experience of what that smelled like, she suspected that might well understate the awfulness of the aroma. She gagged as the Healer held out a full cup.

"Drink it," the Healer said severely. "*All* of it. I know it may not seem appetizing, but the effect is the same, no matter what it smells ... or tastes ... like."

"Tastes?" Mara said in despair, but she had faced worse trials in the past few months and so she took a deep breath (to one side, to avoid smelling the concoction too closely), and then drained the cup.

She choked with disgust, and for a moment thought the contents would be coming right back up again, but suddenly a sense of well-being flooded her. She sighed, a huge sigh of relief, and grinned at the Healer. "Thanks," she said.

"My pleasure," said the Healer. "Now, sleep." She frowned. "Hopefully without screaming this time?"

Mara couldn't promise that, and the reminder of what might await her in sleep did nothing to ease her into rest, but the restorative did. She slept within moments.

If she screamed, the Healer did not tell her about it when she woke. Of course, when she woke, she almost screamed anyway, because the Mistress of Magic's crystalline Mask was only inches from her face. She gasped and jerked her head back deeper into the pillow.

The Mistress of Magic straightened. Beside her stood the Masker. He held a wooden tray in both hands, bearing a small object covered with blue cloth. "No need to shake her awake after all, I think," he said dryly.

The Mistress of Magic laughed, a pleasant sound that surprised Mara, who had been thinking of her as more a cold-blooded reptile than an actual person. "I think you're right." The laughter died. "The Watcher's block will wear off soon. Best get it done."

The Masker nodded. He put the tray down on the table beside Mara's bed. Mara followed it with her eyes. He pulled away the cloth, and she gasped. The object on the tray was a Mask, but not a Mask such as she had ever seen before. It appeared to be made of dark iron, a material she had never seen her father use, and it was only a half-Mask, one that would cover the eyes and the bridge of the nose and leave all else exposed: which meant it wasn't a true Mask at all, but something else.

Something clearly meant for her. The Masker lifted it and brought it toward her face. She shrank back, but of course had nowhere to go; she jerked her face away, but the Mistress of Magic simply came around to the other side of her bed and forced her head around again.

The iron Mask descended, touched her skin. She held her breath, waiting for that horrible squirming sensation she had felt from the real Mask her father had made for her—made so that it would fail and she would be forced into exile—but this Mask did not move. It simply . . . clung. Cold at first, it warmed quickly.

The Mistress of Magic released Mara's head. She flung it to one side, instinctively, trying to throw the strange iron Mask from her face, but it did not budge. One thing, at least, it shared with a real Mask: it felt light as a second skin on her face, despite being made of metal.

"Peace, girl," said the Mistress of Magic sternly. "You cannot be rid of it that way. In fact, you cannot be rid of it at all. It can only be removed by someone who is Gifted *and* has the knowledge of how to do it."

"I don't understand!" Mara raised a hand to touch the pitted iron. "What's it for?"

The Masker responded. "You cannot remain under the Watcher's block forever; it wears off within a day or so, as your Gift finds a way to work around it . . . rather like a wound healing. This . . ." He touched the half-Mask himself. "This is a more permanent solution. As long as you wear this, you cannot use your Gift."

"I've never heard of such a Mask!" Mara said, horrified.

"Really?" said the Mistress of Magic coolly. "How odd. Especially since they are made for us by your father."

Mara stared at her. The Mistress of Magic gazed steadily back, eyes glittering as though they were simply two more facets of her crystalline Mask.

"Unlike regular Masks," the Masker said, with a glance at the Mistress of Magic, "these are not specific to the person wearing them. They work on all Gifted. We keep a supply of them to suppress the Gifts of anyone arrested by the Watchers. The Watchers use their temporary block, then we restrain them more permanently with one of these, until their case is . . . dealt with."

Mara thought again of the corpses hanging outside

Traitors' Gate. How many of those had been Gifted? How many had gone to their death wearing nothing but one of these iron half-Masks, to keep their Gift suppressed until they were dead?

How many had gone to their deaths wearing the very Mask now clinging to her face ... *a Mask made by her father*?

She felt sick.

"Get up, and get dressed," the Mistress of Magic said. "You are coming with me."

"Why?" Mara said. "Where are we going?"

The Mistress of Magic cocked her head slightly to the right. Mara could not see her face, but the tone of sardonic amusement in her voice was unmistakable. "Why, to see the Autarch, of course."

The Masker excused himself. The Mistress of Magic waited and watched as Mara got out of bed, pulled off the white shift, and put on the clothes provided: soft white underwear, a long white dress, supple boots made of pale leather, a yellow belt.

"Much better," said the Mistress of Magic. "You can't meet the Autarch in clothes covered with stains and patches. Now come with me." She led Mara to the door and out into the hallway beyond, where a waiting Watcher fell in with them.

The hallway ran the length of the south wing of the Palace: the windows along the wall opposite the door through which they had emerged looked out over the Garden Courtyard. They were on the top floor, it appeared.

At the end of the hallway, they passed not through a doorway but through a splendid arch, gilded and carved in the shapes of birds and animals. Mara found herself facing a giant mirror in a golden frame, and saw herself for the first time in days.

Her hair, which she normally wore in a neat ponytail,

fell in gnarled, tangled waves around her shoulders. Her brown eyes gazed at her from behind the cruel-looking iron Mask, like the eyes of an animal in a cage, and beneath it her lips had a bruised, frail look in the sickly pale skin of her face. She stared at herself for a moment, amazed and horrified to be standing in this place at this time. Then the Watcher and the Mistress of Magic turned her left, away from the mirror, and took her a short distance to a flight of stairs that wound down four flights to the main floor of the west wing.

At the bottom of the stairwell they emerged into the grandest corridor she had yet seen, all gold-and-white marble, although it did not run the entire length of the wing, being interrupted by a wall behind which, Mara supposed, must be the main entranceway through the golden gates she had seen from the Garden Courtyard. They turned left down a slightly narrower but still grand hallway, which some distance along emerged into a vast entryway with a broad staircase climbing up to high windows and splitting into two more staircases that climbed still higher. Various Palace functionaries scurried through the space on unknown errands they clearly felt were of vital import. Most wore the white, gray, or beige Masks of the unGifted, their particular skills indicated by inlayed patterns: a black scroll, golden fruit, and in one notable instance radiating starbursts of diamonds. Mara took special note of that one, because the woman who wore it turned her head sharply as they entered the foyer, took one look at Mara's iron prisoner's Mask, and then hurried away as though Mara had a fatal illness.

Which I might, if the Autarch decrees it.

They climbed the staircase, turned, and then climbed some more, coming eventually to a broad landing where two massive golden doors stood wide open: and then, at last, Mara was escorted into the presence of the Autarch.

The throne room was two stories tall, with a high, vaulted roof whose golden beams were supported by twin rows of fluted pillars carved of white marble. The floor, too, shone white, while the walls to Mara's right and left, like the beams overhead, gleamed golden.

On a golden throne atop a raised white dais sat the Autarch himself, wearing the golden Mask Mara had last seen from the wall of the city several years before, as the Autarch rode through the Outside Market. Nothing of the man beneath the Mask could be seen: though the Mask had a mouth opening, golden mesh screened it. The Autarch wore white robes belted with gold, white gloves, white boots. A white hood hid his hair . . . if he had any.

Above the Sun Throne, the Autarch's Mask was repeated on a grand scale, the eyes glowing yellow, lit from behind by the enormous window that made up most of the throne room's eastern wall. Sunburst rays of gold, each ten feet long or more, spread out from the giant Mask. Close to the throne, within easy reach of the Autarch, a large basin of black stone stood on a golden pillar: no doubt filled with magic, though it looked empty to Mara while she wore the iron Mask.

Arranged around the Autarch, seated on cushions spread on the steps of the dais, were the twelve members of the Child Guard. Each sat absolutely still, knees together, hands clasped. Like the Autarch, they wore white, but their Masks were silver. Their loose robes and their Masks made it impossible to tell which were boys and which were girls.

Mara wondered what she would feel in the room if she were not imprisoned behind the iron Mask. Would she sense the magic the Autarch drew from the living bodies of those boys and girls, the magic Ethelda believed he needed to ward off the ravages of advancing age; the magic to which he was addicted, as surely as a drunk was addicted to the bottle?

And what would she feel from the Autarch himself, if her Gift were still her own? Would she recoil from him in horror . . . or would she suddenly see him as a kindred spirit?

Never! she thought, but the question hung in her mind nonetheless as the Mistress of Magic led her forward, the Watcher remaining at the door of the throne room. They approached the throne, the impassive Masks of the Autarch and the Child Guard gazing at them, their footsteps echoing from the golden walls.

Fifteen feet from the throne, they stopped. The Mistress of Magic knelt on the marble floor. Mara, after a moment, followed suit, remembering that the man before them held not only her life but her father's life in his hands.

"Rise," said the Autarch. His voice was higher-pitched than Mara had expected, but hard and cold as the northern ice. "I have considered your request, Mistress Shelra. You have told me that this prisoner has that most rare and precious Gift, the ability to see and use all colors of magic. You have urged me not to waste it, but to put it to the service of the Autarchy. You assure me you can train her in the use of her Gift and bend her to my will." The Autarch shifted on his throne. Mara could not even see his eyes behind the Golden Mask: only black pits on either side of the Mask's finely crafted nose. The face on the Mask was incredibly handsome, stern, and wise. Mara wondered if the Autarch's real face looked like that—or ever had.

"Against that, I must consider the threat that she may pose," the Autarch continued. "She has failed her Masking, and that means she can *never* be Masked. What assurance can you offer me that, once she knows how to use her Gift effectively, she will not turn it against us?"

"Her parents, Mighty One," said the Mistress of

Magic, and Mara jerked her head around to stare at her, an icy spike of fear driving into her brain. "She will co-operate with us, or her parents will pay the price. She will not put them in jeopardy." Her gaze turned toward Mara. "Will you, girl?"

Mara could barely speak through the horror that choked her. "No," she said. "No. I won't."

The Mistress of Magic turned her crystal-Masked face back toward the Autarch. "I will supervise her training myself. The responsibility will be mine."

The Autarch drummed the fingers of his right hand on the arm of his chair for a long moment, studying Mara through the blank black eyeholes of his Mask. "Remove her Mask," he said suddenly.

Mara heard Shelra gasp. "Mighty One, I don't think —"

"I am not asking you to think," he said. "I am not *asking* you anything. I am *commanding* you. Obey!"

Shelra stiffened, but bowed. "Yes, Mighty One." She came over to Mara. "Try anything, and you die," she murmured.

Mara hardly heard her. Her eyes were locked on the Autarch, her heart in her throat. She had wondered what she would sense in him if her magic were restored to her . . . but now she realized that the more important question was what he would sense in her. Would he be able to tell at once the full extent of her power? She had not been able to hide from the Masker and the Mistress of Magic that she could see all colors of magic, but they had not detected her far more dangerous—to her, and to everyone else—ability to draw magic to herself, both from the black lodestone that attracted it and directly from living humans. It was that ability, the ability she shared with the Autarch and with his old enemy The Lady of Pain and Fire, that truly made her a threat, and if the Autarch decided she was a threat . . .

She swallowed.

Shelra walked over to the stone basin at the Autarch's right hand, and dipped her right hand into it. Then she returned to Mara. She touched the iron Mask, then raised her other hand to it and drew the Mask away from Mara's face.

And instantly, Mara felt the Autarch's attack.

The breath whooshed from her lungs as invisible, in-sistent fingers scrabbled inside her head, trying to get at her magic, trying to pull it to the man on the Sun Throne, the man she sensed, not by the presence of magic, as she did the Watchers, Shelra, and the Child Guard, but by the *absence* of magic ... no, that wasn't right, by what she could only think of as *negative* magic: for the Autarch, in her restored magical senses, felt to her like a greedy, sucking hole, an insatiable pit trying to pull all magic to itself, including hers.

And yet ... that pull was far weaker than the pull she knew *she* could exert. *I'm stronger than he is*, she thought in mixed excitement and horror. *I am stronger than the Autarch!*

And if I use my power ... I could end up just like him. A black, sucking, greedy, desperate monster, feeding on others ... feeding on children.

She could feel him doing just that, pulling magic to himself from the Child Guard: a flow of magic greater than their bodies could easily replace, a horrifying viola-tion. She could even feel the faint, oh-so-very-faint flow of magic to him from the recently Masked, those whose Masks were made to the new recipe that had convinced her father he had to act to protect her, even if that act put her in terrible danger of another sort.

But he was too weak to pull *her* magic, however much he might want it. That horrifying sense of someone in-side her mind, trying to steal a part of herself, made her feel sick to her stomach—and so, without doing anything consciously, she simply ... stopped it. He could not have her magic, because she would not give it: and he did not have the strength to take it from her against her will.

Nor, she thought, with an almost giddying sense of relief, did he have the power to learn just how strong her own ability to pull magic to herself was. Those nasty scrabbling magical fingers never penetrated her mind deeply enough to learn anything more than that she had magic—and he could not get at it.

How will he react? Mara stared up at the man on the Sun Throne. His golden Mask, of course, remained as impassive as ever. What her own face betrayed, she did not know. But after what seemed an eternity but must only have been a few seconds, the insistent but futile attack on her defenses ended. She heard a sharp intake of breath from the Autarch. He had been leaning forward in his throne; now he sat back again with a nonchalance she was sure must be feigned. "Put the Mask on her again."

Shelra hurried forward, and the cold iron once more touched and then clung to Mara's face. Her Gift vanished again, causing her to gasp in turn. The loss of it seemed even worse after a brief taste of its restoration.

The half-Mask once more settled, Shelra turned back toward the Autarch. The golden Mask turned toward her. "Very well," the Autarch said. "Train her as you will. But I want full reports, and I will also call her to myself from time to time to test her further." He leaned forward again. "And remember this, Mistress Shelra. She is, as you say, *your* responsibility. And I charge you—if you believe she is a threat to the Autarchy, if you have the slightest hint that she poses such a threat, you will inform me and Guardian Stanik at once—or face punishment yourself."

"I understand, Mighty One," said the Mistress of Magic.

The Autarch flicked a gloved hand. "Then go. You are both dismissed from my presence."

Mistress Shelra took Mara's arm, turned her, and led her from the throne room. Mara, head down, staring at the floor as she walked, imagined she felt the Autarch's eyes burning into her back, along with the eyes of all the Child Guard.

They reached the door of the throne room. Mara raised her head. The Watcher stood there. Beyond him stood two more Watchers, flanking a third man, his head lowered, his hands bound behind his back. Mara glanced at him, wondering what crime he had committed . . .

. . . and then gasped as he raised his head, and for one moment, before she was forced on her way down the corridor, her gaze locked onto the startled, wide blue eyes of Chell.

TWELVE

Delving into Mysteries

MARA HARDLY NOTICED her surroundings as the Watcher and the Mistress of Magic led her down hallways and stairs to yet another wing of the Palace. Between her encounter with the Autarch and the sudden appearance of Chell, she had much to think about: but despite what she had felt from the Autarch (and his intention to keep bringing her into his presence, no doubt to continue to try to pull her magic to himself), it was Chell to whom her thoughts turned the most.

Clearly he, too, had been taken prisoner—and just as clearly they knew he was not from Aygrima, or he would be in the dungeons at best or swinging outside Traitors' Gate at worst. Instead, he was awaiting an audience with the Autarch. So what had he told the Watchers—or was about to tell the Autarch?

He doesn't know how to find the Secret City by land, she told herself. *Edrik saw to that.*

But he could find it again by sea, she argued back. *And if he is now bargaining for his life—or the needs of his own people—with the Autarch—he will need something to bargain with. And what better item of barter than the knowledge of a secret conspiracy against the Autarch . . . and where to find it?*

In that moment, she wished she'd left him to die on the frozen beach.

She began paying more attention to where she was as they descended once more into the warren of corridors and rooms underneath the Palace . . . at least two stories underground this time, Mara thought, maybe more. The temperature dropped, and Mara shivered as their footsteps echoed along a long corridor unmarked by doors or anything else except flickering torches in periodic wall sconces.

At the end of the corridor stood a heavy black door. Mistress Shelra unlocked it with a key she drew from a pouch at her belt, swung it inward, stepped through, then turned and nodded to the Watcher. The Watcher propelled Mara through the door, then, remaining in the hall, closed and locked it, leaving her alone with the Mistress of Magic.

Mara stared around at a high-ceilinged room easily as large as the entire first floor of her father's house. A small fire flickered in the hearth set in the far wall, but did little to warm or light the chill, cavernous space. Two plain wooden chairs flanked the hearth. Two more chairs sat by a round table just inside the door to the right: but the centerpiece of the room, drawing Mara's gaze like a magnet draws iron, was a basin of black stone on a pedestal, its round top covered by a heavy wooden lid.

Magic!

The Mistress of Magic stood by that basin, facing her. "This room is shielded," Shelra said. "Walls, door, floor, ceiling, hearth. Magic cannot enter or escape it. This is where we train the most powerful of the Gifted who serve the Autarch ... such as yourself."

Serve the Autarch, Mara thought. The thought sat in her mind like a lump of cold lead. *Serve the Autarch ... or my parents pay the price.*

"This is where you will pass your days, until I deem your training complete ... however many days or weeks or months—or years—that may take. And then we will put you to use." Her eyes, dark behind her crystalline Mask, regarded Mara steadily. "I have suggested to Guardian Stanik and the Autarch, and both are agreed, that it is time we took steps to hunt down and destroy all these troublesome bandits in the Wild. As their attack on the mining camp shows, they have become too strong. You will be a valuable tool in that effort."

The lump of lead in her mind suddenly became even heavier and colder.

"Of course, the only way to train you in the use of magic will be to release you, whenever you are in this room, from the iron Mask you wear," Shelra continued. "You may be tempted, when you can once again see the magic in the basin, to use it to attempt to escape." Her voice hardened. "Do not give in to that temptation. There is not enough magic in the basin to force a way from this room, and any attempt ... *any* attempt ... will lead to dire consequences—not only for you, but first and foremost for your parents. Do you understand?"

Mara nodded.

Shelra nodded briskly. "Good. Then let's get you out of that Mask and begin. But first ..." She reached up and, to Mara's startlement, removed her own Mask. The face thus revealed was older than Mara had expected, as wizened as Catilla's, with parchment-thin and parchment-white skin stretched tight over prominent cheekbones. Shrewd brown eyes glittered at her in the torchlight before Shelra turned to set her Mask on the table by the door.

"Now it's your turn," she said. She walked over to the magic basin and folded back the hinged lid, then dipped one finger into it. Once again, as she had in the throne room, she reached up with the apparently naked finger and touched the Mask, then took hold of it with both hands and pulled it free.

Mara heaved an involuntary sigh of relief as her sense of magic flooded back, this time free of the leech-like sucking of the Autarch. Instead, she felt the magic seething in the basin, the powerful magic bound up in the protected walls of the training chamber ... and the even more powerful magic bound up in the slight figure of the old woman before her. *I could pull it all to me. I could escape. She doesn't know what I can do. She doesn't know that I could tear the magic right out of her and—*

No! she thought in panic. *I can't. My parents ...*

Tears started to her eyes, and she wiped them away with the back of her hand.

Shelra was watching her closely. "Good," she said softly. "Good. I saw your temptation, your desire to rush to the basin and try to use its magic against me ... and you resisted it. You *can* be trained." She gestured toward the basin. "So let's be about it."

She began by having Mara look into the basin. "Tell me what colors you see," she said.

"All of them," Mara said simply.

"Yes, yes, of course," Shelra snapped. "So do I." Mara's head jerked around at that. "I'd be a poor Master of Magic if I did not. But it's not enough to say you see 'all of them.'

You must learn to distinguish every shade, every nuance. You must learn what each color . . . not really color, of course, that's just the way the mind of a Gifted interprets the sixth sense of magic . . . can be used for. *Is* used for. And then you must learn how to draw out just the color you want, in just the amount you want, and how to focus your will on it, and get it to do precisely what you want it to do: *precisely*, mind you. Magic is precious—too precious to waste."

Mara remembered what Ethelda had told her, that the Mistress of Magic might be the only one in Tamita who could tell Mara what her true Gift, the ability to draw magic from others, might mean for her future . . . but Shelra did not know about that aspect of her Gift and *could* not know. How could she learn what she desperately needed to know without revealing her secret?

"Is . . . is this the only way to get magic?" she asked tentatively. "From . . . from the basins? The black lodestone?"

Shelra's eyes narrowed. "For you, yes," she said.

"But for others . . . ?"

"Magic comes from living things," Shelra said. "There have been those who can draw it directly out of them. But it is forbidden, and those who are found to have done it, or are able to do it, are monsters, no longer human. They are killed upon discovery. No exceptions."

No exceptions . . . except for the Autarch himself, Mara thought. She nodded. "I'm just . . . trying to understand how it all works," she said meekly. "Because my Mask failed, I never got to go to magic school."

"You are in it now," Shelra said. "So. Look again into the basin, and tell me the colors you see, in as great detail as you can . . ."

After just two hours, Mara could hardly focus her exhausted eyes on the magic or on anything else, but Shelra remained relentless. A knock at the door, which Shelra answered only after donning her Mask again, signaled the arrival of a lunch of cold meat, dried fruit, bread, and cheese, which they washed down with water before continuing their work. By the end of the day, Mara had begun to see, in the magic basin, that what had always before seemed a random, endlessly shifting spill of color was in fact made up of intertwined threads or rivulets of all the colors of the rainbow . . . and many permutations in between.

Shelra had also begun to demonstrate what each color could do. "Red," she said, "is used to manipulate physical objects; it is the color of engineers and builders. But the different shades of red . . ." She touched the magic pool, drew out her finger covered with red so dark as to be almost black. "For manipulating iron," she said. She touched the surface again; her finger became sheathed with red the color of blood. "Wood and stone," she said. She touched the surface again and this time a layer of glistening pink covered it. "Gold, silver, and other precious metals."

As the afternoon wore to a close, she produced a scroll from the pouch at her belt. "A catalog," she said. "A catalog, as best as I and my predecessors have been able to determine, of all the identifiable colors of magic, and what they seem best suited for. Study it, and tomorrow we will see how many you can draw forth."

Mara nodded, and yawned. Shelra donned her crystalline Mask, then turned to Mara with the iron one. Mara drew back, but Shelra frowned. "You must wear it," she said. "Not only to prevent you from using your Gift but because all adults must go Masked. For those who have failed their Masking, this is the only alternative to execution."

Mara jerked her head in a single nod, then closed her

eyes and held still as the iron, chill from sitting unattended on the table, far from the fire, touched her skin. It clung, and she took in her breath sharply as her sense of magic once again vanished. She swayed a little, and Shelra caught her. "I know," she said softly. "I have donned an iron Mask myself in order to test its efficacy. They are terrible things. But not as terrible as what would be done to you and your loved ones if you were not wearing it."

The Mistress of Magic went to the door. A Watcher stood outside it, a different and much smaller man than had been there when it was locked. "She need not be taken directly to her cell," she told him. "Let her wander in the Garden Courtyard if she wishes, until the supper bell chimes. Then take her to her chamber. Bring her back here tomorrow after she breaks her fast."

The Watcher inclined his head, and indicated that Mara should follow him. But as the door closed behind them, he stopped, looked around furtively, and said, "Hello, Mara."

She stared at his black Mask. All she could see was a hint of his lips and teeth behind the mouth opening, but she knew that voice. "Mayson?"

He nodded. "I heard you'd returned. Traded duty shifts with the Watcher who was supposed to be guarding you tonight."

Mara couldn't believe it. She hadn't spoken to Mayson since two years before his Masking, when he'd begun his pre-Masking apprenticeship with the Watchers. But for all the years before that, she'd been one of his best friends. "Are you supposed to be talking to me?"

He shrugged. "Probably not. But nobody ordered me not to. So I don't think I'm risking anything." He touched his Mask. "Yep, still here." Behind the mouth opening, his teeth flashed in a grin that faded quickly. "Mara, what's happened to you?"

Mara wanted to tell him—wanted to tell *someone*—but he was a Watcher. He might once have been her friend, but now . . . if she told him anything, he would be duty-bound to tell his superiors. If he didn't, his Mask would surely betray him to other Watchers, and he would be interrogated and possibly punished—even executed.

She wanted to trust him, but she knew she couldn't.

One more evil to blame on the Masks . . . and the Autarch.

She realized he was still staring at her, waiting for her to respond. She cleared her throat. "I'm not supposed to talk about it," she said. "But . . . it's good to see you." *If you can call it that when you're Masked.*

"You, too," he said. "Mara . . . I wish I could help you somehow. But . . ." He touched his Mask again.

"I understand."

"I'll try to see you when I can," he said. "If you need anything, extra food, or . . ."

"I'm being well cared for," Mara said. "But thank you."

Mayson nodded. "Not much time until the supper bell," he said. "If you're going to get any fresh air, we'd better get up to the Garden Courtyard." He turned and led the way.

A few minutes and several flights of stairs later they emerged into the open. The sun had long since slipped behind the west wing of the Palace, filling the courtyard with blue twilight. Mayson stopped by one of the pillars of the courtyard's surrounding colonnade. "Wander all you like," he said. "I'll just wait here."

"Thank you," she said again, and ventured out onto the stone paths, leaving him behind. She breathed deep of the fresh air, and glanced up at the stars beginning to prick the darkening sky. Had it only been two nights since she and Keltan and Chell had crawled through the walkway into the city? Less than forty-eight hours since she had spoken to her father?

Where is Keltan? she wondered. *Did he escape? What will he and Edrik do?*

What did Chell tell the Autarch?

She thought again of her father. He would not know she was locked up in the palace, not unless someone told him . . .

And then she felt a chill of fear.

He promised to visit the Palace Library, promised to find out what he can about this strange Gift of mine, she thought. *If he is discovered doing so, and they put two and two together . . . they'll realize he knows I escaped the camp, maybe even realize I went to see him when I sneaked into the city. And if they know that . . .*

Mayson, she thought. *Mayson could get word to him, tell him I'm in the Palace. Stop him from doing anything foolish.*

Or spur him to do something even more foolish?

No! She shook her head. She couldn't ask Mayson to do anything of the sort. He was a Watcher. Maybe not as bad as some of them—at least not yet—but he still wore the black Mask, still answered to Stanik and the Autarch. He would likely report her request—he would have to. And that might bring the very suspicion on her father she was trying to avoid.

She shuddered, and tears sprang to her eyes again. How had everything fallen apart so fast?

And Chell. The thought of him was another cold wind blowing through her soul. What was he doing here? What was he up to?

She had reached the central fountain, the plashing of its water masking all other sounds from the Palace. A stone bench encircled it, and she sat down on it and buried her face in her hands. *I shouldn't cry beneath an iron Mask,* she thought. *It might rust.*

But she cried all the same.

And then she heard, or thought she heard, someone whisper her name. She raised her head and looked to her right. She could see Mayson, still leaning against the pillar. He was not watching her; very *carefully* not watching her, it seemed to her.

"Mara," came the whisper again, and Mara turned her head left to see a shadowy figure on the bench.

"Who's there?" she whispered back. "How do you know my name?"

"It's Chell," came the reply.

Chell? Mara stiffened. "What do you want?"

Chell answered her question with one of his own. "What are you doing here?"

Two could play that game. "What are *you* doing here?" she countered.

"My duty," he said. "To gather information for my King."

"And betray the ones who rescued you from the sea?" Mara hissed back.

"I have betrayed no one," Chell said. He lowered his voice even more, so that even sitting so close to him she could barely hear it above the sound of the fountain; no one else could possibly have heard a thing. "I told them I landed well south of where I actually landed, and made my way inland alone. I have presented myself as an ambassador from the court of Korellia, seeking to restore the trade that once existed between our realms. And so I have had the opportunity to see exactly how your land is ruled, and by whom."

"And how goes your trade mission?" Mara said bitterly. "Will gold from Korellia soon be flowing into the Autarch's coffers and strengthening his hold over Aygrima?"

"It goes poorly," Chell said flatly. "I met the Autarch, yes; but I was not treated as an ambassador: the Watchers took me bound before him as though I were a common criminal." The anger in his voice took Mara aback. "The Autarch, it seems, has no interest in trading magic, and the Gifted who can use it, for anything we have to offer: not gold, not weapons, not food, not even ships. He says Aygrima has all the gold it needs. He says with magic at its beck and call, Aygrima needs no weapons. He says Aygrima has ample food for all. And he says Aygrima has no need of ships, because no one from Aygrima will ever be permitted to sail away from its shores.

"He also warns me that if Korellia thinks to sail against Aygrima in force, that he will unleash such powerful storms against our fleets that not a single ship will return to tell the tale." He shook his head. "He is a tyrant, and these Masks that everyone wears . . . they're an abomination. The whole Autarchy is a prison. Everything Catilla and Edrik told me is true."

"Why are you free to wander the Garden Courtyard, if he has treated you so badly?" Mara said. She heard the bitter tone of suspicion in her own voice, and didn't care. "How do I know you have not traded your knowledge of the Secret City for your freedom?"

"I am free to wander the Garden Courtyard," Chell said, "because I am seen as no one of importance: not even enough of a threat to keep under close guard. I am confined to the Palace, of course—they cannot have an unMasked man seen in the streets. At some unspecified time in the future they will take me to the coast and provide me with a small vessel in which I can sail north to find my own ships. I am to convey the Autarch's warning to my own King. And no one from my land is ever to sully the shores of Aygrima again."

"Then your mission has failed," Mara said. *As has mine.* "So what are you going to do about it?"

"Accept it," he said. "And sail north ... but not to my ships. I will return to the Secret City, and offer assistance from the Kingdom of Korellia to the unMasked Army for their campaign to overthrow the Autarch. The question ... is how I can take you with me."

Mara dared not look at him; Mayson might not be watching, but there were others in the Garden Courtyard, and here in the heart of the Palace, with all its interlocking webs of intrigue, it clearly would not do to assume no one else would take an interest in any conversation between Mara and the stranger from another land. But even though she couldn't see Chell, he had clearly seen her. "What is that on your face?"

"It is an iron Mask," Mara said. "It prevents me from using magic."

"Using ..." Chell's eyes widened. "You're Gifted?"

"Yes."

"But you were captured all the same?"

"I had no magic to draw on when the Watchers found us." *No magic I dared use, at any rate*, Mara thought, wishing now that she had risked it.

"But you were found without a Mask. Why didn't they execute you on the spot?"

Mara hesitated. The reasons for not telling Chell anything about her Gift seemed no longer operative. He could not tell the Autarch anything the Autarch did not already know about her. "I have ... a special form of the Gift," she said at last. "A particularly powerful form of it. I can see, and use, all kinds of magic. They do not want to discard someone with such a rare Gift. And so ... they are training me." She could not stop the bitterness flooding into her voice. "And holding my parents hostage against my good behavior. I must serve the Autarch faithfully, or my parents die."

"Monstrous," Chell breathed, and Mara felt a surge

of gratitude toward him for that. "If there is anything I can do—"

"There's nothing," Mara said.

A bell chimed from somewhere in the Palace. Mara glanced at Mayson; saw him straighten and start toward her. "You should—" she whispered, turning back toward Chell; but he was already gone.

Mayson took her, not down to the dungeon level as she feared, but to a comfortable room (though not as comfortable as the one in Stanik's quarters where she had spent her first night in the Palace) on the second floor of the north wing, with a small window looking out over the Great Courtyard. "Better than my quarters," Mayson said, looking in after her, though he stayed in the hallway. "Good night, Mara." He hesitated. "Be safe." Then he closed the door and locked it.

Mara stared at the door, wondering again if she should have asked him to take word to her father. But the arguments against that course of action hadn't changed. She went to the window and stared blindly out at the starlit flagstones, and the occasional dark figure crossing from the Palace toward one of the outbuildings under the wall or vice versa, until supper arrived: a savory stew, fresh-baked bread, creamy cheese, pickled beets and carrots. She was even given a small pitcher of sweet white wine. She would have felt more like a guest than a prisoner if not for the sharp click of her room's door as the white-Masked servant who served her withdrew.

Still, prisoner or guest, she was ravenous after her day of training. She polished off the meal. She hesitated over the wine, then finally decided there was no reason not to drink it, and poured it into the pewter goblet provided. It tasted far better than the wine she had shared with Keltan and Hyram and the others that had made her so sick a few weeks before, and it relaxed her. She sat by the fire sipping it, staring through the iron Mask into the flames, her thoughts as aimless as its flickering, twitching tongues, until she felt her eyes closing at last, helped no doubt by the wine.

A small door in the room's corner led into the greatest luxury of all, a bath, complete with hot and cold taps like the one in Stanik's luxurious quarters, though the bath itself, of glazed porcelain, was not nearly as grand. She stripped and soaked, dried herself, pulled on a nightgown she found in a chest at the foot of the bed, and crawled beneath the covers.

She was so tired she hardly noticed the Mask still clinging to her face. Sleep claimed her quickly, and during the night she discovered one side benefit of the iron Mask, and possibly the wine: she dreamed no dreams of those she had killed or seen the killing of.

But then, her ordinary dreams, of the Secret City burning, of Keltan or her father naked, hanged, and left to rot on the gallows of Traitors' Gate, of her mother publically whipped and driven into the streets to starve, were quite bad enough.

THIRTEEN

The Prince in the Bathroom

FOR THE NEXT TWO WEEKS, Mara trained with
Shelra eight hours a day, learning to use magic as a
fine tool instead of a blunt instrument. The days fell
into a routine: breakfast was brought to her in her
room, a Watcher (though she kept hoping, it was never
Mayson) took her to the hidden chamber in the basement, Shelra removed her Mask and took the lid from
the basin full of magic, and then the work began.

By the end of the second day she was able to distinguish dozens of unique hues in the swirling mass of the
magic. By the end of the first week, she could tug out the
precise color she wanted and use it as delicately as an
artist might use her finest paintbrush: a sliver of scarlet
to emboss a fine network of molten gold across a black

rock, a touch of turquoise to bring a wilted flower back to full bloom, a bit of blue to heal her own scraped knee after she tripped on the flagstones.

By the end of the *second* week she could dip her hand in red and crush a rock the size of her torso to powder simply by clenching her fist. And on that day, the Autarch once more had her brought into his presence.

The throne room looked exactly the same as before: the Autarch and the Child Guard might have been frozen in place since she'd left. At first everything proceeded as before, as well. The Autarch had Shelra remove Mara's iron half-Mask. Once more she felt him pawing at her mind, trying to tear her magic away from her—and once more she blocked him, without difficulty. But *this* time, once she had done so, the Autarch said, "Put the Mask back on her. Then clear the room. Everyone but her and the Child Guard."

Mara heard Shelra's sharp intake of breath, and waited for her to say something: but the Mistress of Magic clearly thought better of it, because she exhaled in a whoosh. She stepped forward and settled the Mask on Mara's face once more, cutting off her sense of the magic in the room. Then she turned and stalked out, the waiting Watchers following her, leaving Mara alone with the Autarch and the Child Guard. Mara glanced at the Masked youths, wondering which one was the son of the couple she had met at the farm; but her curiosity faded in a hurry as the Autarch gripped the arms of the Sun Throne, pushed himself upright, and came down the steps toward her.

She stared at him through the eyeholes of the cursed iron Mask, anger a hot, bright flame in her mind. *If he'd left me unMasked, I could kill him now. Maybe I could anyway.* For an instant she pictured herself leaping forward, grabbing the Autarch by the throat, throwing him to the ground—he was an old man, she was young, how hard could it be . . . ?

But she didn't move. Just because he had ordered everyone out didn't mean that no one was watching through hidden peepholes, that hidden guards weren't waiting to strike her down with crossbow bolts or magic. And then there were the Child Guard. How those strange Masked children would react to an attack on the Autarch she had no idea.

The Autarch loomed over her. He was tall, far taller than she'd realized while he sat upon his throne, and stood straight despite his age. "You are a problem for me, Mara Holdfast," he said from inside his golden Mask.

"I apologize, Mighty One," Mara said.

The Autarch hardly seemed to notice she had spoken. He began circling her, his boots scuffing across the stone floor, staring at her from all sides, though what he thought he might learn she couldn't imagine. He couldn't even sense her magic while she wore the iron Mask, any more than she could sense his.

At last he stopped in front of her and stared down. "You are a problem," he said again, "because you present me with a dilemma." He cocked his head to one side. "You have a rare Gift: the ability to see and use all colors of magic. The Mistress of Magic shares the same ability. That is how she rose to her exalted position. But aside from her, and you, the only other person currently living in Aygrima with that ability is myself."

She said nothing, keeping her head down, carefully not meeting his eyes.

"Look at me," he said.

She didn't move; but his hand gripped her chin and forced it upward, so that against her will she was forced to look into his eyes: very blue, she saw, a pale, washed-out shade, like a blue dress laundered so often all color had faded from it. "By rights," he said, "I should have you executed. You are past the age of Masking. You were found unMasked in the city at night. The penalty for that is known to everyone in this city from a young age."

She swallowed.

"But your Gift could be of immense benefit to the Autarchy. Shelra has told me what she is thinking: nothing less than grooming you to replace her in a decade or two. The question, of course, is, 'Can you be trusted?' So tell me, Mara Holdfast. Can you?"

He can't sense anything from me when I'm wearing the Mask, she thought. *He couldn't sense anything from me even when I wasn't. He's watching my face; that's all.*

I wonder how good he is at reading faces?

I wonder how good an actor I am?

"Yes, Mighty One," she lied. "I came back to Tamita in the hope of finding mercy; in the hope that if I told what I knew of what happened at the mine I might be permitted to live. I'm only fifteen years old. I want to live."

The Autarch kept his hand on her chin, staring into her eyes; then he grunted and released her. "No doubt you do," he said. "As do we all." And knowing what she knew of the lengths to which the Autarch was willing to go to postpone his own death—she was keenly aware of the strangely silent youth of the Child Guard flanking the Sun Throne—she hoped that he would believe the desire for survival would likewise outweigh all else for her.

He stepped back, but he kept staring at her. She wondered if he was about to say something about the other strange thing he must have noticed, that he could not draw on her magic as he could on others who were close at hand ... but of course his ability to do so was as important a secret for him to keep as her ability to do so was for her to keep. In the end he said nothing, simply turning away and returning to the Sun Throne, grunting as he planted himself on it once more. "Let them back in," he said, and, confirming her suspicion that they had been watched the entire time, the throne room doors swung open and Shelra and the others who had been ordered to leave came in once more.

"Take her away," the Autarch said to the Mistress of Magic. "Continue her training . . . for now."

Shelra nodded. "Yes, Mighty One." She took Mara's arm. "Come." They turned their backs on the Autarch and walked away, but despite the presence of the iron Mask, Mara imagined she could feel that pale-blue gaze burning into the back of her head.

She was glad to return to the magic-shielded room, glad to return to her training. She loved everything she was learning, loved the sight of the magic when the horrible iron Mask came off her face, mourned the blocking of her Gift when the Mask was replaced. She loved the hum and tingle of magic in her fingers, the warmth as it flowed through her body . . . and yet, it wasn't enough.

She felt the magic inside the body of the Mistress of Magic, and she wanted to pull *that* magic to her, as well. *That* was the magic she wanted, even though she knew it would hurt her if she gave in to that desire, even though she knew it might drive her to madness. She hated the thought of being like the Autarch, sucking magic from others like mosquitoes sucked blood . . . and yet there was something about the feel of that pure, fresh, unfiltered power coursing through her, though it had burned her, though it had scraped her raw inside, though it had almost killed her, that made her lust after it.

Lust. The word came to her one day as she soaked in the bath, the day's training running through her mind, and she snorted. *Oh, and you're the world's expert on lust, are you?* she teased herself. *You've never even kissed a boy.*

Well, no, she admitted to herself. *But that doesn't mean I wouldn't like to . . . someday . . . and then, someday, maybe even . . .*

She closed her eyes, thinking about it. *Who will it be?* she wondered. *Keltan? Hyram?*

Mmmmm. Or Chell. Taller, more mature . . . more handsome, really, she had to say. That long, lean body, those strong arms . . . she imagined his lips against hers, his arms around her, pulling her to him, tight against his body . . .

"Mara?" a voice whispered from the door behind her, and her eyes flew open, her head slipped off the edge of the tub, and she plunged into the soapy water, emerging spluttering and choking a moment later. "Mara?" came the voice again. "It's Chell."

Chell? *Chell?* "Don't come in!" she squeaked. Heaving herself out of the water, she grabbed her towel, wishing it was considerably bigger than it was, wrapped it around herself as best she could, and pressed herself to the bathroom wall next to the door so the only way he could see in would be to physically enter the room. "How did you get in here? What do you want?"

"Shh!" he hissed. "We need to talk. Let me come in."

"No!" Mara looked down at herself. The towel could cover her top or her bottom, but not both—not adequately. "I'm naked!"

There was a moment's silence, then her dressing gown, which she had left on the bed, entered the doorway, held by Chell's outstretched arm. Mara dropped the towel, grabbed the dressing gown, wrapped it securely around herself, and then tied it tight. "All right," she said, a little breathlessly. "Now you can come in."

He stepped in. He wore nondescript clothes, gray pants, gray shirt, black vest, black boots, a shapeless black hat jammed haphazardly onto his head.

"How did you get in here?" Mara said again. "The door is locked—"

"I have some skill with locks," said Chell. "And no Watcher currently stands guard. I came in, saw you were in the bath, and—"

"You saw?" Mara squeaked.

"I mean, I saw you weren't in the main room, but I could hear you in here. So I said your name."

He sounded utterly sincere. Mara wasn't sure she believed him, and her ears burned. He could have been standing behind her for several minutes, just watching her.

"I can't stay long," he continued. He was staring at her face; he reached out a hand and touched the iron Mask. "This blocks your Gift?"

She nodded.

"Can't you just . . . take it off?"

"It requires magic."

"Then I will get you some."

Mara blinked at him. "What?"

Chell hesitated. "Mara, I came to talk to you because I have not been entirely honest with you."

No kidding, Mara thought, but did not say.

"I am something more than just a scout," Chell continued.

"You're an ambassador," Mara said. "You already told me that."

Chell sighed. "I'm afraid I am somewhat more than just an ambassador, too. My full title is"—he took a deep breath—"His Royal Highness Chell cor Chell cor Arriken, Prince of the Golden Shore, Duke of the Southern Deep, and Protector of the Holy Fountain."

Mara stared at him. "You're a *prince*?"

He raised his hands in a self-deprecating gesture. "A minor one," he said. "My father had five boys and three girls and I am the youngest of them all . . . and the last; my mother died shortly after I was born. For me to become the king of Korellia, my entire family would have to be wiped out. I am, in short, as expendable as it is possible for a prince to be . . . and thus the ideal candidate to lead what seemed to most within the court a wild and probably fatal adventure to a quite possibly mythical land."

"Then you *have* no captain to report to," Mara said. "You're the one in command!"

"Well, there *is* a captain," Chell said. "Two of them, in fact. Captains March and Gramm. One for each ship. But, no, I don't report to them, they report to me."

"Is anything you told me the truth?" Mara said, feeling a surge of anger. "You told us, in the Secret City, that your kingdom needs magic from Aygrima. But now you tell me it's nothing but a 'wild adventure'?"

"We do need it," Chell insisted. "That was the truth. It's just . . . not everyone believes it still exists." He sighed. "Though we have histories that speak of the magic of Aygrima, there are many in Korellia who think magic is no more real than the sea serpents and giant, ship-crushing flying lizards the old records also speak of. No one has seen one of those in living memory, and no one has seen anyone use magic, either.

"But *I* believed in magic," he went on. "I believed the old tales. I believed I could sail to Aygrima, though the same legends claim that at the time of the plagues no ship could get close because of the vicious storms that swirled constantly around its shores. I reasoned that if magic were real, those storms might have been *created* by the people of Aygrima to ensure their land was not affected by the plague—and since the Autarch has threatened me with them again, I think I was probably right about that. I thought it unlikely those storms would still be active; but I also thought it *likely*, if my theory were true, that Aygrima would be untouched by the plague: just cut off from the rest of the world. After all, the legends also agree that the people of Aygrima were never sailors, always relying on others to ferry them across the seas to ply their magical trade."

Mara shook her head skeptically. "Your father the King mounted an expedition based on nothing more than your *feeling* that old stories *might* be true?"

"Not entirely," Chell said. "I also found, in a tiny fishing village, an old woman who claimed to have been *born* in Aygrima. She said her parents had fled an uprising against the ruler, along with four other couples, in a wallowing old fishing boat unfit to sail across a duck pond, much less the ocean. Yet by immense good fortune they reached our waters, starving and dehydrated but alive—only to run aground on a submerged reef within sight of shore. Her parents strapped her to a spar and put her overboard, and somehow she floated safely through the rocks and the surf, to be rescued, crying and choking on salt water, by a young childless couple who raised her as their own. From her, I learned that Aygrima was real, that it still had magic, and that it was ruled by someone called the Autarch, whom her parents had considered an evil tyrant.

"I do not think my father found her account as convincing as I did, and I am quite sure my eldest brother Corris, heir to the throne, was not convinced at all, since he mocked me mercilessly." Chell's jaw clenched for a moment. "Nevertheless, my father has always indulged me somewhat . . . a perk of being the baby of the family . . . and so he granted me the use of two stout ships and stalwart crews to sail east and north to see what could be seen in the place where the old records said Aygrima was to be found.

"And find it I did. First the Secret City, where a young girl saved me from drowning or freezing to death (or both), and then, with the help of that girl and her friends, the capital city of Tamita itself, where I hoped to negotiate with the Autarch for what my kingdom needs. That hope has faded. But now, unexpectedly, I have a new hope."

Chell spread his hands, his eyes never leaving her face, which was a little embarrassing, since just at that moment a big drop of water that had run down the bridge of her nose from her soaked hair fell off the tip. It tickled, and she flicked the end of her nose with her finger. "What hope?" she said.

"You," the prince (*If he's telling the truth about that*, she thought) replied softly. "You told me by the fountain that you are Gifted. You also told me that you have a very special form of the Gift. And the Autarch has clearly taken a special interest in you as a result. So when I ran across the young Watcher who brought you to the Garden Courtyard the day I spoke to you, I asked him about you—since he must have seen me there, it seemed safe enough."

Mayson, Mara thought.

"He said no one knows what to make of you, but that you are being trained by the Mistress of Magic herself. Rumor has it, he said, that you are being groomed to be her apprentice and eventual replacement. All of that tells me that you are—potentially, at least—magically very powerful."

Mara wanted to deny it, but, remembering the pillar of flame rising above the mining camp, could not. She *was* powerful. Powerful, and dangerous. Not even the Autarch knew how powerful. It made her uncomfortable to even think it.

Of course, at the moment it wasn't strictly true. All of

her magic, all of her potential power, was trapped, locked inside her by the iron Mask she wore. She glanced down at her bathrobe-wrapped body and the puddle of water around her bare feet, and snorted. "Do I *look* powerful?"

"Looks can be deceiving," Chell said. He spread his hands. "Do I look like a prince?"

Actually, yes, now that I know the truth, Mara thought, but didn't say. "Even if I were powerful, so what? What difference does it make to you?"

"Because," Chell said, "there is another reason my father was willing to risk two ships and their crews on a 'wild adventure' many thought futile. He did not do so simply in the hope we could resume the trade in ordinary magic. He did so because . . . we need a weapon."

Mara blinked. "What?"

"Korellia is hard-pressed," Chell said flatly. "We once had the mightiest navy and most powerful army of all the island nations, but in the centuries since the plague a new power has arisen, a bloody, murderous regime called Stonefell. The ships of Stonefell surpass ours in speed and size, and they are armed with weapons the like of which we have never seen before: metal tubes that fling hot iron balls over enormous distances, smashing apart both ships and sailors. They fortunately have far fewer ships than we do, and so have thus far limited themselves to piracy; but we believe they are building a fleet to launch against us. When they do, I do not believe our kingdom will be able to withstand it. Not unless we have some new and powerful weapon of our own. A *magical* weapon."

Mara stared at him. "And you think I could be it? You think I'm powerful enough to use magic to sink an entire fleet?" *Am I?* she wondered, and had no answer.

Chell shook his head. "No," he said. "I have something far more direct in mind." He locked his gaze on hers. "I know even ordinary Gifted engineers can move and shape stone with their magic: we have fortifications and buildings dating back to before the plague that could only have been built with the help of Aygrimian magic. A truly powerful Gifted person might do more.

"I want you to come back to Korellia with me. From there I want you to sail with me to the seawalls of black stone that keep the ocean from the heart of Stonefell. And then I want you to use magic to smash those walls apart, so that the towns and villages and soldiers and shipmakers of Stonefell are swamped beneath the waves, and can never threaten Korellia or any other island nation again."

Mara stared at him, picturing it: the ocean roaring across the protected lands beyond the wall, fields flooding, towers toppling, screams and terror, death and destruction . . . and finally, silence; the silence of the grave. All those lives, snuffed out in moments, snuffed out at her hand . . .

. . . all those bodies releasing their magic, all that magic pouring into her, but with it all that fear and pain and . . .

It would kill her; kill her, or drive her mad. *Or drive me mad and then kill me*, she thought.

She started to say that no, she would never do what he asked, *could* never do it . . . but something stopped her.

Chell was offering to help her escape from the Palace, from the awful choice of either serving the tyrannical Autarch or hanging at Traitors' Gate. It might be the only chance for escape that would ever come.

"And if I do?" she said after a long moment. "What will you do for me?"

"Help you escape from the Palace," Chell said.

"I figured that much," Mara said impatiently. "I mean after *that*."

He met her eyes. "If you do this," he said, "I swear, as a Prince of the Realm of Korellia, that my nation will aid the unMasked Army in the overthrow of the Autarch."

And there it is, Mara thought. *How can I turn that down, not just for myself, but for the unMasked Army . . . for all the people of Aygrima, all the children waiting to be Masked and enslaved?*

But you can't do what he asks, she argued with herself. *You* can't. *You can't kill all those people using magic.*

Or rather, she *could*—but she didn't think she'd like what it would turn her into.

Time enough to worry about that later, she told herself firmly. *The important thing is to get out of here. Escape the Palace, escape Tamita, return to the Secret City.*

"Do you have a plan?" she asked.

"I might be able to get you out of the Palace," Chell said. "I had thought to get out of the city the same way we got in—"

Mara shook her head. "The walkway by the river was torn down the night I was captured. By now I'm sure the iron grates have been replaced as well. There's no escape that way."

Chell said nothing for a moment. "Then," he said slowly, "I must get a message to Keltan and see if he knows another."

"Keltan?" Mara's eyes widened. "You've seen him?"

Chell nodded. "More days than not. He spends his time in the . . . what do they call it, the Inside Market? . . . the shopping area along the boulevard leading from the Palace to the main city Gate. He is obviously looking for you."

"Has he seen *you*?" Mara said, wondering how Keltan would react to the sight of the man they had hosted in the Secret City hobnobbing with Palace nobles.

"I doubt it," Chell said. "I spotted him from the Palace

wall as I was being given a tour, the first time. Since then, during my escorted perambulations around the Palace, I have made a point of asking to be taken up there so that I might look for him. I've spotted him several times, but he's never looked up at me."

Mara studied the prince. "I would approach him cautiously," she said softly. "He might be inclined to stick a knife in you."

"I have not betrayed the unMasked Army," Chell said hotly.

"So you say. But he doesn't know that."

Chell pressed his lips together, then inclined his head. "Point taken. Now—" He stopped suddenly, listening. "Someone's at the door!"

"Supper," Mara whispered, her heart suddenly pounding. "Quick, in here!" She grabbed his arm and pulled him into the bathroom, then cinched her dressing gown tighter to her body, grabbed her towel, and walked out into the main room, toweling her hair vigorously— probably more vigorously than was strictly necessary— as the door opened and a servant came in with a covered tray. "Put it on the table," she said, still toweling. The servant inclined her white-Masked head, placed the tray where Mara had indicated, and went out ... past the Watcher who now stood outside her door. The Watcher's black Mask stared blankly at her for a moment before the door closed.

Mara, heart pounding, threw the towel on the bed and went back into the bathroom. Chell still had his back to the wall, and was holding a bath brush by its wooden handle. Mara stopped when she saw that and couldn't suppress a giggle. "What were you going to do with that? Scrub a Watcher to death?"

"They took away my weapons," Chell said defensively. "Won't even let me have a dagger." He looked down at the bath brush. "Besides," he said, "my arms master has taught me a dozen ways to kill a man with a bath brush." Mara might have believed him if he'd been able to keep a straight face, but the grin that spread across it effectively put the lie to his words. "All right, it is pretty silly," he said. He tossed the brush aside.

"You might want to hang onto it," Mara said, her own smile fading. "There's a Watcher outside my door now."

"He wasn't there before. He probably accompanied the servant who brought your supper, just to make sure you didn't sneak out while the door was ajar," Chell said, but not as if he were entirely convinced.

"Maybe," Mara said. She folded her arms over her chest. "But to return to our conversation. You think you can get me out of the Palace. You hope Keltan can get us out of the city . . . somehow. But how are you going to get my father out with us?"

Chell's eyes narrowed. "Your father? Mara, we can't get your father out. It's impossible. He's the Master Maskmaker! They'd turn the countryside upside down looking for him."

"They'll turn the countryside upside down looking for me, too," Mara countered. "Chell, my parents are hostage, though they don't know it, since they don't know I've been captured: hostage to my good behavior. My mother is in no immediate danger, she's gone back to her home village. But my father . . . if I even try to escape, much less succeed . . ." She let her words trail away.

Chell shook his head. "It's out of the question."

"Then so is what you ask of me."

Chell glared at her, eyebrows drawn together . "Your parents aren't the only hostages," he growled. "Do you *really* think I couldn't lead the Autarch to the Secret City if I chose? I might not be able to get an army there overland, but I could sure as hell get one there by boat. I could offer the Autarch the Secret City and the unMasked Army in exchange for magic to help my kingdom. Maybe that would be enough. My mission would succeed. Shame about all your friends, but . . ." He shrugged. "Casualties of war. Sad but unavoidable."

Mara, who a moment before had been sharing laughter with the prince, felt a surge of fear and anger. "You wouldn't."

Chell let his face soften. "No, I wouldn't . . . *unless there was no other way*. Mara, the Autarchy of Aygrima is a terrible place and the Autarch a tyrant, as much a tyrant as the King of Stonefell. The King of Stonefell holds power through his strange new weapons. The Autarch holds power through the might of his magic. And the ordinary people suffer under each.

"But with Stonefell ascendant, my people, too, may soon fall under tyranny. And my duty, my whole reason for existence as a Prince of the Realm, is to preserve and protect my people. *My* people. Not yours. Not your family. Not your friends. *Mine.* And I will do whatever I have to do to fulfill my duty." His voice became pleading. "Don't make me carry out my threat."

Mara glared at him. *He's a smooth talker*, she warned herself. *Don't get sucked in. For all you know his father is the* real *tyrant and the innocent people of Stonefell are trying to throw off his yoke.* "There is another reason we need my father—a reason *you* need my father."

"And that is . . . ?"

"This." Mara touched the iron Mask.

Chell frowned. "You said you could remove it with magic."

Mara shook her head. "No, I said its removal requires magic. But I cannot remove it myself, because as long as I wear it I cannot *use* magic. Even if I knew the trick of pulling it off, I couldn't do it while it is attached to my face. Only someone else with the knowledge of how to do it can take this from my face, and only when it is taken from my face will I be free to use magic of my own." She drew her hand back from the cold iron surface. "I'm told my father made it. He must also know how to remove it. Quite possibly he is the *only* person who knows how to remove it except for the Mistress of Magic herself—and I hardly think we'll convince *her* to take it off me. So we must rescue my father and get him away from Tamita. With him safe, and my magic restored . . . then I will see what I can do to help your people. But if we simply escape, and I am still wearing *this*"—she gestured at it again—"then I'll just be another girl, with no more magic than the maid who brought my supper."

Chell stepped closer, studying her Mask. She was suddenly aware of how near he was, and of how little she was wearing. She folded her arms across her chest. He reached out and touched the Mask. "It looks like I should just be able to—" He suddenly snatched at it, before she knew what he was doing. She saw nothing, with her Gift blocked, but she heard Chell yelp and jump back.

For what seemed a ridiculously long moment he teetered on the edge of the still-full bath, arms flailing . . . and then he toppled backward into it with an enormous splash that sprayed tepid water all over Mara and the rest of the room. Terrified, she hurried to the bathroom door, ready to intercept the Watcher if he came in; but the door remained closed.

She turned around to see the prince staggering to his feet again, water streaming from his fine clothes. "It . . . it *bit* me!"

"You can't remove it that way," Mara said. Her mouth twitched as she looked at the sodden prince. "I *told* you. You should have listened to me."

"Obviously," Chell muttered. He looked down at himself. "How am I going to explain *this* if I run into a Watcher in the courtyard?"

"Tell them you were dancing on the edge of the fountain and fell in," Mara suggested. "Tell them it's a religious duty where you come from to dance around fountains. At midnight."

"Very funny," Chell growled.

"I thought so," Mara agreed.

Chell glared at her for a long moment ... but the glare faded away into a grin that became a chuckle. "All right," he said. "You've convinced me. Somehow, we have to save your father, too." He shook his arms, spraying more water around the room. "I'll have to talk to Keltan about it." He stepped out of the bath. "Your robe is soaked, too."

"Whose fault is that?" Mara said.

"I'd better go ... if I can," Chell said. "Can you check to see if the Watcher is out there? Otherwise I might have to spend the night."

Mara, remembering what she'd been fantasizing about just before the prince turned up in her bathroom, felt herself blushing and hated herself for it. "I'm sure that won't be necessary." She padded barefoot and dripping to the door, and put her ear to it. Nothing. She knocked on it. "Watcher?" she said. "Are you there?"

Still nothing.

"I think it's ..." Mara began, then gasped in surprise as she turned around to discover Chell standing right behind her.

"I can move silently when I have to," Chell said. He reached inside the pocket of the vest he wore and drew out an oddly shaped piece of metal, with strange curves and right-angle bends in it. Kneeling by the door, he inserted the object into the keyhole. Tongue protruding between his teeth—which made him look about ten years old, Mara thought, and exactly *why* was that so endearing?—he twisted it this way and that, listening. After about ten seconds he pulled the piece of metal out of the lock, stood up, and opened the now-unlocked door a crack. "All clear," he whispered. He glanced back at her and gave her a wink. "Guess I won't have to spend the night after all." And then he slipped out. She heard him lock the door again from the other side.

Mara stared at the door. "He's shameless," she said out loud. "And infuriating."

And cute, said a part of her brain she really wished would just shut up: the same part that had had her thinking about him in the bath. The same part that didn't seem to care that he was a) a foreign prince, b) wanted her to kill his enemies for him, c) had threatened to betray the Secret City and d) had been willing to leave her parents to whatever horrible fate might befall them if she escaped.

It was a part of her she'd only rarely encountered before, a part of her that seemed to be taking more and more interest in things like boys, and what they might be good for, to the exclusion of things like common sense and self-preservation.

Great, she thought. *Something else I've got to try to keep a lid on. No pulling magic from living bodies . . . and no making decisions based on how cute boys are.*

Men, she reminded herself. Chell was a *young* man, but still, definitely a man, not a boy. Not like Keltan (cute, but only a little older than her) or Hyram (older, and also cute, but still just a boy). No, Chell was a man. A handsome man. An *experienced* man.

She shook her head, hard. *Enough!* She might never see him again. Or she might see him again on the gallows outside Traitors' Gate, and Keltan with him, if this mad scheme of his to help her escape did not succeed.

And my father, she thought. *And my mother . . .*

What have I done? she thought then, as the possible consequences of even *considering* escape rushed home to roost, driving all thoughts of boys, cute or otherwise, out of her head.

What I had to, she reminded herself. *Chell has made it impossible for me to just go along as I have been. I have to try to escape, or he'll betray the unMasked Army. And I have to succeed, or my parents . . .*

Her warm thoughts toward Chell, already dwindling, evaporated completely. *He's using me*, she thought coldly. *And that's wrong. As wrong as me ripping magic from other people. As wrong as the Autarch sucking magic from the Child Guard.*

People aren't things. They aren't tools. They shouldn't be used.

A brave sentiment. And yet, as she dried herself (again) and finally crawled into bed, she knew that that was exactly how others saw her: as a thing, a tool, a weapon. Something to be used to strike against an enemy.

It was a bleak thought to take with her to sleep.

FOURTEEN

A Blow to the Heart

ANOTHER WEEK WENT BY. Mara's training continued. She saw nothing of Chell or Keltan. The Mistress of Magic seemed daily more impressed with her process. "It shocks me that your Mask rejected you," Shelra said one day. "No one of your ability has ever before failed her Masking."

"*Are* there others with my ability?" Mara asked. She thought she knew the answer, from what the Autarch had said, but she wondered how the Mistress of Magic would reply.

Shelra hesitated. "I . . . don't think I should comment on that," and her hand went halfway to her green Mask before she caught herself. "Now," she said briskly, "that last water-freezing was a trifle sloppy;

still some liquid around the edges. This time, see if you can . . ."

They plunged back into the training, but Mara wondered what Shelra had not been able to comment on. *Do I really have a greater measure of the Gift than anyone in Aygrima?* she wondered. *Even the Autarch?*

She lived in dread, day to day, that somehow Shelra would detect the other part of her Gift, the part that let her draw magic from others just like the Autarch and all those monsters of the past, the most recent being The Lady of Pain and Fire; but that ability seemed to be undetectable through testing or even close proximity. As far as she could tell, Shelra knew only that she could see, and use to great effect, all colors of magic. She did not know that Mara, whenever the Mask was removed, could also feel the magic inside the Mistress of Magic, an enormous amount of magic compared to anyone else she had sensed, and that Mara ached to tap into that magic, to see if the far greater control she now had over regular magic might allow her to draw the magic out of Shelra more delicately than she had done in the mining camp, to use it to greater effect, to minimize the pain of that unfiltered power pouring into her and maximize the pleasure it had also given her, shamefully but undeniably.

So far, she hadn't given in. But every day it was a struggle not to. *If I do*, she thought, *she will surely feel it, and know the full extent of my Gift . . . and then what will they do with me?*

She thought she knew. *The Autarch can find always find use for a powerful Gifted girl*, she thought. *But one that shares his powers so closely, one with the same powers, potentially, as The Lady of Pain and Fire, the sorceress he forced out of Aygrima in his youth? He wouldn't "find use" for me; he'd kill me. Probably on the spot.*

Her feeling of walking a tightrope increased the day she talked to the Child Guard.

It was rare to see any of the Child Guard away from the Autarch, but one afternoon, when Mara had been freed from training an hour early because Shelra had to attend a meeting of the Circle, she found all of them in the Garden Courtyard, walking among the shrouded bushes, enjoying sunshine with more warmth in it than Mara had felt in a long time. It was still winter, but the days were lengthening, and the unseasonable warmth on this afternoon taunted them with the false promise of imminent spring.

The Child Guard were mostly in twos and threes, talking quietly among themselves, their white robes and silver Masks making them look almost like ghosts as they glided along the paths. But one sat alone by the fountain, near where Mara liked to sit. She thought it was the smallest boy, the one she had noticed from the City Wall shortly before her Masking, shortly before her life had turned upside down. He had already been Masked then, so he had to be at least a little bit older than she, but he looked very young, and somehow forlorn, as he sat there by himself, kicking his legs aimlessly and staring down at the ground.

Mara shot a quick glance at Mayson, who once again was the Watcher who had escorted her from the training room. He was engrossed in conversation with another Watcher, half turned away from her. Taking her chance, she walked over to the fountain and sat down beside the Child Guard. "Hi," she said to him. "I'm Mara."

The silver Mask turned toward her. "I know who you are," said a boy's voice, a voice still changing, so that it squeaked even in that brief sentence. "I've seen you twice in the throne room."

"What's your name?" she said after a moment, when he didn't volunteer anything else.

"We don't have names," the boy said, and once more fell silent.

Not the easiest guy to talk to, Mara thought. She tried again. "Then what was your name before you became a Child Guard?"

The boy hesitated, looked around as if afraid he might be overheard, then leaned close and almost whispered. "Greff. My name is Greff."

Mara felt a chill. "Greff? From ..." What was the name of the village? "...Yellowgrass?"

He sat back, startled. "How did you ...?"

"I've met your parents," Mara said. "Filia and Jess, right?"

He nodded dumbly.

"I slept in your old room! I even met your dog." She laughed. "I thought he was going to eat me, actually, but in the end he turned out to be pretty nice."

Greff laughed, a little shakily. "Stafin's bark has always been worse than his bite," he said. "Unless you're a squirrel." He stared at her, his eyes blue and bright behind the silver Mask. "You really do know them," he said in wonder. "How ...?"

"On my way here," Mara said carefully, reminding herself that this boy spent most of his time in the presence of the Autarch, that the Autarch drew magic from him, and for all she knew could read the boy's thoughts. "I came across their farm. They were very kind to me." *And in return I lied to them,* she thought guiltily.

"They're well?" The boy's voice sounded plaintive.

Mara nodded. "Do you never get to visit them?"

Greff shook his head. "No," he said softly. "Not until I'm eighteen." His voice dropped even further. "Assuming I'm still alive by then."

Mara stared at him. "What?"

But Greff jumped to his feet. "I shouldn't ... I

can't . . ." He held out his hand and Mara, wondering, took it. "Thank you," he said, pumping her arm, and then he turned and scurried away.

Mara watched him rush off to join three other Child Guard under the far portico, then turned back . . . and jumped. Mayson stood close beside her. "What did you say to him?" he asked.

"Nothing," Mara said. "I happened to know his parents. That's all."

"You shouldn't have spoken to him, Mara." Mayson looked at the small clump of white-clad children across the courtyard. "And he shouldn't have spoken to you. The Child Guard aren't supposed to speak to anyone except the Autarch and each other. I should report him—"

"No, don't!" Mara said.

Mayson looked down at her. "Mara—"

"Please," she begged. "I don't want him to get into trouble. I was the one who spoke first. I didn't know it was forbidden."

Mayson glanced back at the Child Guard, Mara following his gaze. As one, the silver-Masked, white-clad youngsters suddenly turned and filed from the courtyard, as though in response to some unheard signal. *From the Autarch?* Mara wondered. Mayson watched them go, then finally sighed. "All right," he said. "No harm done, I guess. But I think it's time you went to your room."

"Thank you," Mara said, and obediently got up to follow him.

• • •

Two nights later, Chell came to her again.

She was already in bed, and already asleep. She jerked awake with a gasp and stared wide-eyed into the darkness, wondering what had roused her. Then she gasped as she heard again, as she had in the bath, her whispered name, "Mara. It's Chell."

She rolled over and sat up and there he was, a barely visible lump of blackness in the dark room. Only a little faint moonglow made it through the open slit of the window, and the embers of the fire, which had burned down hours before, did nothing but thicken the shadows cloaking everything else.

"I have talked to Keltan," Chell said. "He has a plan."

In a low voice, he laid it out for her. He had gotten a message to Keltan through one of the young unMasked boys who served as general dogsbodies around the Palace, running messages and errands as required. He'd told Keltan of Mara's situation and his own. And Keltan had once more proved to know more about the workings of Tamita than Mara would ever have guessed—far more than Mara, and she'd thought herself well-versed in the ins and outs of Tamita, having grown up on its streets ... though not, she had to admit, the same streets as Keltan. Keltan knew of ways in and out of the Palace hidden from public view, tunnels in the warren of passageways beneath Fortress Hill through which supplies such as meat, vegetables, and wine were normally delivered unseen to the kitchens. Of course there were many locked doors, Keltan had warned the prince; but as Chell's presence in her room demonstrated yet again, he had the knack of opening most locks. He also knew, thanks to Keltan, when the tunnels were most likely to be deserted. "I'll take you from this room in the middle of the night, out through the tunnels, into the city," he said.

"And then what?"

"Then Keltan takes over," Chell said. "He says he can get into the shed behind his father's house, where his father keeps a wagon for delivering the furniture he sells in the outlying villages. He says he can hide us in that wagon, and then drive us openly through the gates; the

Watchers still see him as a child and do not question . . . yet . . . his lack of a Mask. 'After all,' he told me, 'no one without a Mask would dare risk being seen on the streets of Tamita, so if someone without a Mask is seen, it must be someone who has not yet donned a Mask.'"

"Provided no one sees him who knew him as a child," Mara said. "It's a terrible risk."

"It's a risk he's willing to take . . . well, for *you, at least.*" Chell chuckled. "I do not think he would take the risk for me. My sense is that he's angry with me."

"You can hardly blame him."

"No, I suppose not," Chell said equitably. "But at least he is willing to allow me to accompany you as he drives you up into the hills, where Edrik still waits—Keltan has been in regular contact with him. And then we will all flee together back to the Secret City."

"And my father?" Mara said.

"That's up to you," Chell said. "On the morning we escape, we will detour to your house, very early, after curfew lifts but before the Gate opens. You must convince him to accompany us. You will have very little time. We must be heading out the Gate the moment it opens, before—hopefully—your absence from your room is noted. If you cannot convince him to come . . ."

Mara swallowed. "I can convince him."

Chell just nodded, the movement barely visible in the darkness. "And now I must slip back to my own room. Every now and then a Watcher pokes his head in unexpectedly. I left a Chell-shaped lump of rolled-up blankets in my bed, but I'd hate to be found missing from a supposedly locked room."

"When?" Mara said, as he started toward the door. "When will we make the attempt?"

"In two nights," Chell said. "In two nights, there will be no moon."

He opened the door and slipped out into the cold night beyond. Mara heard him lock the door with his strange metal tool, and then she was alone in the darkness once more. Her bed was warm and the night quiet, but still it took her a long time to fall asleep again.

• • •

The next day, cognizant she was almost out of time, Mara broached the subject of the Lady of Pain and Fire with the Mistress of Magic. "You've been telling me I have an unusually powerful gift," Mara said to Shelra as they ate lunch together. "But just how powerful? I mean, how do I compare to someone like . . ." she hesitated, as though searching for a name, "um . . . say . . . the Lady of Pain and Fire?"

Was it her imagination, or did Shelra's hand hesitate between her plate and her mouth? If it did, it was only for a moment; then the piece of cheese she had picked up completed its journey and she chewed without apparent concern. "Whatever made you come up with *that* name?"

"Our Tutor told us," Mara said, "that the Lady of Pain and Fire was a powerful sorceress who could do . . . well, anything. So she must have been able to use all colors of magic, too."

"I wouldn't know," Shelra said. "The Autarch's defeat of the Lady of Pain and Fire was long before my time. I'm not *that* old."

"But—"

"Of course she had a powerful Gift," Shelra said. "That much is clear. I cannot say it was the same as yours, but I do know one way in which it differed. The Lady of Pain and Fire suffered from a . . . perversion."

"Perversion?" Mara said. She took a slice of sausage and chewed it thoughtfully, as though all of this was of only academic interest, though in fact her heart was racing. "You mean . . . um . . . sexual?"

Shelra shook her head. "No, nothing like that. Well, not that I know of," she added with a small smile. "No, I mean she suffered from a *magical* perversion." She gestured at the basin. "Normal Gifted use magic that has been drawn to the black lodestone. But the so-called Lady of Pain and Fire could pull magic directly from other humans. It's disgusting. It's a form of rape. And the Autarch quite rightly knew that it could not stand."

"So he killed her?" Mara said, taking another bite of sausage.

"He defeated her," Shelra said. "And that's enough discussion of it." She got to her feet. "Back to training."

And with that, Mara had to be content.

Doesn't she know the Autarch also suffers from this "perversion"? Mara wondered. *Or does she know but wants to be damn sure I don't? And what would she do if she knew I had it, too?*

That hardly bore thinking about. If the Autarch "defeated" the Lady, when he was just a youth, what would he do now to someone who threatened his power as directly as Mara might? Suppose she pulled the magic out of the Mistress of Magic? Suppose she drew it from the Child Guard? Suppose she could connect to the steady streams of magic from the ever-growing number of new Masks, the ones that fed a trickle of power to the Autarch at all times, the power that kept him young and vital, kept his age from withering and weakening him? What would that do to the Autarch's rule?

I could do it, too, Mara thought. *I could . . .*

Except, of course for two things. It might kill her . . . and it might mean the death of her parents.

She needed to get out of the city. She needed to be free of the Autarch's grasp, needed her father free of it.

Then together they could rescue her mother. And then . . .

Then she *would* do something about the Autarch. Somehow. Whatever it meant for her.

Just one more day. It didn't seem to be too much to ask.

But it turned out to be a day too far.

Once again Mara woke from a sound sleep to find someone in her room. But this time she woke in the gray light of morning, not the middle of the night, and this time the figure at the foot of her bed was not Chell.

It was Stanik.

She sat up, blinking. "Guardian Stanik?" she said, her brain still sleep-fuzzed. "I don't . . ."

"Your father," Stanik said, without preamble, his voice cold and hard as frozen steel, "has been arrested."

Mara's heart flip-flopped in her chest. "But—but I've done everything you asked! I've been training, I've promised to help the Autarch—"

He knows about Chell, a terrified part of her mind gibbered. *He knows about the plan. He'll arrest Chell and Keltan, too—*

But Stanik made a dismissive slashing gesture with his right hand. "*You* have done everything we asked. But *he* has betrayed the Autarch."

"I don't—"

"Understand?" Stanik snarled. "Are you sure?" He pointed at her. "Your father," he grated, "was discovered in a part of the Library forbidden to any but members of the Circle. He was researching unusual Gifts . . . Gifts such as yours. That alone was enough to get him arrested. Perhaps he could have talked his way out of that—after all, he is . . . or was . . . the Master Maskmaker. But as a matter of course, one of our most Gifted Watchers examined his Mask closely, and discovered the truth: your father *modified his Mask*. And that raises an interesting question: did he also modify yours? Is that why a child with your unusual Gift suffered an *unprecedented* failure of her Mask?"

Mara felt the blood drain from her face and knew that, even with the iron half-Mask obscuring half of it, she had just given herself away.

Stanik gave a short nod. "As I thought. There is something more here, something I *will* get to the bottom of. But for now, this is all you need to know: your father is in prison, and being interrogated. And tomorrow at dawn, he dies."

"No!" The cry exploded from Mara as though yanked from her soul with a steel hook. "No, you can't!"

"Can't?" Stanik stormed around to the side of her bed. "*Can't?*" His hand lashed out, cracking across her cheek with so much force it drove her back into the headboard. Crying in pain and helpless fury, she slid back down into the bed and stared at him, holding her hand to her face, tasting salty blood where her teeth had cut the inside of her cheek.

"I can do whatever I want," he spat. "And I will do what I must. And what I must do, for a crime of this magnitude, is make an example. To the people. And to you." He pointed a gloved finger at her. "You still harbor rebellion in your heart. It's as clear as the blood on your face. You still think that, once you are trained, you will somehow strike back at us with your great Gift. But hear me, Mara Holdfast, daughter of the disgraced and soon to be deceased Charlton Holdfast: you will *never* strike back at the Autarch. Rebellion is futile. Worse than that, it is fatal.

"You have lied to me. That is clear. Your father designed your Mask to fail. He must have known that the wagon carrying you to the camp would be attacked. Which means he knows who attacked the wagon. Which means *you* know who attacked the wagons, and the camp." He folded his arms, glared at her. "So. You want to save your father? Tell me the truth!"

Mara stared at him, horrified by the dilemma on whose horns she had just been hung. She opened her mouth, closed it again. She didn't know what she could say.

"You have one minute," Stanik snarled. "Or your father dies, no matter what."

"No!" Mara felt as if she couldn't get her breath, as if all the air had somehow been sucked from her lungs and from her breath. "No! I . . ." *I can't betray the Secret City. Hyram, Alita, Prella . . . all those people . . . I can't . . .*

Maybe she didn't have to. Maybe she could give just some of the truth, just enough of the truth to save her father . . .

"I was . . . it wasn't just bandits," she said desperately. "You're right about that. I don't know how my father knew, but . . . there's a story. All the children have heard it, it sounds like a myth, but it's true." She took a shaky breath. "The unMasked Army." Her heart spasmed as she said it. "The unMasked Army," she said again. "It's real. They want to overthrow the Autarch."

Stanik just stared at her, still as a snake about to strike. "And where can we find the unMasked Army?" he said, and like the fangs of a snake, his voice held venom.

"I can't . . . I don't know!" Mara cried. "You have to believe me. I don't. They took me to a . . . a place. Caves. They blindfolded me. They didn't trust me. I don't know how to get there. I don't!"

"Who is their leader?" Stanik said, still cold as frost, implacable as stone. "I want a name. And do not tell me you do not have one, or make one up. If I have the slightest doubt that you are telling the truth, your father dies."

"Catilla!" Mara cried, the name torn out of her throat by the horror of what Stanik threatened. "Catilla is her name. I don't know her last name, if she has one. I don't know anything else."

Stanik stood absolutely still for a long moment. "Catilla," he breathed. He took a step closer to Mara's bedside, and leaned over her, his hands on either side of her body in a horrible parody of a lover's embrace. "Thank you," he said. "That name is enough. I know Catilla's name from the records. I know who her father was. And I know what her father found: a network of caves, along the coast, remote, inaccessible . . . the ideal hiding place for this un-Masked Army we never believed really existed . . . until now." His voice lowered, took on the tones of the purr of a contented cat. "You have given me everything I need, Mara Holdfast. Everything I need to destroy the un-Masked Army. You have served the Autarch well."

Mara felt sick to her stomach. *What have I done?* she cried to herself, but out loud all she said was, "Then you'll spare my father?"

"Spare your father?" Voice dripping contempt, Stanik straightened. "Hardly. Your father is a traitor to the Autarch. Your father will die at dawn tomorrow. You will watch. You will wear the iron Mask. There is nothing you can do to stop it. And once it is done, you will think about what it will mean to see your mother similarly executed, and you will tell me everything—everything— you have held back from me thus far. Or your mother, too, will die." The hand lashed out again, snapping Mara's head around, driving her back into the bed. Fresh blood flooded her mouth. Weeping, she stared up at the Mask of the man who had just destroyed her world. "And after you have watched her die, then you, too, will hang outside Traitors' Gate!" He spun and went out. The door closed and locked behind him, and Mara curled into a ball in her bed and bawled like a baby, tears, snot, and blood staining the fine linen of her pillow.

FIFTEEN

Traitors' Gate

TRAPPED IN HER ROOM, Masked so she could not use magic, left alone without food, with nothing to drink but the water from the taps in the bath, Mara thought she might go mad. She pounded on the door of her room, begging the Watcher she knew must be stationed outside to bring Stanik to her, or Shelra, anyone she could talk to, anyone she could beg for clemency for her father, for her mother, for herself. Inside, she felt like acid was eating away at her soul, as though a pit of darkness were swallowing her whole. She could see no hope, no light. She contemplated trying to drown herself in the bath, but even that would not save her father: it would only mean she would not have to face his death, and that he might well suffer the anguish of knowing she was dead before he joined her. She could not do that to him.

But how could she watch him die? How could she bear that? How could she emerge from the other side of something that unthinkable, that horrific, and remain herself?

She didn't know: but as the day wore down to darkness, and the darkness wore away into gray twilight, and no one came, no one offered her hope, no one offered her succor, and even the sleep that might have given her some relief from the horror of her own thoughts stayed away, it seemed more and more certain that she would find out.

And then it was morning, graying toward dawn.

In a small measure of defiance, she dressed in her old clothes, the ones she had worn on the journey from the Secret City, washed and mended and returned to her many days before. Just as she hung the cloak about her shoulders a Watcher, without knocking, opened the door to her room. She had both hoped and feared it might be Mayson, but it was not. There was a second Watcher in the hallway outside. Both towered over her, head and shoulders and more. They escorted her, one to each side, across the courtyard, down the corridor she had traversed upon first entering the Palace, across the Great Courtyard. Once more she was taken through the Watchers' common room, as empty this time as last. Once more she was taken out onto the barren plateau where the gallows stood like dark, naked trees.

No bodies hung there. All twelve of the gallows stood stark and bare, silhouetted against the graying sky.

There was a kind of stage off to one side, a wooden platform raised several feet above the black rock of Fortress Hill. The Watchers took her to it, guided her up its steps, then turned her to face the gallows. And then they waited.

There was a murmur of voices, down the hill toward the town. Mara turned her head, and saw a crowd of Masked, and a few furtive children, gathering just outside the iron fence that surrounded the gallows. Among the unMasked children she saw a familiar face, pale and drawn: Keltan.

Her cheeks flamed with shame as she remembered what she had done, how she had betrayed the unMasked Army to save her father. She looked away, afraid to meet his eyes.

More people emerged from the door next to Traitors' Gate that led to the Watchers' guardhouse. All were Masked, save one: Chell. To her surprise, he accompanied his escorts to the platform, and climbed up beside her. She stole a glance at him that was not returned. His face, too, looked pale and drawn, but perhaps that was just the early morning light.

She could not imagine her own looked any better.

For what seemed an eternity, they all stood there, silent in the chill air, breath forming clouds of steam around their heads, the official witnesses on the stand, the ordinary citizens forced to the perimeter. Mara shivered. She felt drained, as though every bit of emotion, every thought, had been sucked out of her the same way she had sucked magic from the Watchers at the mining camp, the same way the Autarch sucked magic from everyone. She thought she would never feel again.

She was wrong, as she discovered the moment Traitors' Gate opened, for that was when she saw her father.

He wore only a white loincloth, and he was unMasked. His back was marked with long red welts, and he carried his right hand cradled to his chest. The fingers looked misshapen, and Mara realized with horror that they had been broken.

His eyes flicked around the crowd, and finally found Mara's.

For a long moment, they stared at each other across the stone plateau. Mara couldn't breathe. It seemed everything else had disappeared, that she looked down a long dark tunnel at her father's face, the face she had never before seen unMasked outside their home, the face she loved more than anything else, the face that had been the center of her world, the face whose cheek she had kissed, the face which had kissed her cheek or forehead every night of her childhood as she snuggled into her bed, the bed that had once seemed to have a magical ability to keep at bay everything bad in the world. No monsters could hurt her in her bed, after she had been tucked in by her father. No evil could touch her. No sadness could seep into her dreams.

She longed for that time with all her heart, for here and now, there *were* monsters, there *was* evil ... and there was sadness, so much sadness, so much bitterness and guilt and horror that she thought her heart would break in her chest and she would fall dead on the spot, and it seemed to her that would be a good thing.

But her heart kept on beating. Her father's gaze was torn from hers as he was urged forward again.

The Watchers accompanying him made him climb the gallows. One of them reached out and ripped the loincloth from him. Mara's eyes filled with tears at this final humiliation, but she did not look away from his nakedness; could not look away from what might be the last sight she ever had of her father.

A Watcher fitted the noose around her father's neck. And then Guardian Stanik climbed the gallows to stand beside him. He faced the crowd, and his voice rang out over their heads, a voice that Mara hated as she had never hated anything before.

"Witness," cried Stanik, "the penalty for betrayal of the Autarch. Witness, and learn: however great you may think yourself, however high you may rise in the ranks of the fortunate within Tamita, the Autarch's justice is terrible, and implacable, and even-handed. For this man before you, stripped of his Mask, stripped of his dignity, stripped of his wealth and power, is Charlton Holdfast, Master Mask-maker of Aygrima. He betrayed his duty, his oath, and his Autarch. And now he pays the price."

Stanik turned. The Watcher standing on the gallows next to her father stepped aside, and Stanik took his place. He reached out and took hold of the wooden lever at the gallows' side.

He pulled it.

The trapdoor opened, and Mara's father dropped like a stone into the space beneath the gallows. The sharp report of his neck breaking echoed off the stone walls of the Palace.

Mara opened her mouth to scream, but no sound came out; it felt like an iron vise had clamped around her chest, squeezing the breath out of her, squeezing everything out of her, her vision darkening until she seemed to view the horror before her through a red-lined tunnel.

And then magic came roaring down that tunnel toward her, a tidal wave of magic, the magic released by her father's death. It slammed into her with the force of an avalanche.

The iron half-Mask could not withstand such magic, pouring out of the man who had made it. It split down the middle with a sound like a struck gong, and fell away from Mara's face, clattering to the planks of the platform on which she stood.

Mara's Gift opened. Power from her father filled her, and there was more power crowded all around her, and this time she did not turn away from it. She reached out and ripped magic from the Watchers all around her, as though she were tearing meat from a bone. The magic seared through her body like living flame, but she welcomed the pain, welcomed the way agony blotted out everything but her fury and grief. The Watchers dropped where they stood, falling from the platform all around her, their bodies striking the stones below with cracking thuds and splatters of blood.

But this time was different than the last time, in the mining camp. Thanks to Shelra's training, this time Mara had more control. This time she could *choose* whose magic she would take, and whose she would leave untapped. Chell, standing beside her, remained untouched. The ordinary citizens watching from the perimeter remained standing, though they were beginning to turn and run as they realized that something very strange was happening.

And Stanik—Stanik still stood by the rope that twitched with the death spasms of her father's body. Mara focused her power to a point and hurled it like a spear. It struck him full in the face. His Mask cracked and crumbled away, revealing wide eyes in a pale, angled face. His mouth opened, but whatever he intended to say or scream, whether he intended to hurl curses or beg for mercy, remained unheard, as his head tore from his body, flew across the courtyard, and smashed in a spray of red, white, and gray against the Palace wall.

Spurting blood from its severed neck, the body fell. Stanik's magic slammed into her almost as hard as her father's had. She had too much magic in her now, too much to bear; she had to rid herself of it—

—and so she did. She focused it again, and hurled it away from her over the heads of the fleeing crowd, down Fortress Hill. Chimneys shattered into dust and rooftops exploded into flinders and burst into flames as the mere fringe of that power brushed them. Dust and smoke rose in tortured whirlwinds of gray . . .

. . . and then the magic struck the city wall.

Twenty feet thick at its base, fifty feet high, made of massive yellow blocks fitted together without mortar by the greatest Gifted engineers of Aygrima more than four centuries before, the wall of Tamita had never been breached since its construction, never been damaged by storm, earthquake, or fire. But Mara's magic tore through it as though it were no more than a mud dam constructed by a child playing in a ditch. Blocks of stone the size of wagons sprayed out from the breach, slamming into the ground a hundred yards away, smashing trees to kindling, scraping long scars in the earth before burying themselves in the dirt. An enormous cloud of pulverized rock rose into the air, mingling with the smoke and dust from the damaged buildings to cloud the scene in a gray miasma.

The fire in Mara's veins receded, leaving her cold and weak. She teetered, the whole world spinning around her, and would have toppled from the platform herself if Chell, the only one close at hand whom she had left untouched, had not suddenly grabbed her arm. She clung to him. "I . . . opened a path," she said. "We have to go . . . find Keltan . . ."

"He's coming this way," Chell said. He sounded awed. "Let's get off this platform."

With his help, she descended to the courtyard. Keltan, dashing toward them, skidded to a stop. He stared at her, wide-eyed and white-faced. "If I hadn't seen it—"

"We have to get out of the city," Mara said faintly. "Now. In the confusion. Horses . . ."

"Right," Keltan said. He took a deep breath. "Right. This way."

Keltan led them down to where the crowd had been waiting. Half a dozen Watchers lay unconscious on the ground; near them, lathered, snorting, eyes wide and white, pulling on their reins, stood their tethered horses. Keltan and Chell went to them, soothed them. Mara, swaying, stared down at one of the fallen Watchers. Blood pooled beneath his head; he had struck it on a rock when he fell. But he still breathed. *So I didn't kill all of them*, Mara thought. And then, unbidden, the image of her father falling through the trapdoor of the gallows rose up in her, and her fury almost choked her again. She felt magic nearby, in one of the buildings, the workshop of some Gifted artisan. She reached out for it, and it leaped to her, a flash of multicolored light streaking right through the wall behind the horses, past the oblivious Chell and Keltan. It covered her hand. She drew on the red, so that it appeared to her she'd dipped her hand in blood. She reached out toward the Watcher—

—and then jerked her hand back, horrified. *No!* She couldn't kill him in cold blood, with magic. Her father wouldn't want that. He wouldn't want his daughter to become a killer. He wouldn't . . .

Her rage gave way to horrible grief. She turned the magic to blue, the color of Healing, and let it flow into the Watcher's head. The bleeding stopped and his ragged, uneven breathing steadied, though he did not wake.

"Mara!" Keltan shouted. "Mount up!"

Mara jerked her head around and saw Chell and Keltan already astride two of the Watchers' horses, Keltan holding the reins of a third. She staggered over to it and, on the second attempt, managed to heave herself up into the saddle. She gathered the reins.

Black-clad Watchers suddenly boiled out from Traitors' Gate like termites from an overturned log. "Time to go!" Chell shouted. He clapped his heels to his horse's flanks, and galloped down Fortress Hill toward the wreckage of the wall, Keltan and Mara in his wake.

The streets were deserted, everyone having apparently reacted to the destruction by running away from it, probably not only to avoid collapsing buildings but also to avoid being anywhere nearby when the Watchers arrived. Mara, Chell, and Keltan rode through a choking cloud of dust and smoke, buildings looming out of it, dark and shrouded, and vanishing behind them again. Then they were at the base of Fortress Hill and clattering across the Great Circle Road. Mara, though she had directed the magic that had done it, gaped in amazement at the enormous breach in the city wall, fifty feet wide, the stones set in the earth sheared as cleanly off above as though they were slabs of butter carved by a knife. They galloped through that breach, past the scattered slabs of rock hurled far and wide by the force of the blast, and across the fields beyond. They ran down into a shallow, wooded valley, out of sight of the walls. There they halted. "We must get to Edrik," Keltan panted. "We can flee back to the Secret City . . ."

"No!" The word exploded from Mara, as in one horrifying instant she remembered the other terrible thing that had happened, the other terrible thing that she had done. "It's not safe anymore. Stanik . . . knows—knew— where it is."

"What?" Keltan whirled toward Chell. "Did you betray us?"

"I did not," Chell said coldly.

"*I* betrayed you!" Mara cried. "*I* did!" Tears welled up in her eyes, flooded down her cheeks. "I was trying to save my father," she choked out.

Keltan gaped at her. "*You* told him where the Secret City is?"

"No!" she said. "No. But I . . . I told him about the un-Masked Army. And I . . . I gave him Catilla's name. And Stanik . . . that was enough for him. He knew about the old caves. He knew Catilla's father had known about them."

"But Stanik is dead," Keltan said. "You killed him. Maybe he didn't tell anyone—"

"I would not risk *my* people's safety on such a slim 'maybe,'" Chell said grimly.

Keltan swallowed. He stared at Mara, and his face held so much shock and betrayal that she could not suppress a strangled sob. "Keltan, I'm—" she began.

"Save it," he snapped, and now his white face turned red as anger overpowered every other emotion he might have been feeling. "Tell it to Catilla." He turned to Chell. "All the more reason for us to find Edrik. We have to warn—"

"*You* have to warn him, you mean," Chell said, his own voice still cold. "My duty lies elsewhere." He glanced at Mara. "I have to get to my ships," he said. "Come with me."

"What?" Keltan spun toward Mara again. "Mara, don't be a fool, you can't trust him—"

But Mara hardly heard him. She was imagining returning to the Secret City, to the place that had become her second home, telling Catilla, telling them all, that she had betrayed them, that she had told the Watchers where to find them, that their sanctuary from the Autarch's tyranny had been snatched away from them through her actions, and on top of every other horror unleashed that day, she knew she couldn't do it. She didn't have the strength.

"I'm going with Chell," she said. "I can't go to back to the Secret City. I *can't*."

Chell nodded once. "Then it is decided." He glanced back up at the valley's rim. "The Watchers will be delayed by confusion and uncertainty . . . but not forever. There were witnesses. They will come after us. We must ride."

Keltan stared at Mara for another long moment, as if he had never seen her before; then he wheeled his horse almost savagely and dug his heels into its flanks. He galloped away to the north, vanishing up and over the top of the valley's far slope.

Mara gasped; she'd been holding her breath without realizing it. Tears blurred her vision again and she swiped her sleeve across her face. "Are you recovered enough to ride?" Chell asked her.

Recovered? Mara felt a bubble of hysterical laughter rising in her throat, and choked it down; if once she started laughing, she feared she would never stop. But . . . recovered? The idea was ludicrous. She'd seen her father stripped and hanged. She had absorbed his dying magic, torn magic from the Watchers, killed Stanik and absorbed *his* magic, used all of it to smash the city wall. Her mother had fled to a distant southern village and soon enough would hear of her husband's death, and could face the same punishment herself, and there was nothing Mara could do to help her. She had betrayed the un-Masked Army, which had rescued her from the horrors of the mining camp, and all the friends she had made in the Secret City; and she had once more used the power that could eventually drive her into madness and evil. When next she slept, the ghosts of her father and Stanik and who knew how many others awaited her. Though the morning sun shone bright all around them, Mara felt like she was back in the mine, trapped in a chamber deep underground, all exits blocked by fallen stone, air running out, no life, no light, no hope.

Recovered? She would never recover, not if she lived to be a hundred.

All that swirled through her mind like the muddy water of an unleashed torrent, but all she said out loud was, "Yes."

"Then let's ride." Chell turned his horse so that the rising sun cast its shadow long and black directly in front of him. "West ... to the sea." He clapped heels to the horse's flanks and rode away up the valley, and Mara, setting her jaw and gripping her reins, galloped after him.

SIXTEEN

Flight to the Sea

THEY BURST UP OUT OF THE VALLEY onto open ground, pounding across wheat fields covered with yellow stubble. There seemed little need for stealth, since the Watchers would soon find their trail. Their only hope lay in speed, in staying ahead of pursuit all the way to the distant coast.

Mara had never been west of Tamita, and had only the vaguest notion of the terrain between the city and the sea, knew only that it was supposed to be two days' ride. As a guide she was next to useless, and she knew it; she feared she'd soon be worse than useless, as the impact of everything that had happened in the city made itself felt. She knew that nightmares lurked at the edges of her consciousness, knew they would claim her for certain the moment she slept. And so she resolved not to sleep for as long as she could, but that held its own risks: on the ride from the mining camp to the Secret City, the nightmares had found their way from her unconscious to her conscious mind, manifesting in hallucinations.

At least the first part of their ride was in bright sunshine . . . not that it kept the horrors of the morning from gibbering in the shadows of her brain.

Mara had become a competent rider if not a great one over her weeks with the unMasked Army, or she would never have been able to keep up with Chell, who seemed born to the saddle . . . probably to be expected for a prince, she thought. They could not gallop the whole way, of course; once they had crossed into a shallow valley that hid the walls of the city behind them, they slowed to a walk to give the horses a chance to recover, then proceeded at a steady trot, occasionally alternating with a canter in more open terrain. They passed farmyards and villages, but kept a wide berth, and the day wore on without a sign of pursuit behind or ambush ahead. "Maybe they don't realize we escaped," Mara said to Chell about noon, as they stopped for a few minutes to give the horses a chance to drink and graze, and their own sore muscles a chance to relax.

"They'll figure it out soon enough," Chell said. He looked back along their trail, and frowned. "They may be closer than we think. Look!" He pointed toward a band of trees on the far side of the shallow valley they had just crossed. They had passed through those woods a half hour before. Squinting at them, Mara saw what he had seen: flocks of birds wheeling above the trees. "Something disturbed them," Chell said grimly. "Might be wild animals, or farmers, or hunters. Or . . ."

"Watchers," Mara said. She turned tiredly back toward her horse. "Let's keep moving."

They mounted the horses, who were none too happy about it, and pressed on.

The afternoon ground by. They passed through more low valleys, separated by ridges, each a little lower than the one before, until finally they topped one and, as the sun sank before them, saw at the limit of their vision a bright line of reflected fire.

"The sea," Chell said. He glanced at Mara. "Can you keep riding? If we carry on through the night, we might be there by morning."

"I can keep riding," she said stoutly, though she wasn't nearly as sure about that as she tried to sound. "But what about the horses?"

Chell glanced back. They'd seen nothing else to indicate pursuit since the disturbed birds above the trees, but they'd never since had that clear a view of their back trail. "We'll give them an hour, next time we cross water," he said. There was a growling noise that for a moment made Mara think there must be an animal in the trees, but Chell grimaced and put a hand to his stomach. "I wish *we* could graze," he said. "And I wish I'd eaten breakfast." He clucked to his horse and they trotted on.

They stopped on the shore of a shallow, swift-flowing creek not twenty minutes later. The horses stopped to drink. Mara stretched out in a patch of grass, staring up at the star-studded sky and listening to the rush of water over stones. She only wanted to rest, certainly didn't intend to sleep . . . but her body had other ideas.

In the darkness behind her eyelids, the nightmares waited.

There were old "friends" there: Grute, the boy who had tried to rape her, the first person she had killed with magic. There were Watchers she had slain at the mining camp and at the new magic lode in the mountains that she had found with the geologists sent out by the Autarch. There was the

Watcher who had died in the woods as she, Chell, Edrik, and Keltan made their way to Tamita. But they were pale shades compared to the new nightmares.

Her father . . . and Stanik.

Her father appeared before her naked, head at a grotesque angle, eyes bulging, tongue protruding. "You killed me," he groaned, his voice a choked travesty of the voice she had loved all her life. "You killed me. Your own father . . ."

Stanik came before her carrying his mangled head, face half ripped away, blood dripping from the severed neck. Impossibly, a voice came from the shattered skull and broken, jagged teeth. "You little *bitch*," he snarled. "How *dare* you. How dare you stand against the Autarch. Against the Circle. Against me!"

Closer and closer they came. She tried to back away, but couldn't; her feet were rooted to the spot, her back against a tall black cliff. They reached out their arms to touch her and she screamed and screamed and . . .

. . . woke, jerking upright, but the nightmare continued: for bursting out of the woods bordering the stream came a dozen Watchers, swords drawn, horses thundering down toward her and Chell, stretched out on the ground not far away and as fast asleep as she had been.

There was no time to wake him, no time to do anything but the one thing she knew she should not do, and yet the one thing she longed to do with all of her being: she reached out to all those onrushing men and, screaming in mingled pain and ecstasy, ripped the magic out of them, and flung it, burning as it poured through her body, into the ground in front of them.

The earth turned soft and yielding, writhing and twisting like rotting meat seething with maggots. The horses, their screams echoing hers, sank into the ground, forelimbs cracking like dry twigs. The horses' riders, already unconscious in the saddles, already sliding away, were flung down as well. Necks and arms and legs snapped on impact . . .

. . . and then the ground solidified again, and there was no sign there had been any Watchers or horses there at all, except for one steed's still-protruding head. Eyes wide and white with terror bulged. There was a sighing rush of wind as all the air was forced from the beast's lungs; the head twitched once, madly, swollen tongue protruding from the gaping mouth . . .

. . . and then the wide, white eyes turned red and popped from the skull in twin squirts of blood, and the head was still.

Mara turned her head and threw up into the grass. And then she screamed, as to her it appeared the ground where she had vomited suddenly boiled again, and a man's face exploded out of it, eyes bulging and red, mouth screaming, blood pouring from ears and mouth. She scrambled back on her hands and knees and the entire field before her appeared to erupt with the men and horses she had just killed. Limbs broken, ribs shattered, blood pouring from terrible wounds, they came toward her, crawling, moaning, snorting, snarling, on and on and on. No matter how much she screamed, and screamed, and screamed again, still they came on, and with them were Grute, Stanik . . . and worst of all, her father.

Someone grabbed her and she struck out blindly, felt her hand meet flesh, her foot sink into softness. She heard a grunt, and a curse, and then something hit her head with terrible force, and she collapsed into blessed, untroubled darkness.

• • •

Consciousness returned piecemeal: a sound in the silence, a rocking motion, a cool breeze across closed eyelids.

Warm flesh covered in smooth hair flexed beneath her cheek. Her head hurt, throbbing in time with her heart, sharper pains sometimes stabbing as the rocking motion moved her body. For a long time Mara was half-awake but kept her eyes closed, afraid that if she opened them she would once again see the people she had killed crawling out of the earth-turned-mass-grave she had somehow created through magic. But then she started to slip into that nightmare with her eyes closed, and that drove her fully awake, gasping.

She found herself slung across the saddle of a horse, her head dangling against its left shoulder, her legs hanging down the other side. Only the moon provided illumination, but its silvery light was enough to show her a brown leather boot and a black-trousered leg, beyond that the rear end of the horse, and beyond that a second horse at the end of a long lead. They seemed, from what she could see in the uncertain light, to be riding through a second-growth forest: stumps from massive, long-since-logged old trees interspersed with the much more slender trunks of living ones.

"What's going on?" she tried to say, but her throat was so dry it came out as a nearly unintelligible croak.

"Mara?" said Chell's questioning voice from somewhere above her. "Are you awake?"

"I think so," she grated, her voice a little stronger now. "Unless this is still a nightmare."

"It's real." Chell reined the horse to a halt. "Let me get you down." His boot disappeared as he slid from the saddle. A moment later she felt his hands on her waist, and she was sliding down as well, though if he had not immediately wrapped his arms around her she would have fallen. Her legs felt as limp as overcooked noodles and the pain continued to pound away at her head.

Chell helped her to sit on the pine needle-covered

ground, her back to a tree. He knelt beside her and gingerly touched the side of her head. "Ow!" she yelped as his fingers found a sensitive spot. "What hit me?" She raised her own hand, and discovered a sizable lump.

Chell sat back. "I'm afraid I did," he said.

She blinked at him. "What?"

"You were . . . not yourself," Chell said. There was something odd about his tone. He sounded almost . . .

Afraid? Mara thought. *Afraid of* me?

And then she remembered what had come just before his blow to her head had knocked her unconscious, and knew she couldn't blame him. "I . . . all those people . . ." She shuddered, and looked fearfully around her. "They were . . . coming back. Out of the ground. Or did . . . did I imagine what I did to them, too?" she said, with a sudden surge of hope. "Was that a hallucination?"

"No," said Chell flatly. "No. We both dozed off. The Watchers must have been closer behind us than we thought. They came on us out of the woods. And you . . ." He shook his head. "I've never seen anything like it. Never even *imagined* anything like it. The ground . . . ate them. Swallowed them up, as though they had never been."

Mara swallowed hard to keep from throwing up again. "I didn't . . . I didn't know I could do that. I didn't know *magic* could do that."

"Neither did I." The prince stared at her. "Mara, *what are you?*"

She shook her head miserably. "A freak," she muttered. "A monster."

He regarded her a long moment. "No," he said at last. "I don't believe that."

"You saw what I did."

"I saw what you did," he agreed. "I saw you save both our lives. And back in Tamita, I saw you aid our escape and punish the man who killed your father . . . but I also saw you *not* kill all the Watchers or the people gathered as witnesses, and even heal one you had injured. You had the power then, and the rage, to murder indiscriminately . . . and you didn't." He reached out to her again, and she flinched, but he didn't touch the bump on her head. Instead, he tenderly smoothed the hair back from her forehead. "Mara, you're not a monster. But you're powerful. So powerful, you could rule this land if you wished."

"I don't want to rule this land," she said plaintively. "I'm only fifteen years old." Tears started in her eyes. "I just want to go home. That's all I ever wanted. And now I never, ever can. Home isn't there. My father . . . my father is dead." She could feel the grief clawing up from inside her, like a caged animal trying to escape. "And the Secret City . . . I've betrayed it, too . . ."

"Then perhaps you need a new home," Prince Chell said softly. "Mara, Aygrima is not all the world. It's not even most of it. There are other lands, other kingdoms, oceans and islands, strange shores that have never been explored, lost cities from before the Great Plague . . . so many other places to be than here in Aygrima. Including my own country of Korellia. My father would welcome you there. *I* would welcome you there."

Mara stared at him, wide-eyed. "It sounds . . . wonderful."

"It *is* wonderful," Chell said. He clasped her hands in his. "And I can take you."

For a moment all she could see were his eyes, dark glimmering pools in his moonlit face . . . but then she remembered what he had told her in Tamita, remembered *why* he wanted her to come with him to Korellia, and she snatched her hand away. "You don't want me," she said bitterly. "You just want my power. You want to use me as a weapon. You want me to kill for you."

Chell did not look ashamed. "Of course I want you to use your power for Korellia," he said. "That's why I came, in hope of finding the fabled wizards of Aygrima and convincing them to wield their magic on our behalf against Stonefell. But whether you agree to that or not, I can take you to Korellia. Once you see what my kingdom is like, how much freer and happier my people are than those trapped in the Masks of the Autarch or terrified into submission by the Tyrant of Stonefell, I am confident you will want to help us. But I will take you whether you agree to help us or not. I owe you my life twice over: first on the beach, then again when the Watchers attacked. I hope you will use your power to aid my people. But I offer you safe haven whether you do or not."

Mara closed her eyes. Stanik's ruined face began to coalesce out of the darkness behind her lids, and she jerked them open again. "I could be a danger," she choked out. "This power . . . I don't know if I can control it. You shouldn't risk it. You shouldn't take me back with you, no matter how tempted you are by what you've seen me do already."

"I am a Prince of the Realm of Korellia," Chell said simply. "The risk is mine to take, if I judge it acceptable. And I do." He got to his feet. "You don't have to commit to anything right now. The whole question becomes moot if the Watchers catch us."

Mara shuddered. "I can't use my magic to kill again. I *can't*." But even as she said it, she knew she *could* . . . and that was what really terrified her.

"All the more reason for us to get moving again," Chell said. He held out his hand. "Can you stand?"

Mara let him pull her to her feet. She staggered, and his hand tightened, but then she straightened. "I'm all right," she said. Pain lanced her head, and she winced.

"Except for my head. Did you have to hit me so hard? You could have killed me!"

"Look who's talking," Chell said dryly. "You didn't know who I was. What if you'd decided I was a Watcher?"

Mara grimaced. "I see your point."

With Chell's help, she mounted her own horse again, and gripped the reins tightly. He stood by her left leg, watching her anxiously. "Will you be able to stay on?"

"I . . . think so," she said, a little faintly. "For a while. But I hope we don't have much farther to ride."

"I think," Chell said, "that we should reach the coastline in about two hours. It will still be dark. If we can find a boat . . . we could be out to sea by daylight."

Mara nodded, and wished she hadn't. "I can manage that long. I think."

Chell put his hand on her knee. "Call out if you think you might fall. I'll catch you."

She flashed him a quick smile. He took his hand away.

She rather wished he hadn't.

They rode on. Every hoof fall of the horse jabbed her skull like a hot skewer, but she held on grimly to both her reins and her consciousness, and still had a firm grip on both when, rather sooner than Chell had guessed, they emerged from the trees onto a rocky shoreline and she found herself looking out at the western ocean, waves rolling ashore in long breakers silvered by the setting moon.

Off to their right, where the coast curved out toward the sea, a cluster of lights glimmered. "A village," Chell said. "And any village on the coast will have boats." He slid from the saddle. "I think we walk from here." He began undoing the horse's saddle and the rest of its tack. "We'll set the horses free."

Mara nodded and slid out of her own saddle. She had to lean against the horse's warm bulk for a moment before she had strength to begin unbuckling the saddle.

A few minutes later Chell clapped his hand to the rump of each horse, and the animals galloped away into the darkness, up the coast in the opposite direction from the cluster of buildings. Chell dragged the tack into the cover of the trees, then came back to where Mara had taken the opportunity to sit on the ground, knees pulled up and head resting on them. He sat beside her. "One more push," he said softly. "We walk to the village, find a boat, head out to sea." He paused. "Find a boat, find *provisions*, head out to sea," he amended. "I don't know about you, but I'm a mite . . . peckish."

Mara's stomach growled at the thought of food. Chell laughed. "I'll take that as concurrence. Anyway, once we're out at sea, we're safe from Watchers." He shook his head. "I still don't understand how you can have a kingdom this size with no navy. But so I was told in the Palace."

Safe from Watchers, Mara thought. *But it's not Watchers I'm worried about.* As fatigue wrapped itself around her like a thick, suffocating blanket, she sensed within it all the nightmares she had created for herself with her magic. She couldn't stay awake forever. And when she slept again . . .

She shuddered, and heaved herself to her feet. "Then let's go," she said. "Let's go find food and a boat."

Chell scrambled up beside her. "Lean on me," he said. She nodded and clung to his arm, and together they walked slowly over the wet, rounded stones toward the lights of the sleeping village.

SEVENTEEN

Waves

THE VILLAGE WAS FARTHER AWAY than it appeared, and by the time they reached it, Mara had little strength left. The community consisted of no more than twenty buildings strung out along a single street bordered on one side by a seawall. They stayed on the beach, ducking behind the wall the moment they reached it. The moon, almost set now, cast a long, shimmering trail of light across the restless waves, silhouetting a half-dozen fishing boats drawn up on the shingle.

"Wait here," Chell murmured, and Mara gratefully sat down, hardly noticing the pebbles digging into her skin, and leaned her back against the wall as the prince went through a gate into the village. She waited, wondering uneasily what she would do if someone sounded the alarm . . . but the village, it seemed, slept soundly.

Chell returned within minutes. "Luck," he said, dropping a bag at her side. "Found a smokehouse. Hope you like fish."

Mara's mouth watered. "I love fish," she said. Actually she'd never cared for it very much, but right now it sounded wonderful.

"Now for a boat." The prince left her there, and crept down to the water's edge to examine the craft. He took his time about it, though to Mara's eyes they were all as alike as petals on a starblossom. He climbed into one after the other. She heard soft splashes as he threw something overboard from each boat except the first one, then busied himself around the masts. She took advantage of the delay to marshal what little strength she still possessed . . . and to look this way and that along the dark shore, fearful that her nightmares would once again find their way out of the realm of her dreams and into her waking world.

But the beach remained deserted except for Chell, who finally returned, running, crouched over, up the beach. He took a quick peek over the top of the wall, then plopped onto the rocks beside her. "I've chosen our vessel," he panted. "But I'll need your help pushing her out into the water. Are you up to it?"

"I guess I have to be, don't I?" Mara said. "Let's go."

Chell nodded. He got up, picked up the bag of smoked fish with one hand, and held out the other. She took it, and he pulled her to her feet. Her fingers warm in his clasp, he led her across the rocks to the nearest of the boats, a sailing vessel perhaps twenty feet long. Nets were hung to dry on a rack between that boat and the next, glass floats glistening in the last of the moonlight. Inside the boat, the sail was neatly stowed, wrapped around the boom and yard and tied with twine. There were also two long oars, hung on hooks along both gunwales. Chell let go of Mara's hand and gripped the prow. "Push," he said.

Mara nodded and took hold of the smooth varnished wood. Together they shoved at the boat, which for a moment felt as immovable as a rock of the same size, but then began to slide.

And then came a shout from behind them.

Mara shot a startled glance over her shoulder, and saw a dark figure standing atop the seawall. "Thieves! Thieves! Boat thieves!"

A moment's silence, then more shouts rang out. Doors banged open. Lights appeared.

"Push harder!" Chell shouted. "Hard as you can!"

Gasping, Mara put her back into it. The boat moved faster, grinding across the stones. The stern was afloat, then the amidships. Cold water soaked her feet. "Get in!" Chell shouted, and tumbled into the bow. Mara clambered awkwardly after him. "Grab an oar!"

Mara crawled on her hands and knees to the amidships thwart, and pulled an oar from the gunwale hooks. Following Chell's example, she shoved the blade hard against the bottom. The boat slipped farther away from the shore, and just in time: the villagers had reached the water's edge and were screaming at them, Masks glittering in the moonlight. One man to whom the boat must have belonged waded in after them, cursing, while others started pushing their own boats out to sea. "They'll be after us in a minute," Mara panted.

"They won't catch us," Chell said.

"How can you be so sure?"

"Because I threw their oars overboard and cut their stays once I decided this was the boat we wanted," he said, and sure enough, confusion reigned on the beach behind them. Chell turned his head and looked up at the mast, and Mara, following his gaze, saw a strip of cloth fluttering in the wind. "She'll sail," he said. "Ship oars."

Mara pulled her dripping oar aboard and slipped it back into its hooks. Chell did the same, then scrambled forward. "What should I do?" Mara said, as he busied himself at the mast.

"Stay out of the way," he said curtly, and so she sat and watched (and at one point ducked) as he hauled up the sail. It shook uselessly in the wind until he scrambled into the stern, picked up a rope attached to the end of the boom, and pulled it toward him. The sail swung out to starboard and stiffened, and they began to move, away from the beach and the cursing villagers, still struggling with their crippled boats.

Far out at sea, the moon sank behind the horizon, and darkness swallowed them up. For a long time Mara could still see the lights of the village, tiny flickers of yellow along the shore, but then they rounded the spit of land to the village's north, and there was nothing but darkness.

"You should rest," Chell said, a disembodied voice from the stern. "Lie down on the floorboards."

Mara leaned down and felt the bottom of the boat. "There's water down there," she said in alarm. "Are we sinking?"

"It's just from the oars," Chell said. "I checked her over carefully. She's a good stout craft. Take us anywhere." He sounded different than he had on land; happier, somehow. *He called Korellia a sea kingdom*, she thought. *He's a sailor, the prince of a kingdom of sailors. What must Korellia be like? What are these ships of his like?*

She'd never seen anything larger than the fishing boat they were on now; had never seen a boat at all until she'd reached the Secret City. Aygrima, as Chell had discovered to his astonishment, had no navy. Yet Chell spoke of his ships having dozens of men aboard. How large would such a vessel have to be? How could something that big float?

She hoped she'd get to see for herself. Floating out there on the dark waters, cut off from Aygrima, safe from any pursuit by the Watchers, she suddenly longed to see his island kingdom, its giant ships exploring all the world, everyone unMasked, free of Watchers, free of fear . . . free of magic.

Better for everyone in Aygrima if I never return there, she thought. *Better for the unMasked Army . . .*

. . . if they survive.

And with that thought, she knew that she wasn't done with Aygrima: not yet. She had betrayed the Secret City. Keltan and Edrik would be riding to warn them, but with Watchers hard on their trail, they could be hard-pressed to make it in time . . . hard-pressed to make it all.

"These ships of yours," Mara said. "They're north of the Secret City?"

"Yes," Chell said.

"Then we have to sail right past the City?"

A pause. "Yes."

Mara pressed on. "We're faster than horses in this boat, aren't we?"

Another pause. "Maybe."

"Then we have to sail to the Secret City," she said in a low voice. "We have to warn them in case Edrik and Keltan are delayed."

Another long silence. "Mara, you told Keltan you couldn't face going there."

Her face flushed with shame at the thought. "I know what I said," she said. "But I was wrong."

"Mara—"

"We have to, Chell! I betrayed them. If they are attacked, without warning . . . it will be because of me. And I couldn't live with that." *Add it to the list of things I may not be able to live with*, she thought. "Before . . . I didn't think I could face them. But now . . . now I don't think I can *not* face them."

She waited in the dark for Chell's answer. "All right," he said at last. "We'll try. But I said we *may* be faster than horses. There's no guarantee. I don't know these waters. I've sailed far enough out to sea we should be clear of any shoals and out of sight of any Watchers along the shore at sunup, but we'll have to sail closer to shore to pick our way along the coast. And if we want to be sure of finding the Secret City, we'll have to travel only by day. We may get there to find they have already been warned of what you call your betrayal." His voice dropped. "And how will they welcome you once they know of it?"

Mara had no answer, and so she made none. "As long as we do our best," she said. And then she crawled forward, feeling the floorboards as she went. In the bow, they seemed drier, and so it was there that she curled up, wrapped in a spare bit of sail she found in a locker, closed her eyes, and let sleep claim her, her exhaustion carrying her into it even though she feared what might be waiting there.

• • •

When she woke, gray, fog-shrouded water surrounded them. She sat up, and winced. The floorboards hadn't gotten any softer while she slept, and her head still ached a little. Flexing her shoulder to work out a kink, she stared out at the sea. The sail was now swung out to port. She craned her head to look around the mast into the stern, where Chell sat at the tiller, wrapped in his cloak. His face looked wan in the pale light. "You've slept for four or five hours," he said. "Hungry?"

"Very," she said. She scrambled back to where the bag of dried fish awaited amidships, opened it and took out a fillet of . . . something; her knowledge of fish extended only as far as "they have scales and live in the water" . . . and bit into it.

It tasted salty and smoky and fishy and wonderful. She ate two more fillets in rapid succession, then glanced up at Chell. "Want some?" she said through a full mouth.

He gave her a quick smile. "Had some. Eat what you want."

After yet another two fillets she'd taken the edge off her hunger and could think of other things . . . like thirst. "Water?" she said hopefully.

"There's a barrel by the mast," Chell said. "But it's almost empty. We can go a long way with only a little food. We can't manage without water. We'll have to put in to shore." He looked around at the fog. "If I can find it."

Mara stared at him. "*If?*"

He shrugged. "No compass. No landmarks. Wind died at dawn, shifted when it came back. Usually you get a land breeze at night, a sea breeze during the day. So I'm assuming with the breeze behind us, we're being pushed toward the shore." He gave her another quick grin. "But I'm really hoping the fog lifts to confirm that." The grin faded. "And then there's the question of rocks . . . once you've eaten and drunk, I need you to go forward and keep a lookout."

Mara nodded and went forward toward the water barrel. A wooden cup dangled from it on a length of rope, swinging back and forth as the boat swayed. She filled the cup from the barrel's brass spigot, sniffed the water, made a face, and drank it anyway. It tasted both terrible and wonderful at the same time, and she would have had a second cup . . . but she got only a dribble out of the spigot the second time, and then only by tilting the barrel. She drank the little bit of liquid that had made it into the cup, then returned the barrel to its upright position and glanced back at Chell again. She'd had food, she'd had water, and now . . .

Feeling terribly embarrassed, she called back to him, "How do I . . . um . . . you know?"

"Over the side," he said. "Hang on to a shroud."

"Shroud?"

"Those ropes holding up the mast on either side. The rope going down to the bow is called the forestay." That quick grin appeared again. "Sorry, I forget not everyone is a sailor." The grin widened. "Oh, and don't worry, I won't look. The sail will pretty much hide you, anyway, if you keep to port."

Mara, feeling her face burning despite the cool sea air, nodded and went around the mast again. It was incredibly awkward, embarrassing, and cold, but she managed to do what her body desperately wanted her to do, and felt much better for it.

It was while she was adjusting her clothes that she suddenly froze.

She had slept for several hours, Chell had said. She'd fallen asleep, and waked in the morning light, and she remembered nothing of the time in between. Which meant . . .

She hadn't had any nightmares. Despite everything that had happened in the past two days, the people she had killed with magic, the death of her father, the enormous magical power that had burned through her twice . . . *she hadn't had any nightmares.*

But . . . why?

Her Gift was still there. She could feel the magic in Chell's body. It wasn't like being blocked by the iron half-Mask. So . . . what?

She could think of only one thing that had made the difference, and it was all around her.

The sea.

"If you wouldn't mind keeping a lookout now . . . ?" Chell called. "Sing out if you see anything. Especially anything pointy and hard."

"All right," Mara called back. She made her way into the prow and crouched there on the floorboards, her erstwhile bed. She rested her head in her arms, folded on the curved timber, and peered forward across perhaps ten yards of gray, tossing water to an ever-receding wall of fog. Could the water really have blocked her nightmares, blunted the edge of the magic that plagued her?

Maybe. Why *did* only Aygrima have magic, after all? Korellia didn't have it. Stonefell had something else, called "cannons," which sounded like a kind of magic but clearly wasn't. From what Chell had said of the days before the Great Plague sundered the trading networks of the world's scattered kingdoms, no one but Aygrima had had magic then, either. Something must have made Aygrima special, and she could think of only one possibility: black lodestone, the mysterious rock mined in the terrible labor camp from which she had—barely— escaped, where unMasked even now labored and died and were abused, the mysterious rock that drew magic to it from living things when they died. Pixot, one of the geologists the Autarch had sent out to the labor camp to find a new source of magic, and whom she had accompanied to a cavern in the mountains filled with it, had told her that black lodestone was unlike any other known stone. In the Palace, Shelra had told her that some speculated it had come from outside the world altogether, crashing down from the sky or pushing its way up from far beneath.

If it really had smashed into Aygrima from . . . somewhere else . . . might it not have . . . splashed, like water in a pond into which a rock was tossed? Perhaps all of

Aygrima had been dusted with bits of black lodestone. Perhaps it had even affected those who lived there. Perhaps that was when the Gift arose, though it was now so long ago that as far as any historian of the Autarchy knew, the Gifted had always existed.

And if any of that were true, then perhaps by leaving Aygrima behind, she had also left behind the magic that infused its very soil and air . . . and *that* had somehow blunted the nightmares.

A lot of ifs. But the thought that, away from Aygrima, she might free herself of some of the horrors she had inflicted on herself through her use of magic, made the accompanying thought that she might sail away from the Autarchy forever in the company of the young man at the tiller suddenly more appealing than ever.

And then she frowned. The water ahead, just appearing through the fog, looked different . . . paler, somehow . . . and the waves were piling up on it in an odd way. Suddenly realizing what she was looking at, she jerked upright to yell a warning, but never got the chance.

With a grinding crunch, the boat ran aground.

The impact flung Mara half out of the boat. She caught herself just in time. The mast groaned, but held, but the sail came down with a run, the boom drooping over the side into the water.

Mara stared left and right. The shallows ran as far as she could see in either direction. She shot a look back at Chell. "I'm sorry!" she gasped. "I tried to yell as soon as I saw it, but . . ."

"We were closer in than I thought," Chell said. "My mistake." He shipped the rudder, then crawled forward and freed the oars. He handed one to Mara. "Let's see if we can push ourselves off."

She nodded, and together they prodded at the bottom. It felt like soft mud studded with small stones. The oars sank into it but gave little purchase. After a few moments Chell hauled his dripping oar back aboard. "No good," he panted. "If the wind changes, I might be able to back us off. Not sure where we are in the tides, either; if it's low tide, we may float off after a bit. But if it's high tide . . ." He shook his head. "Either way, we're stuck for now."

Mara stared out at the fog. "But the Secret City . . ."

"I told you, I don't know these waters!" Chell snapped.

"I'm not blaming you," Mara said. "It's just . . ." She shook her head. "I feel helpless. I put them in danger by my stupidity, and I can't do anything to help them."

Chell opened his mouth, hesitated, then said at last, "What about magic? You blew down the city wall. You made the ground swallow those Watchers and their horses. Why can't you get us off a sandbar?"

She stared at him. Didn't he understand?

No, she thought. *Of course he doesn't. How could he? He's not Gifted. He's not even from Aygrima.*

"I don't have any magic out here," she said. "Magic is carried in special urns of black stone." She gestured at the boat. "You see anything like that?"

"I didn't see anything like that when you blew down the City Wall, either," Chell said stubbornly. "Or when you made the ground swallow our pursuers."

"That magic came from the people around me," Mara said in a low voice. *What difference does it make if he knows the truth now?* "I sucked magic right out of those Watchers and used it to destroy them. And in the city, the magic came from my father when he died, and then from all those Watchers who watched him die. There's nobody out here to get magic from." *Even if I dared.*

Chell cocked his head to one side. "There's me."

"You don't know what you're suggesting," Mara said. "It could kill you." She didn't tell him the other reason:

that every time she used magic in that fashion, she drew one step nearer to madness.

"Has it killed anyone yet?"

"Not that I know of," Mara said. "But I don't know for certain."

"Have you talked to anyone you drew magic from?"

"Keltan," Mara said reluctantly.

"He seems unharmed."

"But he wasn't," she said. "It knocked him out. And he was ... odd ... for days. Distant. Withdrawn. As though a part of him had gone missing." She shook her head. "I can't risk it. Even if there's enough magic in you to do the job, and I don't know that there is, what if it knocks you out? What if it ... weakens your mind? I can't sail the boat. I don't know where your ships are. I need you intact. I can't take magic from you."

As much as I want to, she thought, for having him close there beside her in the bow, his body pressed up against hers, she was aware of the magic inside him more strongly than ever, and talking about it made her want it.

And maybe there was another kind of want figured in there, too, that had nothing to do with magic but everything to do with bodies ... and in some ways that scared her even more.

Chell sighed. "All right," he said. "Then I guess we wait."

He left her there and went back toward the stern, and in his absence, she suddenly felt colder than ever. She was about to turn around and join him when she blinked. Something had changed. She could see farther than she'd been able to just a moment before. And a moment after that she could see farther still.

Like a white blanket being lifted from a bed, the fog rose from the surface of the water, thinning as it went. Suddenly she could see twice as far, and then thrice, the circle of water around them widening more and more. Directly ahead, the fog grew darker and darker. A steep, stony shore appeared, and beyond it, a forest of dripping pine trees.

Mara had never been to sea, but she'd read a few stories. She knew the right words. "Land ho!" she shouted.

"I see it," Chell said. "Not that it does us any good."

Mara kept squinting at the shoreline. "There's something in the trees. You see it?"

Chell peered forward. "Where?"

"Just to the right of that dead tree, the white one."

Chell shifted his gaze. "It's the roof of a hut!"

"That's what I thought," Mara said. "And there's smoke coming from the chimney."

"And we're stuck like flies in flypaper," Chell said bitterly.

Mara said nothing.

They waited for the wind to change, or the sea to rise, or someone to come out of the hut and look down into the bay. By the time the sun reached the zenith, the sky was blue, the sea stretched unbroken out to the distant horizon ... and nothing else had changed, except the smoke had quit rising from the hut's chimney. No one had appeared, and Mara allowed herself to hope that whoever had been in the hut had left it and gone inland without ever looking in their direction.

The wind continued to blow from the sea, pushing them onto the mud. The tide had risen, but not enough, and now was receding again. And they were both a lot thirstier.

"I'm going to have to swim for it," Chell said at last.

Mara glanced at him. "This water is like ice!"

"It's not that far," he said. "And once I'm ashore, there's shelter. With a fire, or the remnants of one." He pointed at that tantalizing rooftop. "I'll either get help or get rope. And if I can't get either, then you'll have to swim for it, too."

"I'm not much of a swimmer," Mara said uneasily.

Chell gave her a scandalized look.

"Tamita is a landlocked city!" she protested.

Chell held up his hands. "All right, all right. We'll figure something out. I can rig a raft or something." He glanced out at sea. "We're lucky with the weather. The waves are small. If a storm blew in . . . stuck like this, this boat would be smashed to flinders in no time." He stood. "Well, no time like the present," he said, and began taking off his clothes.

Mara watched as he took off his boots and put them aside, then removed his cloak and coat and vest. When he took off the shirt, revealing a lean body and the strange tattoo on the left side of his chest, she felt her face flush a little, but she didn't look away. Then he put his hand on the belt of his trousers, and she swallowed and suddenly discovered that the cleat to which the forestay was attached was the most interesting thing she had ever seen.

She heard the rustle of more clothing, and then Chell said cheerfully. "You can look, you know. I'm not naked."

She glanced up, and saw that, technically, he was telling the truth, although the thin drawers he wore didn't exactly match her definition of modest. He was in the process of tying one end of a length of rope around his middle. "All right," he said. "I think there's enough rope here to reach the shore. I'll swim it over. If it looks like I'm in trouble, you can pull me back. And if I make it, the rope might give me a way to pull the boat in to shore, as well, or to shift supplies over to it." He took a deep breath. "Here goes."

He lowered himself into the water while still hanging onto the boat, gasping as his bare feet and legs touched the sea. "Not so bad," he said through chattering teeth. He turned toward the shore and waded toward it, the waves quickly soaking him from the waist down . . . and turning those thin drawers all-but-transparent, Mara couldn't help noticing.

She didn't look away, though. After all, she had to be ready to pull him back if he ran into trouble.

The sandspit seemed to end after only a few yards. Chell suddenly launched himself into the water, landing with a splash, and struck out strongly for the shore. A few minutes later he hauled himself out of the water, visibly shivering, onto the stony beach. She watched as he undid the rope and tied it around a broken tree trunk, then began climbing the steep slope to the hut. When he reached it, he pressed himself against the wall, and then edged to the corner. He took a quick glance around it, then another, longer, look, and then disappeared from sight.

She waited, barely breathing. One minute, two . . . and then she heaved a sigh of relief as she saw him again. He had a green blanket draped around his shoulders. He waved and shouted, though she couldn't hear what he said above the noise of the low surf on the sandbar, then began picking his way back down the slope to the shore. Once he was there he shouted again, and this time she understood. "Nobody there! But there's food and water and it's warm. You need to come ashore."

"What about the boat?"

"Once we're both out of it, we may be able to drag it over the sandbar!" Chell shouted. "I think there's a channel down there we could get out through!" He pointed to his right.

Mara swallowed. The fifty feet of water between them looked as wide as the ocean. "But I told you, I can barely swim!"

"You won't have to!" he called. "I'm going to pull the rope taut. All you have to do is follow it."

Mara shivered. "Should I . . . should I take off my clothes?"

He nodded. "Tie them in a bundle if you can, hang them around your neck. You might be able to keep them above water. And bring mine, too."

Mara nodded again. She turned her back and stripped down to her underwear, and used her cloak, mud-spattered and tattered after their ride across country, to make a kind of awkward bag into which she placed her boots, stockings, coat, tunic and trousers. Then she shoved in the bundle Chell had made of his clothes before he left the boat and tied the whole awkward mass around her neck. Feeling self-conscious, she turned around again to face Chell. While she'd been disrobing, he'd been wrapping extra loops of rope around the broken tree stump, so that the rope now stretched reasonably taut from the bow of the boat to the shore, though it dipped into the water halfway. He looked up and saw her. "All right!" he called. "Come into the water."

The air, chill against her mostly bare skin, had raised goose bumps all over her, but the water did more than chill her; it hurt, drawing a gasp from her the moment she lowered herself into it. Shivering seized her almost instantly, but there was no turning back; she gripped the rope in both hands and began to pull herself along it.

At first she had the stone-studded surface of the sandbar beneath her bare feet, but that fell away almost at once, and she gasped again as the rope sagged and the water rose to her breasts. She knew the bundle of their clothes had to be getting wet, but she couldn't do anything about it. Keeping the rope under her right arm, she pulled herself along it as quickly as she could, the water sucking all heat from her, the pain giving way to a frightening numbness. Her arms felt heavy and wooden, clumsy and hard to flex, but she kept moving, and almost to her surprise suddenly found ground under her feet again.

A moment later she collapsed forward into the arms of Chell, who had come down to the water's edge to meet her. He untied the bundle of clothes and set it aside, then pulled her close and wrapped the green blanket around both of them. She clung to him, head pressed against his bare chest, while the shivers gripped her and threatened to shake the teeth from her head. "The hut is warm," he said. "Let's get you up there."

She nodded, and with his help, climbed up a narrow path to the small, square structure, made of weathered logs. Lichen covered the slate roof. The door latch hung crookedly from the smashed wood of the lintel—Chell's handiwork, no doubt. But inside, it was blessedly warm: Chell had obviously fed the fire when he'd first entered the hut, and now it blazed, warm and welcoming, in the hearth. A bed, a chair, and a small table were the only furniture. A second door, closed, promised a second room Mara couldn't see into.

Something about the hut seemed familiar, but all she could think of was the warmth of the fire. She broke out from under the blanket and ran to it, holding out her hands. Chell came after her, wrapped the blanket around her, and said, "I'll go get the clothes," and went out again.

Mara sat cross-legged on the floor as close to the fire as she could get, pulled the blanket around her shoulders, and thought she had never seen anything more wonderful than that blaze. And then she remembered another time she had been grateful to see fire, in another hut, and sudden surmise brought her head around, staring, at the second door, the one that led into a little room in the back . . .

When Chell returned a few minutes later with the

bundle of clothes, which he dumped on the stones by the hearth, he found her standing in the doorway to that back room. "What have you found?" he said, coming up behind her.

She turned to him. "Magic," she said simply. She looked back into the smaller room. Just like in the hut where she had killed Grute, there was the basin of black lodestone, the black lodestone urns set on shelves beyond that, and all of it was softly lit by the sheen of shimmering light just coating the bottom of the basin.

"I can't see anything," Chell said.

"I can."

Chell stepped past her into the room and stared down into the basin. "Is there a lot?"

"No," Mara said. "But it's coming back." She stepped up beside him and looked down at the glimmer of magic she knew he couldn't see. "The smoke we saw this morning ... the harvester was probably here last night. He emptied the basin, loaded up and was gone this morning."

Chell looked at her. "But did he see us before he went? And if he did ... how long before he's back here with Watchers?"

Mara hadn't thought of that, and she wished Chell hadn't, either. "Maybe he didn't see us," she said. She looked back into the warm, cozy interior of the main room of the hut, and sighed. She already knew what Chell was going to say, and he didn't disappoint her.

"But maybe he did. We have to leave, as soon as we can."

Mara nodded. She glanced back at the basin. Already there was a little more magic in it. "If we can delay even a few hours," she said hopefully, "we might be able to take some magic with us. We may need it."

Chell hesitated. "I don't know exactly where we are,"

he said. "Where would he have to go to fetch Watchers, if he did see us?"

"Every village has at least one, but sometimes only one," Mara said. "And the ones in the smallest villages aren't exactly mighty warriors. He'd want to head to a larger town." She tried to think about the maps she had seen of Aygrima and judge how far north they had come along the coast. "Probably Stellit. It's likely the closest good-sized town. It would have half a dozen Watchers, at least." Her heart leaped. "But it's got to be half a day's journey from here. He can't possibly be back with Watchers until evening."

Chell gave her a long look. "How certain of you are that?"

"Very . . ." Mara hesitated. "Well, *pretty* certain," she amended.

Chell grunted. "Well, we can't leave right this minute anyway." He looked at the basin again. To him, Mara knew, it must look like nothing but a lump of black stone. "If I hadn't seen you use magic, I wouldn't believe in it," he said, and then turned around and went back into the main room, kneeling by the bundle of clothes and opening it up.

"Everything is still wet," he said. "It'll take a couple of hours to dry by the fire." He yawned. "I could use a rest. Can you keep watch?"

Mara nodded. "There's only one blanket," she said. She put her hands on it. "Do you want it?"

He shook his head. "You keep it," he said. He yawned again. "It's warm enough in here with the fire going. I don't need it. And you'll need it if you have to go outside before the clothes are dry." He stretched out on the bed. "Wake me if you . . . need . . ." The words tumbled away, and he slept.

Mara studied him. He lay flat on his back, one hand stretched out at his side, the other dangling across his stomach. His bare chest rose and fell, and the dangling fingers twitched. His face, relaxed into sleep, looked younger than it did when he was awake. *How old is he?* she wondered. He'd never said.

She wondered again at his strange tattoo: red circle, green crescent, blue star, all in a line on his left breast. Her gaze traveled down his body. The thin drawers really didn't hide much at all, she realized, and her face flamed. Suddenly she got up, pulled the blanket closer around her, and hurried to the door. It suddenly seemed like a really good time to get a breath of cool air.

She stood just outside, her bare feet rapidly chilling on the flat flagstones that formed the doorstep, and stared up the slope into the forest. A path, narrow but well defined, wound through the trees. The magic harvester, if that was indeed who had been in the hut the night before, must have gone that way. But had he seen them? And had she remembered the map of Aygrima right? If he *had* seen them, and she was wrong about how far he would have to go to get help, Watchers might came galloping over that rise and down that path at any moment.

I could stop them again, she thought. *Like I did by the stream.*

She shuddered, remembering the ground softening and swallowing men and horses alike. *No*, she thought. *I can't ...*

But there was a part of her that *wanted* to, that gloried in her power, the power to avenge her father and all the others unjustly slain by the Autarch and his minions. And an even darker part, deep under that, that loved the sensation of magic rushing into her, magic she pulled from the living or the newly dead. Once she had experienced that sensation purely as pain, as unbelievable agony, the equivalent, the Healer Ethelda had told her, of a grievously wounded man being transfused with the wrong kind of blood from someone else. But now . . . it still hurt, in a way, but it also felt . . . good. Unlike anything else she'd ever experienced. A pleasure that called to her to experience it again, to find an *excuse* to experience it again. She thought back to the way she had felt when the magic from the onrushing Watchers had poured into her, explored the sensation just like, as a child, she had explored the hole left by a missing tooth with her tongue. Her breathing came quicker. Her lips parted. It had felt good. It had felt like . . . like . . .

Mara knew about the ways of men and women, though only in the abstract. But she had imagined what it would be like, often enough, and a horrible thought struck her then, as she stood in the chill doorway of the hut.

What if her Gift were getting . . . tangled up in all of that? What would happen, the first time she was with a boy in that way? Would she lose control? Would she take more from him than he intended to give, leave him a husk, leave him . . . dead?

She gasped, turned, and stumbled back into the hut, pushing the door closed behind her and leaning against it, the blanket slipping from her shoulders. She stared at Chell, lying there all-but-naked, the firelight casting a warm glow over his bare skin, turning each little hair to gold. *I'm not a monster*, she thought. *I'm not! I'm a girl. An ordinary girl . . .*

Suddenly she felt an aching need to prove it, to do something that had nothing to do with her Gift/Curse, to reaffirm she was no different than any other girl. She went to the bed, knelt down beside it, stared at Chell. Her mouth had gone dry. She reached out a trembling hand and touched his stomach. It felt warm beneath her fingers, rising and falling gently. She swallowed, and leaned in closer. His lips, slightly parted, were inches from her mouth. She kissed them.

They felt so warm and alive that she almost gasped with the sensation. She kissed him again, and slid her hand lower down his stomach, to the waistband of the thin drawers, inside them . . .

And Chell jerked awake. His head snapped back. She snatched both her hand and her head back. "What . . . what are you doing?" he gasped.

Mara's blood was pounding in her ears, pounding in her whole body. "I don't want to be a monster," she said fiercely. "I don't want to be a killer. I just want to be a girl. I want you to prove to me I'm a girl!"

Chell stared at her. "Mara, I—"

"Please!" she said. She suddenly found herself weeping. "Please."

"Mara, I can't," Chell said gently. "It would be wrong."

"Why?" she said. She pointed a trembling finger at the door. "You know what's wrong? Wrong is what I did to those Watchers, to Grute, even to Stanik. Wrong is how I felt about it. I'm starting to enjoy it!" Hot tears ran down her cheeks. "I'm starting to *like* killing. Ethelda warned me, she said I could turn into a monster, I thought . . . I *know* . . . I can use magic to help people, too, I thought that was enough, but now . . ." She shook her head. "I don't want to be a monster. I just want to be a girl. I want you to treat me like a girl. Prove to me I'm just a girl!" She flung her arms around him. "Please!"

"Mara." Chell put his arms around her, too, and hugged her close. "Listen to me. You're not a monster. You're still a girl. But I can't . . . doing that would make *me* a kind of monster. I'd be taking advantage of you."

"I *want* to be taken advantage of," she said, her voice muffled. "I want to."

"No," Chell said. He took a deep breath. "Mara, you're only fifteen years old."

"Old enough."

"Physically, maybe, but . . ." Chell sighed. "Mara, how old do you think I am?"

"Eight . . . eighteen?" she said.

He shook his head. "I'm twenty-five. I look younger. It's useful when I want to be . . . incognito." He tilted her chin up toward him and gave her a crooked grin. "I may not be old enough to be your father, but I'm certainly too old to be your boyfriend."

"I don't care," Mara said, but already the heat of the moment was dissipating, and she was starting to feel more than a little silly . . . and ashamed.

"I do," the prince said. "And there's another thing you should know. I'm married. To a wonderful girl named Pim, whom I love more than anything in the world."

Pim. She remembered Chell saying that name when she'd first found him on the beach, wondering who it was. Now she felt even sillier . . . and stupid. She let go of Chell, suddenly embarrassed again by her near-nakedness . . . and his. "When I said I wanted you to make me feel like a normal girl," she mumbled, "I didn't mean I wanted you to make me feel like a silly child who got her hand caught in the cookie jar."

"Better than feeling like a monster, surely?" Chell said. Then he chuckled. "And that wasn't the cookie jar you were reaching your hand into."

Mara felt her face go red-hot. She wanted to melt right down into the floor, but she settled for pulling her knees to her chest and wrapping her arms around them. "I'm sorry," she mumbled. "I don't . . . I don't know what came over me."

Chell snorted. "You're fifteen. I remember being fifteen. I know exactly what came over you." He patted her bare foot. "But, Mara, there's lots of time for that. And when it happens . . . it shouldn't be with me. It should be with someone you love, and who loves you in return." He winked. "Keltan or Hyram are the most likely candidates, I'd wager."

Mara's face flamed again as she thought of the two boys. What would they think if they knew she'd almost . . . ? "You won't . . . you won't tell them what I just . . ."

"I am a man of discretion," Chell said. "No one but you and I will ever know." He stood up then. "Let's see how those clothes are doing."

Mara, who suddenly wanted more than anything else to have both of them fully dressed again, jumped up. "I'm sure they're dry enough."

They were, in fact, still slightly damp in places, but Chell, either divining Mara's desire for more clothing or sharing it, said nothing about that, but pulled on his trousers and tunic, stockings and boots as she donned her own clothes. Then he glanced at the door into the magic room. "Anything happening in there?" he said.

Mara looked in. "The basin is filling, but very slowly. I doubt I could more than quarter-fill a single urn so far."

He grunted. "We'll leave it until the last minute," he said. "First we've got to see about getting off that spit."

He turned to the door, but turned back again as Mara suddenly blurted out, "Thank you."

His steady gaze met hers. "You're welcome. Now let's see to the boat."

Mara nodded, and followed him out of the hut.

EIGHTEEN

Rising Smoke

THE BOAT PROVED EASIER TO FREE from the mud than either of them had dared hope. Without their weight inside it, it turned out not to be grounded very hard at all, and by both pulling together, they were able to drag it over the shallows, clearly formed by silt from the stream that emptied into the cove along that side, and into the deeper and quieter water closer to shore. With the boat afloat once more, they took the water barrel ashore and refilled it in the stream, then loaded it back aboard along with the blanket they had found in the hut, and a single urn of black lodestone, not quite a quarter-filled with magic. Though they had searched, they'd found no food. Then they rowed out of the cove through the clear channel around the north end of the shallows and into the open water once more.

"No more night travel," Chell said as they emerged from the shelter of the cove and the wind picked up, slapping the waves against the side of the boat with more vigor than Mara had yet experienced. She swallowed and held onto the sides while Chell set about raising the sail. "We have to stay in sight of land, and I don't want any more surprises. Shallows are bad, but a rock would be worse. Especially since you're not a strong swimmer."

Mara nodded, and swallowed hard again. Why did it feel like her insides were thinking quite seriously about climbing up her throat? And her head was hurting again. "Is the rocking . . . going to get better?" she said faintly.

"Rocking?" Chell gave her a surprised look. "There's hardly any rocking at all."

"It's more than last night!"

"Well, last night was almost a dead calm." The prince tied down a rope but paused with his hand on the mast, letting the sail shake in the wind, and gave her a worried look. "You're not feeling seasick, are you?"

"Um . . ."

Chell sighed. "Well, just remember, if you throw up, don't do it into the wind, or you'll end up wearing it."

Mara made a face. "Yuck."

"Or worse," Chell said, "*I'll* end up wearing it." He gave her a smile to take the sting out of his words, then made his way back to the stern. He loosened a rope, pulled it taut, then looped it around a cleat, and the sail quieted and bellied out. The motion smoothed, a little, and Mara was able to keep her gorge from rising . . . for the moment. But she remained in the bow, sucking in as much air as she could, as they raced north along the coast.

She had no clear idea of the distances involved and no clear idea of how fast a boat could travel, and thus had no idea how long it would take them to get to the Secret City. She thought she would at least *recognize* the Secret City from out at sea, once they drew near, but she couldn't even be certain of that. One thing she *was* certain of: if it had taken them four days to ride south from the Secret City to Tamita, there was no way they would reach it today, or probably even the day after. Would they get there before Keltan and Edrik? More importantly, would they get there before the Watchers?

Only time would tell.

She watched the coastline slip by. They passed two villages, Chell steering farther out to sea as each one came into sight. They saw other sails, but only in the distance; no one came close enough to hail them or pursue them. Mara wondered what those fishermen thought of the vessel sailing so determinedly north. When they got back to port, would they discuss it among themselves? Would Watchers hear it? Were Watchers even now peering out to sea along the coastline, searching for them?

"Will we camp on land tonight?" she asked Chell as the sun sank toward the western horizon. They'd passed the second village some three hours previously and had seen no sign of human habitation since.

He shook his head. "No," he said. "We can be ambushed on shore. We'll come in closer and anchor, but we'll sleep in the boat."

Mara nodded, but inside she groaned. Her head hurt and she still felt queasy, queasy enough that when Chell suited actions to words and took them in close enough to shore that their anchor could find purchase on the bottom beneath a tree-shrouded bluff, she refused the dried meat and cheese he offered for supper, though she drank some water. The ocean remained quiet, or so Chell assured her, but the motion didn't stop. It bothered her less when she was lying down in the bottom of the boat, though, she discovered, and at least the protective power of the water continued: her dreams were only troubled, not waking-up-screaming nightmares. And maybe the warmth of Chell's body, lying next to hers beneath the blanket they had taken from the hut, helped, too.

But she woke suddenly in the middle of the night when water splashed into her face. She licked it and tasted salt, and sat up abruptly, gripping the gunwale to steady herself. There was a rushing and a roaring all around her. "What's going on?" she shouted into the darkness. Chell was no longer beside her, but instead was fumbling with something in the bow.

For an instant, the darkness was obliterated by light that flashed across the sky, revealing Chell's ice-white face, his eyes and open mouth black circles in the sudden glare, his hands pulling on the anchor rope. "Storm rolling in!" he cried as the darkness swallowed him again. "Came up suddenly. We've got to get farther offshore!" Another flash of light showed him heaving aboard the anchor, a muddy lump of lead. "Move astern!" he yelled. "I've got to get at the oars!"

Thunder rumbled, several seconds after the flash of lightning; the storm hadn't reached them in its full fury yet, but already the boat leaped about like a maddened horse. As Mara moved toward the stern, Chell grabbed the blanket and stuffed it into one of the lockers. Then he unshipped the oars, sat down on the middle thwart, plunged the oar blades into the water, and pulled hard.

The boat leaped so hard it threw Mara onto her back, her head banging against the transom hard enough to make her dizzy. She crouched lower in the boat as Chell, grunting with every stroke, drove them out to sea, away from the wind-tossed trees of the shore, their madly flailing branches visible with every flash of lightning. "Lucky," Chell panted. "Storm came up from the south, over land. If it had come the other way the wind might have smashed us against the shore while we slept." Lightning flashed again, and in its brief flare Mara saw his teeth bared in a grin. Thunder crashed as he vanished into darkness again. "But it's swirling, too. Wind could change any minute. We've got to get as far from shore as we can." He hauled the oars aboard then scrambled forward to busy himself at the mast. The sail rose jerkily, flapping aimlessly in the wind until Chell scrambled back toward her. "Move forward," he said, and feeling like a lump of lead more useless than the hauled-aboard anchor, she squeezed past him. He unlashed the tiller, which he had tied in place when they'd dropped anchor, then hauled in the sheet to quiet the flapping sail.

"The sail is smaller!" Mara shouted at him. "Did something happen to it?"

"It's reefed," Chell said. "I made it smaller, so it won't pull so hard. Safer."

Brilliant light flashed, a blue-white bolt tearing a jagged streak across the black sky overhead, revealing roiling clouds. Thunder hammered them, causing Mara to cry out and throw her arms over her head. "This could get nasty!" Chell cried.

Could? Mara thought, heart pounding in terror. Each new flash of lightning showed angry water all around them, waves piling up like miniature mountain ranges, capped with foam instead of snow, and they seemed to be growing. The boat no longer rocked; now it slid down watery slopes, then up to a teetering pause, then down again. Spray crashed over the bow as it nosed up each new wave. Water sloshed around Mara's feet.

"We need to bail!" Chell shouted.

Mara knelt in the bottom of the boat, fumbling through the lockers beneath the mast, but found nothing but rope and bits of netting. "There's nothing to bail with!" she shouted back.

"Use the water cup!"

The wooden cup attached by rope to the water barrel was swinging wildly, banging against the staves as though trying to smash them in. Mara grabbed it and tried to untie it, but the knots in the sodden rope might as well have been carved from steel for all the impression her fingers made on them.

Neither of them had a knife, and the water was up to her ankles. Desperate, Mara gave up on the mug and instead pulled off her boot and began bailing with that, scooping and swinging, scooping and swinging, trying to stay ahead of the dollops of saltwater that crashed in with every wave and knowing she was losing the battle.

The lightning had become almost constant now, the thunder echoing and crashing all around them, and the wind howled through the stays. The boat labored up the side of each mountainous wave, then fell down the other side as though dropping from a cliff. In the lightning flashes Mara saw white spume flying from the wave peaks, ripped away by the gale. Her arms and back ached and her heart pounded in her chest. If the boat swamped or capsized . . . it would be the end of her. Her magic couldn't save her. Nothing could out here, not even Chell, who would be hard-pressed to save himself, even if he could swim, in the seas surrounding them now.

She'd tried to seduce Chell . . . her ears burned even in the cold and wet of the storm at the still-fresh memory of that humiliating episode . . . because she wanted to feel like an ordinary girl. The storm was certainly accomplishing that. She didn't feel special out here. She felt cold and wet and tired, incredibly weak . . . and incredibly small.

Just when powerful magical abilities would really come in useful, she thought, *they're nowhere to be found*.

And then the heavens opened up and the rain poured

down in buckets, and all thoughts but the need to keep bailing were pounded from her head.

The rain threatened to swamp them, but at least it also flattened the waves a bit, and the wind eased as well. Mara kept bailing, mechanically, almost mindlessly. The lightning became sporadic, the thunder following it at longer and longer intervals. The wind fell further, the rain eased, and finally, almost to her disbelief, there was no longer enough water in the boat for her to scoop it out, and they were galloping along through the dark with a brisk breeze at their stern over waves that had shrunk from the size of mountains to no more than good-sized hills.

Mara, gasping, flung aside her sodden boot and at last sat back on the middle thwart. "I can't feel my arms," she said, shivering and hugging herself.

"You did great," Chell said. With the lightning now reduced to flickers in the distance, he was invisible, but his voice sounded strained and somehow washed out. "If you hadn't kept ahead of the water, we would have swamped for sure." He paused. "How's your seasickness?"

Mara blinked in tired surprise. She hadn't thought about her insides once, and now that she did . . . "I don't feel sick anymore," she said.

"Good," the prince said. "You probably won't, at least not on this trip."

"You mean I might get seasick the *next* time?"

"Some sailors get sick every time they go out," Chell said.

Mara groaned. She massaged her arms and stared around. "How far are we from shore?"

"Not a clue," Chell said. "I don't think we'll see it when the sun comes up, though." He looked up at the sky, and Mara suddenly realized she could see him now.

Their surroundings had brightened from pitch-black to charcoal gray. She could see the waves rolling by underneath them, and scudding gray clouds low overhead. "Almost dawn now," Chell said. "At least we can pinpoint east when the sun comes up . . . if we can see it."

But though the sky grew brighter and brighter, the sun itself made no appearance. "Over there, I think," Chell said at last, glancing over his left shoulder. "Near as I can make it. Which should mean we're heading northeast, and back in toward shore." He turned around and peered forward again. "Nothing in sight." His eyes lit on her once more. "Get some rest," he said. "I'll call you if I need you."

Mara started to nod, yawned, bit it off, finished the nod, and then yawned again. The damp floorboards looked remarkably appealing. She pulled the blanket from the locker, thankful Chell had stuffed it in there to keep it dry when the storm began, wrapped it around herself, stretched out, and almost instantly fell asleep.

The next time she woke, it was to sunlight. She blinked up at bright blue sky, and then sat up. "Ow!" she said as her muscles protested. She looked around. There was no land in sight. "Where's Aygrima?" she said in alarm.

"No idea," Chell said. His voice sounded dull and tired, and Mara, glancing at him, was shocked by how drawn and pale he looked. "We must have been driven farther out to sea than I thought. Or else I misjudged the position of the sun this morning. By the time the clouds cleared away, it was so high overhead I still couldn't be sure of directions."

Mara looked up; the sun indeed blazed almost directly overhead. "We're lost, in other words," she said.

"We're in the ocean west of Aygrima," Chell said. "So we're not *lost* lost. But where we'll intercept land again . . ." He shrugged.

We could miss the Secret City altogether! The thought made Mara feel sick. She had to know what was happening there, had to know the results of her folly . . .

But however much she felt she *had* to know, the world did not order itself so that she *would* know: land remained defiantly out of sight.

"You must be hungry," Mara said, focusing on one thing she could do something about. She rummaged in the locker for food. There were two fillets left of the smoked fish they had stolen from the village where they had acquired the boat, and she handed one to Chell and took the other herself. "That's all of it."

He nodded as he bit hungrily into it. "Another reason we have to get to shore," he said. "But at least we still have water. You can go a long time without food."

Mara swallowed her own fish in three bites and nodded bravely, though her stomach growled as though demanding more.

They sailed on. As the sun began to set, Chell adjusted their course accordingly until they were sailing directly away from it. By nightfall there was still no sign of land, and Chell turned into the wind, bringing the sail ashiver, and then came forward to lower and loosely stow it.

"We're stopping?" Mara said in alarm.

"I have to rest," Chell said. "And sailing in toward an unknown shore in the dark is as good a recipe as I can imagine for disaster." He was rummaging in the locker now.

"There's no more food," Mara said. Food had been much on her mind all day.

"I'm not looking for food," Chell said, his voice muffled by his head-down position. He straightened suddenly. "I'm looking for this."

Mara could barely see it in the dim, fading twilight. It looked like a canvas cone, open at the narrow end, attached by three cords to a length of rope. "Is that for catching fish?" she said hopefully.

"No," Chell said. "It's called a sea anchor. I'll stream it over the bow and it will keep the boat pointed into the wind overnight so we aren't swamped while we sleep."

"Oh," Mara said.

Chell suited actions to words, and sure enough, the bow of the boat swung around into the wind. Then he drank from the water barrel and stretched out on the floorboards. "Nothing to do until morning," he said, and his voice already sounded sleepy. "Get some rest." A moment later his deep, regular breathing proclaimed he was doing as he had instructed.

Mara lay down next to him and pulled the blanket over both of them. The warmth of his body was welcome, but . . . distracting. It brought back disconcerting memories of the hut. She decided not to think about that supremely embarrassing moment and concentrate instead on what would happen when they got to the Secret City . . . but those thoughts weren't much more comforting. In the end she just lay there, staring up at the stars, brighter and nearer, it seemed, than she had ever seen them before, and waited for sleep to come.

When it did, at last, it was blessedly free of nightmares, and she didn't wake (stiff and sore and very, very hungry) until the stars had vanished and the still-clear sky was once more full of light.

Chell was in the bow, his back to her, and when she realized what he was doing she lay back down and closed her eyes until she heard him come back into the stern. Then she looked up at him as he began loosening the ties on the sail. "Good morning," she said.

"Good morning," he said, glancing back down at her. "A good breeze picking up. We'll make land before you know it."

Mara nodded and sat up, wincing a little. Chell raised the sail, left it shaking in the wind, went back to the stern and began hauling in the sea anchor, drops of water shining like rubies in the red glare of the morning sun as they fell from the dripping rope. Once he had it aboard, he settled himself at the tiller once more, pulled in on the sheet to quiet the sail, and set a course toward the sunrise. "Wind is almost dead astern," he called to Mara. "Stay in the bow. If it shifts she could jibe."

Mara didn't know what a "jibe" was, but she needed to go into the bow for a personal reason anyway. She clambered forward, out of sight from Chell behind the sail, took care of that immediate and pressing need, and then settled down to keep a lookout. She feared they would be sailing all day again, but in fact no more than an hour after Chell raised the sail she saw a low line of gray-green on the horizon and shouted, "Land ho!"

"Good," Chell said. "Sing out if you see any rocks or shallows."

Mara nodded and peered ahead, but saw nothing until they were so close in to the gray cliffs, still in shadow as the sun climbed beyond them, that she had to crane her head to look up at the spiky trees clinging to their tops. "Ready about," said Chell, and Mara turned to ask him what that meant just in time to see him put the tiller over. The boom swung across, and the sail began to pull again as they headed north once more.

The gray cliffs slipped by. Mara studied them, looking for anything she recognized. They could have been the cliffs just south of the Secret City . . . or they could have been cliffs a hundred miles north of it, for all she knew.

Then, late in the morning, she saw smoke rising above a particularly prominent headland (they had already sailed around several smaller ones) that blocked their path due north. She pointed it out to Chell. "It could be from the Secret City," she said, but even as she said it, she realized she was wrong: the headland south of the City was much less prominent than this one. "No," she said. "No, it couldn't. It must be a village." And the nearest village, Stony Beach, she remembered, was a full day's journey by horse south of the Secret City.

Chell nodded. "We'll land this side of the headland, then," he said.

"Land?" Mara stared at him. "But that will just slow us down!"

"Not as much as growing weaker from hunger," Chell said. "We need food."

Mara opened her mouth to protest, but at the mention of food her stomach growled violently, and she shut it again.

The cliffs had become more broken as they sailed north, and just south of the headland Chell spotted a tiny cove with a narrow strip of shingle. He lowered the sail and they rowed in toward it, crunching aground about ten feet offshore. Together they jumped out and pulled the boat higher up. Mara discovered to her alarm that the ground seemed to be moving under her feet. Chell, who was tying the boat to the nearest tree, glanced up at her and laughed. "Don't worry," he said. "Your land legs will come back soon enough." He looked up the slope to the north. "Looks climbable," he said. "Let's go see what we can see."

They labored in silence up a rocky slope studded with a few wind-twisted pine trees. At the top they slowed, and crawled the last few feet until they could look down into the cove beyond.

Sure enough, there was a village, and a fairly sizable one: fifty or sixty houses, and some larger buildings near the center of the town. Only a couple of boats were tied up to the three wooden piers. "Probably out fishing," Chell said softly. "That will help. Fewer people around."

Mara, peering down at the village, saw something that made her stiffen. She touched Chell's arm. "Look," she said. "Over there, just on the edge of the woods."

Chell glanced that way. "Looks like a building burned down."

"Not just any building," Mara said. "The Maskmakers' shop."

He gave her a skeptical look. "What makes you say that?"

"Because I know who burned it," she said.

His eyebrows lifted.

"The unMasked Army," she said. "They raided it to get the tools I needed to make counterfeit Masks, and burned the shop to cover their tracks. This is Stony Beach. It's the closest village to the Secret City . . . but it's still a full day's ride."

"Less than that sailing," Chell said. "If we can sail straight up the coast."

Something else Mara had been told when she'd first arrived in the Secret City came back to her. "I don't think we can," she said slowly. "I asked once why no fishing boats ever came offshore of the Secret City. Hyram said there are all kinds of rocks and shoals between the Secret City and here. We'll have to go out to sea again and then back."

Chell shook his head. "Keltan will have made it back before us," he said. "I don't see how we can beat him."

"I just hope he and Edrik beat the Watchers," Mara said miserably.

"It doesn't change anything right now," Chell said. "We still need food. And I think I see where to get it." He pointed off to the left, where a house stood apart from the rest, its back close up against the slope of the headland they had climbed. "There's no smoke rising from that one, so maybe nobody's home. And we can get up to its back door without being seen. Come on."

Mara followed Chell as he wriggled back down behind the ridgeline. They hurried along it until he thought they were just the other side of the headland from the lone house, and then climbed up again. He'd judged it well, Mara saw as they peered down again. The house lay below them and a little to their right, and there were trees between them and the village.

They picked their way cautiously down the slope, and came up to the house from the west, keeping a close eye on the windows to make sure no one looked out: but the house seemed safely deserted.

The back door was closed but not locked. "Keep watch," Chell whispered to Mara, and slipped inside.

Mara crept down to the corner of the house and took a cautious look toward Stony Beach. What she saw made her breath freeze in her throat.

The village, deserted half an hour before when they'd first looked into it, now teemed with people: black clad, black-Masked, armed, armored, and mounted.

Watchers!

Mara jerked her head back and pressed her back up against the rough wood of the house's wall, gasping; then she spun to the door and jerked it open. "Chell!"

Chell, busily filling a bag with the contents of a cupboard in the tiny kitchen, gave her a startled look. "What is it?"

"Watchers!" Mara said. "The village is full of them!"

Chell went to the window and took a quick look, then spun. "Time to go!"

They hurried out and started back up the slope. Mara, panting in Chell's wake, hoped desperately that the woods were enough to hide them. No shouts rang out and no Watchers galloped their way, so it seemed that they were. On top of the ridge, they hurried back to their old vantage point and took another look.

The Watchers were going in and out of houses, returning with bags much like the one Chell carried. Silent women stood by like statues, holding on to crying children. "What are they doing?" Mara said.

"Provisioning," Chell said. "At the expense of those poor villagers." He glanced at her. "Just like we did."

Mara felt a pang of guilt. It couldn't be an easy life in a remote fishing village like this. Who knew how much hardship they had just caused the man who owned the house they had raided, who would return from fishing to find his cupboard bare?

At least he won't be alone, she thought as Watchers emerged from yet another house carrying supplies. *And he'll blame the Watchers.* But that didn't really make her feel any better about it.

"Let's get out of here," Chell said. "Those Watchers are heading to the same place we're trying to get to."

Mara nodded. They scrambled backward from the ridge and then turned and hurried down the slope to the boat, throwing the provisions on board and pushing off. Mara's feet took another soaking and she wondered miserably if they would ever be either dry or warm again.

It took them a long time to reach the tip of the headland, zigzagging back and forth into the wind, a slow process Chell called "tacking." Mara quickly learned that "ready about" meant the boom was about to swing over, and to shift her weight from one side of the boat to the other as needed.

By the time they reached open water and were able to sail due north again, the sun was well past the zenith and sinking toward the west. But there were hours of daylight left yet, which meant they were fully lit and fully exposed to the village as they sailed around the headland and turned toward their destination once more. Still, they were far enough out from it that they would only be an anonymous fishing boat . . . she hoped. All she could see, as she looked back down toward Stony Beach, was a low cluster of roofs and the smoke that had drawn them to the village in the first place.

Twenty minutes later they had sailed past the tip of the next headland and the village . . . and the Watchers, if they were still there . . . were lost to sight.

The food—dried fish, smoked fish, dried berries, hard cheese and harder bread, plus a couple of bottles of sour wine—was hardly a feast, but Mara thought she'd never tasted anything so wonderful. Feeling comfortably full, she almost enjoyed the afternoon's sail through bright sunlight over glittering, friendly waves; probably would have, if not for the frantic feeling that they were already too late.

That feeling intensified when Chell once more insisted on streaming the sea anchor overnight. She would have preferred to keep sailing, but again, he shook his head. "You yourself told me there are dangerous waters along the coast between Stony Beach and the Secret City," he said. "Getting ourselves drowned won't help anyone . . . especially us!" But at least he had sailed until it was almost too dark to see, and they were on their way again at first light.

Chell kept them as far out to sea as he could without losing sight of the coast altogether. More than once he pointed out places where the waves churned over shallows, or splashed white in the sunshine against distant rocks. Mara understood the necessity, but still she fretted that they would sail past the Secret City altogether.

"If we do," Chell said, "I'll know it soon enough. I sailed down the coast from the north, and I remember the landmarks." With that, Mara had to be content.

In the end, though, there was no doubt.

It was late afternoon, the sun already nearing the

western horizon. Its long rays were lighting up the coast, closer now since it had been a couple of hours since they had last passed rocks or shallows, at least any that they could see. The cliffs that had looked forbidding and black in the shadows of morning now looked bright and welcoming in the golden glow of the sinking sun.

But up ahead, Mara saw something that did not look bright and welcoming at all: smoke, and not just the wisps of chimney smoke that had led them to Stony Beach. This was black smoke, black and roiling, smoke that spoke of things burning that were not meant to burn.

Her heart in her throat, Mara pointed it out.

"I see it," Chell said grimly. "We'll go in closer . . . but not too close."

Mara nodded and, clinging to the forestay, stood up to try to get a better look as Chell pointed the bow at that column of ominous smoke.

She soon had all too good a look.

The smoke was rising from the Secret City.

The cove was full of Watchers.

They were too late.

NINETEEN

The Shattered Army

THEY WERE SEEN, of course: though still far out to sea, they were silhouetted against the setting sun. Mara was still trying to understand the horror of what she was looking at, the black smoke billowing from every window in the rock face and from the cliff above, the black-clad Warriors milling around in the cove, when Chell said, "They're launching a boat!" Then he snapped, "Ready about," and the boom swung over as he turned their own craft out to sea again.

Mara tore her gaze from the smoking cliff and saw what he had seen, one of the unMasked Army's fishing boats being pushed offshore, half a dozen men climbing aboard it, the sail rising up the mast. "They can't catch us, can they?" she said. "They'll have to do what we did to get out to sea, that zigzagging thing . . . tacking . . . right?"

"Sun's going down," Chell said grimly. "Wind is failing. And if they've got the oars for it, they've got six men to . . ." His voice trailed off as the sail came down again on the boat and oars flashed out on either side and began driving the boat toward them. Chell looked up at the masthead, where the telltale ribbon hung almost limp. "We can't outrun them," he said. "Not with this wind. And we can't outrow them, either, not with only two of us." He glanced to port. "Our only hope is to lose them in the darkness. But the sun's not down yet."

Mara looked out at the sun, then back at the oncoming boat, and knew at once that the boat would win that race. She swallowed. "We have no weapons," she whispered. "Except . . . for me."

"Can you stop them?"

"I don't know." The strange muting effect the sea had on the nightmares . . . would it also keep her from using her Gift? And if it didn't . . . what would happen if she used magic as a weapon yet again? Would this be the time that tipped her over the edge, plunged her into madness?

Not if I use the magic we brought from the hut, she thought suddenly. But there was so little of it. Would it be enough?

Even if it was, she couldn't use it until the Watchers were nearer. As yet she couldn't even feel the magic within their bodies. But they were growing closer all the time. Their wet oars, reflecting the orange light of the setting sun, might have been ablaze.

She could see them clearly now, rowing in perfect unison, three to a side. A seventh person sat in the bow of the onrushing boat as she sat in the bow of theirs, someone who also wore black like the Watchers, but whose

Mask was a dark red. *Red is the color of engineers*, she remembered. *He can use magic to manipulate physical objects.*

Next to that red-Masked Watcher stood an urn of black lodestone, twice the size of the one they had taken from the hut. As the boat neared them, the Watcher took the lid from the urn and reached inside it.

She wondered later why it took her so long to understand what was about to happen, why it had never occurred to her that she was not the only one who could use magic as a weapon. Her only explanation was that she had never seen it before. But when the red-Masked Watcher straightened again in the bow of the boat bearing down on them, his hands glowing as hot and red as the setting sun, she suddenly understood, and gasped. The red-Masked Watcher thrust out his hands at them. Magic streaked across the water . . .

. . . and Mara, acting on pure reflex, leaped to her feet and called that magic to herself.

The bolt of red magic hurled at their sail improbably swerved in mid-flight. Intended to slam into the canvas, it instead blasted into her. Her clothes vanished in a flash of flame and a cloud of smoke, burned to ash in an instant, but she felt nothing, the magic shielding her from harm even as she absorbed it. She dimly realized she was naked, but it didn't seem to matter. All she could think of was the power brimming inside her, the power she had to release . . . *now.*

She stretched out her hands and flung the magic that had been hurled at them back at the boat full of Watchers.

She saw seven pairs of staring eyes, wide and startled in the final rays of the sun, and then the Watchers' boat exploded. Every bit of it, from bow to stern, from the tip of the mast to the water-buried keel, burst into flame.

The Watchers, screaming, writhed and burned where they sat, then their death agonies were blotted out by an enormous cloud of white steam as the boat crumbled and collapsed into the cold embrace of the sea.

The magic of all those suddenly snuffed lives slammed into Mara. She screamed, whether in agony or ecstasy she wouldn't have been able to say even if she were still capable of coherent thought, back arched, arms flung back, eyes staring at the last orange glow of the sun in the high, thin clouds overhead . . .

. . . and then the whole world whirled around her and disappeared into darkness, taking her with it.

Her last memory was of splashing into the icy sea, the cold water wrapping her nude body in a bitterly cold embrace that she welcomed, for it seemed to quench the fire that still burned through her.

• • •

Mara sputtered awake in darkness. Lost, disoriented, she struggled to move, but couldn't make her arms and legs obey her. She screamed, then gathered breath and screamed again as someone pinned her shoulders.

"Shhh, shhh," Chell said. "You're safe. You're all right."

She bit off the scream, stared up at him. He was only a black silhouette against the brilliant stars of the ocean night. "Ch . . . Chell? What . . . ?"

"You fainted," he said gently. "Fell overboard. Good thing we were barely moving. I was able to pull you aboard. You weren't breathing."

"I wasn't . . . ?" She blinked. "But—"

"I know how to give breath to drowning victims. It's something sailors are taught in Korellia."

Give breath? Did he mean he'd kissed her? While she was lying there without any clothes on?

And she'd missed it?

That thought was so completely inane under the circumstances that she found herself giggling. But once she'd started, she couldn't stop. It seemed her mind stood a little outside her body, watching it giggle helplessly, thinking scornfully that that was no way to be carrying on but unable to do anything about it . . .

. . . until Chell slapped her across the face.

It wasn't a very hard slap, but the sting seemed to snap her consciousness back to where it belonged, inside her skull, and the hysterical laughter instantly dried up. "Ow," she said.

"Sorry," he said.

"It's all right," she said. "I think I needed it." She wriggled. "Can you free my arms?"

Chell nodded, and reached down to loosen the blanket. Mara used one hand to hold the blanket to her chest, and pulled her right one free to rub the side of her cheek where Chell had struck her. "I killed them all again, didn't I?" she said slowly. "With magic."

Chell's reply sounded shaken. "I . . . guess. All I saw was . . . was a flash. You were surrounded by flame and smoke for an instant, and your clothes . . . um . . ."

"Burned off," Mara said, and in the darkness her cheeks flamed, but it was over and done and it wasn't like there'd been anything she could have done to prevent it.

"Yes," Chell said. "And then the other boat just . . . exploded into fire. It broke apart and sank and took the Watchers with it. Since they were burning, too, it . . . it was probably a mercy."

Mara felt sick. More deaths at her hand, more magic hurled at her from dying bodies, more ghosts imprinted on her, ghosts who would lurk inside her, ready to haunt her dreams and maybe even her waking hours. The ocean might protect her out here, but once they returned to land . . .

"The Watchers on shore launched another boat," Chell said, "but the sun was almost down by then, and the wind picked up. They never had a chance to catch us. I doubt they're still pursuing."

Mara nodded. She swallowed. "Is there any water?"

"Water is short," he said, "but we have wine."

"I'll take it."

Chell handed her a bottle. Mara took a long swallow from it. It was dreadful stuff, and she made a face. But it warmed her and created a pleasant fuzz in her head, a fuzz that kept her from thinking about . . . anything. She had another swig, and then another, and another, and after that . . .

. . . after that, she didn't really notice much of anything until she woke in the morning light to find the sail set once more, a high gray haze obscuring the sky, a foul taste in her mouth, and a pain in her head.

"Ow," she said. She'd been saying that a lot, she realized. She sat up, clutching the blanket to her chest. "Ugh," she said, by way of variety. And then, as her stomach heaved, "Urk." She scrambled to the side and threw up a fair quantity of red wine which tasted far less appetizing coming up than it had going down . . . and it hadn't tasted all that great going down.

"Good morning," said Chell from the back of the boat, and Mara, feeling the cold air on her back . . . and lower . . . remembered she wasn't dressed and quickly gathered the blanket around her more securely.

"Good morning," she said. She reached for the water cup, filled it from the barrel, swished out her mouth and spat over the side, then looked around her. The high gray haze overhead was matched by a low gray haze all around, shrouding the sea. But they were close enough to the coast that even through the haze she could see cliffs that were higher and more barren than the ones farther south. Inland, there would be high foothills, and then the mountains. Could you get past the mountains she had always thought of as impassable by following the coast? It had never occurred to her to wonder before.

"We're not far from the islands where my ships are anchored," Chell said. "But since we resumed sailing, I've been searching the coastline."

"For what?" Mara said.

"Survivors," Chell said simply, and suddenly everything that had happened the day before crashed down on Mara with the force of a landslide.

She slid down into the bottom of the boat. "I betrayed them," she said dully. "I told Stanik where to find them."

"No, you didn't," Chell said. "He figured it out. It's not the same thing."

"I don't think Catilla will see a difference," Mara said. "Or Edrik, or Hyram . . . or Keltan. If any of them are still alive."

"Edrik and Keltan should have gotten to the Secret City before the Watchers," Chell said. "They should have gotten everyone away."

"But have you *seen* any of them?" Mara said.

Chell hesitated, then shook his head.

Mara put her head in her hands. It throbbed from the lingering effects of the wine, but that was the least of the pain she felt. She had betrayed the unMasked Army. She had killed again. And her father was—

Unbidden, the image of his horrifying death sprang into her memory, and she gasped. It had only been three days. Three days since she had seen him hang. And the worst of it was that that horrible moment had already faded. So much had happened in the interval that it seemed a lifetime ago.

And her mother . . . what had happened to her? Had the Watchers tracked her to her home village down south? Had she, too, been executed?

Was Mara doomed to betray everyone and everything that mattered to her? Was that her *true* Gift?

Tears started in her eyes and she made no attempt to staunch them. They streamed down her cheeks as she hung her head and wept, the sobs racking her body. She was still weeping when Chell said softly, "There they are."

Mara jerked her head up in mid-sob and saw them, tiny black specks strung along the narrow beach at the base of the towering cliffs, burdened with packs and bags, a handful of mounted riders leading the way, another handful bringing up the rear.

"Can we—?" Mara began, but Chell had already altered course, angling in toward the shore to intercept that crawling line of people.

Somewhere along the way they were seen, and the black dots on shore scurried around, coalescing into a larger group with the horses around the periphery. Mara saw the silvery glint of drawn swords. She wrapped the blankets tightly around herself, stumbled barefoot to the bow, and then drew her chilled feet up onto the thwart to warm them while she sat and watched the shore draw nearer, her attention torn between the remnants of the unMasked Army and the water in front of them. It wouldn't do to run into a rock now.

Closer and closer the shore came, and now she could make out individuals. Among those on horseback she recognized Keltan and Edrik and Hyram. Back in the crowd on foot were Alita and Prella and Kirika. She didn't see Catilla or Ethelda or Grelda, or a handful of others she would have expected to see, like Tishka.

She'd been recognized now, too, and the swords were

lowered . . . but not sheathed. And then Chell was scrambling forward to lower the sail, letting their forward momentum carry them into the shallows. They ground against the rocky bottom still twenty feet from shore, and men and women splashed into the shallows to pull them farther up.

Mara clambered over the prow and splashed into the water, ignoring the icy bite of it as she hurried ashore, blankets clasped, not even looking to see if Chell followed her. She headed straight for Keltan, sitting astride a horse next to Hyram. "You were in time?" she gasped out.

He nodded, grim-faced.

From his own mount, Hyram looked down at her, face cold and grim and unyielding as a Mask. "How could you?" he said, the words strained as though it hurt him to speak. "How could you tell them how to find us?"

"I . . . I didn't . . ." Mara gasped out, stung to the heart; but Hyram turned the horse and rode away.

She looked back up at Keltan. "Keltan . . ."

"It was a near thing, Mara," he said softly. "And not everyone escaped. We sent out . . . Edrik sent out . . . one of the regular patrols to try to harry the Watchers, slow their approach. None . . ." He swallowed. "None of them came back." His eyes bore into hers. "One of them was Tishka."

Mara felt as though she'd taken a dagger to the heart. "No," she gasped.

"Yes," said a new voice, cold as the sea that had numbed Mara's feet as she splashed ashore. She turned to see that Edrik had ridden up into the spot vacated by his son, his face outmatching Hyram's in grimness. "And she was only one of a dozen who fell giving us time to evacuate. We used rockbreakers to bring down the cliff face behind us and block the beach. It will take them

time to find their way over or around that. But it will not
stop them. The Watchers will come north after us. And
where will we go, here in the Wild?" He glared at her.
"Keltan says you did not betray us on purpose," he
growled. "I am willing to ... entertain ... that notion.
But it does not matter. Whether you intended it or not,
you have destroyed the unMasked Army. You have destroyed all of us. And without us ... who will ever stand
against the Autarch?" He reined his horse around so
sharply it neighed in protest, and rode after his son.

Mara looked to Keltan, but with a look almost as
bleak as Edrik's, he, too, turned and rode away. She
glanced at the others of the unMasked Army, hoping for
some smile of welcome, some hint she was not univer-
sally hated, but the men, women, and children who had
fled the Secret City seemed sunk in their own misery and
weariness. Most had simply sat down where they had
stopped moving, clutching their meager belongings to
their chests. Prella did catch her eye, and give her a small
smile; but Alita's look was as cold as the wind and Kirika
and Simona did not look her way at all.

Only one person came toward her: the Healer
Ethelda, picking her way slowly through the clusters of
refugees sitting on the icy, stony beach. Ethelda looked
years older than the last time Mara had seen her, just
weeks before, her face wan and pale as the gray wintry
sky. "Mara," she said, touching Mara's shoulder. "I am
pleased you're all right."

"You're the only one," Mara said miserably. "Everyone thinks I betrayed them."

"And did you?" Ethelda said.

Mara looked down at the stony beach. In helpless
shame, she clenched the fists holding the blankets
clutched to her chest. "I didn't mean to," she whispered.
"I didn't think I had. But I ... I said too much. I men-

tioned Catilla's name. And Stanik knew her. Knew about her father. knew about the caves. He . . ."

Ethelda sighed. "It's of little comfort, I know, but you're hardly the first youngster to think she could pull the wool over a grown-up's eyes only to find out the grown-up is smarter than imagined." A brief smile flickered across her face, but went out like a candle in a storm. "But most youngsters don't then blast the grown-up and a goodly portion of the city wall into oblivion."

Mara shot her a startled look. "How did you—"

"Keltan told me," she said in a low voice. "Mara, I've warned you about the dangers of—"

"He killed my father," Mara said, and her fists clenched even tighter, not in shame now, but in fury. "He killed my father, and I killed him."

"But you drew magic from—"

"I took what I needed and I did what I had to do." She had been feeling miserable and penitent since she'd landed, but now it felt like a hot flame had kindled inside her breast, burning brighter and brighter. "I told Stanik about the unMasked Army and Catilla to try to save my father, because that was what I had to do. I'm sorry it worked out this way, but I would do it again. And I would kill Stanik again. Or all those Watchers the ground swallowed up. Or the ones in the boat. Or—"

Ethelda was staring at her, face horror-struck. "You've killed *more*? Even since Stanik?"

"I've killed the ones I had to," Mara said. The flame inside her leaped up. Suddenly she was keenly aware of all the magic around her, bound up in all the bodies on the icy shore, bound up in the body of the old woman in front of her. She wanted to pull it to herself, rip it from them, feel that wonderful/horrible pain/pleasure again. *And why shouldn't I? Why shouldn't I punish them? How*

*dare they judge me, hate me, blame me, when I only did
what I had to, only—*

She gasped, and loosened her clenched fists, and
crumpled to the ground, weeping, the blanket slipping,
exposing her back and shoulders to the cold air. What
was happening to her? How could she think such things?
She'd killed because she had to, not because she enjoyed
it . . . hadn't she? She'd only taken magic from others at
need, not just because she could . . .

Hadn't she?

Ethelda was kneeling beside her, pulling her blanket
back into place. She reached out and clasped Mara's
hands. "Mara," she said gently. "Now do you understand
what I have warned you about, over and over again?
Your kind of magic, your special Gift . . . it's addictive.
The more you use it, the more you *want* to use it. The
more you *need* to use it. And at the end of that road lies
the Autarch . . . or worse, the Lady of Pain and Fire and
all the other nightmarish figures of legend and terror."

"But . . ." Mara choked out. "But if I hadn't used it, we
would never have escaped."

"I know," Ethelda said. "I know. But . . ." She took a
deep breath. "Well, done is done. Look at you. Wrapped
in a blanket, and bare feet on this beach? You'll freeze
your toes off if we don't get you warm and dry."

Mara nodded dully. "I can't really feel them now," she
said. "I don't think I can walk."

"I'll carry you," said Chell from behind her. He
reached down and gathered her up as easily as if she
were a baby. She snuggled her head to his shoulder and
closed her eyes, suddenly exhausted. "Clothes? Shoes?"
she heard Chell ask.

"There aren't a lot to spare." Ethelda sounded worried and helpless. "I don't know who—"

"I have her spare clothes." Mara's eyes flicked open again and she turned her head to see that Keltan had returned, on foot this time. He was staring at her, nestled in Chell's arms, with a strange, strained expression. "We left our packs with Edrik when we sneaked into Tamita, so they came back with us."

Chell nodded. "Where?" he said.

"This way." Keltan turned and strode toward the head of the long line of refugees. Ethelda followed. Mara closed her eyes again to avoid the stares of the children. Maybe it was her guilt that made her read accusation in those wide, white eyes.

Maybe it wasn't.

"Where is Catilla?" Chell asked as they walked.

"Catilla is at death's door," Ethelda said. "The shock of the attack on the Secret City . . . the cancer . . . I can do nothing without magic."

Mara stiffened so suddenly Chell stumbled a little and stopped to stare down at her. "Magic!" she gasped. She turned her head toward Ethelda. "I have magic!"

"No!" Ethelda snapped. "You must not—"

"Not that kind of magic. An urn . . . not a lot, but some . . ."

Hope warred with disbelief in Ethelda's expression. "Truly?" she whispered.

"In the boat—"

Ethelda gasped, turned, and stumbled back toward the beached fishing boat.

Mara let her head drop back against Chell's chest. "I hope there's enough," she mumbled.

She closed her eyes again.

She felt something change. Chell's arms felt different. The air felt different. The light. The sound . . .

Her eyes jerked open. Chell wasn't carrying her, her father was, her father as she had last seen him, naked, head twisted grotesquely to one side, tongue protruding, eyes staring ... and Keltan had turned into Stanik, leering at her, and the unMasked Army were all dead Watchers, limbs twisted and distorted, ribs showing through shattered chests, bloody, blank-eyed, teeth bared in the rictus of death. She screamed, and screamed again, and kicked and writhed until she freed herself from her father's grip and dropped to the ground, the impact driving the air from her lungs so she could scream no more; all she could do was gape soundlessly as the dead, her dead, crept closer and closer, arms outstretched to tear her apart ...

A hand slapped her face, hard, stinging. The dead vanished. She found herself lying on the ground, blankets twisted around her, ribs aching. Chell straddled her on his knees. "Mara?"

She gulped air, sobbing. "I'm ... I'm back," she said. She pulled the blanket tight around her again, feeling chilled to her core by far more than the cold; as if her body as well as her mind had fallen into that maelstrom of the dead. "Keltan?" she gasped.

"I'm here," he said, and the concern she heard in his voice warmed her a little.

"You said you have my pack from when we went south?"

He nodded. "Your clothes are—"

"Never mind the clothes! The potion. You know the one. There's some left in my pack. If we can light a fire—"

"Fires are already being lit," Keltan said. "Edrik gave the order. He decided we all need to rest, warm ourselves, and have some hot food."

"But the smoke," Chell said. "The Watchers ..."

"They already know we've come this way," Keltan said grimly.

"The potion!" Mara cried. "Boil water, put in the packet, give it to me. Hurry!"

"I will." Keltan scrambled up and ran ahead.

Chell gathered her up again in his arms, grunting only a little with the effort as he straightened and carried her after Keltan. "What happened?" he said in a low voice.

"Nightmares," she whispered. "Those I killed with magic . . . those who die near me . . . I see them. As they were in death . . . or worse. They're in my head, and they come for me when I sleep." *And sometimes even when I'm awake*, she added silently.

"You didn't have them in the boat," Chell said. They were thirty or forty paces from a driftwood fire where Keltan knelt among a cluster of people.

"The sea . . . seems to help," Mara said. "I don't know why."

They reached the fire, the people around it falling silently back. Keltan had placed a small pot filled with water among the coals on one edge of the fire. He picked up a backpack lying at his side and held it out to her. "Here are your clothes, and your spare shoes."

Chell set Mara down on her bare feet. Holding the blanket with one hand, she took the pack with the other, then hesitated. "I'll hold the blanket as a screen," Chell said gently. "I won't look."

Mara's face flamed, remembering her clothes vanishing in a puff of fire and smoke on the boat. "You've already seen," she said. "But thank you." Keltan's eyes widened, then narrowed, his expression so outraged that despite everything she had to fight back a giggle. "Turn around," she told him primly, and he did so, though his stiff back spoke volumes.

Chell closed his eyes. She unfolded the blanket, carefully keeping it between her, Keltan, and all the rest of the unMasked Army as she put it into Chell's hands. Goose bumps erupted as the cold air hit her exposed flesh, and she hastened to don the warm, dry clothes from her pack. "All right," she said. "You can look."

Chell opened his eyes and lowered the blanket as she sat on the beach and pulled on her spare socks and shoes, not as sturdy as the boots she'd lost when she'd intercepted the blast from the Watcher boat offshore from the Secret City, but far better than bare feet on the cold stones.

She took the blanket from Chell and tied it around her neck as a makeshift cloak, since the one thing she lacked was a proper coat, then sat by the fire, sticking her still-chilled feet as close to it as she could. The steam rising from the now-boiling pot smelled as wonderful as she remembered, though Keltan dipped a cup into the liquid and handed it to her with a look of disgust. She sipped the potion, hardly noticing how it scalded her mouth and tongue as it soothed . . . whatever it was it soothed; her soul, she guessed, scraped raw by the use of too much magic of the wrong sort.

It could keep the nightmares at bay, too, or at least make them less horrifying . . . but there were few packets left, and the effect would not last long.

Best not to dwell on that. Feeling more like herself, she let Keltan pull her to her feet. "Where's Edrik?" she said. "I need to—"

But at that moment a youngster ran up to them, puffing, his breath coming in clouds. "Healer . . . Ethelda . . . wants you," he said to Mara, then made a beeline for the fire and stood warming his hands there. "Yuck!" he said, making a face. "What's that smell?"

"It is . . . um, *powerful*, that restorative of yours," Chell said as he, Keltan, and she made their way back along the beach toward Ethelda. "Is the taste as unique as the smell?"

Mara laughed. "It smells and tastes wonderful to me. But if you don't have the Gift . . ."

"I've smelled it a few times now," Keltan said from her other side. "You never really get used to it."

Several more fires had sprung up among the rocks, the unMasked Army clustered around them. Close under the cliff flickered a particularly large one, and beside it lay a blanket-wrapped bundle on a stretcher, Ethelda kneeling nearby. The Healer glanced up as the three of them approached, then got to her feet and came to meet them. Edrik and Hyram stood close at hand, but when they saw Mara, they turned as one and walked away. Mara's heart clenched painfully.

Ethelda looked tired and worn, but there was a lightness in her tone that hadn't been there before as she said, "It worked."

"You Healed Catilla?" Mara's eyes went to the bundle on the ground.

"Not fully," Ethelda said. "There wasn't enough magic for me to completely eradicate the cancer lurking in her body. But I was able to remove the tumors that were causing her pain and keeping her from eating. I have bought her a renewed, if temporary lease on life: time enough, I hope, that we may find sufficient magic elsewhere for me to complete the cure." Her smile faded a little. "The first thing she did when she could speak again was ask for you," she said.

Mara looked at Keltan. His face was unreadable.

"I need to talk to her, too," Chell said. "I'll come—"

"No," Ethelda said. "Just Mara, for now."

Mara gulped. She took a deep breath. Then she walked the half-dozen steps to Catilla's side.

It seemed roughly twice as long a journey as the one from distant Tamita.

Catilla's eyes were closed, but they opened as Mara knelt down beside her. Her face looked more skull-like than ever, like thin cloth stretched over bone, but her eyes were bright, the fire that had always seemed to burn behind them still alight. "Mara," said the Commander of the unMasked Army.

"Catilla," Mara said. "I'm glad the Healer was able to help you."

"I have you to thank for that, I'm told," Catilla said. Her voice was flat, her face unreadable. "You brought magic with you."

Mara nodded.

Catilla's eyes narrowed. "But I will *not* thank you," she said, each word as sharp as a dagger, as though she were plunging a blade into Mara's breast, over and over again. "I would rather have died than see you again. I wish I had *never* seen you. I wish your father had never contacted us. I wish we had never rescued you. I wish Grute had killed you. I wish you had descended into the depths of the mine and never come out. I thought you could help us overthrow the Autarch. Instead, you have overthrown *us*. You have destroyed us, and doomed Aygrima to tyranny forever. Get out of my sight. I never want to see you again."

Mara felt the blood drain from her face. Roaring filled her ears. She opened her mouth, but could only gape soundlessly, like a grounded fish. She stumbled to her feet, Catilla's burning gaze following her the whole time. Turning from the hatred etched on the old woman's skull-like face, she staggered away, pushing past Chell and Ethelda and Keltan. She ran down to the boat, flung herself against the bow, and tried to push it out to sea, but she couldn't budge it, couldn't move it an inch. Her feet slipped out from under her and she fell into the shallows, the cold water wetting the dry trousers she had donned just minutes before. Sobbing, she buried her head on the bow. Footsteps crunched behind her and she raised her head blindly. "Help me, Chell," she gasped. "Let's get out to sea again. Let's . . ."

"It's not Chell." Hands took her by the arm, pulled her to her feet. "It's Keltan."

"Keltan?" She turned, saw him looking at her with an expression of mingled pain and warmth, and flung her arms around him, burying her face in his neck. "How did everything go so wrong?" she choked out, voice muffled. "I've ruined everything, destroyed everything, killed people, killed my father . . . Tishka . . ." Her throat closed and all she could do then was weep, weep as if she would never be able to stop.

Keltan held her without saying anything for a long time. "It's not your fault," he said at last, his voice low, his lips so close to her ear she could feel his warm breath. "It's *not*. It all begins and ends with the Autarch. All the pain you've gone through, all the pain we've *all* gone through, everything bad that has happened . . . it's the Autarch."

She raised her head, blinked at him with tear-dimmed eyes. "But I . . . I couldn't save my father . . . I told Stanik too much . . ."

"You did your best," Keltan said gently. "It's not your fault it wasn't enough. You're only a girl. A fifteen-year-old girl."

Mara straightened and wiped her sleeve across her eyes. "You don't . . . you don't hate me?"

"Hate you?" Keltan's mouth quirked. "Mara, I love you. Don't tell me you've never noticed."

She stared at him. "You . . . you love . . . ? I mean, I knew you liked me . . . and Hyram, too, but I . . ." The icy venom of Catilla's words had seemed to freeze her heart in her chest; now a spark of warmth flared there. "Really? Even after . . . everything?"

"Really," Keltan said. "Even after everything." He took a deep breath, and took her hands in his, and looked steadily into her eyes. "Mara, everything you've done, you've done to help others, to try to save people. It hasn't always worked out. But sometimes it *has*. You saved Prella's life when she was injured. You saved all those lives in the mining camp, mine included. If you hadn't showed up with magic today, Catilla would have died."

"But Katia . . . my father . . . Illina . . . Tishka . . ." So many people she'd loved *had* died, because of her . . . "Keltan, how can I bear it?"

"You can bear it because you *have* to. What other choice do we have? We all do the best we can, day by day." His hands tightened on hers. "And I'll help you," he said, his voice so intense it almost frightened her. "Day by day. Every day. If you'll let me." Then his grip loosened. "Unless . . ." His voice shook a little. "Unless . . . you and Chell . . ."

"Chell?" Mara quickly shook her head. "No, Keltan, there's nothing . . ." She remembered the evening in the magic hut and blushed. Hoping Keltan hadn't noticed, she rushed on. "I thought maybe . . . but I was wrong. I was just being silly. Keltan, he's ten years older than me. And married!"

"Married?" Keltan's eyes widened. He released her hands and glanced over his shoulder at the fire, where Chell, Mara saw now, was kneeling and talking to Catilla. "Really?"

"Really." She reached out and turned Keltan's head back toward her, her hand on his cheek. "I . . . could use your help. I . . ." She couldn't speak for a minute. "I . . . could use your love." And then, as though someone had given her a push from behind, for she never afterward remembered actually making the decision, she put her other hand on his other cheek, drew him toward her, and kissed him on the lips.

The rush of . . . *something* . . . through her body, almost as strong as magic, made her gasp a little, and then his lips tightened on hers, his arms went around her, he pressed her body close to his, and they kissed for a long, long time.

Finally they broke apart, panting a little. Mara stared at Keltan. He stared back. "I," he said: Then stopped. "Um?" He stopped again. "Uh . . ."

Mara kissed him again, gently. "My thoughts exactly," she said as she drew back. The pain in her heart from Catilla's words had eased, the lump of ice that had been there since she'd seen Watchers in the Secret City had melted, even the lurking shadows of the dead vanished, deep into the recesses of her mind. *Keltan loves me*, she thought in wonder. *Keltan believes in me.*

She took his hand. "I've just realized," she said, "that it's not up to me to decide what to do anymore. Catilla leads the unMasked Army. Edrik is her lieutenant. Chell is a prince. And I'm . . ." She smiled at Keltan. "Remember what you called yourself when you were first telling me about the unMasked Army, after the five of us were rescued from the wagons heading to the mine?"

"Least of the last, lowest of the low?" Keltan said, grinning.

Mara nodded. "Exactly." She sighed, feeling as if a huge weight had been lifted from her. "That's what I am now." She squeezed his hand. "And I think I kind of like it."

They sat on the prow of the boat, hand in hand, and waited for others to tell them what would happen next.

TWENTY

Uneasy Alliance

THEY DIDN'T HAVE LONG TO WAIT. Perhaps fifteen minutes passed, then Chell detached himself from the group around the fire and came over to them. If he noticed that Mara and Keltan were holding hands, he gave no sign of it. "It's settled," he said.

"What is?" Mara said.

"The unMasked Army," Chell said, taking in the straggle of refugees with a sweep of his hand, "is defeated and on the run. But it has nowhere to run *to*. It has temporarily delayed the pursuit by bringing down the cliff face north of the Secret City, but it is only a delay. The Watchers are mounted. They have access to boats. And they also have, as you and I well know, magic. Eventually they will catch the unMasked Army, and when they do, they will destroy it . . . if the unMasked Army remains on this shore to be caught."

"And where else is the Army to go?" Keltan said.

Chell turned slowly, making another expansive gesture: but this one took in the sea. "Out there."

"Your ships?" Mara breathed.

Chell nodded. "We're close," he said. "I recognize this coast. My ships should be anchored at an agreed-upon rendezvous point, a cluster of islands northwest of here, out of sight of the mainland, where they were to wait until the deadline for hearing from me has passed. Which it hasn't yet . . . quite.

"I have discussed it with Catilla, and she has agreed: the unMasked Army will continue north with as much speed as it can muster. Meanwhile, I will sail our trusty vessel here"—he patted the fishing boat's blunt bow— "to where my captains are waiting. We will then sail in to the coast and evacuate the entire Army."

"Three hundred men, women, and children?" Mara said. "Your ships can take that many?"

"And keep them fed and watered?" Keltan said skeptically.

Chell held up his hands. "I'm not suggesting taking them all the way back to Korellia," he said. "The islands where my ships are anchored have fresh water, forests, and game: that's why we chose them, to keep the crews fed while they waited and to provision the ships for our return journey. The unMasked Army can survive there, at least for a time."

"For a time," Keltan said. "And then what?"

Chell grinned. "And then I come back with a fleet instead of a flotilla and an army of my own, and we will see how prepared the Autarch and his Watchers are for a surprise assault from the sea. We will land near the very village from which Mara and I liberated this boat, and within a day we will be at the walls of the city." His grin turned a little savage. "The Autarch's Watchers are very good at terrorizing villagers and facing down bandits. But they have never fought a war. And Korellia . . . to our sorrow . . . has been constantly at war for nigh on twenty years."

Mara's heart beat a little faster. To see the Autarch dragged from the Sun Throne and paraded through the streets as a captive, to see Masks pulled from faces and thrown down to shatter on the pavement . . . "Can you really do that?" she said. "Can you really convince your father to launch an invasion? Will he spare the men if you're fighting this . . . Stonefell . . . you told me about?"

"The number of men needed to put paid to the Autarch will barely dent our forces," Chell said. "And the potential payoff will be worth it."

"What payoff?" Keltan said, sounding suspicious.

"Magic, of course," Chell said. "The reason I came here in the first place. Stonefell has weapons we cannot effectively counter . . . not many of them yet, and not as many ships as we have, but they are making more all the time. Eventually they will be able to overwhelm us, if we can't find some way to fight back." He looked at Mara. "I have seen," he said softly, "what magic can do."

Mara said nothing. She knew what Chell wanted from her.

"You have seen what magic can do," Keltan said. "Then you know you will face magic when you attack. What makes you think you can prevail against the Autarch's Gifted?"

"Our numbers will be overwhelming."

"And Catilla *agreed* to this?"

"Why shouldn't she?" Chell said. "She has no use for magic. If we succeed in overthrowing the Autarch, the last thing she will want is a lot of disgruntled Gifted, many of whom have done very well under the current regime, loose in Aygrima. She has promised that I may attempt to recruit them. With the rewards my father will willingly offer to anyone who helps defeat Stonefell"— again he glanced at Mara—"I do not anticipate it will be hard to find Gifted willing to accompany me."

Keltan said nothing more, but he still looked skeptical.

"I'm to set out at once," Chell said.

Mara let go of Keltan's hand and straightened up. "I'm coming with you."

"What?" Keltan's head jerked around. He stared at her. "Why?"

She met his gaze steadily. "Catilla has made it clear that I am no longer welcome in the unMasked Army," she said. "Nor do I think anyone within the Army who knows what I did . . . and can there be anyone who doesn't? . . . will mourn my absence." She turned back to Chell. "Will you take me with you?"

"Of course," he said. "I'd never abandon an old shipmate."

"Then I'm coming, too," Keltan said.

It was Mara's turn to stare at him. "What?"

"You heard me," he said. "I want you where I can keep an eye on you. You get into too much trouble on your own."

Mara blinked, then burst out laughing, while inside a warm feeling welled up and threatened to pour out of her eyes as tears.

Chell just shrugged. "It's all right with me," he said. "Can you scare up some provisions for us? We've got a day's sail ahead of us." He climbed into the boat and clambered out again a moment later with the water barrel. "I saw a stream coming down the cliff face . . . I'll refill this. Meet back here as soon as you can. Daylight's wasting."

He set off across the beach. Keltan held out his hand to Mara, but she shook her head. "I'm staying put," she said. "I don't want to face anyone."

Keltan hesitated, then nodded and trudged off.

Mara sat down with her back to the prow of the boat, and studied the unMasked Army. Away from the Secret City, there was nothing military about it at all. It was only a collection of cold, frightened families, driven out into the cold. Her doing? She shook her head. *No*, she thought. *Keltan's right. It's not my doing. It's the Autarch's. His fault. Tightening and tightening his grip, squeezing the life out of the country, feeding off the magic of his people like some monstrous leech, ready to crush anyone trying to escape.*

If Chell can get these people to safety, she thought, *then I'll do it. I'll use my Gift to help him against his enemies.*

It was a rash thought, and she knew it. She hadn't forgotten Ethelda's warnings of the possible consequences of her continued use of her peculiar and powerful Gift, but she held onto it just the same. Perhaps she wouldn't be able to help him. Perhaps it would be more dangerous to try than not. But she felt she owed it to him.

Keltan returned with two backpacks, his and hers from their journey to Tamita. "Provisions are scant," he said. "But there's dry bread and fish and a bit of cheese."

Mara nodded.

Chell returned hard on Keltan's heels, panting as he lugged the full water barrel over the uneven stones. He grunted as he swung it aboard. Keltan tossed the backpacks in after it.

"Help me push off," Chell said, and the three of them

made short work of what had been an impossible task for Mara alone. When the boat floated, they climbed aboard. Chell took the oars to back them away from the shore, while Mara took her accustomed place in the bow as a lookout, and Keltan moved to the stern. That left her looking back at the shore.

Hyram stood there, Alita close beside him, watching them. Hyram's face was unreadable; Alita's like stone. Mara raised a tentative hand in farewell, but Hyram simply turned and walked away. Alita's expressionless gaze lingered a moment longer, then she turned and followed Edrik's son.

Mara let her hand fall. Her Gift, it seemed, could shatter more than just city walls.

The shore slipped away. Chell, pulling with the port oar and backwatering with the starboard one, swung the boat around until its bow pointed out to sea. Then he hauled in the dripping oars and moved forward to raise the sail, Keltan, as clueless in a boat as Mara had been, scrambling to stay out of the way. With the sail up, Chell returned to the stern, took the tiller, and hauled in the sheet. The sail started to draw, and he steered a course for the open water. Mara watched the waters for rocks and shallows, and resisted the urge to look back.

They sailed all day without raising the islands Chell insisted lay ahead. Mara had to take that claim on faith, although at least they weren't navigating completely blind this time: Chell had acquired a compass from the unMasked Army, which he consulted as they sailed. As night settled in, he strung out the sea anchor and they shared out their meager provisions. "I'll take the first watch," Chell said. "Then you, Keltan, then Mara. For now, get some rest."

Mara and Keltan lay down next to each other on the bit of spare sail and wrapped their blankets around them. The boat's rounded bottom forced them together, and Mara found herself hyperaware of Keltan's warm body, stretched out next to her. A portion of that awareness was simply the fact he was male and the memory of their kiss lingered . . . but an even larger portion was her sense of the magic nestled within him, the magic she had already tasted once, in the mining camp.

She wanted to taste his magic again. She wanted to taste his mouth again, lips warm and alive against hers. She wanted both, and more, and . . .

. . . it was all very confusing, and not very conducive to sleep.

Keltan seemed to have no such problems; his breathing slowed and deepened almost at once. She closed her eyes and tried to emulate him, tried to ignore everything else going on in her body and mind.

It took her a while, but eventually she slept, and the strange protective quality of the sea kept away the nightmares that would surely have brought her screaming awake on land. In fact, so deeply did she sleep that she didn't even notice the first change in watch, waking sometime deep in the night to find that the warm body stretched out next to hers was now Chell's, and it was Keltan who sat in the stern, a silent, shrouded lump.

She slept again, waking the next time to Keltan's gentle shake of her shoulders. "Your turn," he whispered. "I haven't seen or heard anything, and the sea is calm."

She nodded and took her place in the stern. Keltan lay down next to Chell. The boat rose and fell in the gentle swell, its bow pointed into the slight breeze. The stars blazed down from a cloudless sky, pinpricks of light striking answering sparks from the glittering water. She stared up at those glints of diamond. They seemed closer and brighter than they ever had on land. She remembered what she had been told, that some people believed magic had come to Aygrima from the sky. Looking up at the brilliant stars, seemingly close enough to touch and yet impossibly far away, she could almost believe it.

If so, I wish it had stayed up there, she thought. *Then I would never have been born with the Gift, Masks would never have existed, and the Autarch would have no power.*

But then she sighed and lowered her eyes. *For all you know*, she reminded herself, *things would have been worse. You don't need magic to make a tyrant. Think of this Stonefell place Chell seems so worried about.*

"You can't change what has happened." Her father had told her that once, when she was little and he was the perfect, solid center of her world. She had done something wrong . . . broken a vase, she thought, or possibly a window . . . and he had wiped her tears away and sat her on his knee and said, "You can't change the past. All you can do is move on into the future and try to make it better."

She looked back up to the stars, now smeared into halos and comets of light by a sudden flood of tears. Some people also believed that the souls of those who died rose into the sky, that they lived on in the heavens. Mara didn't know if that were true, but in that moment, she desperately hoped it was, that her father was looking down on her and loving her. "I'm so sorry, Daddy," she whispered. "I'm so sorry I couldn't save you. I know I can't change the past. But I promise I'll try to do better in the future. I'll try to save everyone I can." The magic in the bodies of Chell and Keltan called to her, and she swallowed. "I'll try to save myself, too," she added, in a voice so low even she could barely hear it.

The night wore on. The stars faded. The sky in the east turned gray, and then pink. Chell woke, and then Keltan. The sail rose. They were on their way once more.

Three hours after dawn, they sighted the islands.

Mara, in the bow, studied them. Hilly and forested, they were separated from each other by a stretch of water that from here looked narrow enough to wade across, though that was surely an illusion. She didn't see any ships, though.

"They're in a bay on the western side," Chell told her when she asked. "So they could weigh anchor and flee if a force came this way from the mainland. But there will be lookouts in the hills. They will already have seen us."

"You said this was the agreed-upon rendezvous," Keltan said. "You also said there's a deadline. What would have happened if you'd missed it? Would they have come looking for you?"

"No," the prince said. "I gave them strict orders to wait here for six weeks. If I did not return, or send word by one of the men who went with me—"

"The men who drowned?" Mara said, and then could have kicked herself. "Sorry."

"Yes, the men who drowned," Chell said gently. "The men who saved my life first. They and their families will be honored by my father upon my return."

"Sorry," Mara mumbled again.

"If they did not hear from me," Chell continued, "then one ship was to sail back to Korellia to report to my father, while the other would begin a search along the coast."

"Six weeks?" Keltan said. "Cutting it pretty fine, aren't you?"

"Very," the prince said. "But by my count, I still have a day to spare."

"A sail!" Mara cried, and Chell peered around the mast to see what she had seen: coming around the southern headland of the northernmost island, putting the lie to the illusion that the channel between the two was something you could wade across, was the largest vessel she had ever seen—larger than she had ever imagined a ship *could* be. Three masts seemed to pierce the sky above towering wooden flanks that were black at the waterline and gold above. Square sails dropped and blossomed like flower petals as she watched.

"*Protector*," said Chell softly. "My flagship."

The ship swelled in size with astonishing speed. Chell sailed on toward it for a time, then brought the fishing boat up into the wind, sail shaking, and waited. *Protector* came on, slowed, and copied his move, turning into the wind and slowing, sails folding up as it did so, until the two vessels, large and small, bobbed side by side, perhaps twenty yards between them. Chell had a huge grin on his face; he looked happier than Mara had ever seen him.

She turned from him to that amazing ship. She could feel the magic nestled in the dozens of crewmen. Her hands trembled.

"Prince Chell!" boomed a voice from the ship, where sailors were standing all along the guardrail now, staring and pointing. "You're truly a sight for sore eyes, Sire!"

Mara spotted the speaker. High up on the raised deck at the stern of the ship, he wore a black coat whose sleeves were covered with gold braid, and a tall black hat with a golden feather in it.

"As are you, Captain March!" Chell shouted back. "Bring us aboard! And send a message to *Defender*. We must set course for the mainland at once."

"Yes, Your Highness." The captain turned and spoke to someone behind him in a voice too low for Mara to hear. A rope ladder was flung over the side of the ship, while high above, brightly colored flags rose, marked with contrasting shapes: squares and triangles and circles and more. *Some kind of messaging system*, Mara guessed.

Chell was lowering the sail. He stowed it loosely around the boom, then put the oars into the rowlocks and rowed toward *Protector*. Mara stared up at the ship's towering black side and wondered how anything so large could possible float.

A sailor hung easily from the ladder, a boathook in one hand. He hooked the fishing boat as Chell brought it alongside. A moment later, Mara was following the two young men up that giant wall of painted planks. A moment after that, she stood on the deck of the giant ship and looked around.

Dozens of sailors, all dressed in black trousers and black jackets over white shirts, golden scarves at their neck, feet bare despite the chill, stared back at her.

Captain March descended from the high deck at the stern, sailors falling in to either side as he passed. He stared at Chell for an instant, then reached out and pulled the prince to him in a rough embrace that Chell returned. "You're looking thin, Your Highness," said the captain as he released him. Captain March had the same odd accent as Chell. "But I'm more pleased than I can say to see you alive. We feared the worst. Tomorrow I would have sent *Defender* back to Korellia and begun the search."

"It's been an . . . interesting few weeks," Chell said.

"The men who accompanied you?" the captain asked.

"Dead," Chell said simply.

The captain's face tightened. "At whose hand?" He gave Keltan a suspicious look.

"The sea's," said Chell. "Captain, I will tell you everything, but perhaps my cabin would be a more appropriate location?"

March's face colored a little. "Of course, Your Highness." He turned. "Midshipman Lizik! Escort His Royal Highness and his guests to his cabin."

"Aye, aye, sir!" A boy about Keltan's age, dressed in a miniature version of the captain's uniform but with far less gold braid, stepped forward. "Your Highness," he said to the prince, then nodded to Keltan and Mara. "Gentleman and lady. If you'll follow me."

He led them toward the high rear deck, but rather than climbing up the gangway, took them through a red-painted door and down a short hallway into a large cabin that stretched the width of the ship. High glass windows looked out over the sea astern.

Mara stared around. The room dripped with wealth. Red brocade, cloth-of-gold, crystal and silver: everywhere she looked, something glowed or sparkled. She shot a glance at Chell. He looked slightly embarrassed. "My quarters," he said. "I am a prince, you know." He turned to the midshipman. "Thank you, Mr. Lizik. Please tell the captain I will speak to him at his earliest convenience."

The young officer nodded and went out.

Even Keltan looked impressed, Mara saw. "I confess," he said, "that I doubted your story . . . until now."

"I suppose I can't blame you for that," Chell said. He looked down at himself and grimaced. "I must change," he said. He gestured at a sideboard laden with goblets, mugs, bottles, and decanters. "Help yourself to a drink, if you like." He disappeared behind a screen in the corner.

Keltan crossed to the sideboard, Mara trailing him. He ran his fingers over the decanters. "I don't even know what any of this is," he said. He picked up a crystal decanter filled with a bright blue liquid and sniffed it. "Fruity," he said. He poured some into two small glasses and handed one to Mara. "To a successful rescue," he said.

"I'll drink to that," Mara said, and sipped from the glass.

It might have smelled like fruit juice; it tasted like liquid fire. She burst out coughing. Keltan managed not to cough, but he blinked rapidly. "Wow," he said.

"Wow," Mara agreed. She took another sip. It was better than the first, and it certainly had a warming effect on her sea-air-chilled body.

The prince emerged from behind the screen, and Mara gaped. He wore skin-tight white pants, pushed into tall boots of black, polished leather, and above that, a golden jacket over a snow-white shirt whose ruffled collar and cuffs showed at the neck and wrists. He had brushed back his long hair and tied it into a neat ponytail, held in place by a golden bow. As he emerged, he was buckling on a sword with an elaborate basket hilt studded with red-and-green gems. The scabbard, too, glittered; a line of rubies ran its length.

He looked, in short, like a prince, and Mara's ears burned as she remembered the night in the magic hut. *He must have thought me nothing more than a silly little girl*, she thought. *How could I ever have thought...*

Chell saw what they had in their glasses and he laughed. "When I offered a drink," he said, "I really didn't expect you to choose the skyberry brandy. A glass or two of that and you'll be cross-eyed." He came over to the sideboard. "Try the wine, instead." He picked up an unopened bottle, tugged out the cork and poured a healthy helping of the rich red liquid into three glasses. Mara took hers, remembering a night on the beach just a few weeks ago when she had tasted wine for the first time. Keltan had been there, too. So much had happened since then. She sipped the wine. It went down much easier than the skyberry brandy had.

There came a knock at the door. "Enter!" Chell called, and the door swung inward. Captain March came in, removing his tall hat as he entered ... pretty much a necessity, since the captain was so tall even without the hat that his head almost brushed the cabin's ceiling beams. "Your Highness," he said. "*Defender* is on her way and will rendezvous with us within the half hour."

"Good." Chell poured another glass of wine for the captain. "There is much you need to know before she gets here . . ."

For the next few minutes Chell told the captain everything that had happened to him since he had set out to scout the shoreline. It seemed odd to Mara to hear someone else's perspective on events she had experienced firsthand. For Chell, everything was part of his larger mission to find magical help for Korellia's fight against Stonefell. As he described their escape from Tamita, the captain turned startled eyes on Mara. She lowered her gaze and concentrated on her wine.

"We will get no help from the Autarch of Aygrima," Prince Chell concluded. "But if we can help the un-Masked Army overthrow him, then we will have access to magic once more . . . the magic we need to withstand and overcome Stonefell."

Captain March looked from the prince to Mara, then back to the prince. "Permission to speak freely, Your Highness?"

"Always, Captain March." Chell frowned. "I can't remember you ever feeling you had to ask before."

"Your Highness," the captain said, "if what you say of this lass's magical ability is true," (there was more than a hint of skepticism in his voice, and for an instant Mara imagined ripping magic out of him and setting fire to the ship, just to prove how true the prince's account was, but she squelched the notion instantly, horrified it had even occurred to her), "then why do we need the unMasked Army at all?" He pointed at Mara. "She alone could open the sea gates that protect Stonefell."

Chell's eyes narrowed. "We cannot compel her," he said. "She has saved my life and is under my protection. If she chooses to help us, I will welcome it; but as I understand it"—he shot Mara a glance—"she is at great risk if she continues to use her magic in the fashion I have described."

Mara carefully set down her empty wineglass. Between it and the blueberry brandy, she was feeling unusually forthright. "If I continue to use my magic in the fashion the prince has described, Captain March," she said, clearly enunciating each word, "I am told I will turn into a murderous, unstoppable monster who would gladly rip the life out of you and every member of your crew, and then move on to lay waste to all of Korellia and possibly the rest of the world." She gave him a sweet smile. "It's rather tempting at the moment."

The captain's lips drew into a thin line. His attention snapped back to the prince. "As you decree, of course, Your Highness."

"I decree," said Chell, "that Mara and Keltan are my guests, under my personal protection, and are to be treated with all due honor and respect during their time on this ship."

The captain inclined his head. "Of course, Your Highness."

"Good." The prince glanced up and to the left, and Mara, following his look, saw through the port windows that a second ship, smaller than the *Protector* but not by much, had moved into position alongside. "The *Defender* has joined us, I see," he said. "You have your orders, Captain. Set a course: due east to the mainland. We have an army to rescue."

"As you command, Your Highness." The captain inclined his head again, tucked his tall hat under his arm, turned sharply, and went out, the door clicking closed behind him.

"I don't think," Mara said, "that he likes me very much."

Chell snorted. "You told him you could quite possibly

kill him, his crew, and all my subjects," he said. "Not the best way to make friends."

To her own surprise, Mara felt a flash of anger at that. "And he threatened to have me locked up and dragged back to Korellia to be used as an unwilling secret weapon against Stonefell."

"Well," said Chell judiciously, "not in so many words. But I do see your point." He grinned suddenly. "Captain March is a fine man, and a loyal subject, and the best captain in the navy, in my opinion, but he is also a rather stiff and pompous stick-in-the-mud. I confess I rather enjoyed you pricking his bubble like that."

Mara's anger vanished as quickly as it had come, and she chuckled; inside, though, a small part of her worried.

Her words to the captain hadn't been an idle threat. Quite possibly she really *could* do those things. And the worst of it was . . . though she wasn't there yet, she could imagine *wanting* to.

She shivered, and poured herself another glass of wine, then sat down in a comfortable chair to enjoy it.

Perhaps it was the wine or just the general shortage of quality sleep she'd experienced over the past few days, but she jerked awake some time later to find the cabin swinging back and forth with the motion of the ship, and the sky outside already darkening toward night.

Keltan, she saw, slept deeply on a nearby couch. Of the prince there was no sign. Mara got up and explored, finding what she sought in a little chamber nestled in one corner with a rather alarming opening directly above the water. Feeling refreshed and *very* awake—the air coming up through that hole had been *cold!*—she returned to the cabin to find a plate of cold meat, bread, cheese, and pickles on the table, along with three additional plates, two untouched, one covered with crumbs. The prince had obviously eaten and let them sleep. Mara set to with a will, and a few minutes later Keltan, yawning and tousle-haired, joined her. "Where . . . ?" he began, and she pointed to the chamber in the corner. He disappeared into it and reappeared a few minutes later looking happier and as wide awake as she felt.

"Will we sail all night?" Mara asked.

"In a ship this size? I'd think so," Keltan replied. He helped himself to bread and cheese. "We'll probably reach the coast by morning."

"I hope we're in time," Mara said. "What if the Watchers . . . ?"

"We'll be in time," Keltan said. "We have to be."

He had to know it was an empty reassurance, and she certainly knew it, but she accepted it and said nothing more.

Prince Chell came in shortly afterward. "Making good time," he said, helping himself to more food from the platter. "On the course I've set we should reach the coast somewhere north of wherever the unMasked Army has managed to get to. We'll sail south until we find them. With luck, we'll be loading them aboard by afternoon."

The prince retired to his bed, but Mara and Keltan sat up for a long time, side by side on a couch turned so they could look astern at the long white moonlit streak of the ship's wake, stretching straight as an arrow behind them. Keltan put his arm around her, and she snuggled into him. After that it seemed a natural thing to kiss him again. Kissing, Mara discovered, was a fine, fine way to make time pass quickly.

They finally fell asleep nestled against each other, and woke late to find the prince absent once more. Fresh food had appeared: they ate bread and cheese and fruit, washed down with water, and Keltan was attempting to teach Mara a complicated board game he had found in a locker, involving multiple pieces, each with different moves that Mara had a hard time keeping straight, when she heard a distant shout, "Land ho!"

Game forgotten, she and Keltan leaped up. Chell came banging back into the cabin a moment later. "We've raised the coast!" he said. "Come on deck. It won't be long now."

They went out into the cool morning air. Mist, rising from the ocean, shrouded the shore, reducing it to a shadow land of guessed-at hills and hints of trees and rocks. "Damn this fog," muttered Captain March, who stood beside them on what Chell had told Mara, though she wondered if he was pulling her leg, was called the "poop deck." ("Or just 'the poop,' for short," he'd said, and *that* couldn't be true, could it?) "Came out of nowhere."

"We'll have to sail closer," Chell said.

The captain nodded. "Arm the lead!" he shouted, and while Mara was still wondering what that meant, there was a patter of bare feet and sailors rushed forward.

She glanced at Chell. "Arm the lead?"

"The lead is a weight at the end of a long rope, with knots in it at regular intervals," Chell explained. "You fling the lead out in front of the ship to measure how deep the water is. The lead has a little hollow in it that you 'arm' with a bit of tallow. When you haul out the lead, some of the bottom material sticks to the tallow, so you can tell—"

"Eight fathom, mud," came a voice from the bow.

"Ah," Mara said.

They crept in closer to the shore under minimal sail, the sailors in the bow singing out the depth every minute or so. The shore became marginally less ghostly when, at "four fathom, small stones," Captain March turned to the prince and said, "We dare go no closer, Your Highness."

Chell nodded. "We can see well enough," he said. He looked south. "Follow the coast."

"Aye, Your Highness. But we'll keep sounding." Captain March gave his orders, and the ships swung to starboard and began creeping southward.

An hour passed, then another. And then . . .

"People on the shore!" shouted the lookout, high above. "Dozens!"

"We've found them," said Chell. He gave Mara and Keltan a quick grin, then turned to Captain March. "Anchor as close in as you safely can and lower the boats. We need to get them aboard as quickly as possible. Send marines south along the shore to watch for any sign of pursuit."

"What about inland, Your Highness?"

Chell turned and studied the cliff face that loomed, far higher than the one down by the Secret City, dark in the mist above the strand of rocky beach along which the unMasked Army had been making its way. "Unless these Watchers have some magic that allows them to fling themselves into empty space and drop down like feathers, I don't think we have to worry about attack from that direction."

"The mountains inland are impassable," Keltan confirmed. "The northern border of the Autarchy. The only way the Watchers can come after us is along the beach."

Mara gave that tall cliff another look. Like Keltan, she, too, had always heard that the mountains were impassable . . . but she had also heard, from Ethelda, that the Lady of Pain and Fire had been driven into those mountains by the Autarch when he was a young man. *Did she make it through?* she wondered. *Are the mountains* really *impassable, or is that just another lie of the Autarch's, designed to prevent anyone from even* thinking *there might be a way to escape Aygrima to the north? Or did the Lady of Pain and Fire, despite all her magic, die among the peaks?*

She shivered at the thought. Magic didn't keep you from dying. She should know. How close to death had she come now, time after time, despite her Gift? And high in the mountains, far from any humans, the Lady's Gift would have been useless . . . worse than useless, if, as Ethelda said, the Lady had become addicted to magic: the desire for it, combined with the lack of it, might well have driven her mad.

Of course, she was supposedly mad already by that time, so maybe she didn't notice.

Mara shuddered and put the Lady of Pain and Fire out of her head. The Lady wasn't a comfortable topic of thought, anyway, considering Mara had been warned over and over she might turn into the same sort of monster.

Even as she thought it, the magic in the ship's crew tugged at her.

No, she thought. *I'll never become like that. I won't let it happen.*

I won't.

A ragged cheer had gone up from the shore as the refugees saw the ships, and Mara saw Edrik and Hyram, leading the column on horseback, wheel around and gallop to the water's edge. She imagined how she would have reacted to see such enormous vessels looming out of the mist, offering rescue unhoped for, and a grin split her face.

"Lower the boats!" shouted Captain March; and with a splash, the evacuation of the unMasked Army from Aygrima began.

TWENTY-ONE

The Sea Arises

BOAT BY BOAT, the unMasked Army fled the icy shore for the towering ships of Korellia. Keltan and Mara stood on the poop, watching as the members of the Army were helped aboard: men and women, clutching their belongings and their babies; frightened, tired children, faces white, eyes wide, wondering even through their exhaustion at the astonishing vessels on which they found themselves. A dozen at a time, until the decks were full and both *Protector* and *Defender* rode much lower in the water than they had.

Prella and Kirika came aboard together. Prella gave Mara a big wave, and she waved back, a grin spreading across her face that died when Kirika gave her a look so cold she would have feared a knifing had she encountered it on someone in the street. She let her hand fall, remembering again that none of this would be happening if she had not thought she could outwit Stanik.

The last boat to come alongside held Edrik and his wife, along with Catilla, Ethelda, Hyram, and Alita. Catilla's eyes slid up the side of the ship to where Mara stood, then slid away again as though she were beneath notice. Edrik did not look up at her at all, but Hyram did, and Mara actually gasped and stepped back a little at the fury that flitted across his face. Her fingers found Keltan's, and he took her hand comfortingly.

In the boat, Alita took Hyram's hand, too, and the look she turned toward Mara was cold . . . and more than a little smug. "Hyram and Alita?" Mara said to Keltan.

He nodded. "Shortly after we left," he said. "And when I arrived with word of what was about to descend on the Secret City . . ." he let the words trail off.

Mara felt a pang. She had liked Hyram. He had liked her. He and Keltan had even fought, once, over her. But she had turned him against her. *Forever?* she wondered, and remembering the anger she had glimpsed in his gaze, very much feared it was so.

With the last of the unMasked Army aboard, Prince Chell ordered Captain March to weigh anchor. To the chants of sailors manning a windlass, the clanking chain rose link by link, sails began to pull, and *Protector* and *Defender* slipped away from the shore.

Mara looked down from the poop at the mass of people sorting themselves on the deck, and decided to stay put for the moment with Keltan. Captain March glanced at them, then at Prince Chell, who stood looking astern at the vanishing coastline with his hands clasped behind his back, and said nothing.

Mara and Keltan joined Chell at the rail. "Will the Watchers really just let us go?" she asked.

Chell shrugged. "Even if they put two and two together and link my escape . . . and the ships I have already told them I have . . . to the otherwise impossible disappearance of the Army from this shore, what can they do? They have no navy."

"They have fishing boats," Keltan said. "We sailed to the islands in a fishing boat. They could do the same."

"But they'd have to know that's where the unMasked Army has gone," Chell said. "Even if they scout every island along these shores, they cannot determine that for months. And in that time, I will return with a far more formidable force . . . and then we will take the fight to the Watchers." He glanced sideways at Mara, and smiled. "Mark my words, and mark this day," he said. "Today is the beginning of the end of the Autarch's tyranny."

Mara gave him a half-smile back . . . and then clutched at the railing. The ship had given a sudden lurch. The prince glanced over his shoulder. "Captain?"

"Sea's rising," Captain March said. "I was right about there being something unusual about this mist. There's bad weather coming."

Mara looked up at the sky. Before she had been able to see blue, even through the thickening mist, but now . . . black clouds were rolling in from the sea, thick black clouds with thin, white outriders that swept overhead with frightening speed, like hurled javelins. The ship lurched again. The waves grew even as Mara watched. She clutched the railing tight.

The rigging thrummed. Cold air blasted into her face. "It's straight out of the west!" Captain March shouted. "We'll make no headway against it! Best we can do is sail close-hauled to the northwest and hope we can keep off the shore!"

"As you see fit, Captain," Prince Chell said.

Captain March began shouting orders. The ship

turned ponderously, sailors pulled on ropes, the sails shifted to a new angle, and the wind began blowing more from port. They galloped along, the shore now lost behind them and to starboard, through a shrinking circle of dark sea surrounded by white mist, waves rolling through from white wall to white wall . . . but each wave was a little bigger than the last, and increasingly they were capped by white foam and flying spray. "She'll weather this," the captain said, staring to the west. "But is this all that's coming?"

It wasn't.

The wind rose from moan to howl to shriek. The waves grew to the size of hills, and then to mountains. The sky turned black as night. The mist blew away in tatters in the rising gale, but it hardly mattered, because hard on its heels came snow.

It arrived as a wall of white hissing across the waves. *Defender*, which until then had at least been visible as a dark bulk on the edge of the mist-shrouded circle of water, vanished in an instant. And then the snow swept over *Protector*.

Mara gasped as a million flakes of ice, borne on a howling wind, stung her face like nettles and drove into every crevice in her clothing, chilling her to the bone. The poop deck was suddenly a tiny island surrounded by swirling snow, the rest of the ship invisible. Drifts piled up on the deck, turning it white. And still the waves grew, the ship crashing into one, riding up and up to the crest and then falling down the other side to crash into the next. Mara was pleasantly surprised to discover her time at sea had inured her to the motion; she didn't get seasick, a small mercy.

"North-northwest!" Captain March shouted to the helmsman.

"North-northwest it is!" the helmsman shouted back.

But then March came back to the rail, where Chell clung along with Mara and Keltan.

"We can't hold it," he said flatly. "Not in this wind and this sea. We're heading north-northwest, but we're being driven east, back toward the coast. And in this weather ... we'll see nothing of it. If we're driven ashore, we're dead men ... and women," he said, with a glance at Mara. "And children," he added under his breath.

Mara thought of what conditions must already be like on the deck in the wind and spray and snow, and her heart went out to the little ones clinging to their mothers and fathers. *At least they still have mothers and fathers*, she thought, and hated herself for that pang of self-pity. Her own self-disgust drove her away from the rail, across the heaving deck to the gangway. Chell put out a hand to try to stop her. "You're better off up here!" he shouted over the gale.

"And those women and children would be better off in your cabin," she snarled. "Your Highness."

Chell's face darkened for a moment, then he pressed his lips together and gave a short, sharp nod.

"I'll come with you," Keltan said, and together they picked their way down the slippery gangway steps to the deck. Behind them, Mara heard Chell ask March, "What do you recommend, Captain?"

"Fight it out as long as we can," said the captain. "It's all we can do. We have no sea room ..."

Mara felt a chill at the fatalism in the captain's voice, but she shoved it away. "You take port, I'll take starboard!" she shouted to Keltan.

He nodded and disappeared into the flying snow.

The ship slammed hard into a wave. Water sluiced across the deck. Mara staggered to the rail and began pulling her way across it. Faces appeared, refugees from the unMasked Army huddled on the wet deck. "Women and children to the aft cabin!" she shouted. "It's warm and dry. Women and children to the aft cabin!"

Mothers staggered up, holding their children, helped by husbands and fathers, and began making their way toward the stern. Mara continued along the rail until she was certain she'd spoken to everyone. The motion of the ship grew worse, and great dollops of spray crashed over everything with every wave. Shivering, she turned to make her way back to the stern.

Her foot slipped on the icy deck. Her hand flew off the railing. She fell hard on her rear end, and began to slide, down a deck that seemed suddenly steep as a mountainside.

A hand grabbed her, her body swinging around to slam into the railing. She seized the wood gratefully and pulled herself upright, twisting around to see who had saved her. "Thank you," she gasped out . . . and found herself facing Hyram.

For a moment he just stared at her. Snow had crusted his eyebrows and his blond head, as though he had turned old overnight. He still had her hand in his.

"Hyram . . ." she said. "I'm—"

He released her hand and turned away without a word, vanishing back into the thickly falling snow that shrouded the bow as another wave crashed aboard.

Shivering, Mara turned and fought her way back to the poop deck. The groups of people huddled together, wedged against the masts and railing, were noticeably smaller and mostly made up of men and older boys now.

At least no children will be washed overboard, Mara thought. But if the ships foundered, it would make no difference.

Keltan met her at the gangway. "You should go into the cabin, too," he shouted.

"No," Mara said flatly. The children might not know,

but the women would certainly know that the fall of the Secret City could be laid at her feet. She couldn't face them, and even if she could, she couldn't cower in the cabin waiting to see if they would all die. Better to freeze on the deck.

She climbed the gangway. Captain March, Prince Chell, and the helmsman were all little more than dim shadows in the thickly falling snow. "Ship's sluggish, sir," she heard the helmsman say as she reached the poop once more.

"Aye, she would be," March muttered. He went to the front of the poop. "All hands! Clear snow and ice!"

How long they fought the seas Mara didn't know. She stayed where she was, miserable, wet, and cold. The light began to fail as, somewhere beyond the clouds, the sun reached the horizon. The snow never stopped, and despite the best efforts of the crew and the unMasked men and boys who also threw themselves into the effort, soon even she could feel the difference in the motion as the ice built up on rigging and deck. The ship seemed to plunge harder into each wave, and stagger up more slowly. They had long since lost touch with *Defender*.

The end, when it came, came quickly.

The sun had set. Mara and Keltan had sunk to the deck and were huddled together for warmth. Chell had gone down the gangway and hadn't come back. The captain had never budged from his spot beside the helmsman. Running lights made pale circles of light in the still-falling snow.

Then—

"Rocks!" screamed the lookout, high above them in the crosstrees. "Rocks to starboard—"

They hit.

A terrible crunching sound, then the tortured shriek of splitting planks, mingled with the whip-snap sound of breaking wood high above as masts cracked and spars shattered. The lookout's shouts turned to a scream of terror, a scream that plunged down from the top of the mast and ended in the sea. Mara felt the burst of magic released by his body as he died, but it was distant and did not flow to her.

Mara and Keltan, tangled together, were flung across the poop deck and crashed into the forerail. The wheel spun so suddenly and viciously that it clubbed the helmsman to the deck, where he lay moaning.

Captain March picked himself up and charged down the deck. "Damage parties!" he cried. "Clear the boats! Sparl, Thimon, with me." He vanished into the swirling snow.

Mara hauled herself up by the railing and peered into the darkness. "I can't see any—"

Another horrendous crunch. Shouts and screams rang out on deck as she was flung to the planking again. "It's *Defender*!" Keltan shouted. He turned toward her, and she saw blood streaming from his nose, black as tar in the dim light of the running lamps. "She's run into us!"

Mara, picking herself up, saw that he was right. The other ship's starboard side was pressed tight against *Protector*, listing toward them so that masts and rigging were entangled. The heaving sea ground the ships together, the vibration groaning through the planks with every wave. More splintering sounds came from starboard, as the waves pounded *Protector* against the rocks.

"We're all going to drown!" Mara cried.

"Boats," Keltan said desperately. "There are boats . . ."

"They'll never be able to launch them!"

And then, in the space of a single breath, the frantic panic filling her vanished, replaced by a preternatural calm. *It's up to me,* she thought. *I have to use magic.* She closed her eyes, feeling the power all around her, filling every living body on both doomed ships. *Even Ethelda would say I have no choice. I can pull it to me. I can . . .*

And then she gasped, and her eyes flew open, as she felt magic such as she had never felt before, power she would never have felt possible—*and it wasn't hers*. It was all around her, in the sea, in the ships, in the very air . . .

The storm . . . stopped. One moment the wind was howling, screaming through the tattered ropes of the rigging. The next . . . dead silence.

The sea raged on for one long minute . . . and then, just as suddenly as the wind had dropped, the waves quieted. They sank in a moment from mountains to hills to little more than ripples.

The air warmed. Water began to drip from the ice-coated rigging.

Mara spun and stared to the east, to the shore. She could see nothing, but she knew, beyond a shadow of a doubt, that that astonishing surge of magic had come from there.

"Did you do that?" Keltan asked in an awed voice.

Mara shook her head. "No," she said, and she knew she should be glad she had not had to risk her soul to save the ships . . . but a part of her wished that she *had*, wished she really had had no choice but to draw on the magic of the men and women in the ships, wished she had had an excuse to once more feel the pain/pleasure of her Gift.

And *another* part of her was furious that someone *else* had had both the nerve, and the power, to use magic to save the ships.

Chell came rushing up the gangway. "Did you—" He began, and Mara cut him off.

"No!" she snapped. She looked off to starboard. "It was magic, all right, but it came from over there."

"Watchers?" Chell said. "Could they have someone with them Gifted enough to stop a storm in its tracks?"

"Maybe," Mara said. "But I wouldn't have thought they'd be carrying that much magic."

"Well, whoever did it saved all our lives," Chell said. "We would have been ground to sawdust between *Defender* and the rocks. But if it stays as calm as this, we can last the night . . . and ferry everyone ashore in the morning."

"But . . . the ships," Mara said. "The unMasked Army. The islands . . ."

"These ships won't be taking anyone anywhere," Chell said, voice grim. "*Protector* is hung up on the rocks; we'll never be able to get her free and eventually the waves will return and smash her to kindling. *Defender* . . ." He glanced at the other ship, clearly visible now that the snow had ended, the running lights glowing on the torn, tangled sails. Sailors, already aloft, hacked at the rigging with long knives. "She might be salvageable. But she can't carry all the unMasked Army and all the crew of both ships as well." Chell's shadowed face looked like that of some ancient statue hewn out of gray stone. "There's nothing to be done. The unMasked Army must take its chances on shore. If *Defender* can be repaired, I will return to Korellia with her and bring aid as soon as may be."

"Weeks later," Mara said. She thought of the cabin full of women and children, of that rocky, unforgiving shore. "They'll all be dead by then."

"We will leave what supplies we can," Chell said. He turned to face her. "Damn it, Mara, I don't like it any more than you do. But I have a duty to my king . . . my father. We're in a fight for survival as well. *We need the magic from Aygrima*. I must tell him what I've found here. I am certain he will send me back, with a significant force, so that we may gain access to that magic. But I can no longer help the unMasked Army as I had planned. My duty to my own realm must come first."

Mara turned away from him and stared at *Defender*. Then she turned again and looked inland. "Whoever stopped that storm may have his own ideas about what happens next," she said slowly.

"That has occurred to me," Chell said. "Which is why, if *Defender* can be sailed, we will flee these shores in it tomorrow and worry about repairs as we limp away."

"But what if whoever stopped the storm is the one who started it in the first place?" Keltan put in. "Captain March said it came out of nowhere."

Chell shook his head. "Then we are all doomed. We have no way to fight such power." His gaze slid to Mara. "Unless you ... ?"

Mara remembered how that vast wave of magic had crashed over the ships and sea, negating the immense energy of the storm, and she shook her head. "No," she said. "Whoever or ... whatever ... did that, they're beyond me." *Maybe not in power*, she thought, remembering flame and smoke spearing the sky above the mining camp as she contained the explosion that would have destroyed it, *but certainly in control.*

And then she thought, *What could I learn from someone like that?*

"Then all we can do is make our own plans as best we can without regard to what some mysterious superpowerful magic-user may or may not decide to do," Chell said. He glanced up at the sky. Stars were beginning to prick the darkness in the ragged gaps in the drifting cloud cover. "At first light, we abandon *Protector*."

The night continued to warm as time passed, as if whoever had stilled the storm wanted to ensure that they did not freeze as they waited for daylight. Keltan and Mara dozed where they were, on the slanted deck, propped up against the railing. The helmsman, arm broken, had been taken below. Captain March and Prince Chell, busy elsewhere on the ship, did not return. Mara thought of the women and children in the cabin below them, surely more comfortable than anyone else on the ship, and took that warm thought with her into ...

... nightmares.

The ship was on the rocks, and the protection of the sea had deserted her.

They were all there: her father, dead Watchers, Stanik, Grute. In her dream, she stood alone on the poop deck, and they came lumbering across the deck toward her, up the gangway, reaching for her with dead, clawing hands. She tried to scream, but nothing would come out. And then they were on her, grabbing her. She struck out violently with feet and hands, but she couldn't shake them from her, couldn't break their deathlike grip—

"Mara, stop it! Stop! Wake up!"

Mara gasped, eyes snapping open. She was still held in a tight grip, but the hands on her arms belonged to Keltan. She looked wildly around. She wasn't lying down, she was standing up, and her back was pressed against the rail as though she were trying to push through it.

"Keltan?" she said weakly.

"You got up, in your sleep, you were kicking and punching the air, I thought you were going to fall right over the rail ..." Keltan was panting. He let go of her arms. "You could have killed yourself!"

"Keltan ..." Mara flung her arms around him and hugged him tight. "The nightmares," she whispered. "The sea helps, but on land ... I've killed so many people in the past few days ... Keltan, hold me. Keep me safe from the nightmares."

His arms went around her and returned her embrace. "I will, Mara," he said. He kissed her gently on the cheek. "I will."

She squeezed him harder. Then they sat down again

by the rail, arms around each other, and remained there in silence through the final hour of the long night.

First light revealed they were far closer to shore than any of them had guessed. "If we hadn't hit the rocks we'd have been aground soon after," Captain March said, as he stood on the poop deck with Prince Chell, surveying the scene. "Look at that." He pointed north and a little east, where the splash of water showed a long spit of just-submerged land stretching out into the sea. "We'd never have cleared that the way we were being pushed east."

Chell grunted. "If we'd run onto that, we might have been able to wade ashore. But not from here." He turned inland again, hands on his hips. "Still, it's close enough, and looks like good landing for the boats. That damnable shore cliff is finally gone, too. Those hills are climbable." He glanced at Mara. "The unMasked Army will be able to get inland from here," he said. "There could be game . . . water . . ."

Mara said nothing. She was looking much farther, at distant, snow-covered peaks. There were some, very far away, directly inland, but there were more and closer ones to the south. "I think we're north of the mountains," she said. "Beyond Aygrima's borders."

"Then let's hope the Watchers have given up the chase," Keltan said.

Mara said nothing, but she looked down the shore to the south.

"Let's get everyone except the salvage parties ashore," Chell said. He nodded at Captain March. "The captain thinks *Defender* can be floated."

"She'll have to be put up on legs and her hull gone over with a fine-tooth comb," the captain said. "Weeks of repair work, I'm guessing. And we'll need bits of *Protector* to pull it off. But, yes, I think she can be made seaworthy again, and Captain Gramm agrees."

"Let's be about it, then," said Chell.

Captain March nodded, and turned to shout orders to the waiting crew. No boats could be lowered from *Protector*, trapped as she was between *Defender* and the rocks that had ripped apart her hull, so the unMasked Army refugees aboard *Protector* had to first cross gangplanks to *Defender*, then make their way down ratlines to one of the only two boats that were still usable ... one of which, Mara saw, was the fishing boat in which she and Chell had made their way north from Tamita.

It was a slow, laborious process, and the day had worn away to late afternoon before it was complete. As the hours passed, the broad, flat beach grew cluttered with groups of people and mounds of supplies, some the belongings the unMasked Army had brought with them from the Secret City, some supplies from the two ships.

Mara and Keltan were among the last to leave *Protector*, crossing to the shore with Chell, Captain March remaining aboard to continue supervising the work parties trying to free *Defender* from its tangled embrace with *Protector*. As Mara climbed out of the bow of the fishing boat, she saw Catilla and Edrik talking to other leaders of the Army. Hyram stood nearby. Neither Catilla nor Edrik paid her any attention, but Hyram once more gave her a long, measuring look before turning away.

She whirled about abruptly and blindly, seized Keltan's hand, and began walking south along the beach. "Where are we going?" he said, after trotting a couple of steps to catch up with her.

"Away," Mara said. "I don't want to be here right now."

"But—" Keltan looked back over his shoulder.

"They don't need me," Mara said.

For a few minutes Keltan didn't say anything, just crunched over the stones of the beach alongside her.

"When *Defender* is repaired," he said slowly, "you're going to go aboard, aren't you?"

"I don't know," Mara said.

"Really? It seems pretty clear to me," Keltan said. "At sea, the nightmares don't trouble you. At sea, you don't have to face your guilt over what you told Stanik. At sea, you're the treasured guest of Prince Chell. Why *wouldn't* you go to Korellia?"

"Why, indeed?" Mara snapped. She let go of Keltan's hand, spinning to face him. "I didn't ask for any of this," she cried. "I didn't ask for this Gift . . . this curse. I didn't ask to be rescued by the unMasked Army to try to make counterfeit Masks for Catilla. I wish I were still living in my parents' home in Tamita. I wish I were Masked!"

"You don't mean that," Keltan said.

"Don't I?" She turned and looked back at the refugees scattered along the beach. "How many have died because of me, directly or indirectly? How many more will die? And that's even without . . ." She choked off what she was about to say. How could she even begin to make Keltan understand the way her Gift burned inside her, urging her always to use it, to taste the magic of others, draw it to herself, experience that mingled pain and ecstasy? *I need to talk to Ethelda*, she thought. *She's the only one who has a clue . . .*

"Mara," Keltan said. "Stop it. You can't go back. You can only go forward. And going forward . . . I . . . I don't think you should go with Chell."

She snorted. "I'll bet you don't."

"Not because of me," Keltan said angrily. "Because it would be running away." He pointed at the unMasked Army. The sound of a crying baby pierced the cool, still air. "You think it's your fault they're out here, that they're homeless and on the run? Then do something about it. Help them! You have magic. Use it! Use it to keep them alive through the coming weeks and months. Don't run off to sea just because you're feeling guilty. If more people die when you could have helped prevent it, then it *will* be your fault! And you won't be the girl I thought you were, the one who has always tried to *help* people."

She stared at him. "Keltan . . ." He didn't know what he was offering. An excuse to use her magic. A reason to use it. A *good* reason. She could take just a little, here and there, as she needed it. She wouldn't abuse it. She wouldn't take more than she needed. She wouldn't . . .

She wouldn't become their own little version of the Autarch, stealing magic from others to meet her own needs. She'd never become that.

Except, deep in her heart, she feared she *would*.

"You don't know what you're saying," she whispered at last. "Keltan. You don't . . ."

She turned from him and ran farther up the beach. She heard him running after her. Ahead, the beach curved back to the west. She dashed up to the bend, rounded it . . .

. . . and skidded to a stop.

"Mara!" Keltan called. He reached her. "I . . ."

His voice trailed away.

The beach was black with Watchers.

TWENTY-TWO

Pain and Fire

SHOUTS RANG OUT. Two mounted Watchers galloped toward them, swords shining in the late afternoon sun.

"Back!" Mara screamed. "Warn them!"

Keltan turned and ran. Mara ran after him. "Watchers!" Keltan screamed. "Watchers! To arms!"

Mara fell farther and farther behind as he ran. She
could feel the magic in the Watchers, the magic in the
unMasked Army, magic all around her, tugging at her,
slowing her. All she had to do was reach out for it, all she
had to do was pull it to herself, all she had to do was turn
and hurl it against the Watchers . . .

No, she thought, sobbing as she ran. *No, I can't kill
again, I can't . . .*

She reached the unMasked Army. Families were scrambling north along the beach, running toward the men, who were drawing swords and nocking bows and running toward the enemy. She glanced behind her. Watchers boiled around the bend in the beach, the front rank, mounted, galloping over the rocks, splashing through the shallows. Edrik raced up, grabbed her, spun her around. "How many?"

"A hundred," Mara gasped. "Maybe more."

Edrik swore and pushed her aside, then ran on.

Mara, behind the line of armed men, turned.

"Loose at will!" Edrik bellowed, and bows hummed. Arrows flew, found marks. Three Watchers tumbled from the horses. Two died: Mara gasped as their magic slammed into her. She fell to her knees.

Oh, no, she thought. *Battle . . . so many deaths . . . so much magic . . .*

She shuddered with pain . . . but also with pleasure, enhanced by the knowledge that more would surely follow. *Kill more*, a part of her panted. *Kill more . . .*

What's happening to me?

The mounted Watchers swept down onto the unMasked Army. Swords clashed. Men fell. Magic roared into Mara. She found herself on her feet again, screaming.

More Watchers died. Horses galloped through the camp, riderless. But now the main body of the Watchers came sweeping over the beach, shouting . . . but slowing. Out of bowshot, they stopped, black Masks giving them the look more of a horde of insects than of a force of men.

"What are they doing?" Mara heard Edrik say, but she already knew. She could sense it: a store of magic, and the Gifted to use it.

"They're going to attack using magic," she said. It

seemed that her voice went nowhere. "They're going to attack using magic!" she said, louder, and Edrik turned to look at her.

"How do you know?"

"I can feel it," she said. She walked forward. She was hardly aware of what she was doing, only that the magic she sensed drew her.

"Mara, no!" she heard Keltan cry. She heard him running after her, felt him grab her arm. But she was full of magic from the men who had died, and she exerted just a little of it then, just enough so that his hands slid away from her as though she were a statue made of ice. She strode through the defenders of the unMasked Army untouched and to the front of the line. She waited.

It didn't take long. The ranks of Watchers parted. Three men strode forward, wearing Masks of red. Red, too, sheathed, not just their hands, but their whole bodies, turning them in her sight into walking flames of magic. She had never seen any Gifted draw that much magic to himself, and each carried, slung on harnesses, additional containers of black lodestone, open so that she could see the multicolored seethe of even more magic within them. But it didn't matter. She'd stopped a magical attack before, in the boat. She could do it again.

Then the attack came, and she found out how wrong she was.

To her Gifted eyes, the magic surrounding the three men suddenly leaped up, twining together into a vast, seething sphere of red flame, like a second sun come to Earth.

And then that ball broke apart into a hundred flaming spears that streaked across the beach toward the unMasked Army.

Mara reached for that magic, tried to draw it into herself . . . but she was already brimming with the magic of those who had died, and she suddenly discovered that her Gift had limits after all. Perhaps half of those flaming spears turned aside from their path and thrust into her. This time she was better prepared than she had been in the boat, and contained the magic so her clothes did not burst into flames . . . but the magic she took in filled her to the brim, filled her with so much magic she screamed. She could absorb no more, and so the remaining fifty spears slammed into the unMasked Army.

She heard screams, felt a wave of magical pressure as men, women, and children died beneath that hail of magic. The force drove her to her knees. She gaped soundlessly, burning inside; but she also felt fury, an echo of the fury she had felt when her father died. She had to get rid of the magic within her or die, and so she flung it, shrieking her hatred, at the ranks of the Watchers.

It roared across the beach like a wall of fire. Some of the Watchers, those with their own measure of the Gift, saw it coming and tried to turn and flee; others had no clue; it didn't matter, the magic moved too fast. Two score men screamed and died, burning, smoke and flame erupting from their writhing bodies. The stink of burning cloth, leather and meat spread across the beach.

But the three red-Masked Gifted were not among the dead. They had turned aside her magic with contemptuous ease, and already were drawing more from the urns they carried. Once more they flamed like giant, walking torches. The red, seething ball formed again.

Edrik had not been idle. He could not have seen the flaming spears of magic, but he had seen his own people struck down and had certainly seen the front rank of the Watchers burn and die. "Attack!" he screamed, and the fifty or so surviving men and women he had in arms rushed forward, swords drawn.

Mara wanted to scream at them to turn back, warn

them of the magic about to tear them apart, the magic she could see and they could not, but she had nothing left, no breath to make a sound, no strength to use any of the magic pounding down on her like heavy surf from the dying people all around. The force of it had driven her to her knees; now she dropped to all fours in the rocky sand. It took all her strength just to raise her head to watch that hopeless charge.

Impotent, she awaited the final blow that would destroy Edrik's fighters and leave the women and children helpless ... but then she felt a new force of magic, and recognized it at once as the same unbelievable power she had felt when the storm that had arisen so mysteriously had quieted just as mysteriously.

The Watchers' Gifted struck. Their flaming spears leaped at the unMasked Army—and just ... blinked out. Mara could not see their expressions through their Masks, but she saw their jaws drop ... and then that incredible magic spat their own magical weapons back in their faces.

The three Gifted died instantly, riven by javelins of fire, their bodies exploding into bloody chunks and gouts of red-tinged steam. Twenty Watchers behind them died, too. The magic from all of those deaths should have hit Mara like an avalanche, driven her into unconsciousness— but it didn't. Instead, she felt it sweep over her head like a giant bird passing in a rush of wings, speeding somewhere else ... to *someone* else.

The remaining Watchers tried to flee. Edrik's men cut many down from behind. A few turned and fought, only to be overwhelmed. Flashes of magic struck down those who were out of the Army's reach. Not a single Watcher made it to the bend in the shore.

The entire battle had taken no more than ten minutes. Mara tried to get up, but instead fell over on her side and lay curled there, gasping. The shouts and screams and weeping from all around seemed to be coming from far away and have nothing to do with her. All she could think of was the rush of magic that had passed her by.

Where had it gone? And to *whom*?

Hands tugged at her. "Are you all right?"

It took her a long moment to recognize the voice — Keltan — a longer moment to register what he had said. She gathered the bits of her consciousness that seemed to have been scattered as explosively as the dismembered bodies of the Watchers' Gifted. "I . . ." She swallowed. "I don't know."

Keltan pulled her upright. Her head swam and she leaned against him for a moment, closing her eyes. When she opened them again, she found herself staring at the beach, soaked with blood, littered with the corpses of the Watchers, smoke still rising from those she had killed. The sight was like a slap to her face; she jerked her head the other way, only to see still more bodies behind her, bodies of the unMasked Army, men, women, and . . .

Her heart broke in her chest.

Children. Not twenty feet away, a little girl, chest a smoking ruin, stared sightlessly at the sky. A woman cradled the body, weeping helplessly.

"How . . . how many dead?" she whispered. "Keltan, *how many*?"

"I don't know," Keltan said. He sounded numb.

"Injured. There'll be injured." Mara focused on that. She couldn't undo what had happened, but maybe . . . "Help me up!" With Keltan's assistance she managed to stagger to her feet, though she had to lean heavily on him to keep from falling. "The Watchers will have had more magic . . . a wagon, maybe . . . Ethelda can use it. We have to find it. We have to find *her*." Almost dragging

Keltan with her, she set off through the camp toward where she had last seen Ethelda, with Catilla.

She saw Catilla first. The diminutive old woman was kneeling by a body. Asteria knelt beside her, face in her hands, shoulders shaking with sobs. As Mara and Keltan approached, Catilla turned. The stark pain and sorrow on her face brought Mara up short. "Grelda," Catilla grated, "is dead. I have known her since I was a girl."

"I . . . I'm sorry . . ." Mara whispered. She put out a tentative hand toward Asteria. "Asteria, I'm so—"

Asteria only sobbed harder.

And then, looking past Catilla and Grelda's granddaughter, Mara saw another body, and her blood ran cold. "Oh, no," she whispered. "Oh, no!"

She pulled free of Keltan and ran . . . stumbled, really, for her legs seemed to have no strength left . . . past Grelda's prostrate form. Like Catilla before her, she knelt beside a body: the body of a small woman, her lined face slack in death, her blue eyes open and staring sightlessly at the sky. Blood soaked her blue robes, which still smoked slightly in the late afternoon sun.

"Ethelda," Mara whispered. "No . . ." She felt desperately for the slightest bit of magic in the body before her, any hint of life, but found nothing.

Ethelda was dead. She had died in the hail of magic from the Watchers . . . the magic *she* had been unable to turn aside.

The magic whoever had ultimately destroyed the Watchers certainly *could* have turned aside . . . if he or she had chosen to.

Cold fury filled Mara. She staggered to her feet. "Come out!" she screamed. "I know you're out there. Come out and face us! Show yourself!"

Catilla stared at her as if she had gone mad. Chell, fifty feet away, bending over one of his sailors who had suffered the same fate as Ethelda, straightened abruptly, his head also turning toward her. Keltan put a hand on her shoulder. "Mara . . ."

She shrugged him off and stepped inland, screaming at the forested hills. "Come out, damn you!"

And she came.

Mara felt the magic before she saw its source: a wave of it, a *wall* of it, magic such as she had never imagined, power such as she had never conceived. The magic had a center, a glowing, sunlike heart. It appeared out of nowhere, sudden as lightning, and she knew it had been hidden from her until its owner chose to reveal it, and that she could not match it.

Now that the source had been unveiled, she knew exactly where it was, would have known where it was with her eyes closed, and she faced that place, a forested fold in the hills that rose above the beach, a ravine down which the person to whom she had called slowly walked.

It was a woman wrapped in a coat of silver fur above boots of soft brown deerskin. Her head was bare, revealing long gray hair, loose around her shoulders. To Mara's eyes she glowed white from within, as though she were a clear vessel with the sun somehow trapped within it, like a living lamp.

Keltan gasped, and for a moment Mara thought he saw what she saw . . . but then she realized he was reacting to something far more physical.

The woman was accompanied by wolves.

There were thirteen of them. They had silver fur, the same silver as the fur of her clothes. They had green eyes, and grinning, fanged mouths from which hung bright red tongues. They seemed to be laughing at everything and everyone, laughing . . . and wondering what they would taste like. They would have terrified Mara if not for the fact their mistress was far and away the most frightening person she had ever seen.

Even stranger, the wolves, too, glowed white with magic.

The woman strode down into their camp. One of the sailors, moved by fear or foolishness, drew his cutlass and ran toward her. She flicked a finger at him and he flew back through the air a good twenty feet, crunching to the ground and lying there stunned.

Chell stepped forward. "Who are you and—" His voice dried in his throat. He made gagging noises and clutched his neck.

Catilla had gotten to her feet. Her eyes blazed, but she said nothing. The woman, wolves flowing around her feet, stepped by Catilla without a glance, then stopped, barely ten feet from Mara. The wolves arranged themselves around her feet and stared at Mara with their green eyes, tongues lolling.

The woman cocked her head to one side. "My name is Arilla," she said.

The name meant nothing to Mara.

The woman smiled slightly. "You know me better as the Lady of Pain and Fire," she said. "I have come to take you home."

TWENTY-THREE
The Lady

THE BEACH MIGHT HAVE BEEN EMPTY of everyone except Mara, the strange woman, and the wolves. No sound seemed to penetrate the space between them, so that it was in utter silence that Mara breathed, "I should have guessed."

"Indeed you should have," said the Lady. "Unless my reputation has faded with time. Which I doubt."

"Your reputation remains," Mara said. "But nobody seems to know much about you *except* for your reputation."

"And that reputation is . . . ?" the Lady asked.

"Murderess. Slaughterer of the innocent. Destroyer of villages," Mara said. "Cast out from Aygrima in the earliest years of the Autarch's reign through the force of his magic and the glory of his cause."

The Lady laughed. "I suppose I could expect nothing less." The laugh faded. The smile that had birthed it faded in turn. "I am not what my reputation makes of me," she said, "except in one thing: I am the enemy of the Autarch. I have been his enemy for sixty years. For sixty years I have awaited the opportunity to move against him. And now . . ." She spread her hands, encompassing the unMasked Army. "And now, such an opportunity is delivered to me."

"You'll have to talk to Catilla"—Mara glanced at the old woman, who stood apart, glowering—"if you wish the help of the unMasked Army."

"The unMasked Army?" The Lady of Pain and Fire looked at Catilla. "Is that what you call it, Catilla? It looks like a piss-poor army to me!"

"I have kept it secret from the Autarch for sixty years, Arilla," Catilla said. "Sixty years of freedom for those within its ranks."

"Yet the Autarch still reigns," said the Lady.

"The Autarch still reigns," agreed Catilla. "And you still lurk north of the mountains. Which of us has done more in the fight against him since we each chose our own ways all those decades ago?"

Mara stared at Catilla, mouth agape. "You two . . . know each other?"

"Knew each other," the Lady said softly. "Once." Her gaze fell to the ground, where Grelda and Ethelda lay side by side. A sound of pain escaped her. "Grelda?"

"Slain by the Watchers' magic."

Mara's anger, forgotten for a moment in her astonishment at the Lady's arrival, waxed hot again. "You could have stopped it," she cried. "You could have saved them both, could have saved all of them. You have the power! I tried, but there was so much magic, I couldn't hold it all . . . why didn't you stop it?"

"Even my power has limits," said the Lady. "I was still too far away." She suddenly strode forward. The wolves didn't move, though she had given them no command Mara had heard. Mara gasped as the Lady put her arms around her, trembling as she felt the magic burning like the sun in the Lady's small body. "I'm so sorry," the Lady whispered into her ear. "I know just how hard it must have been for you, to bear so great a Gift alone."

The Lady's touch burned her like fire and chilled her like ice . . . and excited her; excited her like Keltan's touch, like the feel of Chell's skin beneath her questing fingers . . .

She tried to push away, but the Lady's grip tightened. "Do not fight it," she breathed. "Do not fight it. It only hurts when you fight it. You must learn to *welcome* it, if you are to control it . . . if you are to use it to overthrow the Autarch."

Now she did push the Lady away, and stood trembling. "Me?" she said. "Overthrow the Autarch? I can't—"

"You can," the Lady said. Her mouth quirked. Up close, her face seemed ageless: eighteen or thirty or a hundred. *Closer to the latter*, Mara thought, *if she's really an old friend of Catilla's.* Yet there was nothing of age or infirmity about the Lady, despite her long gray hair.

The silence intensified around them. Mara could hear nothing but the pounding of her own heart, the rush of her own breath, and the voice of the Lady. *More magic*, she thought. "I did not come for the unMasked Army, Mara," the Lady said, and Mara knew not a hint of what she said could be heard by anyone but her. "I came for you—the one I have awaited for decades. The one who shares my Gift and my power. The one who, joining forces with me, can throw down the tyrant who now sits upon the Sun Throne and set all Aygrima free."

She smiled. "But I can see this is overwhelming to you. We will talk later, in detail. For now . . ." She took a step back, and the feeling of impenetrable silence vanished, the noises of the beach, wails of grief, the roar of surf, the rush of wind, the crackle of fires, crashing in on Mara so suddenly she flinched. "Catilla," the Lady said, turning to the Commander of the unMasked Army. "Gather your people. There is food and shelter a short march inland. I will take you—"

"Your pardon," said a new voice, and Mara turned to see Prince Chell watching the Lady with narrowed eyes, his voice clearly restored but his face set in anger. He had his hand on his sword hilt, though what possible good he thought a blade could be against someone who had just slain a hundred Watchers single-handedly, Mara couldn't imagine. *Probably a soldier thing*, she thought. *Maybe it just makes him feel better.* "I am Chell, Prince of Korellia, commander of the flotilla that has foundered on the rocks of your shore."

The Lady's eyes glittered as she turned her head to look at Chell. She stepped away from Mara and closer to him. The wolves flowed forward, arranging themselves around their mistress and the prince. Chell glanced down at the animals, all of which were staring at him, then returned his gaze to the Lady. "Korellia," she said. "One of the old Island Kingdoms. So it still exists."

"It does," said Chell. "But it is sore beset." He studied her. "I have come here," he said, "because the Kingdom of Korellia faces a foe whose machines of war threaten our survival. I have come in search of magic, as was traded with Korellia of old. I seek power to overthrow our enemies. I thought I had found it"—he glanced at Mara, then back at the Lady—"but now I think I beheld only a reflection of the true power in this land."

The Lady laughed. "Your body is fair, your face is

handsome, your tongue is silver," she said. "These things work for you." But like a snuffed candle, the laughter vanished in the next instant, leaving nothing of merriment behind. With a face white and smooth as polished ice, in a tone as cold as the winds of the storm that had driven them ashore, the Lady said, "But hear me. I do not say I will not aid you. I do not say I will. What I do say is that until the Autarch is overthrown, your wishes and the concerns of your little land mean nothing to me."

"But I can help you with that," Prince Chell said persuasively. "If you help me get my ship afloat, I will sail to my kingdom and return with an army. I will—"

The smooth visage of the Lady cracked in an instant, gave way to fury. "I do not need your help, interloper!" she screamed at him, and if before she had wrapped silence around her words, now they cracked across the beach with the force of a thunderbolt. Fresh crying broke out from children just beginning to calm after the terror of the battle. "The Autarch rules by magic, and by magic he must be overthrown!" Mara, with her Gifted sight, saw the white fire shining within her wax even brighter. "What good would your armies be against *this*?" She raised her hands and flicked them as though directing an unseen choir.

Defender rose from the sea. Water cascaded from its sides in sheets, pouring across the deck of the stricken *Protector*. Masts and spars shattered like kindling; ropes stretched and snapped. Trailing the wreckage of its own rigging and much of *Protector*'s, *Defender* floated majestically over the water, the work party clinging desperately to its shrouds and railings. One man slipped and fell, and with contemptuous ease the Lady flicked a finger and caught him in midair, lowering him almost gently to the beach; almost, for his breath whooshed out as he thudded onto the sand.

Defender she was less careful with. Trailing green weed, the ship rode up above the beach a hundred yards north of where they stood. . . .and then dropped twenty feet, shaking the ground as it slammed onto dry land, the keel snapping with an ear-splitting crack. Broken-backed, *Defender* heeled slowly onto her port side and lay still.

The Lady's mouth was slightly parted, and she moaned a little as she turned and faced *Protector*. Prince Chell, with a furious cry, drew his sword and stepped toward her; she flicked a finger and he was flung backward, sword skittering from his hand as he, too, thudded to the beach.

The Lady reached out her hand. Mara felt magic flowing to the Lady, pouring into her, though where it came from she could not tell. The Lady opened her hand, then closed it again, forming it into a fist. Her knuckles turned white.

Out on the rocks, *Protector* . . . crunched. Its sides stove in with a terrible rending sound, its remaining masts shattered and fell, and suddenly there were two pieces of ship where before there had only been one . . . and then there were none, as the Lady turned her hand over and pressed it down, and the remnants of Chell's flagship sank beneath the waves in a flurry of white foam.

"Stop it!" Mara said. "Stop it!"

The Lady's head jerked toward her, and Mara took a step back, for with the magic pouring through her skin, the Lady looked like nothing human at all: only a skull with eyes on fire and teeth bared in a horrible death-grin.

But then the Lady seemed somehow to gather herself together. The magic-light faded from her, pulled back inside her skin. She looked normal again . . . or as normal as anyone dressed all in fur and surrounded by wolves could look, Mara thought. "I trust I make my point," the Lady said to Chell, who had picked himself up and was staring at her, holding his arm. Then she turned to Catilla. "I offered you food and shelter," she said quietly. "Will you accept?"

If Catilla had been horrified or startled by what she'd just seen, she gave no sign of it. She inclined her head slightly, her eyes glittering in the pale sun. "For the sake of my people, it would seem I have no choice."

The Lady turned again to Chell. "I will not let the Kingdom of Korellia interfere in the affairs of Aygrima," she said. "But I will make the same offer to you. Food and shelter for your men. Will you accept? Or will you stay here . . ." Her gaze moved past him to the shattered hulk of *Defender*, and her lip curled. ". . . with your ship?"

Prince Chell bent over and picked up his sword from the sand. He slid it into its ruby-encrusted sheath. He stared at the Lady for a long moment. "It seems I, too, have no choice."

"Excellent," said the Lady. "Food and shelter it is. And then . . . talk." Her eyes turned back to Mara, and even though she had pulled her power back into herself, Mara could still see a glint of it gleaming in those dark brown pools. "I have plans," she said softly. "Plans I have spent many a weary year perfecting. It is time to put them into action."

She turned away from Mara. The wolves flowed around her. "I will wait upon the hill," she said. "Follow me when you are ready."

She strode away.

Chell came up beside Mara. "That," he said softly, "is the most terrifying woman I have ever met."

"That," Mara said, her eyes locked on the departing Lady, "is what I may become."

Chell looked at her, shocked, but Mara was only peripherally aware of it. She turned and looked at the broken ship on the shore, at the scattered debris that was all that was left of *Defender*, and then turned once more to stare after the Lady of Pain and Fire.

What she had told Chell was true. The Lady of Pain and Fire was what she might become. And what frightened her most was that she didn't know if she feared that . . . or longed for it.

She saw Keltan staring at her, and went to join him.

Around her the unMasked Army and the shipwrecked sailors of Korellia gathered their supplies and their dead, and prepared to follow the Lady of Pain and Fire into the unknown.

Available July 2015 in hardcover from DAW,
the third novel in *The Masks of Aygrima*
by E. C. Blake:

FACES

Read on for a special preview.

THE DEAD LAY ON THE BEACH, row upon row, the snow gently wrapping their disfigured forms in shrouds of purest white, hiding the horror, hiding all differences. Had she not known how they were arranged, Mara could not have told which were Watchers and which members of the unMasked Army.

Except for the smallest corpses. There had been no children among the Watchers.

She stood, Keltan to her right and the Lady of Pain and Fire to her left, on the landward side of the gathered corpses. No one else dared come close, with the Lady's wolves arranged around her feet. The survivors of the unMasked Army huddled together in small groups across the rows of dead from the Lady. Edrik stood with his wife, Tralia, both of them supporting Edrik's grand-mother, Catilla, commander of the UnMasked Army. Hyram was there, too, his arm protectively around the shoulders of Alita, the dark-skinned girl who had been rescued with Mara from the wagon taking them to the mining camp. Two other girls who had been in that wagon, Prella and Kirika, held each other close. The survivors of Chell's men stood with their Prince and their captains on the seaward side, where the sinking sun turned them into faceless silhouettes, as though they wore the black Masks that had crumbled away into dust from the Watchers' faces when they'd died.

Whatever words were to be said over the dead had already been said, by the surviving members of the families . . . those families where anyone survived; not far from where she stood Mara saw three corpses gathered together, man, woman and young daughter. An entire family wiped out.

A family like mine once was.

Among those corpses lay that of Simona, the baker's daughter who had been the fourth girl rescued from the wagon with Mara.

No tears dimmed her vision. Her ability to weep, like so much else, seemed to have been stripped away from her this day. Instead, her grief coiled, with her anger and fear, somewhere deep inside her, down where the monsters lurked, the monsters created in her mind whenever she used her Gift of magic to kill, whenever she absorbed the magic of those who died in her presence.

Though she had killed few if any of those on the beach before them now. The Watchers had killed those of the unMasked Army. And the deaths in turn of those Watchers, and the psychic burden they imposed, could be laid directly at the feet of the Lady in white fur by her side.

"The burial ceremonies are complete?" the Lady said now to Mara, in a voice only she—and the wolves; she saw their ears flick at the sound of their mistress's voice—could have heard.

"Yes," Mara said.

"So." The Lady raised her hands. In Mara's Gifted sight, they began to glow brighter and brighter, until they seemed like twin suns come to the beach. She knew that those around her who were not Gifted, like Keltan, saw nothing at all. She still found that hard to believe.

The Lady made a pushing motion. Mara saw a ball of white fire spring forth from her palms, spread into a towering wall of flame, and sweep across the beach. As the fiery wave passed, the bodies vanished, dissolving into white dust that the flame pushed ahead of it into the sea.

One instant, the corpses were there. The next, they were gone, and the snow fell onto empty, level ground, already softening the human-sized blotches of bare stones where the bodies had lain an instant before.

Mara heard a kind of collective gasp from the un-Masked Army and the men of Korellia, followed by renewed weeping from those whose loved ones' remains had just vanished. She'd gasped, too, but for a different reason: for the first time she had seen *where* the Lady obtained her power. This close to her, she had sensed its flow.

Most Gifted could only use magic collected and held in containers of black lodestone, the strange mineral that attracted magic to itself. A very few—Mara, the Autarch, and the Lady of Pain and Fire among them—could draw magic directly from other living things, including people, though the Autarch's power was limited in that he required those people to be wearing magical Masks for him to access their magic.

The Lady had just drawn magic from the wolves.

Mara looked down at them. They grinned back at her, tongues lolling.

"I see you glimpse the truth," the Lady said softly to her. "But this is only the beginning of your understanding. Once we reach my stronghold . . ." She shook her head. "But first, we must reach it." She glanced at Keltan. "Boy."

"Keltan," he muttered, but she hardly seemed to notice.

"Tell Catilla we must leave at once." She glanced out at sea. "There is a storm brewing."

"Your doing?" Mara said.

The Lady shook her head. "There are other magics than mine. The defenses of Aygrima against invasion from the sea were established long before my time — long before the Autarch's time. I do not know how they are activated, but I am sure he does. I suspect he was behind the storm that drove Prince Chell's ships ashore. But this one . . ." Her eyes unfocused for a moment, as though she were reaching out with all her senses. "This one," she said, "feels natural to me — though it may still be in reaction to the previous storm. I do not see how you can magically produce a storm without disrupting the natural patterns of nature for days afterward." Her eyes focused again, and she looked back at Keltan. "If we are not off this beach before full night, there will be more deaths. Tell Catilla there is shelter inland, but we must move *now*."

Keltan frowned, glanced out at sea, froze for a moment, and then dashed off without another word. Mara followed his gaze, and saw what had given him pause.

The sun was vanishing, but not yet behind the horizon: instead, it was being swallowed by a rapidly rising line of black cloud, cloud whose towering peaks it outlined in flame as it disappeared behind them.

"I'm not sure they can be off the beach before the storm hits," Mara said, turning to the Lady. "Can't you delay it?"

She shook her head. "You overestimate my power," she said. "I came to the shore holding as much magic within myself as I could, and I drew much more from the dying Watchers, but I also used a great deal destroying the remaining Watchers, disabling the ships, and cleansing the beach." She smiled slightly, the expression revealing deeper lines in her face than were usually apparent, so that for the first time Mara had a hint of her true age. "The wolves provide some, but they are not inexhaustible. I can do nothing against the storm, or stop the rising seas that will soon lash this beach. But as I said, I have prepared shelter a short distance away, to see us through the night. After that. . . ." She glanced inland. "We are three days' journey from my stronghold, and that is three days as *I* travel. It may be a week with this ragtag bunch, and the journey is difficult."

Mara felt a surge of anger. "Then leave without us, if you're so worried. Save yourself. What do you care about this 'ragtag bunch'?"

The Lady raised an eyebrow. "I need them," she said. "I need people. And, as I have told you already, I need *you*. If I—if *we*—are to overthrow the Autarch, then we must all help each other." She looked across the now-empty beach at the unMasked Army, and Mara, following her glance, saw Edrik already beginning to chivvy people inland. Beyond Edrik, the water, almost calm a few moments before, now tossed restlessly against the shore, and out to sea, the waves advanced in white-capped rows growing ever larger.

The sun suddenly vanished completely behind the rising clouds, and an even colder wind than usual swirled the snow across the beach.

"I will use my magic as I can to make the journey easier for them," the Lady said, "but I cannot remove all hazards or discomforts." She snorted. "If I could, I would not have suffered them myself on my journey here."

Mara stared out across the beach, at the weary, crying children being urged to their feet, at the weeping widows and walking wounded turning their backs on the rising sea to start the long, uncertain journey inland. "Is there anything I can do to help? This suffering . . . it's all my fault."

"It is the *Autarch*'s fault," the Lady said sharply. "Don't forget that. And don't forget that he *will* pay. Now that I have you, he will fall, as hard and fast as his father." She took a deep breath. "And no, there is nothing you can do to help. I have no magic you can use, and I do not think you are yet ready to take magic from either the wolves or your companions."

Mara shot a horrified look at her. "I'll never be ready to do that. It's . . . I don't dare."

"Really?" The Lady gave her a cool look. "I can see we have a great deal to talk about . . . and a great many misconceptions on your part to clear up. But all that must wait." The wolves, sitting at ease around them, suddenly rose to their feet as one animal. "We are moving at last, and I must lead the way." She turned, tugged the hood of her white fur robe into place, and strode inland. She did not move like a woman of at least Catilla's age. Like the Autarch, she seemed to have the secret of perpetual youth.

Like the Autarch, Mara thought, and shivered. She knew how the Autarch achieved his long life: by draining magic from the Child Guard and, through the newest version of the Masks, from many others. So how was the Lady achieving the same effect?

Mara had a lot of questions for the Lady of Pain and

Fire. But first, of course, they had to survive the night. *What did she mean, she's prepared shelter? How? And what kind of shelter?*

Despite her questions, she didn't follow the Lady to the front of the column. Instead, she went in search of Keltan.

She found him at the rear, gathering the belongings of a woman who was carrying a squalling infant. "Lost her husband," Keltan grunted as Mara came up. "Needs help."

Mara said nothing, but turned to the woman. "I can carry the child, if you need to rest," she said.

But the woman glared at her, hatred plain on her face even in the fading, dim blue twilight. "Don't touch her. Don't come near her, you . . . monster!"

Mara gasped. "I—"

"Don't talk to me!" The woman could barely choke out the loathing-filled words. She turned and strode blindly toward the forested hills beyond the beach, clutching her infant to her breast.

Keltan, still carrying the woman's bundle slung over his back, paused beside Mara. "She didn't mean it," he said. "She's just upset . . ."

"She meant it," Mara said. *And the worst of it is, she may be right. I may really be a monster.*

"I thought you'd be up with the Lady," Keltan said. "What are you doing back here?"

"I don't want to walk with the Lady," Mara said. She wished she could take Keltan's hand, but they were both full. She contented herself with falling beside him, trudging through the snow, the wind swirling it around their feet and already biting deep through the flimsy coat she wore. "I want to walk with you. With someone ordinary."

Keltan shot her a glance. "Thanks . . . I think."

"You know what I mean." Mara shook her head. "The Lady—she wants me for something. She wants me to become like her, I think. To help her overthrow the Autarch. But if I do what she wants . . . Keltan, I don't want to be a monster. I just want to be a girl."

"You *are* a girl," Keltan said. "I've kissed you, I should know, right? You're definitely a girl, not a monster." He shook his head. "But if you mean you just want to be an *ordinary* girl . . . Mara, I'm sorry, but you can never be that. After what you've done . . . after what you've seen . . . you'll never be ordinary. You never have been."

Mara said nothing. Her life in Tamita, before her failed Masking, seemed dim and distant as a pleasant dream that had vanished upon waking, leaving behind only a faint sense of wellbeing . . . and longing. Had she ever really been a carefree child, playing barefoot in the streets, sitting on the city wall and watching the crowds in the Outside Market, sneaking out at night with a friend to swim in a fountain, secure in the knowledge her mother and father loved her and she had a hot supper and warm bed awaiting her every night?

Now her father was dead, and maybe her mother, too, for all she knew. She'd seen so much death, had *caused* so much death, had done things she would never have dreamed possible less than half a year past, things she wouldn't have believed if they'd been in one of the tales she'd enjoyed reading as a child. Everyone wanted to use her, to turn the powerful abilities she had never wanted to their own ends: the Autarch, Catilla, Chell, and now the Lady of Pain and Fire. None of them seemed concerned with what *she* wanted, or needed, or longed for. They just saw her as a tool, a tool they would use until it broke.

But if I break, she thought, *with the power I have to rip magic from the living, to kill and destroy . . . how many more will die?*

"You're not a monster," Keltan said again.

Mara wasn't at all sure she believed him.

Michelle Sagara
The Queen of the Dead

"Brilliant storyteller Sagara heads in a new direction with her *Queen of the Dead* series. She does an excellent job of breathing life into not only her reluctant heroine, but also the supporting players in this dramatic and spellbinding series starter. There is a haunting beauty to this story of love, loss and a teenager's determination to do the right thing. Do not miss out!"

—*RT Book Reviews*

"It's rare to find a book as smart and sweet as this one."

—Sarah Rees Brennan

SILENCE
978-0-7564-0799-5

TOUCH
978-0-7564-0800-8

And watch for the third book in the series, *Grave*, coming soon from DAW!

To Order Call: 1-800-788-6262
www.dawbooks.com

DAW 192

Edward Willett

"Their moral dilemma is only on of the reasons this novel is so fascinating. The Selkie culture and infrastructure is very picturesque and easily pictured by readers who will want to visit his exotic world." —*Midwest Book Review*

"Willett is well able to keep all his juggling balls in the air at the same time....It's a good story, a great mate to the first volume." —Ian Randal Strock at *SF Scope*

The Helix War
Omnibus:
Marseguro   Terra Insegura
978-0-7564-0738-4

And don't miss:

Lost in Translation
978-0-7564-0340-9

DAW 177